ALEXANDRA GARDNER

KING OF CHAOS

LIGHT OF CHAOS: BOOK 1

PUBLISHED BY TRUE BEGINNINGS PUBLISHING.

true_beginnings_publishing@yahoo.com

Formatting and all artwork by True Beginnings Publishing.
Original stock photos are not covered by copyright.
All text and characters are Copyright Protected.

ISBN-13: 978-1-947082-71-7
ISBN-10: 1-947082-71-X

King's Chaos, Light of Chaos: Book 1.
© Alexandra Gardner.
First Printing, 2019.

To the assholes who said I couldn't,
and to those who said I could:
This one's for you.

I lounged on top of my mother's grave, staring up at the graying sky. The dew from the grass clung to my hoodie and jeans, one hand resting on my bow. Its metal length felt like the comfort of a blanket, draped across my stomach and ribs. I twirled an arrow between my fingers, contemplating my pending demise, and crossed my legs at the ankles, one foot shaking lazily. My toe *tap-tap-tapped* against her headstone.

"Winter's almost over," I told her, watching the clouds pass by overhead. "My birthday's next month...the big one-eight."

Well, I'm already eighteen, but time travel just has that effect on a girl. I heaved a sigh. *It's amazing I've lasted this long.*

I stopped tapping my foot to stare at the headstone.

> *Sarah Samantha Anders*
> *U-we-tsi-a-ge-yv*
> *u-ni-tsi*
> *u-s-da-yv-hv-s-gi*

"I know, I know," I murmured, settling back onto the grass. "Your little girl grew up so fast these last ten years. You probably wouldn't recognize me now. Although, dad says I'm the spitting image of you." I smiled, moving my hand from my bow to finger the feathers braided into my hair. "You know him—always with the flattery."

"Getta loada this," a man drawled from atop the tall angel tombstone nearby. "She at it again."

"Even in death, we can't git no peace," the other ghost, a woman this time, muttered. "Goin' t' talk t' herself 'til my ears're bleedin'."

"Yer ears can't bleed, Doreen. Yer dead!"

"Hush-up, Earl! Nobody ask ya."

Ignoring the magnificently whiny duo, I forged on. "Dad's fine. Still working hard and all that. I know he worries about me, but I'm okay. I haven't told him how easily they've been tracking me down lately. I don't want him to worry, y'know? I can handle myself."

"I pity the poor chil'," Earl said. "Her mom ain't listenin'."

"*I'm* listenin'—not that I damn want ta. Dronin' on an' on 'bout nonsense again an' again—*ridiculous!*"

My jaw clenched. I was careful to stare vacantly through the two unwanted onlookers when their heads appeared above mine, obscuring my view of the late afternoon sky. It would be more of a hassle if they knew I could see and hear them; I'd learned that one the hard way. Not all ghosts were friendly. Even if they were, a lot of them were drama queens. *I should know—I live with one.*

I wasn't sure how long ago Doreen and Earl died, but their southern drawls and old-era clothing told me they weren't native to contemporary Seattle. Why ghosts traveled the globe, I'd never know. I knew why my resident ghost had, but I'd avoided speaking to others after that one time...I shuddered at the memory.

"She chatty as ever," the dead man said. "At least she not ramblin' about magic 'n mages."

"*Yet*, ya mean," Doreen scoffed. "As if such thins exist!"

Norms, I thought cynically. Only a non-magical being wouldn't believe magic existed, even as she was a damn ghost floating on the astral plane.

I heaved a sigh, sitting up and getting to my feet. Daylight was burning. If I didn't want to miss the bus back into the city, I needed to get moving.

Or, something devilish inside of me piped up, *you could use your magic.*

I frowned at myself.

No, I told it. *The mages will find me if I do that.*

Ignoring the two squabbling ghosts, I slung my quiver over my shoulder and touched my fingers to my lips before placing them against the top of my mom's tombstone.

"Daughter, mother, wife," I read aloud in the familiar Cherokee. Mom excelled at all three roles and so much more. "I love you," I murmured, smiling sadly.

I weaved through the headstones, moving toward the gate that would lead to the road. Few people bothered to visit the graveyard this time of day; they were either at work or bustling home for dinner. City life was busy and the dead easily forgotten. Just not for me.

When I was halfway through the graveyard, my step faltered. Every hair on the back of my neck rose and every nerve prickled. A menacing tingle slithered up my arms, feeling the presence of five—no, *six*—mages nearby.

Really? Do we have to do this today?

I gripped my bow, fingers hovering over and brushing the feathers of my arrows. Their soft tickle helped ground me, even as my heart raced in my chest. I lengthened my strides toward the exit, hoping to get some distance from the latest batch of executioners sent to find me. Eyes darting left and right, I scanned the grounds for threats. My eyes landed on the black-cloaked man staring at me from across the cemetery. The overlapping sun and moon insignia on his chest told me he was a mage of the Bronze Eclipse guild.

I began to jog, picking up speed, but before I could slow my momentum, I collided into a large, hulking man when he stepped out from behind one of the tall crypts. His magical energy stung my arms on impact.

"Watch where you're walking!" I snapped.

The hulk wasn't amused. Faster than my eye could track, he grabbed me by the throat and slammed me against the tomb. I wheezed.

Ugh! Why do they always go for the throat?

He was too close to shoot, so I settled for a lovely knee to the groin. Once the mage doubled over, cupping himself, I put an elbow into the back of his neck. He slumped to the ground, and I nocked an arrow, pulled back, and let it fly. As my bow string *thunked* and vibrated, I winced at the carnage I'd wrought. Blood sprayed as the arrow unwound his calf muscle, mangling it with its power.

Running again, I sensed the other pursuers.

Dammit! I didn't even use magic today! So much for that tactic.

I accessed the power coiling in my core, the vast center of magical energy raging inside of me like a volcanic inferno. It shivered through me, and I reached for the metaphysical plane between this world and the void, ready to get the hell out of here. Before I could flee, someone crashed into me, disrupting my concentration and my connection to my magic. My back hit the ground, knocking the air from my lungs. The weight of my bow smacked my hand painfully against the earth, but I squeezed it tighter, unwilling to lose my only means of defense.

A fireball shot past my head, the heat enough to make my skin tighten uncomfortably as the moisture was sucked from the air. I wheezed under the mage's crushing weight as he pushed himself up. Intentional or not, this new assailant had managed to land on top of me right as his friend had tried to go for the crispy -Samantha approach.

That would've been a horrible way to die.

I muttered, "Thanks, buddy," to the man now straddling me.

With him hovering above me, it was all too easy to bring up my knee, fast and hard. When the air hissed from his lungs, I shoved him off me, rolled over, and drew another arrow while he writhed in agony, holding himself. Adding insult to injury, I pulled the string back, and *thwack!* I popped an arrow into yet another victim's leg.

"Catch ya later!" I waved cheerily, smiling as I sprinted away. "*Sucker.*"

Two down, four to go.

Panting, I wove in and out of gravestones, dodging fireballs until I had no choice but to duck behind someone's headstone. I winced, knowing there would be scorch marks marring the stone. The second I could leave the safety it provided, I leapt into a sprint, weaving through the graveyard. My lungs burned, my throat throbbed, and my legs protested as I dodged more fire, blinking sweat out of my eyes.

I clamped my jaw shut until it hurt and tightened my fist around my bow. *He's going to destroy my sanctuary!*

Even from a distance, I felt the heat on my back, almost roasting my neck and drying the feathers in my hair. The coolness of the wet, winter air stung my face but couldn't chase the heat away. I yelped when one of the fire elemental's flames flew a little too close for comfort.

The smell of singed hair had me glaring over my shoulder. *Mother. Trucker.* My hair was frizzy enough in the humidity as it was; I didn't need Flame-On making it worse. I whirled, only stopping long enough to return fire. He incinerated my arrow with a well-aimed fireball before it could reach him, the smell of burning plastic permeating the air between us.

If it wasn't such bad news for me, I would've been impressed.

I pivoted toward the tree line, hoping Flame-On would be wary of causing a large city fire. There were waist-high shrubs just a few feet from me. I jumped the hedge—more like dove—ducking into a crouch and rolling. I grunted, my spine grinding into my quiver, tree roots, and fallen branches.

I sprang to my feet and sprinted deeper into the brush. Crisp leaves crunched under my heavy footsteps, and twigs snapped as my feet pounded the uneven ground. A root hidden underneath the foliage tripped me up, and I barely managed to stay on my feet as the pull of gravity gave me momentary vertigo. Rocks, dew-slick leaves, and other nuisances hindered my escape.

I pumped my arms and ran harder, my shallow pants puffing in the cold air. My nose and fingers were going numb, and snot dribbled down my lip. I wiped my sleeve across my face, licking my lips and tasting salt from the sweat permeating my skin.

One thought filled my mind like a driving force. *Run, run, run, run!*

I'd lost sight of my assailants, but they'd also lost sight of me. I weaved around greenery, being sure to stay hidden as I left the mages in the dust. Climbing a sturdy tree near me, I perched, bow at the ready.

Flame-On sauntered into the woods, his remaining three friends flanking him. He wasn't close enough for me to line up my shot, so I waited, breath lodged in my throat as he got closer. I noticed—now that I was looking—just how young he was. He and his companions couldn't have been any older than me. In fact, Flame-On looked like the youngest of the group, and it made my disgust with the guilds that much greater.

At the same time, it was their young age and inexperience that had kept me alive so far. Maybe they were a new squad. Maybe they didn't work well together. Whatever the case, it had worked in my favor. If they'd been a squad from the Crimson Sun guild, I would've been dead ten times over by now.

They came into range, so I took aim and let loose, catching Flame-On in the thigh. I tried to feel bad about hitting my mark, but I didn't. He'd destroyed something precious to me, had taken away the last thing I held dear. After this, I'd never be able to come back here again. Rumors of this battle would reach the ears of those in the Magical Community, and the graveyard would be yet another haunt I couldn't visit.

I'd never be able to speak to my mother's grave ever again.

These guys should be glad I wasn't taking kill shots. Unlike the Hunters chasing me, I wasn't a murderer. I planned to keep it that way, but it didn't mean I would let them return to their guild, boasting like I was some sort of coward. If they were stupid enough to take on the "dangerous"—who decided that nonsense, anyway?—Sibyl, then they would just have to return to their guild, tails between their legs. A little street cred never hurt a girl anyway.

I snorted because street cred actually *was* my problem.

I hopped from tree branch to tree branch, numb fingers slipping and catching pitch with each grab of my free hand. My boots thudded against the branches, the sound of the bark cracking under my feet making my heart lurch in my chest. I was making too much noise but staying put after my last shot was too dangerous. They'd locate me soon.

I bit back a curse, teeth grinding when I slipped on a branch that had had the bark peeled back by some forest critter. My boot glided over the surface, and my torso crashed into the trunk, the metal of my bow clanking against it. I wheezed, fingers digging painfully into the bark while my heart raced. Squeezing my eyes shut, I slowly uncurled my death-grip from the Evergreen.

Trying to get a different angle, I squatted on the branch before the other three Hunters could find me. I could sense that two of the remaining mages were fairly weak, but I wouldn't count myself victorious yet. The third was packing some serious magical energy. They clustered just close enough together that I couldn't tell if the strongest energy was coming from the guy in the middle of the two flanking him.

Come on, show me your power, I silently pleaded.

If I knew who the threat was, then I could take him down, shoot the other two without much struggle, and be home before "curfew." Considering I worked later tonight, it was less of a curfew and more like, "If you're not home before dark, so help me, Samantha Anders, I'll haunt you in your afterlife!" I pursed my lips, knowing Phoenix was going to rip me a new one because the sun was setting already.

Russian roulette it is, I decided and took aim.

Something curled and snaked around my ankle, magic tingling along my skin on contact.

Take the shot!

My arrow hit just as I was pulled airborne. *Crap!* It was an earth elemental, and whichever mage he was, it wasn't the guy I'd just knocked on his ass. I dangled upside-down from my ankle, feeling the branch twining up my calf.

You got this, Sam; only two left, I told myself.

Psh! With your luck, you'll manage to get yourself killed.

If Phoenix could hear my mind-babble right now, *he'd* kill me.

At least we'd be dead together.

I briefly wondered if I would chill on this plane like Phoenix or move to the next—if there even was a next plane. I couldn't be sure; he sure as hell hadn't moved on or whatever.

I plucked an arrow from my bow. *Thank the goddess for clip-on quivers*. I was down to back up arrows now that my large quiver's contents lay scattered on the ground. Three arrows. Two Hunters.

More than enough.

I scanned the brush, looking for Mr. Mother-Nature and Mr. Unknown-Entity. Leaves rustled to my left and I whipped my bow into position, took aim, and fired.

Direct hit!

Feeling particularly cocky, I smirked, taunting, "Come out, come out, wherever you are, Mr. Mother-Nature. It's just you and me now."

"Wow," a man's voice came from my right, his tone dry. "So original."

I shrugged, feeling the twining branches crawl along my hip and up my waist. "What am I supposed to call you when you haven't introduced yourself?"

"Right, like I'm going to stop to greet my enemy? 'Hi, my name's Lucas; what's yours?'" He mocked in falsetto.

"Captain Shoot-Your-Ass, at your service." I gave a firm, two-finger salute, paired with a wink and a click of my tongue.

"Clearly." Flat. Deadpan. Mr. Mother-Nature wasn't impressed.

"Well, this has been fun, Mr. Mother-Nature"—I got a sick thrill out of watching his aura flare with irritation—"but I think I'm about overdue for my curfew. I'm gonna have hell to pay when I get home. Thanks for that."

I let loose an arrow, but the jerk had the audacity to dodge it. I mean, *how rude!* Grabbing my last arrow, I sent a prayer to Hecate. My arrow sailed toward my target, burying deep into his shoulder. I immediately regretted my decision. After knocking out newly dubbed Mr. Fainty-McFainterson, his control over the earth magic dissipated.

Frickin' figures, I thought to myself, careening toward the Earth. At the last moment, I wrapped my magic around me and shifted into Chaos, the void swallowing me whole.

"Home late again, I see." Phoenix glared at me from just inside the door.

I glared back, slipping my body through the narrow opening. "Are you keeping tabs on me again, *old man?*" My comment was meant as a jab, and I knew he wouldn't appreciate it. He wasn't a day over 20—at least, he hadn't been when he'd died two millennia ago…give or take a few centuries. Who was counting? The guy was older than dirt.

I slammed the door shut behind me and stared through his translucent body. Haphazardly, I tossed my bow and quiver into the open, pathetic excuse for a closet. His colors were vibrant today, no doubt a testament to his foul mood.

Round one; let the fight begin.

"Really, Sam?"

"'Really,' what?" I quipped, heavily slumping onto my bed with a hiss. My fall through Chaos had injured my shoulder, the not-so-smooth landing ending with me in a heap on the asphalt in a back alley uptown. It had been a long, horrible ride home on the crowded bus. This time of night, there was only standing room. My shoulder *so* hadn't been up for holding onto the stand-ee strap hanging overhead.

Although I could've, coming directly home would've been a mistake. I needed to be careful when and where I used my magic. Otherwise, I would draw mages directly to me. It wasn't a perfect system, but I depended on Phoenix to take care of the rest. That had worked so far, but lately, it wasn't enough.

"A brat—I'm dealing with a colossal brat," he muttered, swiping a hand down his face. Normally, his Demotic accent was beautiful, but right now, it reminded me he came from another time—forever-and-a-half ago. Since then, he'd had plenty of time to learn the perfect colloquialism to annoy me.

I studied him out of the corner of my eye; his accent wasn't the only thing that reminded me he was ancient. His goatee was wound with braided cloth. His long, black hair was woven with feathers, turquoise, and clay beads, a ghost of decoration from his lifetime. Similar trinkets of bangles, necklaces, and even earrings adorned his wrists, neck, and ears. Some of it was gold.

I liked to make fun of his "man-skirt," but it was actually a shendyt, typical garb from Ancient Egypt. I counted my blessings he wore a linen tunic, which wasn't always typical of men in his time. I wasn't sure how I would feel about having a per-petually shirtless roommate, even if Phoenix was dead.

"Careful, old man, your grumpy-old-grandpa is showing."

"That's because your bratty teenager is showing, Sam. If those Hunters get their hands on you—"

"Yeah, yeah." I waved a hand dismissively. "They'll kill me. They didn't succeed today." I shrugged, gritting my teeth at the pain the motion brought. "Not for a lack of trying, though." I averted my eyes, waiting for hell. A slight thrill surged through me; I enjoyed our arguments, even if that made me a tad maso-chistic and just a touch sadistic.

"Come again?" *Let the meltdown begin.* "Years later and you're still acting like a suicidal maniac! When are you going to learn to take threats seriously?"

"If I die, I'm dead. The world goes on. Besides, oh Ghostly One, you're one to talk."

"And you're a fool!"

Knock out! Round one: point to Phoenix.

That seemed unfair. I wasn't a fool—or suicidal, for that matter.

"Don't get your man-skirt in a twist. I'm just...*livening* things up a bit. You know, as opposed to resigning myself to *this* boring existence." I gestured toward the messy room I called home.

A heap of clothing lay in the corner, piled up to my knees. Bras littered the room—*a girl can never have too many.* A pair of heels appeared to be on two different planets; one was strand-ed near the door, and the other had found its way onto my bed. I slapped at it, knocking the heel to the floor like a mischievous cat. I glanced at the suitcase in the front entryway, still half packed. Always ready to run, to disappear, and to never return. This studio apartment was number three in the last six months. I had to remain elusive.

I stared at the counter where my prayer candles sat neatly, the only semblance of organization in my life. No matter where I ended up, my candles gave me a sense of home and belonging. Mom had loved her ritual candles; having my own felt like having a piece of her with me wherever I went. Even Dad's house didn't quite feel like home anymore. Not without her.

"Sam, I know you're not satisfied with your situation…" Phoenix sighed, and I rolled my eyes. The sigh was just for effect; ghosts didn't need to breathe. "But these are the cards the gods dealt."

"Whatever." I bounced my head against my mattress.

"You're unique, your magic a gift and a blessing."

At that moment, some random ghost decided to float through the wall of my apartment. I pretended not to see him, though his presence made my face fall into a hard line. He floated over my head. The translucent specter spotted Phoenix and changed route, fleeing feet first down through my floor.

"Only you would believe that nonsense! Look at what I have to put up with because of these *gifts*." I pointed to the patch of floor where the ghost had disappeared.

He shrugged, unperturbed by my fifth temper tantrum today.

Grumbling under my breath, I moved across the room, heading for a heap of laundry.

"Sam."

Ignoring my friend, I bent down to pick up the clothes.

"*Samantha.*" The power in his voice had me frozen still, slivers of energy vibrating up my spine in a sensation that tingled to the top of my skull. Phoenix's power was captivating and addicting when he manifested enough emotion to exert it. It never ceased to amaze me, considering he insisted he'd been a Norm when he'd been alive.

Perhaps being a ghost somehow made him inherently magical. Maybe his extreme age gave him some power. Or, maybe I was feeling a modified version of my own excess power, which Phoenix had absorbed over the years, both fueling his spectral form and reducing my magical presence in the Magical Community. It was how I'd managed to stay hidden so far.

If today was evidence of anything, it was that my luck was running out. Phoenix normally did a draw on my powers before I went anywhere. He'd done so ever since my magic had started to have a mind of its own a few years ago. Those magical outbursts were how the guilds had found me in the first place.

Frustrated, I turned to confront him.

Round two: fight!

"I'll be more careful about making an *appearance* in the 'Big, Bad World,'" I air quoted.

"I'm not saying you can't go out; I'm merely trying to say–"

"Don't even go there." I dumped the heaping armful of clothing into my stacked washer-dryer.

"Sam, if you would embrace your power, learn to master it, you wouldn't need…"

I stopped listening. This was the same old argument we'd been having for a while now, and I was getting suspicious. I relied on him to help keep my magical energy in check, which meant I wasn't as practiced in my powers as I could be. Lately, it seemed like every time I turned around, a new ability was cropping up. I was starting to wonder if Phoenix was taking less energy from me in hopes I'd be forced to learn how to better control my abilities.

Joke's on him, I mused. *I'm as stubborn as a mule.*

So's he, I shot back at myself, *and he's been at it a lot longer than you.*

Shaking my head, I made a noise of disgust. "Every time we toy with my magic, I get hurt." I unconsciously rubbed my shoulder. "Or worse, I draw mages to me. Remember?"

"Which is exactly why I think you *should* keep trying. Send them chasing you all over the world! Chaos will take you to any time, any place. Why not use that to your advantage?"

And why shouldn't I try? I thought devilishly, already thinking of new ways to piss him off.

Slowly, I straightened up, a mischievous grin spreading across my face. "Maybe you're right, Phoenix. It would be good practice."

"What's that look?" He sounded panicked.

"I *should* try again. And I have just the time in mind…" I gathered my magical energy, pulling it to my core.

Round two: point to Sam!

"Sam…" He reached for me, but he was too late, too insubstantial, too dead.

I closed my eyes and pictured a pair of forest-green eyes, crinkled with love, joy, and laughter. Wavy, brunette hair, loose tendrils escaping a braid and blowing in the wind. A wide smile on thin lips. A laugh like tinkling bells.

My aura expanded, and energy spread over me, making the hair on my arms rise. I felt cocooned in gentle warmth. My magic was manifesting stronger than it ever had before. It filled me, sparking from my head to my toes. I couldn't stop now, even if I wanted to. The room felt so far away. I felt far away. Everything felt far away.

I blinked out of existence.

J didn't actually blink out of existence. It only felt like it for a few moments, but once I took in the scene around me, I sincerely wished I hadn't. Phoenix was in a frenzy, and my body lay limp on the floor. *Funny*, I thought; I hadn't heard the *thud* it would've made on impact. *Ugh*, there was going to be a bruise on my cheek when I woke up…

If I wake up. Shuddering, I willed myself not to be so pessimistic. *Ha!* I would be dead before *that* ever happened.

But…I could feel magical energy swirling within me, so I had to be alive. Instead of going into Chaos like I'd tried to, my spirit had separated from my body. I floated in front of Phoenix, but he didn't see me. Weird, considering ghosts can see other ghosts.

Unless…

Despite not having vocal cords, I laughed, the sound not reaching Phoenix. He must've been P-I-S-S-E-D—*pissed!* Or, he would be when he realized I wasn't dead. Whatever I was, pure essence or otherwise, it was some sort of new ability. I tried to let him know I was here, but my incorporeal fingers passed through him. I resembled a human-shaped, ghost-like entity of myself, even though I didn't seem to be a ghost or human in this form.

Phoenix floated down toward my crumpled body on the floor, reaching out a hand and touching my cheek. That wasn't possible—ghosts couldn't make physical contact with human bodies. But he was touching me. *Since when could he do that?* His expression relaxed before pinching into a hard scowl…He'd realized I was still alive. Then came the anger. I was in for it; the argument would be explosive.

The room suddenly went dark, and a swirl of colors engulfed me. Red, orange, yellow, green, blue, purple—over and over they swirled around me until it seemed they were one and the same yet separate. They were pastels, watercolors dripping around me. They were soft, dull, and turning clear. My form vibrated, resonating with the colors engulfing me. When they faded, I was all alone, dizzy, and pulsing, electricity vibrating through me.

My surroundings came into focus, and I realized two things like a smack to the face: I was still a spirit, and this was not my apartment. An open, rolling field stretched out in front of me, a light breeze blowing through the grass. The sun was beginning to set over the hill, an orange glow lining the horizon.

"See, Sarah? I told you—it's beautiful!" a giggling, dark-haired girl exclaimed, dragging a young girl by the hand to the crest of the field. "And, if we wait, magic will happen!"

"Slow down, Anna-Banana!" Sarah laughed breathlessly.

"Come on! Almost there!"

"Okay, okay!"

The two girls sprinted past me, enraptured by the scenery before them.

I stared, my mind reeling to catch up. *Sarah? As in...*

I willed myself forward, chasing hot on the heels of the girls who couldn't be older than nine or ten years old. Anna released Sarah's hand, pumping her fists before launching into a cartwheel. She twisted until she could safely fall onto her back, arms and legs spread, making a star.

"Show-off!" Sarah shouted.

Anna stuck out her tongue. "Hurry!"

Sarah sprinted hard, skidding to a stop before turning and falling across Anna's stomach, forcing her to grunt.

Sarah grinned. "Gotcha!"

Anna grimaced, pointing to the sky. "Here it comes!"

The girls stared, enthralled by the stars beginning to twinkle as the sun dipped past the horizon.

I crept closer, hovering above them and staring intently into Sarah's face. I couldn't believe my eyes. *I did it!* I'd found her. I didn't even care that I'd gone further back in time than I'd meant to.

I reached out, wanting to touch the youthful girl who would someday be my mother. Before I could, Anna excitedly flailed her arms, making contact with my incorporeal body. I vanished, and an ear-piercing scream ripped through the peaceful quiet.

Sarah sat up, turning to see what had her friend wailing like a siren. "Anna? Anna-Banana, what's wrong?"

I shot upright, hands flying to a throat that I could feel burning from the bloody-murder scream just moments before. I whipped my head around, realizing the pain that had torn through me was from being sucked into Anna's body.

"Sarah?" I tested Anna's now-hoarse voice.

How surreal.

"What, Anna? What happened?"

"N-N-Nothing."

Phoenix had told me ghosts could perform possessions, but I didn't realize I could. *Of course, I didn't know!* I didn't even know I could separate my essence from my body. *Well, hasn't today just been lovely?*

Sarah didn't seem appeased by my response.

"Really. I was just startled by, uh…" I grappled for an excuse. "How dark it got."

She arched an eyebrow, still doubtful.

"Look." I pointed to a constellation, tracing the lines. "It's Aries."

Distracted, she whipped her head around to look at the stars. "So cool! How do you know that?"

"Because that's my zodiac sign, duh."

"But I thought your birthday was in January?"

Oh, crap. Not my body, not my birthday, not my zodiac. I'm screwing this up!

"Right." I shrugged, feigning nonchalance. "I always mix up the zodiac."

"That's okay, Anna-Banana, I still love you. Even if you *are* a forget-me-not." She winked, wrapping her arms around me.

I inhaled, breathing in the familiar scent of her—lavender and earthy musk. I savored the feel of her arms around me—

arms that would never hold me again. I patted her hair, coveting every bit of contact I could get.

Then, I felt a sharp tug in Anna's chest. It pulled again, this time with some oomph, the force knocking me down. Scowling, I tried to sit up. Before I could, a massive heave flung my spirit across the field, rolling head over feet. Dizzy and disoriented, I finally manage to get myself righted. I looked back and saw Anna shaking her head, appearing disoriented.

Suddenly, my magic took over, conjuring snippets of the pending future. Maybe it was a result of merging into Anna. Maybe it was a result of being flung from her. Whatever the case, it was pitiless. Memories assailed me, flickers of images: Mom, in her hospital bed; Mom, telling me everything would be "okay"; Dad, dressed in black, crying in front of a casket. *Her* casket.

I shrieked, trying to get the awful images to stop.

Help! Please, Hecate. Someone. Anyone? Help!

Phoenix. Phoenix. Phoenix!

Colors began to dance around me. *Flash!* Red. *Flash!* Blue. *Flash!* Green. Yellow. Purple. Orange. I whirled around and around, trying to get my bearings. *Flash! Flash! Flash!* The colors swirled, becoming murky. Dark, darker still. Then…nothing.

 hen I came to, my hands flew to my throbbing temples. My *everything* didn't feel good. Damn, I had a migraine. I groaned, pushing myself up, and rubbed my hands down my face, my cheeks and eyelids pulling with the motion.

"Goddess, I hurt." My eyes widened in shock. "What the—?"

"Sam?" Phoenix got right up in my face. "If you're awake, you better open that sassy mouth of yours right now! What's two plus two?"

I winced at his shrill voice. "Fish. And what crawled up your ass? Turn down the decibels. Can't you tell I'm in excruciating pain?"

"If I weren't already dead, you would've given me a heart attack!"

"What the f—"

"*Samantha Rosalind Anders!* Stop the obscenities and talk to me!"

Focusing on my throbbing temples again, I grabbed my head. Not only was I in my own body, I was still on the floor—the dirty, hard floor. *Nasty.*

"Earth to Sam, I'm talking to you."

Through bleary eyes, I stared up at Phoenix, the room warbling at the edge of my vision.

"What happened?" he demanded. "It was like…your very essence had been ripped from your body. You were so empty, I thought you might have destroyed yourself. Thank Ra, you're alive."

"You call this alive?" I snapped, wincing at the noise.

"Sure. You're talking and breathing, aren't you? Now, tell me what happened."

"Mom."

One word, but the meaning rang clear.

He blanched, an impressive feat for a translucent being such as himself. Then, his eyes narrowed. *Oh no.* I felt a lecture coming, and I resisted every impulse telling me to roll my eyes and groan.

"How long ago?"

"I'm…not entirely sure…" I trailed off. "She was a girl. Maybe somewhere around nine or ten?"

His jaw dropped and then began working. "I thought you couldn't go very far!"

My eyes rolled toward the back of my head, and I massaged my temples. "Would you stop yelling?"

"That kind of time jump could've killed you!"

I covered my ears at his outburst. *Apparently not.*

Phoenix looked ready to strangle me.

I scooted away. "I never said I *couldn't* do large time jumps. I just choose *not* to. Besides, you know I've gone back *way* farther—"

"That was different! Your powers *surged* when they unlocked. They've stabilized now."

"They have not!" I snapped, knowing he was both right and wrong. They had stabilized in comparison to my thirteenth birthday but still fluctuated regularly. "It's not like I've made a habit of using Chaos to go into the past. I avoid moving outside of present time—when I don't accidentally over or undershoot my destination. Granted, that's probably because I never take the time to practice my abilities. Isn't that something you always get after me to do? You can't have it both ways."

"Fine." His tone implied it was anything but. "Say I concede your point. Now, care to explain why you went limp?"

"I would if I could."

"Pardon?"

"I haven't the slightest inkling what happened. One minute, I was charging my power. The next? My body was sprawled on the floor. My consciousness took a joyride with a spirit-version of myself."

"Like…a *ghost?*" Phoenix flickered, more translucent this time.

"Not quite. I was me…but also hazy, white light. And I could see you, but you couldn't see me."

"Not a ghost. Not visible to ghosts…Perhaps"—he tilted his head to the side, brow furrowing—"a spiritualized collection of magical energy?"

I nodded; my gut told me it was something like that. That would explain why Phoenix couldn't see me—magical energy and spirits were two different things. Sometimes I loved the intuition that came with these "Sibyl" powers, but the perks didn't seem worth the drawbacks.

"It seems dangerous. Don't do it again. If your body had been attacked while you were gone, I would've been helpless to defend you…" He trailed off as if he had just had an epiphany. "Unless…Now, I'm not saying I would do it." His eyes shifted around the room. "At least, not without good reason—it would be for your safety, that is."

My gut tightened. "Phoenix?"

"I would take care not to be intrusive," he rambled, "but in extenuating circumstances, I think you could find it in your heart to forgive me…"

I'd had enough of his stalling. "Phoenix!"

He coughed uncomfortably.

I'm going to strangle him!

"Ah, yes. What I'm trying to say is…" He finally looked me in the eyes. "If your consciousness was absent, I think I would be able to perform a full-body possession."

My jaw dropped. "You *pervert!*" I picked up the high heel I'd knocked off my bed earlier, throwing it through his plasmatic body. It crashed into the wall before clattering onto the floor.

"*No-no-no-no-no!*" He threw his hands up in defense. "It would be to keep you safe!"

"Sure! And I'm supposed to assume that's *all* you would do?"

"Yes, Sam! I'm not some creep. What do you take me for?"

"A male—a young male who hasn't had a body in over two thousand years! A *hormonal* young male who would be in the body of a teenage girl!" I shrieked, and he looked indignant, his mouth gaping in horror. "*Psh!* The experience would be a man's dream. So why wouldn't I expect you to be a pervert?"

"Because you trust me, and I'm not into violating people—least of all *you*, Sam."

"Oh yeah?" I challenged, not letting up. "It would be over-whelming, wouldn't it? I know I was overwhelmed when I got sucked into Anna's body."

His eyes narrowed. "Come again?"

It was my turn to fidget. "Mom had some little friend named Anna with her. The brat threw her fist through me and five agonizing seconds later, I was in control of her body."

"You performed a full-body possession?" His eyes went wide. "With the host in residence?"

"Yeah…but it only lasted a few minutes before it felt like I got sucker punched. Next thing I knew, I was being ejected like a jack-in-the-box." My eyes glazed, remembering the horrible feeling of complete loss of control.

"I'm surprised the full merge didn't rip you to shreds. That's a delicate skill to master. I've seen eager, newbie ghosts torn to bits for trying. Tampering with another living creature's entity is nothing to play around with. It's one thing to submerge into a person's mind to pick up their thoughts, but it's suicide to take possession of a body with its soul in residence."

Despite kneeling on the floor, I felt dizzy. "It's not like I initiated the merge. She swung her arm through me, and it just *happened*."

"If you'd practice your magic, then you'd know how to shield against intruders in your body and others pulling you into theirs!"

"We're back to this again? 'Practice your powers, Sam.' 'Don't time travel, Sam.' 'Learn how to control your abilities, Sam,'" I mocked. "You keep contradicting yourself! Make up your frick-frackin' mind! This yo-yo game is gonna give me a serious case of whiplash!"

"Oh. I see." Phoenix's golden eyes became cold, calculating slits. "*I'm* the bad guy. I protect you, encourage you, and try to help you. Clearly, I'm the problem here."

My eyes widened, staring into his. Twin orbs goaded me, daring me to place the blame solely on him. I leaned forward, putting a hand down in front of me, ensnared by the fire flickering in his eyes. An arched eyebrow coaxed me to come closer, daring me to own up to my unfair accusations. I put my other hand down, crawling nearer until inches separated us.

He growled low in his throat, baring his teeth at me. "I'm *waiting*, Samantha."

"Um…"

"Yes?" He floated toward me, making my thoughts scatter.

I rocked back on my knees. "I, uh…um. I'm sorry?"

Phoenix advanced, and I reached an arm behind me, crawling backward.

"Go on." He continued to encroach on my space.

I scooted back further. "What I mean is, you're right. You *do* scold me."

"And?" He came closer, crawling toward me.

"And I never listen…" I stopped and gaped, staring at his hands and knees, which were *touching* the ground.

"Samantha," he growled between his teeth, snapping my attention back to his eyes.

"You touched me," I accused, which sounded way worse than I'd intended, but ghosts were incorporeal beings, incapable of making contact with anything in the living world. Phoenix shouldn't have been touching the floor right now.

His eyes were wild. "What?"

I backed up again, my back coming flush with the wall at the end of the room—a whole lot of good that did since he just followed me. I sucked in a breath of air and held it.

Up close and in my face, he hissed, "What did you just say?"

My body vibrated, adrenaline and Phoenix's palpable energy tingling along my skin. My heart pounded in my ears, and I swear I could feel his breath on my cheek.

"What. Did. You. Say?" He bit out between his bared teeth, his lip curling back in a snarl.

I advanced away from the wall, turning the tables on this crouching lion. "*You touched me. I saw* you!" Our noses were almost touching as we stared each other down.

"You're wrong," he stated as if I hadn't just spit molten lava words in his face.

"What?"

"You. Are. Wrong." Blasé, he punctuated each syllable.

No retort came to my mind, despite the blatant lie.

His gold eyes stared into mine, a thick lining of kohl surrounding them, making them breathtaking and highlighting the unique color. His thick lips curled into a scowl, pulling his sharp cheeks down. He had a long nose, which flared with his barely restrained anger. Even as a muted version of himself, his russet skin tone set off his features nicely.

I heaved a sigh, feeling the fight leave me. *Let Phoenix have his secrets—for now.*

"My mistake." I shrugged, turning my head to hide my resignation. "You keep giving me advice, and I keep being a jerk. Same-old, same-old."

"I'll always be here for you. Even if it's as a verbal sparring partner." His lip twitched into a half-grin. "I know you think I'm contradictory, and I concede that I am. I just worry." He reached out to touch my cheek, but I only felt a chill.

Turning my head back to meet his gaze, I imagined his hand as if it were solid. I pushed my energy out, forcing it into his palm. To my shock, his hand changed from prickling chills to solid warmth. I gasped, reaching up and putting my hand over his. Then, I closed my eyes and leaned my cheek into his palm, reveling in the touch of the dead man. My eyes snapped open when he snatched his hand away with a hiss. It faded, becoming transparent again.

Our eyes met, and silence passed between us.

Then, he faded into the ether, leaving me with questions burning inside me. Like many arguments we'd had before, this one would go unresolved. Round for round, our sparring went nowhere, as always. Phoenix was dead-set on keeping his secrets, but I'd find a way to pry them out of him. It would be a waiting game.

How has my life become so bleak?

I laughed bitterly, considering my childhood. I'd spent countless days at my father Henry's office after school in my youth, especially after Mom died—cancer took her in the blink of an eye. I'd been sad about her passing, but Dad and his boss, Richard Morley, had more than made up for the hole she'd left in my heart. Ricky had been like a big brother, letting me hang around the penthouse offices whenever I was there.

But I'd shut out a lot of people once my magic had started going haywire. I didn't want to endanger the people I loved, so I didn't have friends. Well, I had Phoenix. He'd been my one and only constant over these last several years. Friendships were so hard for me to make and keep, I'd started to develop a complex.

Besides my powers, which had always been dangerous to the people around me, my intuition magic had helped me ace my classes. I ended up skipping a grade and was a freshman by age thirteen, meaning I'd been a year younger than my classmates and therefore a little bit of an outcast. I'd graduated last June, just two months after my seventeenth birthday.

I'd had friends, but those friendships hadn't worked out...I shuddered, repressing memories best left forgotten. If it weren't for Phoenix now, I wouldn't have any friends. I supposed I should consider myself lucky to have a companion at all. My track-record was unfortunate in so many ways.

Tears stung my eyes, but I wouldn't cry about a past I couldn't—*wouldn't*—change.

Maybe I would apologize for pushing Phoenix to tell me his secrets. Maybe I would put more trust in his reasoning. I knew I wasn't easy to get along with, and I trusted him to do what he felt was best when keeping me safe. It was a fulltime job, no doubt.

I wished—not for the first time—that he understood my magic. Neither of us knew the full extent of my abilities. As far as we could tell, there was no one else like me. Everything would be so much easier if we could just figure out why I had powers other mages and witches didn't. While I wasn't exactly clear on the details, I knew mages and witches had different magical energies, and even practiced different magic than each other, but they couldn't do the things I could do.

There were necromancers and mediums; they could see ghosts. I wasn't sure if I was one or the other. Clairvoyants could get glimpses of the future—usually just feelings—but I could see full visions. Elementals had an affinity with one of the five elements. So far as I could tell, I wasn't an elemental.

The list of magical classifications went on and on, but what stumped us was how I could do so much. I could see ghosts; get visions of the past, present, and future; enter Chaos to move through time and space; manipulate magical energy; and see auras. Not to mention the intuition powers, which had saved my life a time or two—*thousand.* Today, I found out I could separate my essence from my body. Who knew what else I was capable of? I wasn't inclined to find out, but it appeared as if I didn't have a say in the matter.

I'd never heard of a mage or witch having so many gifts—let alone ones so powerful. My gifts made me a target, and my blunders stumbling around in the past had made me a "threat" to the Magical Community and the world as a whole, at least according to the guilds. They wanted me dead. It wasn't fair, but life never was. Especially not mine.

I entered the bathroom and, looking in the mirror, saw my jade-green eyes had dark circles under them. My frayed eyebrows arched down, matching my thin lips. My brown hair was shaggy and mussed, falling out of its braid, the edges singed. There were scratches all over my light-brown skin from today's chase through the graveyard. Basically, I looked like hell. Cursing under my breath, I grabbed a hairbrush and undid my braid. Ripping noises ensued while I pulled the brush through the jungle that was my hair.

How had I gotten myself into this state?

I let out a curt "Ha!"

Rolling my eyes, I recalled the day I'd ruined my entire life. Thirteen and unaware of my abilities, I'd managed to slip my way into the past. Frustration flared at the memory, and magical energy seeped from me. I began to pant, my energy draining. I dropped the hairbrush, and as if from a distance, I heard it clatter to the ground.

Images began flashing in rapid succession: a birthday crown in mud, cave walls that lasted for miles, never-ending darkness, light at the end of the tunnel, hand-crafted candles, and an elaborate, round table with five chairs. I could feel magical energy swirling out of me.

No, I don't want to see this. I backed against the wall and sagged to the ground. *Make it stop.*

Events from five years ago conjured from Chaos and manifested into my mind:

"Sibylla!" the ancient guild mage yells at Samantha, locking her in a prison cell. He leaves her there, afraid, confused, and all alone.

"Let me help you, Chibale," she says to the slave who tends to her in her cell. He nods, understanding her intent, even if they don't speak the same language.

"I'm sorry," she says, panting and out of breath, "I don't know how to use my magic very well. If I knew how I did it, I bet I could take us to your home instantly."

He smiles at her, encouraging her to be strong on their long journey.

"How much farther?" she asks, the sand storm buffeting the pair as they trek across the desert hand-in-hand.

He doesn't understand the question to provide an answer. He squeezes her hand, somehow knowing she needs reassurance.

Samantha collapses, barely conscious as they enter Chibale's village. He scoops her up in his arms despite his own fatigue and hunger, carrying her, delirious and ill with fever, the rest of the distance to his home.

*She writhes and moans in her sleep, something soft
and cool dabbing her forehead.*

*She awakens and sits up, bleary-eyed and exhaust-
ed, in an unfamiliar bed. It takes her a minute to realize
she doesn't remember coming here. Terrified, Samantha's head swivels, catching sight of a tall man's back.*

"Chibale!"

*Startled, he jumps and turns around. He isn't Chi-
bale. Her heart pounds in her chest, fear surging
through her veins.*

*The young man smiles, and it's with genuine happi-
ness, not malice. The colors wavering around him are
soft, warm, and comforting—like sunshine and happiness. She is reminded of Chibale, and the longer she
studies the young man's face, the more she sees the re-
semblance.*

*"Is Chibale your dad?" Samantha asks, knowing
the young man won't understand her any more than
Chibale had.*

*The young man's face scrunches in confusion. He
approaches her, making her worry she'd misread the
colors surrounding him. She isn't sure how to interpret
auras, but his isn't threatening; it seems intrigued and
curious. He sits in a chair next to the bed, reaching to
his side to grab a washcloth from a bucket on the floor.*

*The man speaks in a beautiful, lyrical version of the
same language Chibale spoke. His voice is a rich bari-
tone, and it fills the room as he speaks with confidence.
By the inflection of his words, Samantha is certain he's
asking a question as he holds out the wrung-out cloth
and his free hand.*

She tilts her head, not sure how to respond.

*He smiles, taking her small, dirty cheek in his palm,
wiping the cloth gently over her face. His touch makes
her skin hum, tingle, and vibrate. Her eyes go wide, trying to understand the feeling. Chibale's hand hadn't*

had this effect on her, but the evil mage who'd locked her up had had a threatening tingle and hum when he'd grabbed her.

The young man chats at Samantha, quickly distracting her from the strange sensations. She watches his lips form the words as he talks and wipes the grime from her face.

"What's your name?" she asks when he rinses the cloth in the bucket.

His brow furrows.

"I'll go first," she says, pointing to her chest. "I'm Samantha."

His face lights up and he nods. "Sam-anta," he repeats with some difficulty, his accent turning the name choppy.

"Did Chibale tell you my name?" she asks.

The young man replies, but the only word she understands is Chibale's name.

She points to herself again. "Samantha." Then, she points to the young man's chest. "Chibale's son?"

He shakes his head in confusion.

She tries again, repeating until understanding lights his eyes.

"Bennu," he says, pointing to his chest. Then, pointing to hers, he repeats, "Sam-anta."

She beams at him, and he smiles back. "Bennu. That's a pretty name."

Excited, he gets up to grab a parchment of some sort. He roves over it, finally stopping on a symbol before flipping the page to show her. She tilts her head to the side, studying the drawing.

"It's a bird." She chews her lip, looking more closely. "It's not just a bird, it's a phoenix," she says.

He points at the bird, then at himself.

Her eyes widen. "Bennu means phoenix?"

He smiles at her, and she smiles back.

Chibale enters the room, surprise on his face. A genuine smile lights his features as tears of gratitude roll down his cheeks. Tears fill her eyes too, and Samantha reaches a hand toward him.

I came out of the vision, panting, cold sweat permeating my skin.

"Chibale," I whispered under my breath, pulling myself upright. I had to use the bathroom counter as a crutch, having just expelled even more of my energy on the vision. I became weaker thinking about my savior, Chibale, even if he thought I'd been the one to save him.

After we'd escaped the mage's lair I'd been imprisoned in, and he enslaved in for years, I'd gone into hiding with Chibale. It had taken a few weeks, but he and I had made the long trek to his homeland. I still wasn't sure how either of us survived. The longer I'd stayed in his time, the more I'd felt my powers building within me.

Worse, I hadn't known the full extent of the damage I'd done by visiting the past. That understanding came later—much later. As in, after I'd returned to the twenty-first century—on the very day I'd left so many weeks prior—and a little birdy filled me in. The rumors about the powerful, dangerous Sibyl had spread far and wide, the young time-witch who'd disappeared without a trace.

When I'd returned from Ancient Egypt, I'd found a familiar-looking young man floating in my bedroom. A ghost. Not just any man's ghost, either. Not a day older than when I'd last seen him, Bennu had grinned at me.

"Hello, Samantha," he'd said in heavily accented English.

I'd screamed, he'd grimaced, and my dad had come running into my room. More screaming had ensued over my filthy and near-dead state—it had been a long day. *Yeah, long.* I'd learned how absolutely draining manifesting my powers across centuries of time travel could be. I'd been hospitalized for several days following the event.

Apparently, I'd kept mumbling about meeting a phoenix in my delirium. Dad had been concerned I was delusional. Bennu had smiled a secret smile at me, and soon, the ghost had a special nickname and a home with the world's most powerful, most dangerous Sibyl in all of history.

I shook my head, letting my mind come back to the here and now. Looking at myself, I could see the scrapes and bruises I had from fighting the mages earlier today. There was sap on my palms from Tarzaning through the trees. My skin was clammy from the exertion of my flashback. Was that the outline of a handprint on my neck?

Just great! I'm gonna have to wear cover-up for a week!

Rolling my eyes, I began to strip. Thirty minutes later, I was showered, toweled-off, and wrapped in a robe. Opening the door, I headed for my dresser, digging through it and looking for a rockin' outfit that wouldn't get me kicked out of work but would let me have some fun after I clocked off. Tonight, after waiting and bussing tables, I would get to dance.

"Sam," Phoenix said.

So, he came back, hmm?

I ignored him.

Crop-top, plaid miniskirt, black leggings, and heels in hand, I reentered the bathroom to dress. After adding my super awesome concealer to my neck and donning an intricate, lace choker to avoid unwanted questions, I applied make-up and fixed my hair with a few thin braids, leaving the rest loose around my shoulders. I exited the bathroom, grabbing my purse, keys, and cellphone.

My live-in ghost was now nowhere to be found. I would probably get an earful for leaving without Phoenix later, but it wasn't like he didn't know where to find me. Besides, if it was so important to him that he accompany me places, he shouldn't have taken off again.

hen I arrived at Club Cadence in downtown Seattle, there were already several customers lined up outside the door. As I strode up to the bouncer, I received several aggravated glares and curses thrown my way. I shrugged, putting a hand on my hip.

"Hey Drake," I said to my colleague.

"Hey-hey! It's Sammy Girl. How you doin'?"

"Never better," I said, lying through my teeth, and we bumped knuckles.

"Go on in, the boss is waiting for you."

"Thanks, Drake. Try to stay out of trouble."

"You know it."

I shook my head, my magic giving me a glimpse of the trouble he would have tonight. Poor fool was going to be in a three-on-one brawl. My lips quirked. Why anyone would mess with him was beyond me. Over six-feet tall and at least two hundred and forty pounds of pure muscle, he could intimidate a WWE fighter. With a fierce, sharp scowl, Drake was the epitome of kick-ass.

I wound my way through dancers, making a beeline for the bar.

"Hey, Tina," I shouted to be heard over the music.

"Hey there, hun." She leaned over and gave me a one-arm hug. "Boss Woman is looking for you. She says she needs your skills, pronto."

"Yeah, Drake told me she was looking for me. Any idea where she's currently hiding?"

"I'd try backstage. Something about wires and messes."

"Thanks, Tina."

I took an apron from behind the counter, wrapping it around my waist, and grabbed a notepad and three pens—I never knew when a kleptomaniac would strike—and made my way toward the stage.

"Yo, Samantha! Lookin' fine, girl."

"Sup, Kenny. Seen Terry around?"

"Yeah, she's backstage losin' it hard."

"You know what's going on?"

"Yeah, I guess the new girl tripped over some wires in the back. Terry's having a panic attack. Better hurry."

Great, I thought cynically. *Day one and Shanelle's replacement is already screwing things up.*

"Roger that." I saluted him, heading backstage.

Someone nearly tackled me to the ground.

"Thank God! What took you so long? I'm at my wit's ends here!" Tear tracks were evident on Terry's face.

"Aunty, I just got here. Everyone on staff told me to hurry back here. So, what's the problem?"

"That's my girl! Just the attitude I need." She ran her hands through her short blonde hair, trying to gather some semblance of composure. "Our new girl tripped over some wires back here when I was showing her around. I've been trying to plug them back in, but I don't recognize half of these plugs. What happened to standardized USB?"

I shrugged at her, but she barreled on in typical Aunty Terry fashion.

"All I've managed to do is get the strobe lights back on, but the colored lights and surround-sound are still down. Lord knows what the rest of these do! Anyway, I know you're good with these kinds of things, and I could really use your help right now."

"Is that all? Take a breath, Aunty. I'll have your system back up and running smoothly in no time."

"That's my favorite niece! I swear, if it weren't for you, I would've gone out of business the same day I opened!"

I rolled my eyes. "That's not true and you know it. You could've asked Shanelle at any time." Shanelle was my tech-savvy cousin and former coworker. One might say Club Cadence was like a family business.

"Nells is always busy these days," Terry said with a pout. "Hence the new girl."

I shook my head. "Go on. I've got this. You've got more important things to do—like running the club."

"Bless your soul, sweetheart. Thank you."

With that, I turned to the wires to assess the damage. *Yeesh!* She wasn't kidding. What was half of this nonsense? It didn't matter; I just needed to see where the wires had been plugged in a few hours ago, so I closed my eyes, accessing Chaos. I guided my mind's eye back through time, waiting until I saw the image I needed. *Gotcha!*

Feeling a little dizzy, I pulled my mind from the vision and began picking up wires. Ten minutes later, bass from the surround-sound vibrated through my body and colorful lights shone through the opening leading to the stage.

Kenny stopped me on my way out. "Girl, you seriously rock!"

"No, Mr. DJ, *you* rock. If you wanna thank me properly, you can play the good stuff after I get off shift tonight."

"Anything for you, goddess of my heart." He winked at me, and I blew him a kiss.

Oh yeah, tonight is gonna rock!

Tonight so totally didn't rock.

My shift felt like it dragged on forever. Some rude customers had seriously pissed me off, killing my vibe and putting me in a sour mood. Worse, self-confident Austin, a disgusting, college frat boy, had hit on me for the fifth time this week—*and I only work two days a week! Really, can't the guy take a hint?*

Frustrated, I headed for the bar and sat down on one of those really cool spinning stools, rotating back and forth while I waited for Tina to take my order.

"Hey hun, done with your shift already?" She gave me one of her winning smiles, and I perked up a bit.

"Yeah. Terry doesn't like me working long shifts. The extra cash is enough for me to get by, and I get the perk of dancing in a twenty-one and up club."

"Girl, you and your crazy dancing addiction! What can I get you?"

"A root beer, please."

"Coming right up."

She set my soda in front of me, and I was just taking a sip when my whole body exploded with sensation. Wave after wave of tingles shivered from my tailbone to the top of my skull. *Crap, they found me!* My head whipped around, searching for the ridiculously powerful mage in the club. When I couldn't spot him, I hunched over my drink. My stomach churned as I sipped my soda, trying to blend in with the crowd.

"Hello," a deep voice said from next to me, the mage's power zinging over my skin as he spoke.

So much for blending in.

I turned begrudgingly to face my next problem and opened my mouth to respond…then closed it the second my gaze collided with his hazel eyes. They bore into mine, making my mouth go dry despite the soda I'd been sipping. Sandy-colored, ear-length hair was swept back from an undeniably handsome face. Stubble ran the length of his jawline, emphasizing his sharp chin. He looked menacing yet oddly disarming.

He took the stool next to mine and waved Tina over.

"What can I get ya, hun?"

"Mountain Dew, please." He smiled before turning back to me. "Cool place, isn't it?" He had to shout to be heard.

Besides already majorly wigging out, I got this strange feeling as I looked into his eyes. There was a deep sense of sadness about him despite the smile on his face. Silent darkness wavered at the edge of his aura. It wasn't malicious; it was just empty. It spoke of betrayal and despair greater than I could imagine. For some reason, that bothered me, and my heart clenched for this stranger.

When his smile faltered, I realized I hadn't responded to his question, too caught up in his overwhelming presence. "Uh," I mumbled lamely, followed up with another incredibly intelligent comment. "A soda?"

The mage's smile grew, and he leaned closer to me. In a conspiratorial tone, he asked, "Can you keep a secret?"

Wary, I nodded. *What kind of game is he playing?*

"I used a fake I.D. at the door, but the alcohol isn't why I'm here." He shrugged. "Besides, after the day I had, I could use the caffeine."

Before I could even begin to question why he would share that information with me, Tina returned with his soda. She set the Mountain Dew in front of the mage, her eyes trained on me, giving me a *look* that insisted I needed to up my game.

Her face said: *Damn, that boy is hott!*

I rolled my eyes at her, my face saying: *He's so not my type!*

So not the point, Sam, I thought, wanting to bang my head against the counter. With my luck, I'd be dead by the end of the night.

Tina gave me another look: *Girl, you crazy if you think a fine specimen such as* that *isn't your type.*

I glared her down. *Still not my type, and I'm outtie.*

The stranger laughed, making me jump.

Startled, I snapped, "What's so funny?"

"I'm sorry, it's just you two must be pretty close. Your facial conversations are entertaining."

I turned ten shades of red, before clearing my throat and trying to save face—with sarcasm. "Yeah, so glad to hear I'm providing you free entertainment. Besides, who are *you?*"

Offering me his hand smoothly, he said, "My name's Evander, what's yours?" There it was again, that disarming quality that both invited me in and made my hair stand on end.

I stared at his extended hand, wondering what kind of trap this was. The magical energy rolling off him indicated he was a crazy-powerful mage, but other than that, he seemed almost normal. He wasn't in a guild uniform, although his crimson shirt didn't endear me to him. Crimson was the mark of the Cardinal Sun, even if I didn't see the sigil anywhere on him.

He was also making conversation with me, which was a first for any mage I'd met—well, at least for guild Hunters, which, with an energy like that, he had to be. I'd met plenty of people in the Magical Community—they weren't all bad. Guild mages, however, were bat-shit crazy.

I scrutinized Evander further, trying to figure him out. An impossible task, considering he was so contrary. So much power, yet so much restraint. So much violence, yet so much compassion. It all warred within him, and I found myself baffled. I was disarmed by the melancholy in his aura and the kind, sincere smile on his face. Something in my gut told me to trust this stranger, even though my amygdala told me to *run, run, run!*

"Sam," I replied cautiously, shaking his outstretched hand.

His response was lost to me when his magical energy assaulted my palm, shot up my arm, and burned along my shoulder. When he let go, my skin stung with pins and needles. My arm felt heavy and numb, and I gritted my teeth.

"What was that?" I asked, trying not to appear as breathless and shaken as I was.

He smiled patiently. "Would you like to dance with me?"

My eyes widened in shock. *Me, dance with the enemy? Oh, hell no!* I looked at Tina, my mind grappling for an excuse. When she grinned at me, wiggling her eyebrows, I realized I wouldn't find help there.

"Actually, I was on my way out," I lied, and Evander looked pointedly at the half-full soda sitting on the bar in front of me. *Crap.* "That is, I wanted to enjoy a soda before I went home."

"Now, if that ain't the biggest crock I've ever heard come out your mouth."

Dammit, Tina! I leveled my glare on her.

She hooked her thumb sideways, pointing at me. "This fool here dances like a madwoman until just before closing."

"Oh, so you come here often?" Evander asked, wry amusement in his tone.

"Tina, stop helping," I hissed, glaring at her.

"Sorry, hun. I see you in here all the time, dancing to the beat of your own drum. I can't let you tell this handsome young man 'no.'"

I. Am. Going. To. Die. I am going to die, and it will be because my coworker tried to play matchmaker.

Desperate, I put a haughty sneer on my face. "Actually," I said, sucking air between my teeth, "I was trying to spare your feelings. You're totally not my type, and I'm just not interested." Flicking my fingers at him and turning back to my soda, I made my tone sickly-sweet. "Run along."

Tina gasped my name like a curse.

Evander laughed and leaned in again. "Truth be told, princess, you're not my type either."

"*Excuse me?*" I snapped.

He leaned a bit closer, saying, "You heard me. I'm not into petulant, spoiled brats like you."

I leaned away from him, anger boiling in my veins like an inferno begging to be unleashed.

Tina snorted and walked up the bar, taking another customer's order.

With another wry smile, he offered his hand again. "Now, are you going to dance with me, or would you rather risk getting hit on by the creep three seats behind you? He's been leering at you since before I sat down."

With a grimace, I casually looked over my shoulder. Sure enough, Austin was sitting three seats behind me, his eyes darting away when he saw me looking. I heaved a sigh, getting stalker vibes from the guy. Unfortunately, Evander was right. Austin was probably just waiting for Evander to leave so he could ask me to dance, and I would have to turn him down. Again. My options were a dance with the devil or a dance with the creep.

I cleared my throat, turning back to Evander. "Sure. That would be…*great.*" I wouldn't have sounded more repulsed if someone had dumped a bucket of pig guts on me.

Better it be pig guts than my *guts…The night's still young.*

Evander stood up. Hesitantly, I took his outstretched hand. Another round of jolts shot up my arm, and I ground my teeth together when he didn't let go. He led me to the middle of the dance floor, twirling me out and then back in as he stopped in place. Glancing over his shoulder, I watched Austin get up, kick his stool, and head for the door, violent anger muddling his aura.

I shivered, hoping I never saw him again. My situation wasn't preferable, but *that*…I didn't even know how to deal with a violent Norm. Mages I could attack with arrows—which I didn't currently have—magic, or whatever I thought would save my ass. A Norm was a risk. Exposing my power would lead the guilds right to me, and attacking a Norm would bring the cops to my doors and land me in a prison cell…where guild mages would eventually find and kill me.

For the moment, Evander wasn't a threat, and trying to leave with Austin stalking the night would be a mistake. *Time to make the most of this.* I looked over at Kenny and gave him a wave, pointing down to the ground. Understanding my meaning, he changed the song to something between rock and pop.

I turned my attention back to Evander, resting my hands on his shoulders while his hands held my waist, and then our dances began. "So, what brings a guild mage to Club Cadence?" I asked with as much nonchalance as I could muster, shouting to be heard over the music.

His step faltered, nearly tripping over his own two feet. *Not so suave now, are you?* Apparently, he wasn't expecting me to play my hand.

"Noticed that, did you?" He pursed his lips.

"Considering my arms have all but gone numb from the sheer voltage you're giving off?" I shrugged. "Look, I'm not down for playing games. If you're going to attack me, attack. If you're just passing through, I'd prefer you get out. Leave, or let's take this outside."

His eyebrows shot into his hairline. "What if I said I really did just come here to dance?"

"Bull," I quipped. "Don't insult my intelligence."

"Fair enough." He twisted me away from him, pulling me back in close.

It was then that I noticed something shimmering just left of his heart on his shirt. I squinted my eyes harder, noticing the hazy outline of a sun. *Cardinal Sun Hunter!* I stopped dancing, pulling away from him.

"So, are we going to do this or not?" I crossed my arms, tapping my foot.

He raised his hands as if to placate me. "I'm not here to hurt anyone."

"And I only trust you as far as I can throw ya, and pal, you're a large dude."

He snorted. "Look, princess, I'm not exactly pleased to run into you here either. This complicates things for me."

"For you? *For you?*"

"Yes, for me. I took my sweet time getting here, hoping whoever had been stupid enough to send out several massive, magical homing beacons all over downtown Seattle would have the brains to high-tail it out of here. God, I waited hours— *hours*—expecting no one to be here, cuz, clearly: being hunted." He gave me a meaningful look. "But *nooo*. The stupid girl waits around after drawing the attention of every major guild in a 100-mile radius. Please, Sam. Do you have a death wish? Do you really want the Cardinal Sun's Elite Hunter to kill you?"

Not sure which point to focus on first, my mouth opened and closed.

Evander sighed, running a hand through his hair. "The worst part is, your corpse would earn me a pay raise—and I'd be known globally in the Magical Communities—but guess what? It just happens to be your luck that I'm not actually here to kill you."

"I—"

He held up his hand, silencing me. "Let's just hope the other guilds' Hunters haven't pinpointed your location yet. Nice job bouncing energy all over the city, but it won't deter them much longer. Not with the other signatures nearly faded."

"What?" I had no idea my energy lingered after I used it.

"If you want to stay alive, I suggest we get moving." He grabbed my arm and began pulling me toward the exit.

Brain finally working, I shouted, "*We* aren't going anywhere."

"Unlike other Elites, I'm not trying to kill you—and if they did, it would be the least of your problems. Trust me, princess, if someone takes you in alive, you'll *wish* you were dead."

I held my ground. "Isn't that what *you're* trying to do right now?"

Exasperated, he stopped and turned to face me. "No, Sam. If you would just listen—" He stiffened, his head snapping up, eyes alert. "I suggest we get a move on. *Now!*"

Grabbing my hand, he took off at a full sprint for the door. Caught off guard, my heels slipped on the floor, causing me to trip. Catching me around the waist, he lifted me, throwing me over his shoulder like a sack of potatoes.

Oh, hell no. I kicked and punched his back as he continued for the exit.

"Sam, not that I'm trying to be rude or anything, but you're practically giving these people a free peep show."

I went limp at once, my face burning crimson. "I can walk, y'know!"

"Yeah, but I need you to *run.*"

I growled in frustration.

Evander stopped mid-stride, causing my face to damn near leave an imprint on his back. Faster than I could blink, I was back on my feet and in front of him. He leaned over me, coaxing me to dance. Physical and mental whiplash left me standing there, glaring a hole in his head. He gave me a wide-eyed stare as if I were the unreasonable person.

I went rigid, tingles of magic brushing along my subconscious. I felt the power signatures of four mages as they came into the club, their signatures fanning out. *How did I not notice them before Evander did?*

"Friends of yours?" I asked, eyes narrowing.

"Not on your life."

I let out something between a hysterical laugh and a scoff.

"Shhh!" he hissed. "Don't draw attention to us."

"Can't they sense you? Or me, for that matter?"

"I've used a concealment spell on you and have since hidden my own energy—someone mentioned feeling numbness." He looked at me like I was an idiot. I had to be because I was letting a Hunter drag me around. "They know we're here somewhere, though."

"If I'm concealed, then I'm going home."

"You can't. If you go too far from me, the spell will wear off."

"Of course, it will," I snapped sarcastically. "Y'know, I really think I'd rather take my chances with these mages. This isn't my first rodeo, pal."

What are you gonna do without your bow, Sam? I pursed my lips. *Improvise, obviously.*

Dodging around him, I made a beeline for the door, but he caught me around the waist and spun me to face him.

"You know I'm getting really sick of—!" My rant was cut off. By a pair of lips.

I tried to shove Evander away, but his fingers dug into the back of my head, holding me firm. Wrongness and disgust flitted along my subconscious, his aura screaming, *no, no, no!* I gave another shove, my heart drumming panic in my ears. When that didn't work, I bit his lip. He flinched, pulling away but only a fraction.

His eyes were open and alert, scanning the room.

If he isn't trying to cop a feel, then what...? Magical energy surged directly behind me. *Oh.* My blood ran cold, then filled with angry heat. *There had to be a better way of discreetly scoping out the room than that!*

The mage passed by us, heading to the dance floor, and when Evander finally exited the personal space of my face, I slugged him.

He grabbed his cheek. "I deserved that."

"Touch me again and we're going to have problems."

He lifted his hands to placate me, nodding toward the exit.

First chance I get, I'm outtie.

urning, I headed for the door, Evander hot on my heels. Just as we reached it, a blood-curdling scream stopped me in my tracks. I whipped around, racing back into Club Cadence, not caring who I shouldered and shoved on my way across the floor.

No, no, no, no, no!

I slid to a halt in front of two Hunters, more stooges from the Bronze Eclipse. One of them had Terry by her hair, a knife at her throat. Fury ripped through me.

"Let her go!" I snarled.

They were momentarily stunned by my sudden appearance. Then, the one holding the knife smirked, letting up on his hold. Tears streamed down my aunt's face, making my blood boil.

"I said"—my teeth ground together—"Let. Her. Go."

Laughing openly now, the mage holding Terry finally addressed me. "No-go. We've got business with her."

"Scram, kid," the other mage taunted.

I flushed with rage, my magic rushing to the surface. The spell Evander cast on me shattered, and the men blanched from the force of my magical energy. I took advantage of their open-mouthed stares to rush forward and duck. Then, I struck upward, slamming my palm into the nose of the mage holding my aunt. He dropped the knife and released her.

I grabbed Terry, pushing her to run into the crowd and out of harm's way. When I turned back around, a sharp pressure pierced my abdomen. I stared into the murderous black eyes of the Hunter I hadn't attacked, then I found myself sprawled on the ground, unsure how I got there. The throbbing in my stomach wasn't from the bass pulsing through my body. Gagging, I tried not to choke on bile and managed to get on my hands and knees. Wrapping one hand around the hilt, my fingers clasped the blade protruding from my gut. I dry-heaved, despite my best efforts not to.

"Yew 'roke my noze, yew bich," the other Hunter yelled.

This statement was followed with a kick to my abdomen, catching my hand and driving the knife in deeper. I screamed, the edges of my vision blurring black, and fell onto my side. Several hazy forms danced around each other, fists flying. I blinked slowly, trying to clear my vision.

The bass vibrated through me as I bled on the floor, unable to get up. Vaguely, I wondered why no one was stepping on me. Why no one was offering to help me. Why no one had helped my aunt. Why people weren't screaming, considering the rival Hunters were fighting. It was like the Norms didn't even know we were there. I had no doubt it was one of the mages' doing.

Goddess, I hate mages!

Strong arms lifted me from the floor, cradling me against a broad chest.

"Jerk," I panted. "Took you long enough." The arms holding me in place were searing my flesh with the familiar magical energy resonating from them. "Put me down. You're hurting me!"

Evander gently set me on my feet, a grim expression on his face. I wobbled, bloody hands reaching for his shoulders to steady myself. He placed his hand firmly on my hip, fingers digging into my skin. The other wrapped around the hilt of the knife. My eyes met his, and I saw the apology in them.

"This is going to hurt. *A lot.*" He grimaced before ripping the knife from my gut.

I screamed, loud and shrill, and blackness clouded the edges of my vision. He grabbed my jaw, pulling a vial from his belt and biting the cork in his teeth. He put the vial to my lips.

"Drink!" he barked.

Not having the strength to fight him, the fluid passed my lips and trickled over my tongue. The bitter taste made my mouth pucker and my stomach churn. I dry-heaved again, and he slapped a hand over my mouth. Muffled screams replaced the need to puke. My stomach seared with agony and I clutched it, tears sliding down my face. When I stopped screaming, he released me.

Looking down, I saw healing flesh surrounded by enough blood to make me gag again. Whatever the hell that disgusting thing had been, it was knitting my flesh back together—painfully. At this point, I was beyond shock—beyond surprise—I just wanted to go home, curl in a ball, and cry.

Seeming reassured, Evander dragged me toward the exit by my hand. Exhausted, I let him.

"Y'know, you're a real jerk," I yelled.

"It just warms my heart to hear you call me that—and after I saved your life." He threw a glare over his shoulder. "I'll keep that in mind next time you're bleeding out on the floor."

"There won't be a next time."

"Somehow, I doubt that."

"Where's my—" I quickly corrected myself. "Where's the woman they attacked?"

"She'll be safe now. She's the least of their worries."

Note to self: call Terry after I ditch Evander.

"What happened to the Hunters?"

His silence made chills crawl down my spine. It was only made worse when I saw the sliver in his aura that burned with resentment, anger, and guilt. I suddenly didn't want to know.

We barreled through the open club doors, shoving a couple out of the way in our haste to escape.

"What the—Sam?"

"Bye, Drake! In a hurry!"

He called after us, but my ears were pounding too hard to understand him.

I glanced over my shoulder just in time to see Drake grab a bloodied mage by the scruff of his neck. *Oh.* I suddenly realized why I had that vision of him having a scuffle. Guilt racked me. Kick-ass or not, he wouldn't be able to stand up to Hunters for long. I really owed my coworkers an apology when I came back. *If* I survived the night.

"This way." Evander ran down the street, and we turned a corner at the end of the block. "It's not much farther."

"What isn't?"

My question was met with him doing yet another one of his ninja tricks. One moment we were on the street; the next, he spun us into an alley. In one fluid motion, he pulled me deep into the darkness, pressed my back against the wall, and boxed me in with his body. I shoved him, and he stumbled in surprise, quickly catching his footing. Before I could start yelling, he pushed me back against the wall, into the shadows and out of sight of the alley. One hand covered my mouth, the other rested against the wall next to my head, pinning me in place.

The seconds ticked by, Evander breathing down my neck. It was grating along my nerves. His forehead was pressed against the wall as if it held him grounded, and his chest rose and fell with each labored breath he took. Heat radiated from his body, while the damp, brick wall behind me chilled my spine.

Just when I was about to push him again and demand to know what he thought he was doing, I felt the tingle of the approaching Hunters—only three of them. *What happened to the fourth?* With sudden clarity, I understood Evander's silence when I'd asked earlier.

If that's how he treats a rival guild member, then how does he treat people he's been tasked to hunt?

That was a stupid question, considering I'd gotten to see him up close and personal all evening. With a growing sense of dread, I waited until I felt all the Hunters' power signatures pass by before trying to say something. Evander pressed his hand more firmly over my mouth.

Oh, no he didn't!

Irritated, I did the only thing I could think of. I opened my mouth and licked his hand. It had the desired effect. He wrenched it away from my mouth so fast, one would've thought I'd lit it on fire. I took pleasure in the look of incredulity on his face.

"That's disgusting!" he hissed under his breath.

"So's feeling you breathing down my neck," I hissed back.

"That's totally different. My God, what if I hadn't washed my hands?"

"Considering they've been all over my face, I think you'd owe me an apology either way."

He pointed a finger at me like he was about to say something, but then just stared at me. Clearly, he hadn't thought of that. "Whatever. They've passed by us for now, but I can't keep shielding us the rest of the night. Please tell me you don't live in the city."

"I, uh, don't live in the city?" I phrased it like a question, licking my lips.

Groaning, he turned away from me, putting a hand over his eyes. "And I don't suppose you have a way of cloaking your magic?"

I gave him my drollest stare.

His eyes went wide. "You've got to be kidding me!"

"What do you want from me?"

"For you not to be some helpless child! Newsflash, I'm not a babysitter!"

"Excuse me?" I scoffed.

"You're like a goddamn neon sign of magical energy!"

"So?"

"So? Do you have any idea how *distinct* your energy signature is? They'll be able to track you home."

I shrugged. It wasn't like I didn't already know that. Like auras, magical energies were unique to each mage and witch. It was part of the reason the Hunters eventually pinpointed my location. It was also how they knew they were attacking me and not some random witch who happened to look like me.

He began cursing me under his breath, muttering, "Of course, Princess lives in the same city she likes to spend her time in. The same city where she just lets her powers leak all over the place! Could you be any more careless?"

"Goddess!" I threw my hands in the air. "Have you been talking to Phoenix? Does everyone have to constantly remind me just how incompetent they think I am?"

"Who?" He looked momentarily dumbfounded before going off on another tirade. "And yeah, people *should* keep telling you. You're going to get yourself killed. How you've managed to survive this long is beyond me."

I growled, curling my fingers, miming strangling him. He glowered before his face became a mask of horror, his head whipping toward the end of the alley. We'd gotten too loud while arguing. We were supposed to be hiding.

He grabbed my hand, and we ran.

Minutes later, we piled into Evander's black Jeep Wrangler. The thought occurred to me: *I'm being kidnapped.* I could practically hear Phoenix berating me already. The Jeep peeled into the street, and the electric locks clicked.

"Where are we going?" I asked, annoyed with myself.

"Isn't it a little late to be asking me that?" He rolled his eyes. "To my compound. The wards will keep them from sensing our magical energy. I can't keep shielding us both for much longer."

My eyes widened and I couldn't breathe. I wanted to use Chaos to get the heck out of this Jeep, but I'd just draw other Hunters to me. There were over eight floors in my building but going straight to my apartment was out of the question. It might take a while, but they'd be able to narrow down which unit I was in eventually. It was also late enough that most of the buses weren't running. Anywhere I escaped to, I'd be forced to walk home…in the dark…in heels…with Hunters stalking me in the night.

Evander glanced over at me, sensing my rising hysteria. "Calm down. I'm not gonna hurt you."

"Of course, you aren't!" I snapped. "Wouldn't want to accidentally kill your precious cargo before you got paid."

"What?" His head whipped around to stare at me, incredulous. "Do you really think I helped you just to turn you in? Be reasonable."

"I *am* being reasonable!" I shouted. "You're a guild mage."

Something flickered in his aura too quickly for me to catch it. "You'll just have to take my word for it."

"Why should I believe you?"

"I don't expect you to believe me or to understand."

"Try me," I challenged, staring intently at his profile.

His aura flickered with irritation. "Let me break it down for you, princess."

"Asshole," I muttered, but he ignored me.

"There have been rumors about strange energy leaks in this area for a while now. Several hours ago, a huge beacon of magical energy caught the attention of the Cardinal Sun. Due to certain...*qualities* I possess, I was assigned to survey the area."

I knew my trip through Chaos wouldn't go unnoticed, but it sucked that I didn't have a choice. It was use Chaos or make-nice with the ground after I was dropped from the tree. Not to mention, those Hunters wouldn't have stayed down for long. *Resilient creeps.*

"My orders are to take you directly to the Cardinal Sun's Council upon capture." Evander frowned, contemplating his next words. "It's the highest level of treason if I'm caught aiding you."

"Well, you've captured me," I said drolly.

"No," he ground out. "I *rescued* you."

"So you say."

"You have got to be the most ungrateful brat I've ever met in my life. How about saying, 'Thanks for risking your neck to save my damsel ass, Evander.'"

What a dick.

"Fine. Say I believe you for a fraction of a second. Why risk yourself?"

"Short version? I hate my job."

I arched a brow. "Long version?"

"Since I'm a second-generation member, I was raised on the guild's politics. I was told not to ask questions. The more missions I went on, the more I found myself questioning the morals of the guild."

"Go on?"

He sighed, throwing a glance my way. He didn't want to say more, but he wanted me to believe him. "My father was proud of his position within the guild, so I thought I'd be happy there too." He snorted. "I was wrong. Now, I'm treated like a weapon; my master points, and I deliver the finishing blow."

"You're an executioner?" My stomach plummeted. Of course, he was. Just like the Bronze Eclipse mages earlier today, Evander was a Hunter. Hunters only had one job.

His expression became grim. "Not by choice."

I felt an overwhelming urge to reach out and comfort him. His aura was somber, resigned, defeated. Yet there was something else glowing there, something calculating, and it gave me pause. I shoved my compassion down, refusing to lower my guard.

"Quit then," I said, folding my arms over my chest.

His lips twisted into a bitter smile. "Unfortunately, guild membership is for life at the Cardinal Sun. Want out? Die."

The darkness that flared in his aura rendered me speechless. *He's thought about it*, I realized with sickening clarity. *He's weighed his past against his future, and it's brought him to this—to risk.* My heart ached again; he knew what his punishment would be.

He was a dead man walking.

Trying to understand him, I said, "That still doesn't tell me why I should believe you're not going to kill me or hand me over."

Evander chewed his split lip and stared ahead. "Neither option is in my best interest."

He pulled onto a dirt road, turning on his high beams and illuminating the forest ridge ahead of us. The vehicle bumped along as we drove over rocks and divots. I half-expected us to get stuck in the mud, but he navigated the worst obstacles with ease, impressing me with his off-roading skills.

"Care to elaborate?"

When my question was met with prolonged silence, I thought he wasn't going to respond. Finally, he said, "I get the sense you're not what the guild thinks you are. But if you're as powerful as the Magical Community believes, then you'll be able to help me with something."

Great. Quid pro quo. At least I'm alive...for now.

When he parked, I jumped from the Jeep, my heels betraying me as I toppled forward. *Deceitful, treacherous shoes!* Thanks to his ninja speed, I was caught and hauled to my feet, moments from face-planting into the gravel.

"Thanks," I muttered, pulling out of his grasp.

His compound looked more like an underground bunker. There was a small, concrete structure cleverly hidden between some boulders in the mountainside. The only distinguishing trait was the door, which looked like it could withstand the force of a bomb exploding next to it. There were no windows visible from the outside. The sheer number of magical wards covering this building told me Evander was prepared for an army to attack. Maybe one would.

"If you think I'm staying here, you, sir, are nuts." I turned, reaching for the Jeep door.

He caught my arm, a habit that needed to stop. *Right now.* I glared at the offending hand and he released me.

"Unless you want either my guild or the others to find you, you don't really have a choice." His attention shifted, his eyes cutting to the trail we'd just come from. "Get inside."

"I don't want—"

"Sam, *now!*"

Sensing the shift in his demeanor, I took off my heels and sprinted for the door, Evander right beside me. The cold, sharp gravel bit into my feet, and I gritted my teeth to keep from screaming. He kept pace with me, despite his aura telling me he wanted to turn me into a sack of potatoes again. We reached the door, and he whispered an enchantment, making the barrier ward pull away. He unlocked it and shoved me in, hastily recasting the enchantment and relocking the door.

"There's not much time," he breathed, leading me into another room. "Be quiet! I'm serious—*not a peep.*" He closed the door in my face and locked it.

Enraged, I was just about to scream and pound on the door when I heard another door open and close. I heard muffled talking and feet shuffling as someone followed Evander into the compound. He was either trying to hide me to save both our asses, or he was trying to keep me out of the way while he sold me out. I was leaning toward the former, considering he was doing a lot of showboating and acting just to betray me now.

Then again, my fearful mind piped up, *he could be saving you only to use you for his own nefarious purposes.*

I pressed my ear to the door, listening for conversation. Evander was talking, but the words were too muffled to make out. I wiggled to various spots on the door, hoping to pick up pieces of the conversation. Shifting again, I overbalanced, my hand catching and rattling the doorknob.

The conversation stopped.

I was just getting my balance back when three things happened all at once: I heard Evander yell, "Wait," the door opened with most of my weight still supported on it, and I fell against a man who most definitely was *not* Evander.

"Hello there." His voice was rich, melodic, and had a touch of an accent I couldn't place.

I stared into dark brown eyes, glinting with cruel, mischievous intent. This man was full of deadly power. If I thought Evander had caused my magic-radar to flare, then this mage was set to eleven. I could feel the edges of my vision blurring just from contact with him. His hands held my wrists in a tight grip, letting me know he had no intention of releasing me anytime soon.

I gaped at my assailant, taking in his high cheekbones and the stubble lining his chin, jaw, and full lips. A strong nose was framed by two almond-shaped eyes, lined with the longest lashes I'd ever seen. His skin was a smooth, medium-brown. His brunette hair was wild, his locks curling at the nape of his neck. A dark line peeked out of his shirt, and I wasn't sure if it was his hair or the end of an elaborate tattoo. I couldn't see straight to tell.

My ears roared, and I had to strain to hear Evander's shouting over the *whooshing* sound in my head. Darkness enveloped me, making it difficult to see him, the room, or anything but the man holding me. My knees had buckled at some point, and I was pressed up against the terrifying mage. He felt like molten lava. I wasn't sure if I should be worried that my nerves were shot, or worse, that he might be a fire elemental. I'd nearly been crispified enough for one day.

Drowning in shadow and misery, I only heard every other word Evander yelled: "Stop," "Jeph," "Hurting."

Blinking slowly, I stared into the man's—Jeph's—eyes. "I'm okay," I mumbled to Evander, trying to look for him.

Jeph's lips quirked, and the magical energy seeping into me receded, pulling away from me in waves of black tendrils so fast I wasn't sure I hadn't imagined the darkness that had just enveloped me. I could suddenly think clearly; my ears weren't roaring, and I had control over my body. Steady on my feet again, I shoved Jeph away from me, irritated at all the men who had grabbed me today.

"Can I help you?" I snapped.

This time, the mischievous glint in his eyes was palpable, the twist of his smug smile loaded with humor. "Brave little thing, aren't you?"

"Braver than a man with no balls who picks on a woman he's just met."

Evander gasped, and Jeph's eyes were all but glittering now. *What a sicko...he's enjoying this.*

"Evander, who's your friend?" he asked, eyes never leaving mine.

I wanted to smack him for speaking about me as if he wasn't pinning me with the weight of his stare.

"No one who concerns you," Evander replied tersely.

"'No one who concerns you, *sir*.'"

"*Sir*," he amended, spitting the word like venom.

"I'm right here, y'know," I snapped, but Jeph ignored me, turning to Evander.

Dick.

"This is my cousin," Evander lied, pulling his hand through his hair.

My eyes widened in incredulity before I schooled my features.

Jeph returned his focus to me, a smirk on his face. "Evander, it would do well for you to check with your superiors before you involve *family*"—his mocking tone made my gut churn with dread—"in your affairs. One might think you were trying to hide something."

"It's none of the guild's concern whether I have my family in my home or not!"

Jeph growled low and threatening. "Change your tone, *Hunter*." He spit Evander's title like it was disgusting and lowly.

"I'd hate to have to report back to the Council that their favorite pet had to be put down."

"Apologies, *sir*," Evander ground out, teeth bared. "It won't happen again."

I clapped my hands, slow and sarcastically. "While all this testosterone is the highlight of my night, I'd like to get back to what I was doing." I scowled at Jeph, then addressed Evander. "Where's the bathroom? You forgot to tell me in your haste to get the door for your"—my eyes flicked to Jeph, my eyes narrowing as I mimicked his disdainful tone—"*superior*."

"It's down the hall, first door on your right."

I grabbed my heels from the floor, pointing one at Jeph on my way out of the room. "Nice meeting you." I winked, used the toe of the shoe to salute him, and turned, sauntering down the hall like I owned the place, his bark of laughter chasing me. When I reached the bathroom, I locked the door, pressing my back against the cool wood and sliding down. I sat there for a moment, pulling myself back together.

Can tonight get any worse?

The goddess answered my call faster than I could finish the thought.

"Sam!"

I heard the screech in my mind at the same time I felt my brain become a popsicle.

"I got to Club Cadence just in time to see you sprinting, hand-in-hand, with a man!" Phoenix yelled in my head. *"And not just any man—nooo—you can't just meet a normal guy. You were being dragged along like yesterday's trash. By. A. Hunter! What in Duat is going on?"*

Not sure if the mages were spying, I decided to answer him through our current mental connection. *"I met Evander at Club Cadence. I tried to leave, but Tina heard him ask me to dance and wouldn't let me say 'no.' You know how crazy she can be. Next thing I know, the club is being invaded by Hunters from the Bronze Eclipse—and they attacked Terry. You saw the aftermath of our brawl and us running for cover."*

"I knew I shouldn't have taken my eyes off you. I should've never let you go to work tonight. I take full responsibility for your stupidity. Now, let's go."

I scoffed out loud. *"One, I'm not stupid. I had to go to work—it's my job. Two, I can't leave; several guilds in the area are watching for my magical signature."*

Phoenix growled, hissing, *"For your sake, I hope this doesn't end badly."* He slipped from my mind, appearing in front of me. "What on Geb's green earth is *that?*"

I followed his gaze to the huge bloodstain on my shirt. I looked at him, fear and anger lurking in his eyes.

"Sam…"

"Tis nothing—just a scratch," I joked, trying to lighten the mood.

He gritted his teeth, looking away from me. "Get patched up. I'll go eavesdrop."

Before I could respond, he was gone.

The goddess was particularly generous today with surprises because then my phone chimed.

<Samantha Anders! Where the hell did you go!?!?>

I grimaced, fingers numbly typing a response to my aunt. *<Went home. Y?>*

<Don't play dumb with me! What happened!?>

<Calm down, Aunty. I'll explain next week.>

<NO! You'll explain right now!>

<Not safe. Trust me. Next week?>

<Fine! But you better TELL me what the HELL is going on!>

<Yes ma'am! And Aunty…please keep quiet about what you saw tonight. It's dangerous.>

It was eerie that she didn't respond. But the goddess was nothing if not consistent today. My phone chimed with a different text tone this time. I groaned.

<Hey-hey! How's my Sammy Girl?>

<Fine, Dad.>

I hated lying to him, but what else was I going to do? Say, *"Gee Dad, I dunno. I was nearly incinerated this morning, was stabbed this evening, and now I've been kidnapped by the very mages I've been trying not to get killed by"?* Yeah. That would go over well.

It wasn't like he could do anything anyway. Even if I chose to leave, I'd be leading other Hunters right to my doorstep. If I wasn't willing to do that to myself, there was no way in hell I was going to lead them to my father.

<I just got off work. Want me to stop by your apartment? I can pick you up and we can go do something. I've got Sunday off.>

I wanted to scream. It figured the one time Dad had some time off, I was a prisoner in some crazy mage's home.

<Sorry, Dad. I'm out with>—I stumbled over the next word as I typed the lie—*<friends.>*

<Good to hear it! Maybe next week—if I get time off?>

<Maybe.>

<I love you, pumpkin.>

<Love you too, Dad.>

I wanted to chuck my phone across the room.

When I exited the bathroom, Evander was alone in the living room, elbows on knees, chin resting on his clenched fists. He was staring into space, deep in thought. Since Phoenix hadn't sounded the ghost-alarm, I figured I wasn't in any immediate danger. I'd taken advantage of the amenities available to me and had showered the blood from my body. However, I hadn't wanted to redress in my bloody clothes, which left me with a bit of an issue.

I cleared my throat, causing Evander to startle. He stared at me in disbelief, probably shocked by my blatant disregard for other people's property. I'd wrapped my hair in a towel and had borrowed a robe—without asking. He was probably reconsidering just how stupid he thought I was; I *had* showered in my enemy's lair, after all.

"You're something else," he muttered as he led me down the hall and around the corner, stopping in front of a door. "For the time being, this will be your room. It's enchanted, so you should be able to find anything you need—like some clothes," he said dryly.

"Thanks, pal."

His eyes dipped to my bruise-necklace, a frown creasing his features. He opened his mouth as if he wanted to say something, but closed it and turned on his heel, walking up the hall. I stared after him, his aura a chaotic mess I couldn't sort out.

I slipped into the room, closing the door firmly behind me.

Phoenix reclined on the bed, arms folded behind his head. "This is a bad idea, Sam."

Ignoring him, I walked across the room to where a dresser stood. I open a drawer and found it empty. Frowning, I reached in, my hand touching soft fabric. I grabbed it, pulling out a pair of plain underwear. *If it's enchanted, then maybe if I concentrate...*I reached back into the dresser, groping around again. This time, I pulled out a pair of cute, lacy panties. *A girl could get used to this.* After assembling an entire outfit, I turned my back to Phoenix and began dressing under the bulk of my robe.

"I really think you should go home," he murmured. "But I know it'll be dangerous if you do." He sighed, and I closed my eyes, praying for patience.

"Gee, Phoenix. That's exactly what I told you earlier." I pulled a t-shirt over my head. "While you've got nothing better to do, why don't you fill me in on your spying?"

"As it turns out, the creepy, eerie one is apparently on the Council."

Shocked, I almost fell over putting on my pants. Catching myself against the wall, I steadied myself and zipped up my jeans before turning around to face my BFF.

"You've got to be kidding me."

"No, Sam. I'm not. I tried to merge into his mind to read him, but that man has crazy-high defenses. It was almost like he knew I was there, but I was able to get a few thoughts. He knows the surly one is lying about your identity. And"—he scowled, disgusted—"you've seriously piqued his interest."

"Lovely," I muttered sarcastically. "What else?"

"As far as I can tell, a man named Phantom asked Creepy to come check on Surly's progress—in hunting *you*." He glared at me.

"I already know about Evander's mission. Next."

His expression turned menacing. *If looks could kill…*

"Phantom is Surly's direct boss and is also Creepy's equal on the Council."

I flopped face-first onto the mattress, the top of my head passing through Phoenix's thigh on my way down. I shuddered, the chill of touching the ghost sending gooseflesh down my neck and arms, making my hair stand on edge. It wasn't as bad as mind-melding in the bathroom earlier, but it still sucked.

"Sorry." The mattress muffled my apology.

"Sam, I want to continue our talk from this morning."

"Hmm?"

"I'm…sorry," he said, and I shrugged my shoulders, keeping my face in the mattress. "I want you to practice your magic and anything else you feel is necessary to survive. I won't contradict myself again."

I rolled over, sprawling onto my back, legs dangling over the edge of the bed. "I'm sorry, too. And you're right. I'm starting to realize just how vulnerable I am without proper training. I'll work on it."

"Thank you, Sam. I just want to see you safe." After a pause, he said, "I also want to say—"

There was a loud knock at the door.

"Come in?"

Evander pushed the door open. "Were you talking to yourself just now?"

I continued to lie on the bed, staring up at the ceiling. "Were you eavesdropping?"

"No, I—"

"Pretty sure you were."

"I wasn't. I just heard talking through the door."

"Don't tell Surly I'm here," Phoenix said.

No duh.

"Yes, Evander. I was talking to myself." I crossed my eyes, turning my head toward him. "The crazy lady strikes again."

Unamused, he stared at me. I uncrossed my eyes, staring into his.

He was silent for a long time, his aura raging between caution and indecision. "What happened to your neck?"

I bounced my head against the mattress, staring at the ceiling again. "A Hunter decided the best way to greet me was by shaking hands with my throat. Typical day. Typical nonsense."

"How can you be so nonchalant about someone choking you?"

"In case you haven't noticed, I'm not exactly on the top of everyone's best friends list. Although being stabbed was a new experience for me." I rubbed my finger along the raised, puckered skin that was somehow (magically?) healed, except for the forming scar.

Phoenix scowled at me, and I glared back, lifting the edge of my t-shirt, just enough for him to see my wound was mostly healed and I wasn't going to die. I only succeeded in making his form ripple and waver with anger.

Seeing the cut, Evander scowled. "That wouldn't have happened if you'd just listened to me."

I bristled, sitting upright. "Screw you, pal!"

"No need to thank me," he said sarcastically. "I only saved your ass."

"Which wouldn't have needed saving if you hadn't cornered me."

"I didn't corner you!" he snapped. "And from where I stood, you looked like you needed some help. Do you even know *how* to fight?"

"I took self-defense classes," I said, thinking back to the *one* beginner's class I'd taken a couple years ago.

"Clearly," Evander muttered, seeing right through my bullshit.

"It is what it is. Do you need something? Or did you come to tell me about your boss and his *lovely* friend who damn near smothered me to death earlier?"

His eyes narrowed. "What do you know about my boss?"

My eyes met Phoenix's, then Evander's. "Not much. Just that his name is Phantom."

Evander paled. "How do you know that?"

"I have my ways."

We proceeded to have a staring contest.

"Right." There was suspicion in his aura.

"Seriously though, can I help you?" I asked sarcastically.

"God!" he shouted, his temper snapping. "You're such a... such a..." He growled, his fists balling. "I should've just let them kill you and saved myself the headache."

Phoenix's form rippled again, his face contorting in rage.

"Then kill me already and we can both be headache free," I muttered.

Evander blanched, and I could tell he regretted his words. I didn't care. Neither did Phoenix, who began putting ghostly punches through his face, swearing up a storm. He flinched, the chill of my BFF's hits seeping into him. I stared, watching my spectral friend continue to take futile swings at the mage...until the unthinkable happened.

Evander suddenly pitched forward, face planting into my lap.

"What the—?" I glared up at Phoenix, lifting my eyebrow again, daring him to deny that he just partially took solid form.

Sheepish, he grimaced before winking out, disappearing into the ether or wherever it was.

I pushed Evander's head off my lap. "If you would kindly stop sexually assaulting me, that'd be great."

He jumped away like I'd branded him with a hot poker. "I didn't—I wasn't—did you hit me?"

"Totally," I muttered. "I just enjoy stranger's faces in my lap."

His face a deep shade of pink, he muttered, "Good night," before hastily retreating from the room.

I blinked, eyebrows raised as I stared at the closed door. *Did I embarrass him?*

Getting to my feet, I began investigating my temporary prison. The queen-sized bed rested on an ornate, golden frame, a white, floral bedspread covering it. White, purple, and gold throw pillows were arranged neatly on top. The floor and ceiling were trimmed in royal purple, gold filigree snaking throughout, and lavender and violet floral prints decorated the white walls. Near the head of the bed, a white bedside table sat empty.

There was a moderately-sized bathroom attached to the bedroom. It was also decorated in white, gold, and purple. There was a sink and mirror, a toilet, and a shower. Like the dresser, all of the cabinets and drawers appeared empty until I reached inside with an item in mind. Just to be certain, I checked for extra toilet paper and feminine hygiene supplies.

Still curious, I decided to explore the compound. If I went back around the corner, I would find the living room, the room I was shoved into, the bathroom I'd showered in, and the front entrance. I turned the opposite direction, continuing down the hall, noting two more doors. At the end of the hallway, there was a large kitchen and a dining room.

When I opened the fridge, I found boxes of leftovers and various other food items. To my dismay, the fridge wasn't enchanted. Sighing, I grabbed a box of leftover rice and orange chicken. Much like the fridge, the drawers and cupboards in the kitchen held real silverware and flatware. Frustrated, I went on a wild goose chase until I found a damn fork. I ate the food cold, too hungry to bother reheating it.

After my impromptu dinner, I paced the kitchen and dining room, noticing this was the end of the compound. But my gut told me there was more than I was seeing. Listening to my instinct, I wandered back down the hall and opened one of the doors. It wasn't a bedroom; it was another hallway. Multiple doors lined either side of the passage. I followed it to a "T." To my right, I could see a spiral staircase leading up and, to my left, a spiral staircase leading down.

Which way? My power responded, making me turn to my right. *Up it is.*

Once at the end of the hall, I placed my hand on the rail and one foot on the bottom step. I glanced over my shoulder, suddenly feeling nervous. When I turned back around, I screamed, falling on my ass.

A ghost loomed before me.

"**G**o away!" a harsh voice commanded.

"I…" Breathless, I got to my feet.

"You're not welcome here." His voice was cold as ice.

Finally pulling myself together, I glared at the ghost. "Unlike you, I'm a guest."

"You are, are you?"

"Yes."

Looking at the shadowed face, I could tell he'd been at least a decade older than me when he'd died. In life, this ghost had brown eyes and cropped brunette hair. He had a perpetual five o'clock shadow. He was also built like a tank with muscles that rivaled Drake's. He was wearing modern clothing, but that didn't tell me much about him except he was likely a Seattleite and died sometime in the last fifteen years.

Intrigued, I asked, "Are you haunting Evander?"

"Don't be stupid!" If he wasn't a ghost, I'd be cleaning spittle off my face.

And this is why I don't talk to spirits.

I pursed my lips. "So…you're what? Just hanging around?"

"You might say that. Who're you?"

"Samantha Anders."

His eyes widened before they narrowed. "Neil Hunter. I'd say it's nice to meet you, but it's not."

"The feeling's mutual," I retorted. Then, I tilted my head, brow furrowing. "Do I know you?"

"Of course not."

We glared at each other, and the longer I stared at Neil, the more something felt…*off*. It was as if I was trying to remember a word, but it was at the tip of my tongue. Just as the thought formed in my mind, it was snatched away, leaving me dizzy with the effort of trying to remember it.

"If you're quite done, leave."

"Not on your life," I muttered to be spiteful and nodded to the staircase. "What's up there?"

"None of your business," he sneered.

Getting progressively irritated, I gritted my teeth against the cold and stepped through him, continuing up and saying, "It was nice chatting with you. *Not.*"

He tried to chase after me but hit a barrier.

Odd. The only thing capable of deterring spirits is...I inhaled, smelling the burning sage. *Ah.* Sage naturally repelled negative energy, which included some spirits.

Even more curious now, I continued up the stairs, Neil screeching at me the whole way. I came to a landing, finding a lone door and turned the knob slowly, pushing it open. Feeling around for a light switch, I peered into the room, seeing the glow of the burning sage. My hand found a switch on the wall, and when I flicked it, dim lighting came on overhead.

I wandered in, frowning at the bottle-lined shelves across the room. Each bottle held a different colored liquid. There were jars lining shelves on the adjacent wall, too. I grimaced, noticing the small, wrinkled objects floating in each of the jars. I didn't want to know what they were.

In the other corner, there was a bookshelf lined with books. Several old, thick, and dusty books were strewn about in piles on the floor, some open, some closed, and some flipped over. Some were in languages I didn't recognize or had symbols I'd never seen before. Crumpled paper also littered the floor, along with tattered and crinkled drawings. There were chalk drawings on the wood floor; chalk and pencils lay scattered nearby.

On a table next to the bookshelf, I noticed various colored prayer candles. Some were barely used, and others so well used the melted wax spilled in a dried puddle at their bases. I took a step toward them. They were set in a circle, yellow to the east, red to the south, blue to the west, green to the north, and silver in the center. Whoever set them up had knowledge of rituals.

I turned, further surveying the room. That was when I found it. It was by the open door, resting against the wall. Beautiful, huge, and handcrafted, the chest was old. Swirls of pale pink and purple radiated from the chest as if magically enchanted. Entranced, I crept toward it and kneeled in front of it, placing my hands atop the age-worn lid.

The chest spoke to me, the pink and purple wisps wrapping around my wrists and swirling up my arms. I could actually *feel* the chest wanting to be opened, which was nuts—it was an object, not a person. Call me Pandora, because I was going to open this box. Carefully, I lifted the latch on the front, grabbing the lid on either side. I pushed it up...and heard it slam shut, the swirling lights flickering out.

The room went dark and a blade pressed against my throat at the base of my jaw. From this angle, one sweep of the blade would slice me open from ear-to-ear. I trembled and gulped, causing the dagger to bite into my skin. My assailant's other hand grabbed me around the neck. It took every ounce of willpower I had not to whimper at the pressure on my bruises. The blade remained firmly in place as I was pulled to my feet.

Bloodlust assaulted my senses, his aura palpable in the air around me. I could practically taste his fear and anger, his confusion and betrayal, his determination and vindication. The combination spelled bad news for me if I didn't stop him from following through.

"Evander," I breathed.

There was a pause, then I heard the metal clatter of his weapon as it impacted with the floor. Everything became a blur as I was whirled around, light flooding my vision and blinding me. Then, I saw him. His hair was matted to his face, and sweat trickled down his forehead. Dark, wary circles shown under his eyes. But it was the raw anger blazing in those eyes that brought me back to reality.

"What are you doing in here?" he growled. "How did you get in?"

I shook my head, not sure what he meant.

"Answer me!"

I flinched backward, tripping over the chest, and his hand reached out, grabbing me. Pivoting, he flung me further into the room, away from the door. I stumbled, trying not to trip over my feet.

"Phantom sent you, didn't he? He's testing my loyalty—and I failed...again." He ran an angry hand through his hair. "Figured I wouldn't kill a woman this time. Bastard."

A sick feeling churned in my gut, and I stared at him, speechless.

"I should've known the moment Jeph let up on his attack. Careless, so damn careless, Evander!" he snapped, working himself into a frenzy.

I trembled, his ferocity grating along my subconscious as his aura and his magical energy flared. He was like a caged animal, pacing as his energy bled from him in waves. I could barely stay standing under its assault.

"Well, go on then." He flung out his hand, palm down, re-calling the dagger and flipping it, catching it by the blade and pointing the hilt at me. "Dispatch me. That's your job, right?"

I couldn't breathe and my eyes began to water. *This is wrong...so wrong!*

"No," I whispered weakly.

"*No?* No, you aren't a spy?" He advanced toward me. "Or no, you won't kill me?"

I took a step back, shaking my head, silent tears sliding down my face.

"Which is it?" he roared.

My shoulder bumped into the shelf behind me, the glass jars rattling and shaking. He snatched my dominant hand.

I'm going to die, I'm going to die, I'm going to die!

He put the hilt of the dagger in my palm and wrapped my fingers around it, pulling my arm up and pressing the tip of the blade to his jugular.

"Well?" Evander held my trembling hand there, eyes full of fury and resignation.

I couldn't breathe. "I'm not..."

"You're not...?" He loomed over me, his aura a riot of ago-ny—so much emotional anguish it suffocated me.

Tears burned my eyes, rolling down my face. *What did that man do to you?* I wanted to ask, but my voice wouldn't come. Teeth chattering, I reached my free hand up to comfort him, but my hand went to my jaw instead, my skin stinging. My fingertips came away with a mixture of blood and tears.

His gaze flashed to my wound, finally noticing the cut. When his eyes met mine again, the fire that had raged in them was extinguished, replaced by something I couldn't identify. *Guilt? Self-loathing?* He released my hand, the dagger like a lead weight in my grip. I dropped it, the clatter of metal filling the silent room.

This was too much, the whole night too much. My shock and fear were quickly replaced by anger. "What the hell, pal?" I snapped, shoving him. "I don't know what your problem is, but I'm not working for anyone!"

"Right, and I'm the Tooth Fairy."

"Really, pal? Pull your head out of your ass!"

He searched my gaze. "You're—"

"Not here to kill anyone!" I yelled. "By all means keep posturing, though. I'll wait." I crossed my arms over my chest, tapping my foot.

He stared at me in horror. "I could've killed you…"

"Gee. I hadn't noticed," I said sarcastically. "Didn't you know I was up here? Magical energy and all that?"

"I thought you were asleep. I should've noticed your energy sooner, but I was…distracted." He looked away from me. "Let me get something for your neck."

"No, thanks. I can take care of myself."

His head whipped back around, my anger refueling his own. "Then I'll leave you to it," he snapped. "*After* you tell me why you're in my attic! How did you even get in here?"

Exasperated, exhausted, and over this stupid argument, I started for the door.

He grabbed my arm, stopping me. "Answer me."

"His Lordship and Grace—that's *you*, BTWs—didn't tell me I wasn't allowed to look around."

He glowered at my sarcasm, but I was far from done.

"I smelled sage, so I got curious. The door was open and the rest is you trying to make me piss my pants. Satisfied?"

His grip loosened on my arm, slowly at first before his hand dropped limply to his side. Red speckles of annoyance, anger, and confusion muddled the otherwise soothing blue of his aura. Then, all the fight drained out of him and he sighed.

"Will you let me patch that up?" He gestured to my wound.

I shrugged. "As long as you don't choke me again. I swear, I'm going to have a permanent bruise-necklace until I die."

"It won't happen again," he said with conviction. "Not by my hands or anyone else's."

I patted him on the shoulder in mock-sympathy. "Don't make promises you can't keep."

His hazel eyes held mine as he said, "I'm not joking."

"Neither am I."

His eyes narrowed, but I didn't back down. I didn't flinch or look away, despite everything inside me still screaming from our near-encounter. Evander could've killed me if he had wanted, but he was keeping me alive. I wanted to ask what he had in store for me, but then he might ask me for a favor.

If I gave him what he wanted, would he let me live? Would he kill me here and now, once I was no use to him? I couldn't be sure. Even if he kept me alive, he could still turn me over to the guild. Once I was in their clutches, would they care that he had delayed handing me over to them? I could tell them and possibly get him executed as a rogue for disobeying orders, but what purpose would it serve to kill someone who had already been so tormented?

Could I live with myself if I was the cause of his death— even if he'd be the one to seal my fate, one way or another?

Several moments passed with neither of us saying anything. He blinked, his eyes softening as he stopped glaring, and I pursed my lips, tilting my head to the side. Something about the color and shape of his eyes reminded me of someone, but I couldn't think of who. The longer I stared at him, the more something else nudged the back of my mind. It was like walking into a room to search for something, but forgetting the moment I got there, just to turn around, leave, and do it all over again because every time I remembered, it slipped my mind.

I opened my mouth to ask if maybe I'd run into him somewhere before—he was around my age, so it was possible—but my ears started ringing. My hands rose to cover them when the ringing turned into a pulsing heat. Then, I doubled over. Evander was instantly at my side, hand on my back as he tried to catch my eye again. The pain increased and my vision began to swim as he called my name over and over. I couldn't respond, too busy curling in on myself.

The chest by the door pulsed, then my head did as if they were linked.

"Sam!" he shouted again, and it took me a minute to realize I'd crumpled to the floor.

Through blurry vision, I stared at the pink and purple aura swirling off of the chest. It reached for me at the same time Evander did. It had just wrapped around my wrist, a hissing, *"Open, open, open,"* filling my head, when he lifted me up into his arms, breaking its hold. My ears continued to burn, the pain only lessening when we exited the attic, Evander moving so fast it was like flying as he ran down the stairs and up the hall to my guest room.

My vision slowly refocused, and the noise gentled to a dull roar. I could hear my pulse, could feel it behind my eyes and in my throat. My whole body felt leaden as he gently set me onto the mattress. I sat on the edge, trying to breathe and stop trembling. I didn't know what kind of hex was on that chest, but it had to be something sinister if it could cause me so much harm.

"What," I began, panting, "is in that chest?"

His brow furrowed, and he leaned over me, hands on my shoulders to help me stay sitting up. "What?"

"The…chest." I pointed up, indicating the attic.

"Nothing, so far as I know."

I shook my head, still trying to catch my breath. "Hexed."

"Hexed?" He shook his head next. "That thing has been in there as long as I can remember. It's just a box that I don't have the key for."

I shuddered. "You didn't see—" I cut off, realizing what I'd almost said, what I'd almost given away. I was one of the rare people who could see auras; he probably didn't see it attack me.

"See what?"

"Nothing. I'm...a little dizzy." I grabbed my head to emphasize the point.

He moved his hands to the base of my jaw, gently turning my head side-to-side, looking me over. "I don't see any damage, but you did hit your head when you fell." He touched my temple and I hissed. That would explain the throbbing.

"I'm fine," I said through gritted teeth.

He snorted. "You just said you were dizzy, princess. Wait here a second," he said as if I had any intention of getting up while the room was swimming.

It seemed like no time at all passed before he was back, and I wondered briefly if I hadn't blacked out for a minute. How hard had I hit my head?

"Here," he said, squatting down in front of me and holding out a vial with green liquid. "This is a healing potion—they're all the rage at guilds."

I grimaced, eyeing it like it was a snake about to bite me. "Pass."

"Don't be a baby," he held it under my nose.

The smell was worse than rotting eggs, so I pushed his hand away. "Double pass."

"It'll help you feel better. Just take it."

"Hmm. Must be poisoned," I said, not entirely joking.

"Are you always this irritating?"

"Yeah, actually."

He stared through me, frustration rolling off him in waves. "Fine. If you want to keep your throbbing headache and that cut"—he poked the side of my neck—"then be my guest."

"I'm your prisoner," I retorted.

"You—" He shook his head, grumbling under his breath.

"What about Norm pain killers?" I asked, pretty sure he'd just insulted me.

"Don't have any." He wiggled the potion in front of my face.

I snatched it, sick of the heartbeat in the side of my head. His expression was smug as I shotgunned the potion, trying not to choke on it. I nearly spit it in his face; it really was the most horrible thing I'd ever tasted. Sour Patch Kids and farts, that's what it tasted like. I slapped my hand over my mouth when I started to sputter, trying to hold in my laugh at my own deranged thought. I couldn't stop my shoulders from shaking, my eyes already beginning to water. I lasted another second before I snorted.

Stick a fork in me, I'm done!

I blew a raspberry, dissolving into giggles.

Evander's eyes widened in horror. "How hard did you hit your head?"

I laughed harder, falling back on the mattress and holding my stomach at seeing his expression. That lasted another two seconds before my breath wheezed from my lungs, the searing pain of healing enough to steal my breath. I gasped, unable to scream as the potion worked to heal my neck and head. My neck burned like lava was stitching it together, and it felt like someone was driving a stake through my temple. When it finally stopped, I stayed there, curled in on myself. I'd thought my gut had hurt when it had healed at the club, but I'd been hopped up on magic and adrenaline. Right now, I was bottomed out and lacking the same hormone spike as before.

"You...you okay?" Evander asked.

I gave him a shaky thumbs-up.

"You really are something else," he muttered. It still wasn't a compliment. "So, I have a proposal for you."

I groaned.

"You suck at combat," he continued, ignoring my whining. "While you're here, how about I help you?"

Still laying on the bed, I opened an eye, peeking at him through the tangle of my hair. "You're a smooth talker, aren't ya?"

"The way I see it, you're gonna get yourself killed if you don't learn to defend yourself—no, if you don't learn to *fight*."

"Thanks for the vote of confidence," I muttered, rolling my eyes.

"Look, you've gotten by on what *has* to be sheer dumb luck so far—"

"Rude!"

"—but they're sending in the Elites, now. If the Cardinal Sun had sent anyone but me, you'd be dead right now."

I sat up, pushing my hair out of my face and staring into his eyes. "Oh, yeah? And you 'saving me'"—I air quoted—"is the safer of the two options? I'm not buying it. You're only keeping me alive cuz you want something."

His gaze didn't waver. "You're safe here."

His aura burned so brightly, full of determination and conviction, I wanted to believe him. I wanted to, but I couldn't. I couldn't trust a man I didn't know, a man who worked for my enemy, a man who wouldn't admit to his own selfish reasoning. I was a tool to be used.

"Fine," I said, more to gauge his response than because I meant it.

Relief flared through his aura, and I had to fight the urge to scowl. Was that relief because I had caved to his demands? Or was he relieved because he thought he'd get what he wanted? Or…was it genuine?

No, Sam, don't let yourself hope. Hope never ends well.

"Okay," Evander said, heading for the door. "First thing in the morning, we'll start."

"The *morning*?" I whined. "But it's after midnight!"

"When you wake up, then." He stopped, hand on the doorknob, his back to me. "G-Good night," he murmured before leaving, shutting the door behind him.

Eyes narrowing, I frowned, chewing my lip in thought. *What's his angle?*

"Finally," Phoenix said, popping into the room next to me and making me jump. "I thought he'd never leave."

I arched a brow. "It's not like he can see you, y'know?"

He shook his head. "Yeah, but I can't talk to you if he's around either."

"True." I pursed my lips, stretching out on top of the mattress. "What's up?"

"You gonna do what he suggested?" he asked, hovering near the foot of the bed and watching me.

My lips twitched. If my life was a horror movie—I was still waiting to find out it wasn't—then this would be a very different scene. Phoenix would be a bloody, gray-scale creature of nightmare, arms raised, nails jagged and sharp, as he slowly closed the distance between us. I would be cowering in fear, screaming bloody murder, trying to hide under my blankets. Then, I would die.

Instead, the sight of his sepia form, highlighted with the dusting of his coloring from life, gave me comfort. His friendship, no matter how unorthodox it was, meant a great deal to me. Without him, I'd be lost. Without him, I'd be dead already. Evander had been wrong about one thing. It wasn't sheer dumb luck that had kept me alive for the last five years, it had been Phoenix. It would always be Phoenix. The thought sent a pang through my heart.

I don't deserve his friendship. I've never deserved it.

"Because," he continued, "I think you should."

"What?" I screeched, wincing and looking at the door, waiting for Evander to come busting in. When he didn't, I lowered my voice. "*You*, the most suspicious, paranoid ghost I've ever met in my entire life, wants me to *train* with the enemy?"

His expression told me to stop being dramatic. "Technically speaking, you're safe here, right?"

"Right."

"And he wants something from the Sibyl, right?"

"Right," I repeated.

"So, there's no reason to believe he'll harm you until he gets what he wants, right?"

"Well, I mean—"

"And it's not like he can keep you here thanks to Chaos."

"Phoenix!" I shouted, exasperated. "Get to the point."

"He's trying to charm you," he said, lip curling down in disgust.

I blew a raspberry. "Well, if he is, he's doing a shitty job of it."

He shrugged. "Regardless, he wants your favor."

My mouth opened and closed. "What's your point?"

"Play his game, accept his training—the relative safety of this warded compound—and then..." His golden eyes held mine. "Then, we disappear."

"You mean...ditch him?"

"No, I mean save yourself—*before* he can betray his empty promises."

"So," I drawled, blinking slowly, "if I'm hearing you right—and I *think* I am, but I did hit my head earlier—"

"When?"

"—you're telling me to *manipulate* Evander, *use* him to learn a thing or two about combat, and then dip out? Is that about right?"

"That's exactly what I'm saying."

"Wow, Phoenix. That's calculating, even for you," I said, not sure if I was impressed or slightly disturbed—both, most likely.

He shrugged. "I was a vizier, Sam. If I could run a country, I think I can stay a few steps ahead of a teenage boy."

I gritted my teeth, my heart clenching at the reminder of his title in his former life. It was a reminder of everything he'd had and everything he'd lost, everything that was gone and everything he could never have. My eyes watered, guilt and anger warring inside of me.

"For now," Phoenix continued, oblivious to my inner-turmoil, "get him to play his hand. No one helps anyone out of the kindness of their heart, especially not when that help comes at the risk of their own life. Whatever he wants, it's either dangerous or costly. Either way, he'll want to be sure he's gained your trust before he strikes. It's *your* job to pretend to be playing into his hands, and then stab him in the back before he can get you killed."

"I..."

I chewed my lip, staring at my hands as emotions warred inside me. Could I *pretend* to accept Evander's help without letting myself get caught up in the web he was spinning? Could I spin the lies he was weaving and unravel the threads holding me here, all while reaping the benefits of this mock-truce? Or would

I be the fly the spider finished off, the false safety of his cocoon the real coffin in the end? Was this compound going to be my tomb, or was I going to be the one to crush the spider?

I looked up, meeting Phoenix's eyes again. I hardened my heart, putting trust in him, in the friend who had seen centuries of war and battle as the world had changed around him. He'd been a vizier, the right-hand man to one of the most powerful men in Egypt. His planning had never failed me before.

"You know what they say about friends and enemies," I said.

His lip twitched. "It's never a simple 'yes' or 'no' with you, is it?"

I grinned, and he rolled his eyes, trying to hide a smile.

Eight

he next morning, I examined my neck in the mirror. The healing potion must've worked because my bruises had faded to a dull yellow. The cut from Evander's dagger was just a slightly puckered pink line. I supposed I could get used to magic, spells, and potions if they came with these kinds of perks.

Satisfied, I went to find Evander. He was in the kitchen, an empty plate of food in front of him. His hair was combed out of his face, and he wore a t-shirt that was strikingly close to the natural, sky blue of his aura. He was also wearing sweats and tennis shoes, and it looked like he'd already done a workout because they were still damp with sweat.

"Are you ready to train?" he asked, not looking up from his phone.

"As ready as I'm ever gonna be."

After a light breakfast and some godly coffee, Evander took me back to the hallway with stairs. As it turned out, the left end of the corridor led down to training grounds. I examined the wide array of exercise equipment, weaponry, targets, and the climbing wall and rope, slowly beginning to appreciate the effort that went into every muscle on his body.

"We'll start over here." He pointed to a secluded part of the room.

Padded mats lined the floor and walls, letting me know that sparring wasn't a gentle sport. It looked like I was about to get roughed-up and thrown around like a rag doll. At least he had more healing potions, but either way, I wasn't looking forward to this.

"From what I've seen, you've got some *basic* skills. I was shocked when you broke that Hunter's nose. Few people know how to use their body weight the way you did." He gave me a nod of approval. "So then, show me what you got."

He took a boxer's stance. I decided the best tactic was to mimic his posture. His lips twitched in amusement, then he came at me. *Have I mentioned how fast this boy is?* I sprawled on the floor, pinned under his forearm. He hovered above me, straddling my hips.

"No good. You can't have reflexes that slow and expect to survive a battle." Not letting me up, he pursed his lips. "I'm gonna have to run you through the mountain to build your speed and endurance."

In response, I brought my knee up, and his thighs squeezed, catching my leg.

"At least I don't have to teach you to take cheap shots," he muttered, putting some distance between us and taking his starting stance. "Again."

This time, Evander slowed down, allowing me to track his movements. He circled me, and I watched his stance and technique. Praying for guidance from Hecate, I rushed him, dropping and sweeping my leg at his ankles. His legs came out from underneath him. Instead of falling, he rolled forward and reached for me, and I threw my weight sideways, rolling away from him. I crouched, searching for him. He shoved my back with his foot, and I flopped onto the floor. He twisted my arms behind my back, putting a knee on my neck.

"You know, you're really not good at this," he said pityingly.

I bucked, trying to free myself. As soon as he released me, I got to my feet. He crouched on the floor and I charged him, feinting left. Then, I ducked right, and he braced himself. I threw a punch, but he caught my wrist and fist in his hands. I tried to wrench free, but he held me firmly. I brought my knee up, aiming for his head. Keeping hold of my wrist, his right arm snaked around my leg, stopping me.

He pulled me toward him, and my balance wavered. Bracing my core, I jumped, throwing my weight. I fell backward and kicked with my foot. He released me, but my momentum carried. My foot hit his cheek, but my back smacked the ground, forcing all the air from my lungs. I gasped, and Evander put his foot on my sternum.

He pointed his thumb and forefinger at me like a gun. "Bang, you're dead."

I glared up at him, not dignifying his comment with a response. It was a stupid notion anyway; mages couldn't use guns. Magical energy made gunpowder sporadically combust. It was a fine way to lose one's hand.

"When you're in a fight, you don't have time to breathe," he said, scowling. "No matter what, don't stop moving."

I'd only landed one hit, while Evander had mopped the floor with me. Frustrated, I grabbed his ankle in both hands. With a hard twist and pull, he fell on his ass. I jumped up, put my knee on his chest, and pointed my finger at his bewildered expression.

"Bang, *you're* dead," I mocked.

Loud, slow clapping came from the far side of the training room. We flinched, turning our heads to see Jeph leaning against the wall. Evander's magical energy flared, his aura radiating shock and anger.

"That was quite the show." Jeph leered, his gaze fell on me. "Want a true master to show you how it's done?"

Evander pushed himself off the floor, putting himself in front of me. "*Sir*," he said sarcastically, "I would love a chance to spar with you."

Jeph's eyes danced with mischief. "*Tsk, tsk,* little Hunter. Remember who taught you everything you know?"

"Not everything."

Jeph smirked. "I'm going to enjoy putting you in your place." He flicked his fingers in my direction. "Shoo, shoo."

I walked to the side of the room, and the spectacle of my life began, or it would've if I could've seen it. As it was, all I could discern were two blurs of movement dancing across the mat. I could only tell which one was Evander because he was wearing blue while Jeph was in black from head to toe.

Straining my eyes, I willed myself to see them clearly, to keep up with their movements. I felt magical energy rise within me, and my eyes began to burn. I blinked rapidly, rubbing them to stop the pain. When the burning stopped, I looked back out to the room—and I could track the mages' movements. My magic had somehow enhanced my sight.

Is this how Evander and Jeph move so fast?

My hands flew to my mouth when Jeph landed a hard blow to Evander's jaw. His head whipped to the side. He retaliated, pegging Jeph across the face with his elbow. Jeph grinned widely and punched Evander in the gut. He doubled over. Jeph brought his knee up, hitting him in the face. While he was dazed, Jeph did a spin-kick, sending Evander across the room. He hit the padded wall with a *thud!*

Horrified, I ran to him.

Jeph got there first, grabbing a now-growling Evander by his shirt and yanking him to his feet. It was like watching predator and prey stare each other down. Magical energy radiated and crackled around both men like a miasma of choking darkness. I could feel Jeph's bloodlust as his dark aura sliced along my skin.

"Stop!" My voice rang with power.

They turned their heads to look at me. Their magical energies and auras wavered and flared with emotion, Evander's with fear, Jeph's with delighted anticipation. If I was going to stay safely hidden, I needed to play along with the ruse that Evander was my cousin, needed to interfere before they took their sparring match too far. Knowing I had no chance in hell, I approached Jeph.

"It's my turn now." I put my hands on my hips, glaring at him. "Unless the *master* is too busy being a dick to show me *'how it's done?'"*

Evander's face paled. "Don't…"

I shot him a look, telling him to back off.

The shift in Jeph's aura was instantaneous, sending a surge of trepidation through me. The deadly intent of it changed to something sinister and dark yet exuberant and delighted. His eyes sparkled with anticipation, letting me know I was about to regret my entire life. *Wait, that's nothing new.*

I walked toward the center of the room.

He all but threw Evander back onto the floor in his excitement. Then, he lifted his hand, muttering something unintelligible under his breath before throwing a glowing orb at Evander. It stretched into a large, solid bubble, trapping him inside. He pounded his fists against the bubble, but it silently absorbed his blows.

"Can't have you interfering, now can I?" Jeph taunted, waving his fingers at him.

Evander yelled, but I couldn't hear him through the ward.

Turning, Jeph approached me like a snake, deadly and focused. I was entranced by his graceful walk, dread running up my spine. A smirk lifted his full lips at the corners, drawing my eyes. Heat rushed through me when he sized me up, and I returned the gesture. He wore a snug t-shirt and a pair of exercise pants that clung to his lean muscles. I was able to get a better look at the dark, curling lines on his neck. A similar design was also peeping out from under the sleeves of his t-shirt. The tattoo was pitch black, but I couldn't tell what it was.

"Ready to play?"

I rolled my eyes, calling on false bravado. "I'm gonna take you down a few notches."

"No, precious, I don't think you will."

He came at me, his fist landing in my gut. I doubled over, wheezing, and I threw myself sideways. I fell to the floor, barely avoiding his knee. If I wasn't already aware, I now knew for sure I lacked both the speed and skills needed to win this match.

"Here, kitty, kitty," he purred.

"Asshole," I hissed through clenched teeth, getting to my feet.

Arching a brow, he cracked a crooked smile, causing my heart to do a pitter-patter. He reached for me, catching my arm. I kicked, but he caught my leg. He yanked, spinning and holding me flush against him. The heat and magical energy radiating from him felt like it was electrocuting my skin.

Jeph bent his head, putting his lips right next to my ear. "You're *her*, aren't you?"

My heart stopped. *Do something!* my inner voice screamed. "'Her'? Sorry pal, not looking for a boyfriend at the moment." I wanted to groan; sometimes my mouth was faster than my brain. Sarcasm was going to get me killed.

His breath danced over my sweat-slick skin as he chuckled. The hair on the back of my neck and my arms rose. He put his lips closer to my ear, rubbing them against my earlobe. "No, precious. You're the *Sibyl*, aren't you?"

Ice ran through my veins, and I trembled.

He chuckled again, nipping my earlobe with his teeth. I couldn't stop the shudder that coursed through me. His body temperature was just so hot, it was doing weird things to me. Never mind that being near him was making my skin vibrate and hum in a way I hadn't felt for a long, long time.

He suddenly pushed me away, and I practically fell on my face. "If you kill me now, who else will know?" His eyes smoldered, and his smile was alive.

And what am I gonna kill him with? My hands? He's an idiot.

"I like the angry fire in your eyes, precious."

"That's cool, cuz I like the thought of my fist in your face!"

One second, we were staring each other down, the next, we were going at it. Punches flew left and right. I dodged, parried, ducked, and rolled. He came at me, catching my punches and throwing his own. Picking up on his pattern, I avoided the worst of his blows. When I would kick, he would catch my ankle, pulling me off balance.

"Not bad." He gave me an amused grin as we circled each other. "But it's not going to be enough."

"Don't be so sure," I countered as if I had a chance. "I've dealt with your kind before. Cocky, confident—you're all the same. Pride before the fall, isn't it?" I didn't know why I was baiting him. I just knew I needed to stand my ground.

His aura shone with interest. "Think you know me, do you?"

"I don't need to know you; your attitude says it all." I shrugged. "Besides, I don't make it a habit to get to know psychopaths."

His eyes widened. Then, he threw his head back and laughed, deep and throaty. The rich sound filled me, making the barest of a smile creep onto my own lips. When his eyes met mine again, there was something there I hadn't seen before… respect.

"You get more and more interesting with each passing second."

"And you just get more and more annoying," I retorted. "Do you make it a habit to beat up on women, or do you just attack every new person you meet?"

A wry smile pulled at his lips. "It's my motto to shoot first and ask questions later. Hasn't failed me yet."

"That's just sad. Makes it difficult to make any friends that way."

"I have friends. Well, one."

My eyebrows went up. Somehow, I couldn't fathom a man like him having friends. Then again, I wasn't exactly friendly myself. I had Phoenix; he'd been my best friend for years, but I didn't exactly commune with the living, now did I? Even Terry, Drake, Tina, and Kenny were kept at arm's length; I couldn't trust them with the truth of my dark secrets.

"I can only imagine what kind of friend you have. He's probably a complete douche—like you." I wasn't sure why I added the last part, but I sure enjoyed watching his feathers ruffle.

"Vincent's nothing like me—it's his best quality."

The self-deprecating tone shocked me. Whoever this Vincent guy was, he was someone special to Jeph. Just by the shift in his aura when he talked about him, I could tell their friendship meant a great deal to the mage. It was disarming to think of this cold predator as someone capable of that kind of loyalty and dedication.

"If you say so," I muttered.

"I do say so, precious."

He lunged at me, our match carrying on and on. He kept moving, never actually going in for the kill. It was as if he enjoyed the battle more than he coveted the win. Panting furiously, I wiped at the sweat on my forehead. Sweat glistened on his body too, but he didn't look nearly as exhausted as I felt. I was ready to be done with this fight.

I ran at him, ducking and sliding between his legs. As I did, I grabbed his calf, making his balance waver. I punched the back of his knee, forcing him to kneel. Then, I grabbed him in a chokehold, wrenching backward.

Jeph chuckled. "Like me on top, precious?"

Caught off-guard by his scandalizing tone, my hold slipped. He knocked my arm away and sat up. I sat up too, scrambling away. Before I could get far, he kneeled and reached for me. He grabbed my ankles and yanked. *Hard.* My head hit the ground, dazing me. He pulled me closer, perching between my legs and staring down at me.

Terrified, I tried to punch him. The floor prevented me from getting momentum, and he stopped my attack with ease. He held my fist in his palm, pulling my body toward him. Desperate, I threw my other fist at him. I clocked his cheek, but he didn't even flinch. We stared at each other, frozen.

I felt the muscles in his jaw work as his lips stretched into a mischievous, lopsided grin. My heart stopped, and my breath caught. Panicked butterflies skittered in my stomach. *I'm so dead!* I pulled my fist from his face like he'd burnt it. Maybe he had; a fiery glow seemed to play just below the surface of his skin.

Jeph shoved me down, trapping my hands above my head. I was now nose-to-nose with my opponent, his weight pinning me. I could feel every terrifying, lithe muscle of his body pressed against mine. It made my body tingle with unbearable heat: my thighs, my hips, my stomach, my breasts. We were both panting from our prolonged sparring match, and I couldn't tell if I felt my erratic heartbeat or his. I also didn't know whether to keep staring into his fiery eyes or to close mine and pray he'd go away.

I was completely defenseless, trapped—unable to use Chaos unless I resolved to kill him. *Am I willing to kill to keep my secret safe?* The thought made me sick; I wasn't sure if that made me weak, naïve, or human. I closed my eyes and licked my lips, anticipating my death.

Please, goddess, let it be painless.

Nothing happened.

When I opened my eyes again, I saw Jeph staring at my mouth. A flush crept up my neck and into my cheeks. His eyes met mine again, fire blazing in his irises.

Fight, Sam. Fight!

I began to wriggle and yank on my wrists, trying to buck him off me.

Growling, he put his lips next to my ear. "Hold. Still."

I stopped breathing, flexing every muscle in compliance. When he pulled back, I saw renewed hunger dancing in his eyes. I gulped for air, sensing his bloodlust. And then fear spurred me on.

He already suspected I was the Sibyl; what was the point of hiding it? If I could save my ass, then why was I laying down to die? I'd never backed down before. I'd started this when I'd challenged him, when I'd taunted him. I didn't have to kill him to get away. I only had to escape into Chaos.

I pulled on the void...and instantly knew something was wrong. Never had opening the rift between dimensions felt so heavy or sinister. It was stifling. It was suffocating. It was *wrong*.

Before I could cut my link to it, we hurtled into Chaos.

Nine

I screamed as Chaos ripped my breath away from me, yanking us through time. Years sped past me like physical barriers as we slammed through each of them. For small jumps, it didn't feel like this. For minutes, hours, days, years, it was like passing through dense air or thin water. These weren't mere years. These were *centuries*.

Each century was like slapping the surface of a lake, like a belly flop, my skin screaming at the impact as the tenth, eleventh, and twelfth one passed. Each jolted through me like an electric shock. I wasn't even sure I was breathing anymore as magical energy tore from my core. Worse, it felt like magic was being pulled from me just to be shoved violently back in and then ripped back out again. I was pretty sure I was going to hurl.

And when I smacked the sixteenth barrier, reaching the fifth century, I thought I would die. I screamed something feral—a howl containing all my fear and agony—as I ripped us from whatever had sent us hurtling into the past. It took what little strength I had left within me, but I pulled us through the wall of Chaos, dropping us from some height off the ground.

I couldn't even scream when my back hit the dirt beneath me. It was made worse when Jeph's weight crushed down on top of me. I saw stars—blackness and stars. I was pretty certain I even died for a minute, but I couldn't be sure. I didn't think dying felt so hollow, so numb—so *agonizing* when feeling began to return to me. It was like there was so much fire coursing through my veins that lava and sandpaper made up my blood and muscles.

"What the hell was that?" Jeph demanded, but I couldn't be sure if he'd actually spoken or if I'd just imagined it. My ears were roaring.

But as he scrambled off me, I knew I had to be alive. He must've spoken, too, because I could hear people talking around us. Gasps, frantic chattering, and language I couldn't even begin to comprehend filled the area. There were also screams and shouts.

There was even one goddess-damned word I understood.

"*Sibylla!*"

"Shit," I hissed, regretting the word as it left my mouth. My throat was raw and papery from screaming. It just frickin' figured these people recognized my power—or me. I was pretty hard to miss, especially when crashing into a crowd of people the way we just had.

"Where are we?" Jeph demanded, grabbing my arm and yanking me to my feet. At least, I assumed it was him. I was still seeing stars and blackness, speckles and never-ending death.

"Dunno," I wheezed. "Fifth century or so."

He was silent, eerily so as his hand dug into my arm. But his silence didn't mean it was quiet. A chorus of, "*Sibylla! Sibylla! Sibylla!*" chanted from every direction, men and women voicing their anger and dissent at my presence.

I was so screwed.

"That's not a joke, is it?"

"Not even a little," I breathed.

"Take us back," he growled.

"Can't...no magical energy." As I lay there, I was finally starting to catch my breath. "Pretty sure I'm dead."

"You're going to wish you were if you don't take us back. Right. *Now.*"

"Threats aren't becoming of you," I muttered, managing to blink away some of the darkness. I wished I hadn't.

"I'm not the one threatening you, precious."

Eyes swimming, my gaze landed on the moshing crowd. "*Oh.*"

"*Oh,* indeed."

There was more than just a crowd around us—there was a sea of angry faces. They were close enough to see the fear and hatred in their auras, but far enough away their faces all seemed to blur together. The men reached for swords on their belts or magic gathered in their hands. They were ready to defend themselves from the Sibyl.

Their shouts and hollers died off as one man stepped a few paces forward. He held his sword toward us. He looked from Jeph to me, then he said something I didn't understand. His eyes never left mine, but the way he spoke told me he wasn't speaking to me. The crowd rippled with calls of ascent, and someone took off, heading deeper into the town—because that's where we were, some sort of run-down, dirty-looking town.

"Shit," Jeph muttered.

"What?" I hissed.

"Hunters are coming."

"How do you know that?"

"Because I'm superior," he said, tone haughty.

"Oh, shove it up your—"

A blast of magic hurtled toward us, and we hit the deck. If my nose wasn't broken, then I would consider it a Christmas miracle. Well, a March miracle. Whatever. It probably wasn't even March wherever we were right now.

New voices shouted at us, and they sounded commanding, *threatening*. They weren't townspeople...*Those are Hunters!*

"What do they want?" I asked, inhaling dirt.

Jeph held my head down. "Your death, so far as I can tell."

"Tell them to get in line," I muttered.

"Is that supposed to be funny?"

"No. I'm being serious."

More commands were thrown our way, probably something along the lines of, "Come out with your hands up." Not that we were inside anywhere. Not that I could get up.

"There's something wrong with you," he said in disbelief.

"I'm aware. Now get off me!"

"No can do, precious. These idiots kill you, then I'm stranded here."

"Wouldn't that be a shame?" I asked sarcastically.

"You're not very nice, are you?"

"Nope."

"Fine by me." There was a smile in his voice. "Just don't die."

"Would be easier without you suffocating me."

"*Sibylla!*" one of the Hunters yelled.

"Jesus," Jeph hissed. "You've got enemies wherever you go, don't you?"

"Like I said, tell them to get in line."

"Working on it."

My brow furrowed. What did he mean by that? He muttered something under his breath, magic washing over me, and I could finally understand the shouts raging around us.

"It's her!" a woman screamed shrilly. "She's real!"

"She'll kill us all!" came another accusation.

"She'll steal our children and make them her slaves!"

"Get up, Sibyl!" one of the Hunters commanded. "In the name of the White Paladins, you're to stand trial."

"Are they serious right now?" I hissed. "Trial? For what crime?"

"Breathing, apparently," Jeph muttered. "And be careful, the translation spell goes both ways—they can understand us now."

"You could've said something."

"Didn't think I had to, *Si-byl.*"

"Power doesn't equate to knowledge, *ass-hole.*"

"Then what's the point?" he asked sarcastically.

"The point is, you need to get the hell off me so we can get out of here."

"Already working on it."

"Plan to fill me in?" I demanded.

"Mmm, no."

He was the most infuriating person I'd ever met in my life.

Then, the pressure on my back lifted, and I risked raising my head. Magical energy flitted to me from every person in the immediate area. Where had we fallen? In the middle of a literal Magical Community?

I'd heard that towns with only magic users had once existed, hence the modern-day term for the Magical Community, but I had no idea they *actually* did. I supposed when the Norms outnumbered us 10,000 to 1 in modern society, it made sense that we were mixed bodies of people. In times where people were more spread out, I could almost believe in settlements filled with only magic users.

The terrifying thing about being here was that, nearly one thousand years ago, thirteen-year-old me had earned the title of "Sibyl." It was apparently still fresh in the minds of the Magical Community. I'd wondered how the tales and legends had managed to make it all the way to the twenty-first century to haunt me. Apparently, I was just that infamous—and this little jaunt through time wasn't going to help me with anything.

We got to our feet, and power gathered in the hands of mages, fear modeling their auras. Fear, determination, and vengeance for crimes I hadn't committed. There was no way I was making it out of here alive. And then I *knew* I wasn't going to when Jeph put his hands in the air.

"Help me," he said, tone pleading. "She's taken me hostage."

"*Excuse* your ass!" I snapped, jaw dropping.

The Hunters—the ones wearing some ridiculous knightly getup with a horse embroidered on their tunics and cloaks—shifted their focus between Jeph and me. They were wondering if he was really a hostage or if he was trying to create a diversion. At this point, I was confused enough to be wondering the same thing.

"Keep your hands up," one of the Hunters instructed. I assumed he was their leader or something because he had the strongest magical energy out of the bunch. He also had an arrogance about him that boasted, *I'm too good for you.* Then again, he was a Hunter; they were just like that. "Now, come over here. No magic, or my archer shoots."

Jeph's eyes flicked to the archer holding an arrow taut on his bow. I wanted his weapon. *In fact...*I gasped, doubling over when I appeared next to him, and he jumped, releasing his arrow. It sailed past Jeph's face.

Why had I thought using Chaos when I was drained was a good idea? Instead of getting the weaponry I wanted, I was grabbed from behind. At least I'd caused a distraction. Jeph stole a sword from the lead Paladin, slicing the man across the chest, and he went down.

"Don't kill them!" I screamed, sweat rolling down my forehead. "The timeline!"

Jeph glared, blade flashing at his next opponent. Their weapons clashed, impossible sparks flying.

My captor jerked me around, scooping me up and carrying me away. Since it was easy to do and I really was wiped, I went limp in his arms. We toppled to the ground under my extra weight. Clearly, he hadn't expected me to pull a stunt so simple and stupid. I did stupid well. I rolled away from him, screaming when someone's foot almost smashed into my face. I lurched backward, knocking into my captor. He fell forward, his body pinning me.

I could still hear blades clashing nearby, which meant Jeph hadn't been subdued. I wasn't sure how he was still alive. There were ten Hunters and a town full of goddess only knew how many magic users. It didn't mean they were trained to fight—*that's what guilds are for*—but if they joined the battle, we were as good as dead. Now to pray guild law banned the Magical Community from interfering in Hunter affairs.

Jeph roared, and I looked through the throngs of Hunters' legs to see him charging forward, his side slashed open. It looked deep, and I wasn't sure if all that blood was his or the Hunters'. Probably both. He had a sword in each hand, and he was swinging them so skillfully, my heart shriveled. If this man was my enemy, then I was so, so screwed.

"Get up!" Jeph yelled, parrying a Hunter's attack. He used his short sword to force the man back, then used his longsword to gore him. "Get up and run!"

"Easier said than done!" I snapped, trying to crawl my way out from under the man pinning me. His fingers dug into my spandex. If I kept crawling away, they were going to come off. What was more important, my life or my modesty?

Flames roared to life all around us. Embers exploded from the fire, streaking toward me and the Hunters. I couldn't say where the hell it came from—one of the White Paladins or the crowd—but whoever it was, they weren't being conscientious of who got caught in the blast. It scalded the hand of the Hunter holding me, which would've been great—if it didn't also burn my pants.

Screaming, I slapped the flames until they died. Then, I bucked and squirmed, wriggling out from underneath the Hunter and kneeing him in the face. As soon as I was on my feet, someone grabbed both my arms, twisting them painfully behind my back. I was back where I started but with a different mage. This was getting old.

Jeph now had five men at his feet, bleeding and groaning in pain, and two on either side of him. I had three men with me, the one on the ground, one holding me and...the archer.

I grinned. "That's a nice bow you've got there."

He eyed me warily. "Don't talk."

"I was just complimenting your weapon."

"Shut it," the man holding me rumbled.

I liked this translation spell. It translated their jargon into English slang I could understand. I had no doubt what he actually said sounded more like "Speaketh not," or something, but I could dig a spell that did colloquialisms.

"There's no need to be rude," I muttered.

The archer lifted his bow, arrow nocked, and aimed at Jeph.

"While you'd be doing me a favor," I said conversationally, "I'd really like it if you didn't kill him."

"He's killing us. Now, quiet." The archer took aim again.

"He's not killing them," I said, rolling my eyes. "He's incapacitating them. There's a difference."

"Gag her," the archer told the Hunter holding me.

He sighed, putting a hand over my mouth, and I bit him—*hard.* He yelped, the archer jumped, and the arrow hit one of the men fighting Jeph. Their heads whipped around to stare at us. Jeph recovered first, short sword slicing along the remaining man's chest. The Hunter fell to the ground, howling in pain. Then, Jeph turned to us, his sweats, shoes, and skin covered in their blood. He looked like an avenging angel—a dark, gory, *sinister* angel.

My captor threw me to the ground, his shoe pressing against my throat. As it turned out, mages really did have a fetish for choking me—no matter what time period it was. And he was doing a damn good job of it, because he wasn't small by any means. That guy was a frickin' tank, unlike the slender archer.

The archer, who'd thrown down his bow in favor of a sword as Jeph approached us. I reached for it, knowing it wouldn't do me much good without any arrows, but having a weapon would make me feel better. My fingers grazed it, and the pressure on my neck increased. I couldn't breathe, agony assaulting my senses. My eyes pulsed, my hand went limp, and blackness crowded the edges of my vision.

Jeph must've taken down the archer because the darkness receded when he attacked the tank standing on my throat. Raw, angry magical energy blasted the Hunter off his feet, sending him colliding into a tree. I coughed and choked, rolling and getting to my hands and knees. They wobbled and protested under my weight.

"Get up!" Jeph hissed, wrapping an arm around my waist, and I barely managed to grab the bow as he lifted me to my feet. He released me, and I almost fell over. "Damn it!" he snapped, catching me against his side.

He gasped, a sound raw and agonizing, when my free hand found the gash on his waist. My hand became slick with his blood. I really shouldn't have looked, but I did. I put my mouth in my elbow, trying not to throw up. It was deep, crimson, gruesome, and...I gagged.

"We need...to run..." he panted.

"Arrows. I need—"

He flung a hand out and the quiver floated to us. He gave it to me, and we began to wobble away. I could barely stand after losing so much magical energy, and Jeph was losing blood fast, looking worse for the wear. Sweat plastered his hair to his forehead, and he was shaking. We didn't get far before magic blasted us off our feet. We hit the ground, and Jeph gasped, an "O" of silent pain on his lips.

"They took out the White Paladins!" someone shouted.

"Stop them!"

"Kill them!"

"Shit," Jeph hissed. "Forgot about them."

"You don't say," I wheezed.

"Less bitching, more running."

I gritted my teeth, struggling to push myself up. "Trying."

I got to my feet, stomach curdling when I saw the angry townspeople marching toward us. It was mostly mages since the witches probably didn't know many attack spells. If they used energy blasts, we'd be screwed—not that I was going to tell them that.

An eerie calm filled me, and I squared my shoulders, lifting the bow and firing. Arrow after arrow soared toward the approaching men. I landed attacks in shoulders, hands, calves, and thighs. I was trying not to mortally wound anyone; I didn't know who was important to the timeline. My intuition spiked with panic when I aimed at various people, so those were the ones I was careful with. When I shot the eleventh man, the townsfolk stopped approaching. They stared at me, fear coloring their aura and faces. They were afraid of me, of my power, but they were also in awe. They watched me, and I could only imagine what they saw.

A young woman with her unruly hair billowing around her face? A powerful witch with a bow and quiver ready to knock them down? A sweating and pale girl with strange clothes and blood soaking her? I wasn't sure. Whatever the case, they were entranced by my power. It was both flattering and stupid. I'd literally done nothing up until just now. Worse, this moment would haunt me through the centuries. These people would tell the tale of the Sibyl, wild, powerful, and fierce.

"Let's go before they try to attack again," Jeph said, taking my elbow.

I let him lead me away but watched over my shoulder until the town was a speck on the horizon.

Ten

e hobbled along a dirt road until Jeph collapsed, his face hitting the ground, arms out in
front of him. He'd lost a lot of blood and really
needed medical attention. There wasn't much we could do, however, not with enemies potentially lurking nearby. We'd only
knocked the Hunters down, but they would've alerted the guild
to our presence by now. If they hadn't, one of the townsfolk
likely had. There was no way we'd be safe out in the open.

I bent down, reaching for him. The motion sent my head
spinning and my vision sparkling. I'd lost so much magical energy I was surprised I could even stand. *But really, standing is
overrated*, I decided, when my legs gave out and I fell to my
hands and knees. I panted, sweat trickling down my forehead
and spine.

"Hey," I said hoarsely. "You alive over there?"

He groaned.

"I'll take that as a maybe." I shook his shoulder.

Very slowly, his head lifted, eyes glossy and distant. He
blinked a few times, face contorting in pain.

"We need to get something for your injury."

"It's fine," he wheezed, pushing himself up. He was as
sweaty and pale as me, which was saying something, considering he was a shade darker than my light-brown coloring. His
hair was plastered to his forehead. Mine probably was too.

"You don't look fine, pal. In fact, you look like a corpse."

He glared pitifully. "I said I'll be fine."

"Will you, though?"

He ignored me, pushing himself onto shaky legs. "We need
to keep moving. They'll be hunting us before long." He laughed

bitterly. "Unbelievable. *I'm* being hunted by the mages hunting you—and I'm technically on their side!"

"You're the one that started slicing them up."

"They didn't believe me for a second anyway. They were never going to let me live if they moved to execute you."

"At least we would've been put out of our misery."

His lips twitched, and I could swear he was trying not to smile. "You're kinda morbid, you know that?"

I shrugged. "You get a morbid sense of humor when every day could be your last."

"Right." He stared up the dirt trail. "We should probably get off the road."

"And then what? Get lost in the woods?"

"We're sitting ducks out here."

"You can't even stand straight," I pointed out.

And he couldn't; he kept favoring his uninjured side.

"Just...let's just get somewhere a little more sheltered, okay?"

I bobbed my head, finally pushing back to my feet. The world spun around me, and I started to fall. Jeph reached out, barely catching my arm before I would've kissed dirt. Gritting his teeth against the strain, he helped pull me back up to a half-standing position.

"And I'm the one who can't stand straight?" he muttered, putting an arm around my waist.

Whether it was to hold me up or lean on me, I wasn't sure, but that was the result either way. We leaned against each other, using each other as a crutch. It kept us both on our feet as we made for the tree line. That proved to be a horrible idea; our already-clumsy feet snagged every root and fallen tree branch, our shoes tangling in the plants and underbrush.

We tripped and stumbled our way through the woods, and to my horror, it began to rain. Jeph stopped walking—just stopped—his face a mask of *unbelievable!* I felt the same way. After a minute of internal screaming from us both, we started moving again, my shoes and clothing chafing with each step as we were quickly drenched.

When we were deep enough into the woods that Jeph felt we were safe, he stopped walking and pointed to a mossy spot near a tree. We hobbled over, and I helped him sit down, his back resting against its trunk. Then, I kneeled next to him, steeling my resolve before I lifted his shirt to examine his wound.

"Don't!" he hissed, slapping my hands away.

I arched a brow. "It needs attention."

"I already told you, precious, it'll be fine."

"Keep your BS to yourself, pal."

I shoved his hands out of the way, lifting his shirt again. *Goddess*. Did I really think I could look at something that gory? I choked on bile, staring at the wound.

"I don't suppose you have any healing potions?" he asked.

"Does it look like I have pockets on this outfit?"

His gaze raked over me. "This is what I get for being careless. Never go anywhere without our belts—that's like the first damn rule they teach us."

I wasn't sure what that meant, but not having medical supplies wasn't going to help him.

"Do you know emergency first-aid?" I asked hopefully.

"Mages don't *do* emergency first-aid. We've got potions and healers for that."

"Well, it sure is screwing you over right now, ain't it?"

"You're an optimistic one, aren't you, precious?"

"I like to consider myself a realist."

He shrugged. "Let me rest for a bit and I'll be good to go."

"I'm not a doctor or anything, but rest isn't going to magically make that wound go away."

"You know what?" he asked, not waiting for me to answer. "Train tickets don't talk."

"What?"

"Train tickets. As in, you're the only way I'm getting back home. Now, close your mouth and mind your own business."

My jaw dropped. I had half a mind to dig my finger into his cut just to show him how useless he currently was. Just to hear him scream.

"How about *you* rest and I'll leave you here to rot?"

He scowled. "You wouldn't dare."

"Oh, I would." I got to my feet. "In fact…"

I kicked his knee, and he roared, reaching for it.

"Nice knowing ya—*not!*"

I wiggled my fingers, walking away…and was promptly knocked to the ground, getting a mouthful of grass and mud. I spat and sputtered, screaming in rage as I kicked and flailed. Jeph held me there, saying nothing as I continued to throw a tantrum under his weight. When I finally stilled, he spoke.

"If I'm on my deathbed and you can't even get out from under me, what makes you think you're going to survive ten minutes in this time period all alone?"

"Get. Off."

"No, I don't think I will. I'm quite comfortable."

I snarled.

"Anyone ever tell you you're like a feral kitten?" he taunted. "All claws, no bite."

Just to be spiteful, I turned my head and bit the arm closest to me, locking my jaw and digging my teeth into his flesh. I tasted blood but didn't care. It was his turn to snarl as he rolled us, my back laying across his front as he tried to pry my jaw apart one-handed. He finally gave up and wrapped his fingers around my neck, digging his thumb and forefinger into the pressure points just below my ears.

A silent scream escaped my lips, and I reached up to pull at the wrist assaulting me. He yanked his arm from my mouth, and I dragged his hand away with some effort. We both panted, more energy wasted as we struggled against each other. I shoved off of him, and he sat up, a scowl leveled on me as he cradled his injured arm to his chest. Now that I was staring into his fiery, angry eyes, the heat of him not pressed against me, I realized just how sodden and cold I really was. I started shivering, much to my annoyance.

I rocked back on my heels, wiping a muddy arm across my mouth. It tasted like sickly sweet iron and dirt, and I ran my tongue along my teeth trying to get the gritty feeling off of them. But it wasn't just the dirt bothering me, it was tasting his blood. I'd only just barely broken the skin, but I could still taste the coppery tang of it. I was disturbed by the weird urge that had me licking my lips next, trying to get the last of it, one last taste of dark crimson.

Jeph pressed his lips together, a twinkle of amusement in his eyes. What could he possibly find funny? We were trapped in the fifth century with guild mages hunting us. We'd just attacked each other. We were both exhausted, he was wounded and bleeding, and it was cold. We were also both covered in filth.

"What?" I snapped.

"Your face is covered in mud," he said, making me think of an old rock song.

"I swear to the goddess—if you start singing, I'm gonna strangle my own damn self and hope I die."

He grinned. "I hadn't planned on it, but…"

I glowered. "You're not funny."

"Neither are you."

A beat of silence.

"Anyways, I'm outtie," I muttered, getting to my feet.

"Where do you think you're going?"

"Away from the psycho-Councilmember who tried to kill me this morning."

"I didn't tr—if I wanted you dead, you'd be dead."

"Obviously. You're just the sick, twisted asshole who likes to play with his food."

"*Oh*, precious," he said, smirking. "There you go again, pretending you know me."

"Tell me I'm wrong." I crossed my arms over my chest, staring down at him.

He was still sitting in the mud, looking perfectly at peace. "You're not…but if you're right, does that make you food? Come here and let me have a bite."

I blushed crimson. "Rot in hell!"

"Every day."

I scoffed and made to walk past him, but my stupid shoe snagged on a long vine. I went tumbling toward the ground… and landed right on Jeph. We knocked foreheads, and he cussed while I groaned in defeat. Then, I gulped. My legs straddled his hips and he held my waist, my hands resting on his shoulders, our faces just a breath apart. I stared into dark brown eyes, unable to breathe as his gaze held mine transfixed.

A grin spread across his lips. "Awfully obliging, hmm, precious?"

And then I could breathe, my face falling into a hard line. "Nope. Just decided to strangle you instead." I put my hands around his throat, seriously contemplating it—not that I'd be able to. He could kick my ass across the clearing before I could ever suffocate him.

"You're a kinky, naughty girl, aren't you?"

"Y'know what? Just kill me. It'll be better than listening to you for the next however long we're stuck here."

"Keep that up and you just might hurt my feelings."

"What feelings?" I muttered.

"Hmm. Maybe you do know me."

I rolled my eyes. "Whatever. If you're done being an ass, you can let go now."

"You first." He arched a brow.

Grudgingly, I pulled my hands from his neck; I really would be safer without a Councilmember following me around, but it looked like I didn't have a choice in the matter. He held me for a second longer, eyes boring into mine before he finally released my waist. I braced my hands on his shoulders, pushed myself up, and put some distance between us.

"We should get moving," he said. "It'll be dark soon, and we're not going to want to be caught in the elements. If that doesn't allow a predator the chance to catch us, then the Hunters will."

"Y'know, I really don't like you."

"Noted," he muttered, getting to his feet. "In the meantime, let's agree to disagree about our present-day differences. Right now, we need to work together if we're going to survive this."

"Mhm…"

"I give my word, in this damn time period, I'll do everything in my power to keep you alive. You die, I might as well die too. I'm not staying here." He held a hand out to me.

I eyed it like it was a snake. "And when we get back?"

"We can cross that bridge if we live long enough to get to it."

He had a point. If I died, he was stranded. I wouldn't want to live here for several reasons, so I didn't blame him for wanting to go home. We also had no guarantee I'd recuperate enough magical energy to get us there before we died, whether from poor provisions or from being tracked by Hunters, only time would tell. If he wanted to get back, he'd have to ensure my survival, all while knowing I could choose to leave him here.

It was a gamble for him as much as it was for me, but truth be told, he needed me and I needed him. While I was the transportation home, I was so far out of my element here, I'd likely get myself killed. I didn't have Phoenix to watch my back. I didn't have the luxury of my magic to escape—and wouldn't because using it at all would prevent me from recovering magical energy. And with a measly five arrows left in the quiver I'd stolen, I would be out of my only means of defense before long.

Jeph, on the other hand, was some sort of badass all unto himself. After getting a glimpse of him dual-wielding, I had no doubt he could've annihilated the Hunters without breaking a sweat. Instead, he'd been forced to hold back or risk distorting the timeline. Having him at my side was my best bet for survival—for now—but there were no guarantees when we got back.

If we got back.

I wasn't confident in my ability to get us home in one fell swoop. I hadn't even done that going home from Ancient Egypt. It had been painstaking days as I'd stepped century by century in and out of Chaos, hiding in backstreets, nooks, crannies, the wilderness—wherever was discreet—as I made the long journey home. I was able to make it a handful of centuries at a time, but it left me shaken and dizzy. And that was when I'd had weeks to recover my magical energy before leaving Egypt.

Right now? I was completely drained and couldn't even do that much. If I tried, we'd be entering a new time, with new rules, and new, unknown threats. I couldn't keep risking more Hunters finding me throughout the timeline, couldn't keep risking the stories and legends growing. I'd been completely ignorant of the reputation I'd had when I'd done that at age thirteen.

Now, I knew better, and I'd already done enough damage to the timeline over the last five years.

We'd have to stay here as long as possible until I regained my magical energy. I didn't think I could get us all the way to the twenty-first century in one jump, but the fewer stops we made along the way, the better. Which meant I was stuck here—with *him*.

I put my hand in his, and we shook on it. He held onto me a minute longer than was comfortable before letting go, his gaze never leaving mine. I couldn't help but stare back; everything about him commanded my attention. From the intensity in his eyes to his magical energy that screamed, *I'm here, so fear me*, I was trapped within his gravity.

He smirked, and I got the distinct impression he was laughing at me. That, or I'd just screwed myself over somehow. I wasn't sure how yet, but he was too damn smug for it to be nothing. I scowled, stepping around him and heading deeper into the woods.

Eleven

*B*y the time it was dark, I was chafed from head to toe, my legs were made of rubber, and I was starving. My stomach lamented, singing the song of its people. I wasn't the only one who was hungry; I'd heard Jeph's stomach rumble several times as we'd trekked through the woods. The good news was we'd found a Norm town.

Like the first town, it was a collection of small, wood and thatch-roofed houses, some with the straw almost reaching the ground. They were little things, no bigger than a moderate-sized bedroom. Creeping toward them, I noticed some had smoke coming from the top, others had no apparent heat source inside. We kept walking until we came to a larger structure that was a little way away from the main town.

Jeph held up a hand, indicating for me to wait outside. He was in and out in a flash, opening the door wider to let me in. I shivered, glad to be out of the cold. The building appeared to be a storage shed since all it held was hay—probably to replace their roofs as the weather broke them down. It wasn't a bad idea to store extra supplies. It also meant no one was likely to find us.

"Stay here," Jeph whispered, heading back for the door.

"Where are you going?"

"To hopefully find something to eat. I'll be back."

He left before I could offer to help. A lot of good I would've been anyway. My legs, now that I was sitting down, refused to move. I wasn't getting back up anytime soon. But exhausted or not, Jeph still had his gaping wound. He shouldn't have been moving at all. We'd walked at least fifteen miles today, maybe more, and he had to be exhausted.

Before I could contemplate that thought further, or the fact that I was sitting in pitch-darkness, unable to see, he came back in. He held a lit torch in one hand. It was dangerous, considering we were surrounded by hay and wood on all sides. A basket, filled with all sorts of things, was in the other. It took me a minute to realize what that meant.

"You stole that!" I hissed under my breath.

"I don't think they accept plastic."

"That's not fair to them."

"No," Jeph muttered, sticking the pole of the torch into a hole in the floor. "'Not fair' is being attacked for no reason."

"Sucks, doesn't it?"

His eyes narrowed, but he didn't comment.

He sat down across from me, putting the basket between us. He pulled out a few things, setting them at his side before revealing the food within. There was a wooden bowl holding a small loaf of bread, cooked fava beans, and cabbage. I grimaced, not sure what I'd expected. It didn't look particularly appetizing, but it wasn't like beggars could be choosers. Sighing, I reached in and grabbed the bread, breaking it in half. I held out half to Jeph, taking a bite of mine. He accepted the offering, his nose crinkling as he sniffed it.

"I's nah tha' bahd," I mumbled around a mouthful of food.

His lip curled back. "Don't talk with your mouth full."

"You're not my real mom," I muttered, taking another bite.

He arched a brow, taking a bite of his own bread. Deciding I should use the bread as a palate cleanser—just in case the beans and cabbages were disgusting—I set it back in the basket, grabbing the bowl of food.

"Is this...sanitary?"

"A little late to be asking," he mumbled. "I think so. It didn't look dirty, but that doesn't mean much."

Resigned to my pending demise, I lifted the dish to my lips, letting some of the beans and cabbage slide into my mouth. I chewed and let out a soft moan. I was so hungry it was like tasting heaven.

His lips quirked up. "That good, huh?"

"Mhm," I murmured around another mouthful. "Heaven."

"I don't suppose you're going to share?"

I hissed, pulling the dish out of reach, and he smirked, taking another bite of bread. Once he finished it, he took the piece I'd set down and ate it too. I supposed that was fair but felt bad because bread wasn't very filling, and there were plenty of beans and cabbage to feed us both. Besides, I didn't need nearly as much food as a calorie-burning man.

I held the dish toward Jeph, and he arched a dubious brow. The flame of the torch seemed to chuckle along with him, each mocking me. I handed over the dish, and he put it to his lips, his head tilting back. I watched him in the firelight, the flames dancing over his rain-slicked skin and hair. His throat muscles worked as he swallowed the last of the food.

Trying not to stare, I let my eyes glide to the tattoo curling under his ears. My eyes then traveled to his muscular biceps, where the other end of the tattoo peeked out, before landing on the bite I'd left in his forearm. I couldn't believe I'd done that, but I'd done worse to get away from my pursuers before.

Yeah, but they'd been attacking you...

Before I could linger on that thought, my eyes were drawn to the blood-soaked cut in his t-shirt. Leaning overtop the basket, I reached for his wound. I wanted to see if it had become infected or inflamed—especially after rolling around in the mud like pigs. Just as my fingertips grazed his shirt, the dish clattered to the floor, and Jeph held my wrist in a vice grip.

My eyes widened, darting up to meet his.

"What are you doing?" he asked coolly.

"Trying to see if it's infected."

"It's not."

"I don't suppose you found some water?" I barreled on, thinking of how to tend to it without anything to stitch it up. "We could definitely wash this out if you can find..." I trailed off, noticing the supplies he'd set next to him. "Oh."

"I can bandage my own wound."

"I can help."

"I don't need your help."

"I'm not gonna hurt you."

"Says the girl who literally kicked me while I was down *and* bit my arm."

"That was before we called a truce," I reminded him.

"You need a truce to be nice to someone?"

"No, but you were being mean!"

He snorted. "So that constitutes you drawing blood like a rabid dog?"

"You called me a feral kitten!"

"You are."

"You—!" I pointed my finger at him, wanting to clobber him.

That stupid brow arched again, a self-satisfied smirk on his face. He finally released my wrist, turning to dunk a cup into the pail of water before holding it out to me.

I took it, frowning. "You going to let me help after all?"

"No. That's to drink. I had some when I was at the well."

"So, it's poisoned."

"It's—oh, for the love!" He snatched the cup from my hand, taking a long sip of it before giving it to me again.

I tried not to think about how we'd been sharing food and beverage from the same dishes. What if he has cooties!

Restraining an eye-roll, I sipped the water. I hadn't realized I was thirsty until I was gulping down water like it was life itself. When I came up for air, Jeph was staring at me. He held his hand out for the cup, refilled it, and gave it back. I sipped slower this time, trying not to embarrass myself. Again.

Shaking his head, he grabbed the pail and a linen cloth, gently peeling back his t-shirt. He gasped when the cotton clung to the wound, dried blood crusting it to his skin. I felt woozy seeing pieces of flesh peel away with the cloth, the injury red, puffy, and swollen. He tried holding his shirt up while he reached across his torso, dabbing at the wound, but no matter where he held it, either his hand, elbow, or arm blocked his line of sight. He scowled, grabbing the hem of his shirt like he was about to…

Oh, hell no!

"Can I…?" I murmured, holding my hand out.

He paused his stripping, pursed his lips, and sighed, relinquishing the cloth to me. He held his shirt out of the way, and I avoided looking at the ab muscles staring up at me. Instead, I dunked the cloth into the pail, being careful not to get my filthy hands in the water. I sat crisscross on the floor, contemplating the best way to go about this.

"Lie down," I said.

"I'm not a dog, you don't have to bark orders at me."

I ground my teeth together. "Lie down, *please?*"

He did, laying with his injured side up, and I scooted in front of his stomach. He rested his left arm above his head, stretching his muscles and laceration taut. I imagined that didn't feel very good, but it gave me full access to the wound. I pushed his shirt up to his armpit to keep it out of the way, and he jolted. I placed one hand on his ribcage to hold him steady while I dabbed at the dried blood on his hip and waist. It was disconcerting feeling his warmth and muscles under my palm.

He let me work in silence, and it was probably a good thing. If he distracted me, I might accidentally hurt him, and if he said something stupid, I might hurt him—*on purpose*. The thought had my lips tilting up in grim satisfaction. It made me wonder if I was a cruel person. Then again, Jeph just seemed to bring out the sadistic side of me. *I'd* bitten *the guy, for goddess' sake!* And for a comment—*not* because he was threatening me, *not* because I was defending myself, but because he'd insulted me one time too many. I still wasn't sure if I felt guilty or not.

Once the crusted blood was wiped away, I wrung the cloth out as best as I could. Then, I looked over at him, finding him watching me intently. I tried not to let the surprise show on my face, but my heart leapt in my chest. How long had he been watching me? I thought he'd maybe closed his eyes—*you know, to try to relax or something.*

"This is probably gonna hurt," I told him.

"Just be quick."

I bit my lip, my fingers digging into his ribcage to keep him still, and gooseflesh broke out along his skin, starting from my hand and trailing down his side. I tried not to think about that as I gently touched the cloth to his wound. His whole body went rigid, and I gnashed my teeth, trying to work as quickly as I could. Jeph made a noise between a growl and a snarl, and it made the hair on the back of my neck stand on edge. I wrung the cloth out again before giving one last scrub over the length of the wound.

Jeph let out a string of curses, impressing me with his foul language.

"Okay, all clean. So, what else did you bring? Did they have a salve or anything?"

"Supposing that's what that is"—he pointed to a goo-like substance in a small, wooden container—"then yes. If not, then I have no idea why I found it stored with bandages."

I picked up the salve, lifting it to my nose. It smelled grassy and earthy, which was about as good as we were going to get. It didn't look dirty, so that was promising, right? I dunked my fingers into the water, trying to clean them off before I stuck them into the salve. Then, I held Jeph's rib cage, digging my fingers in to hold him steady in case he jumped or tensed. Gooseflesh spread down his side again, and I got the feeling it was my grip that was making him…I didn't want to think about it.

I gently wiped the salve near his raw flesh, and he hissed, clenching his teeth on a growl. His eyes closed, his neck and back arched in agony. If I was slow, it would only drag out his suffering. The thought might've appealed to me earlier, but seeing him in so much pain now, I felt horrible. He'd gotten this injury because of me. Because I'd brought him here on accident. Because he'd been trying to protect me—even if his motives were selfish.

Grimacing, I decided gentle wasn't what he needed right now. I grabbed a large dollop of salve and splattered it onto his side, smearing it around the cut as quickly as possible. I was careful to avoid packing it into the wound in case it brought on an infection.

Jeph panted, his chest heaving and a cold sweat breaking out along his skin. How had he thought he could've dressed his own wound? If I was trying to be careful, I could only imagine how the awkward angle would've made it more painful for him to treat himself.

"Almost done," I said, reassuringly. "If you sit up, I can wrap it."

He nodded, attempting to sit up, and gasped, nearly falling back on his side. I reached out, catching him around the waist with my left arm and grabbing his bicep with my right hand. I pulled him upright, holding him steady. We sat there, panting each other's air, him from the pain, me from the strain and adrenaline. I swallowed, licking my lips nervously. He was entirely too close for comfort, and I was about to be closer.

I grabbed the bandages, not meeting his eyes. The weight of his gaze stayed on me as he lifted the hem of his shirt above his abdomen. With a shaky breath, I put one end of the linen bandage just past the far side of his wound, then I leaned forward, wrapping the cloth behind his back, nearly hugging him in the process. The inside of my wrist rubbed along his bare flesh as I passed the bandage from one hand to the other. This close, it was impossible to miss his slight shiver.

My pulse spiked, and my breathing became shallow. I prayed he couldn't see the flush in my cheeks, couldn't feel the sudden warmth that had flooded me from the brief contact, knowing it was *me* who'd made him shiver. I couldn't begin to let myself think about his reaction to me...of my reaction to him.

Enemies, enemies, enemies, I chanted. *Annoying, rude...*I let other insults fill my mind, trying to think of anything but the magnetic pull he had on my thoughts and attention.

I quickly wrapped the bandage around him a few more times, making sure his wound was covered and well protected. Once satisfied, I tore the end of the linen into ribbons, tying them around slits I poked into the bandage to secure it in place. Then, I extracted myself from Jeph's personal space, avoiding eye contact as I backed away.

He pulled his shirt down, then sighed, holding his wrist out. "While you're in a charitable mood..."

I pressed my lips together, picking up the filthy rag again and dunking it in the water. I wiped dirt and grime from the grooves in his arm. Grooves in the shape of my teeth. Grooves that, now that I was washing away the muck, were deeper than

I'd thought. Guilt prickled along my subconscious. When it was as clean as it was going to get, I wiped the salve on it and wrapped it with the remaining bandages.

Before I released his arm, I met his eyes. "I shouldn't have bit you."

Jeph snorted. "You don't say."

I glowered, tossing his arm at him and getting to my feet. "Whatever. See if I ever apologize again."

"Hey!" He caught my ankle, and I nearly tripped.

I floundered before regaining my balance and turning a glare on him.

"Thanks."

"What?"

He released my ankle, scratching his cheek. "I said, *thanks*. You know, it's this thing people say when they're trying to show their gratitude."

"*Pfft!* Yeah, okay."

He glared up at me. "You really aren't nice, are you?"

"You're one to talk."

He didn't respond.

I turned to find a patch of hay to lay on, settling down and trying to get comfortable, but it was a moot point. There was nothing comfortable about this place, about this situation, about this century. The torch extinguished, and I closed my eyes to sleep.

J shivered, and my teeth chattered, the barn providing little in the way of warmth. It didn't help that the temperature outside wasn't much better. At least we weren't exposed to the elements.

"Come here," Jeph said.

"What?" I demanded incredulously.

"You're shivering. Come here."

I turned over to glare toward the dark shape of him. Without things like artificial light—a building, a streetlight, a car passing by—it was dark as pitch. It was also quiet—*too* quiet—and the rain barely made up for it. I didn't like how foreign and eerie it was.

"N-N-No th-th-thanks, pal." My teeth chattered despite me. "I'll t-t-take my chances w-w-with the hay."

"You're being ridiculous!"

"Am-m-m I?"

"Yes! If you contract something and die, I'm stuck here."

"Gee. So s-s-sorry to hear t-t-that."

We fell quiet, nothing but the sound of my teeth chattering and the rain falling outside to fill the silence. Then, there was some shuffling on his side of the shed and something sinister wrapped around my wrists and yanked. I screamed, colliding with Jeph's chest. I wanted to protest, but the instant-heat was enough to make me moan from the prickle of my numbed fingers as I splayed my hands over his pecs.

I half-groaned, half-sobbed, toeing off my sodden socks and tennis shoes before sliding my feet under the hem of his sweatpants, seeking the unimaginable heat his body was providing. He was like a furnace and completely dry despite being caught in the downpour right alongside me. I didn't even stop to question it, didn't even care that I was being extremely intrusive.

"Jesus Christ!" he hissed. "Your skin is like a corpse."

"I-I-It's...c-c-cold."

"No shit."

"W-W-Why aren't y-y-y-ou cold?"

"Hot blooded," he muttered, wrapping his arm around my waist and giving me more warmth.

I shifted my toes, riding up his sweats as I sought warmer flesh on his calves. He flinched but didn't say anything. Not even caring anymore, I ran my fingers up his arms, putting them under the sleeves of his t-shirt. I sobbed at the warmth, feeling like a big baby after roughing it for a whopping day. I was a city girl. The wilderness—especially the foreign terrain of the *fifth frickin' century*—was *not* for me.

"And to think, you wanted to take your chances with the hay."

"Sh-Sh-Shut up," I chattered, burying my face in the crook of his neck.

"God damn! Is your nose made of ice?"

"Dunno," I mumbled, pressing it against his neck.

"Stop that," he breathed.

I shivered, but this time, it had nothing to do with the cold. Thank the goddess he couldn't possibly know that. It was bad enough I'd done it at all, but now that I was starting to warm up, I was all too aware of how intrusive I was being. And the breathy words that had just come out of his mouth, in combination with the pulse jumping under my nose, had my heart racing in my chest.

Don't react to it, I told myself. *Just because he's warm, and pretty, and pressed up against you...*I gritted my teeth, stopping that train of thought. *Don't think about it. In fact, I should punch him in the face for dragging me over here against my will.*

Only...I was finally starting to feel my toes again. *My fingers and toes!* They'd been so numb I wasn't entirely sure I knew what they were supposed to feel like. Right now, they felt like static mixed with a bowl of Rice Krispies, but it was better than the nothingness they'd been before.

"Stop what?" I whispered, feeling his entire body tense when my lips grazed over the pulse jumping in his neck. Gooseflesh rose on his skin, and I had the traitorous urge to press my lips against his throat. "Stop trying to get warm?"

"No." It was gravelly.

My stomach flipped. "Then what...?"

"Move your face."

"Move...my face?"

"Yes."

"O-Okay." I pulled back. "Better?"

Jeph relaxed but only slightly. "Yes."

Needing to fill the silence, to provoke him, to break the tension building between us, I asked, "Afraid I'm gonna chomp a vein open and leave you here to bleed out or something?"

"After what you did to my arm?" he scoffed, rising to my bait. "I wouldn't put it past you."

"Whatever," I muttered, moving my toes from his calves to his shins and my fingers to his biceps.

He jolted when my finger grazed the skin near his armpit. "Would you stop that?" he snapped.

I cocked my head to the side. "Are you...ticklish?"

"No, precious. You're freezing. Keep this up, and you just might steal my soul with those reaper hands and feet of yours."

I snorted. "This is your fault."

"And how's that?"

"You *literally* pulled me over here."

"So?"

"Haven't you ever cuddled a woman? Icy toes come standard—and you better believe that makes *you* the heating pad. Surely your girlfriend has put her popsicle-toes under your butt while sitting on the couch before?"

"One, I don't have a girlfriend. Two, I've never had that experience. Are you sure you're not just cruel? I pity your boyfriend."

"I don't have a boyfriend."

"And yet, you mentioned you weren't looking for one."

I blushed. "I..."

"Besides, aren't you Evander's girlfriend or something?"

"Don't make me vomit." I gagged and shuddered. The kid was nice—ish—but he gave me this over-protective, brother-like vibe. Even if he hadn't kidnapped me, after that weird not-kiss in Club Cadence, I'd rather make-out with a bar of soap than ever repeat that experience. "We're—"

"Cousins. Right." His tone told me he knew we weren't. Far be it from me to disillusion Evander's pathetic attempts at deception.

Then, my brain caught up with his insult. "And I'm not cruel!"

Jeph snorted. "Right. That's why you—*ah!*"

I grinned evilly. "Ticklish?" I stroked the tip of my finger lightly against the underside of his arm again, and he jumped.

"Keep that up, precious, and you're not going to like what I do," he growled.

My heart leapt in my chest.

"Stop calling me that," I said breathlessly. "My name's Sam."

"And my name isn't 'Pal,' but that's what you keep calling me. Besides, *precious*," he said, just to piss me off, "when you name a pet, you get attached to it."

"I'm *not* a pet!"

He chuckled, and being this close, it rumbled through me. "Who said I was talking about you?"

My brow furrowed. If he wasn't talking about me..."Not gonna happen."

"Because I'm your enemy?"

"Thanks for the reminder," I muttered. "But no. You're an ass. I wouldn't get attached to you if you were the last soul on the planet."

"Not even a person—the last *soul*." His tone was mocking as his hand splayed on my back, running up my spine. "You've got mighty strange standards, precious."

"What are you do—" I gasped when he pulled me flush against him.

"You're still cold. Can't have you getting hypothermia and dying, now can I?"

"I'm not gonna die..."

"Of course not. I'm keeping you alive, aren't I?"

"That's…not very reassuring."

"You know"—he put his lips against my ear—"you'd get warmer faster if…"

"If…?" I breathed, trying to stop the erratic heartbeat in my chest, the tingling in my palms, the butterflies in my stomach.

"If you weren't wet."

"It rained. I can't do anything about that."

"Don't play dumb, precious." He chuckled, and I suppressed a shiver. "You can always…*strip*."

I'd had just about enough of his crap.

"I'm going to bed." *Before I try to kill you!*

I pushed away from him, turning to get up, but Jeph's arm caught me around the waist, pulling my back flush with his chest. I stopped breathing when his breath tickled over my neck. His heart beat against my back, strong and steady against my erratic one.

"You'll just get cold again," he murmured against my ear.

My jaw clenched, even as my eyes closed at the silk and honey of his voice. "I'm *so* not sleeping like this."

"Like what?"

"With you sp—" I choked on the word. "Spooning me. And let go of my waist already."

"Haven't you ever had a man spoon you?" he taunted. "An arm around the waist comes standard with spooning."

I wanted to strangle him. Absolutely wanted to kill him dead.

"If you would let go, I could be on my merry way—"

"To freezing to death," he said, cutting me off.

"Like I said, I'm not sleeping like this."

"What, do you want to be big spoon?"

I guffawed. "No thanks."

"Then what's the problem?"

"You're…"

How did I even begin to put all the embarrassing things into words? I could feel *all* of his front pressed up against *all* of my back. It was…it was…*Ugh!* Every muscle. Every. Frickin'.

Muscle. Was pressed up against me. And it was…it was… mildly concerning.

Totally concerning, I amended.

I'd never been closer to a man other than to kiss—and that was standing, not laying down. Not pressed up against a man more gorgeous than sin. *And why am I thinking about this at all? Who cares if he's touching me? He's only doing it so that he can get home*—I rolled my eyes—*and kill me later.*

"I'm…?" he drawled.

"Touching me."

"That's what happens when people spoon." His tone was rife with amusement. "Don't take it personally. I'm just trying to keep you alive."

"Yeah, well…Get your arm off me and I *might* actually believe you're not gonna molest me or something—you creep."

He tensed. "You think I'd…" His tone was hard, disbelieving, angry. "I'm not a pig, precious. I'm not going to rape you in your sleep."

"Sure, you're not," I ground out. "After you just told me to strip? Not buying it."

"Good night," he muttered, pulling his arm away and turning over to his injured side. His back pressed against mine and it was almost enough heat to keep me warm, but little enough that I was shivering before long. "Keep quiet," he called over his shoulder. "I'm trying to sleep."

"Screw you, pal."

"Not interested," he deadpanned.

"Asshole."

"Just admit you were wrong."

"I'm never wrong," I lied.

"Whatever. Stop your chattering. It's annoying."

"I could strangle you to death, then you'll sleep soundly."

"Promises, promises," he muttered.

My head whipped around. "What's even wrong with you?"

"With me?" He turned his head to look at me. "I'm not the one trying to shiver to death."

"You're infuriating!"

"You're insufferable," he replied calmly.

I scoffed. "I am *not!*"

"Yes, precious, you are."

Jeph turned over, and I did too. I could barely make out his scowl but glared right back.

He blew out a breath. "We need to rest. There's no telling what tomorrow's going to bring. Are you going to keep being difficult?"

"I'm not—"

"Yes, you are. Now, either roll over or come here." He lifted his arm, indicating to cuddle up against his front.

I gnashed my teeth, scooting closer. He heaved an impatient sigh, putting his hand on the small of my back and pulling me to him. Then, he rolled so that he lay on his back. I was cradled against his rib cage, my head resting on his chest. I froze, barely breathing. This was worse.

"Now, go to sleep," he commanded.

"I—"

"For the love of the stars, Sam"—the sound of my name on his lips sent a thrill of something racing through my veins—"stop arguing and get some sleep. You're the one who needs to recharge her Sibyl batteries to get us home."

I didn't reply, choosing to readjust to get comfortable. I tried not to think about how much of a hypocrite I was when I nestled my head in the crook of his neck, my hand resting over his rapidly beating heart, my leg, bent at the knee, coming to rest over his thighs. I inhaled the smoky scent of him—like a campfire in summer—and was asleep within seconds.

 hen I woke up, I was alone. That would've been great and all, but I shouldn't have been. I sat up, rubbing my bleary eyes. As I looked around the shed in the light, I realized why I'd been so cold last night. There were gaps between the wooden planks used to build the shed.

Shaking my head, I frowned when straw fell from it. I groaned under my breath, missing the comfort of my bed and the safety the four walls of my apartment had once offered me. They weren't much, but they'd been something. Even that had been stolen from me in the last twenty-four hours.

"Here," Jeph said, materializing out of nowhere and throwing something at me. "Put this on."

Fabric slapped me in the face, and I pulled the garment off my head, glaring up at him from my spot on the floor. "The hell is this?" I asked, studying the tan and brown bundle.

"Clothing. You know, from *this* century."

"Do I wanna know where you got this from?"

"Probably not," he said, shrugging.

"You didn't steal it off some poor, unsuspecting girl, did you?"

"Why?" He smirked, making something churn in my stomach. "You jealous?"

"Pig." I thrust the fabric back at him. "I'm not wearing this."

"Just put it on."

"I'm not wearing the clothing of one of your conquests."

He rolled his eyes. "I stole it—from a clothesline. Now put it on. It's cleaner than what you're wearing, especially after you rolled around in the mud."

"Don't. You. Dare." I wanted to throttle him. "It's *your* fault that happened."

"Wear it, don't wear it. See how quickly our enemies find us. In the meantime, I'm changing. So, I suggest you turn around—unless you're secretly a pervert."

He turned his back to me, pulling his shirt over his head. I gulped, turning around before I saw more than I needed to see. Then, I stared at what was essentially the boxiest tube-dress I'd ever seen. It had nothing to the shoulders, which meant I'd either need to wear a shawl at all times or…or go braless. *Not. Happening.*

"You picked this on purpose," I muttered, pulling my shirt over my head. My heart pounded, hoping he wouldn't turn around. Worse, I could hear him stripping behind me.

"Yes, precious. It's my life's goal to make *your* life a living nightmare."

"I told you"—I pulled off my ruined pants, grimacing—"this isn't my fault."

"*No*, of course, it's not. I'm the one that took us nearly two millennia into the past and stranded us here."

"Are you always this friendly in the morning?"

"Only after my daily routine of a mini-crime spree," he quipped.

"Can you even be serious for two seconds?"

"Nope."

"You're an ass."

He didn't respond, and we dressed in silence. Rather, he did because I heard the fabric rustling as he pulled the tunic over his head. Heard the sound of his socks scraping along the wool trousers. He was nearly done and I was still standing there, staring at the dress in confusion.

"You decent yet?" he asked.

"Uh…"

"What does that mean?"

"I don't…How does…?" I turned the dress side-to-side, trying to figure it out. "I hate my life."

"It can't be that confusing, can it?"

"No…? Maybe?"

"If I turn around—"

"Don't. You. Dare."

"Well, hurry up. I'm starving."

"Trying! Stop rushing me!" I yelled, sick of him already.

"Whatever. Door's on your side, so hurry up."

"When I figure out which end goes up and which end is the front…"

"You're really not even…" Jeph trailed off, and there was a note in his tone that made me feel even more naked than I already was. I was standing there, in my bra and panties, in a small building—*alone*—with a man.

"It's not like I'm from this era, pal. Like I know how this works."

"It's not that complicated. Just put it on already and let's go."

"Give me a minute, I'm still—" I screamed, Jeph's hand reaching around me to snatch the dress.

"Arms up."

"What are—"

My wrists were gripped by something dark and billowing. They pulled my arms up, and Jeph yanked the garment over my head, spinning it around. He grabbed my shoulders next, turning me to face him. Then, he looped the straps around my neck and fastened the clip-thingy that came with it, somehow securing it in place.

"That's how other women are wearing it," he said, looking it over.

Humiliated rage filled me and I threw my fist. He caught it, a scowl on his face.

"You *pervert!*" I screeched.

"Don't flatter yourself, precious. I'm just hungry and you were taking forever."

"I *hate* you!"

"Good to know. Now, what are you going to do about…?" He gestured to my bra straps.

Through gritted teeth, I asked, "I don't suppose you grabbed me a shawl or something?"

"I grabbed what was available. This was it."

I was frustrated by his poor acquisition skills. All he found was a basic dress for me and the bare minimum for himself. He had a long tunic, trousers, and leggings. But I'd seen other men wearing cloaks. He didn't have a belt either, which was another period-centric accessory men wore.

Grumbling under my breath, I looped each of my arms out of my bra straps in turn, tucking them into the side of the dress—until I had a better idea. I pulled them back out, lengthening the straps to the farthest setting, and started tying them behind my back for extra support. I fumbled before Jeph grabbed my bare shoulders, spun me again, slapped my hands away, and did the task for me.

"Tighter," I growled, furious. This man had zero boundaries—and it was grating on my last nerve.

He laced the straps down so tightly I nearly wheezed, but I knew—at the very least—these ta-tas weren't going anywhere. I didn't care what demon-ass time period we were in I *so* wasn't going braless. Especially when I *knew* there was going to be running in our foreseeable future.

"Done now?" he asked as I stuffed the knot under the top of the dress.

"I don't know, *pal*. Are *you* done harassing me yet?"

"It's not harassment. It's practicality."

"You…" I put my finger in his face. "You *looked!*"

"No, actually." He pushed my hand out of my face, scowling. "I didn't."

"Liar."

"Believe what you want, but I'm not actually a creep."

"Sure, you're not."

"Whatever." He shook his head, stepping past me. "The sooner we get moving, the sooner we'll find food."

"You mean, *steal* food."

"It's not like we have money. Now, pack up. We're leaving—and we're not coming back."

Scowling, I bent to retrieve my discarded clothing, folding them up, not sure what to do with them. I also picked up the stolen bow and quiver—I supposed that made me a hypocrite—and buckled the quiver around my waist. I was used to mine being slung across my back, but I could see the perks in having the arrow next to my dominant hand. It would allow me to refill my bow faster. Maybe I would switch to one of these when I got back to Seattle...

If I get back to Seattle.

Shaking away negative thoughts, I turned back to Jeph. He'd slung the short sword across his back—we must've lost the longsword somewhere along the way—and adjusted its fit on his shoulder. His profile was to me as he played with the strap, and I studied him, noticing again how threatening he was. Easily six-foot tall and made of lean and lithe muscles, he was terrifying. I'd gotten to see first-hand just how fast he was. Watching him dual-wield while taking down Hunter after Hunter was... disconcerting.

That wasn't all that caught my attention. I wasn't blind. Jeph was...well, the guy was gorgeous, what with all the striking features he had. Young—maybe twenty-one or twenty-two at most. Brown eyes like chocolate, lashes long and thick, lips sensual and full, and that stubble—*hott*. The guy was cut straight from the fabric of sin and sewn together with threads made of sex appeal. It should've been a crime to be that good-looking, especially with the social skills of a leper and the disposition of a predator. And that was the part I needed to remember. Hott or not, this guy had threatened me yesterday. He'd told me to kill him to protect my secret, but then he'd toyed with me. Now, we were here.

"Ready?" he asked, turning to take my filthy clothing from me. He tucked them into a little leather pack I hadn't noticed before. He buckled the pouch around his waist in place of a belt. I tried not to notice how well the tanish-white clothing suited his dark features.

"How's your side doing?" I asked, trying to pull my head out of my ass.

"It's fine—just like I said it would be."

"Does it hurt?"

He stared at me. "What do you think?"

"Oh."

"It's not that bad." He sighed, scratching his cheek. "I've honestly had worse."

"Worse?" I couldn't imagine anything worse than the deep gash in his side.

"Believe it or not, I wasn't always a badass."

I rolled my eyes. "Modest, aren't ya?"

"Did you always know how to shoot a bow?"

"No." I unconsciously rubbed the tips of my calloused and scarred fingers together. Years of practice had marked me.

He nodded. "Everyone starts somewhere. Even the best of us."

"Whatever you say, Mr. High-On-My-Horse Councilmember."

"Let's just go find something to eat and get going. We're burning daylight."

"Where are we going?"

"Away from here. We're too close to the last town to stick around too much longer. I'm not sure what protocol is in the fifth century but, in the present, Hunters keep the same mark until the target is captured or neutralized." His expression turned serious. "After the scene we made yesterday, I'm betting they'll send Elites in place of the Hunters we battled—and trust me when I say you don't want to deal with Elites."

"What's the difference?"

"Hunters are like the police force. Elites are assassins."

"Yeah." I'd assumed so but was suddenly dizzy with trepidation. "Let's get going."

When we stepped outside, I was surprised to see so many people milling about. It had been so dark when we came through—and I'd been so exhausted—I hadn't really taken the time to appreciate the size of the town. It was massive, so massive I couldn't even begin to wrap my mind around all the people walking from place to place.

Besides the thatch and wood houses, there were also cobblestone and mud buildings. They weren't much larger than the thatched homes, but I had no doubt they were sturdier. Straw littered the muddy ground, trying and failing to sop up the moisture. The pouring rain hadn't done anyone any favors last night, and my sneakers were mucky and cold in seconds.

As I looked at the dirty faces of people we passed, I was made painfully aware of how much we stood out in the community. It wasn't just our darker features amongst all the fair hair, blue eyes, and pale skin. It was how ragged, broken, and exhausted so many of these people looked. They'd had to work for everything in their lives while we'd lived in luxury and convenience. They stooped when they walked and moved with purpose from place to place.

Jeph stood tall, shoulders back, eyes forward. He walked with confidence, grace, and a threat in every step. Me? I felt like Pocahontas being invaded by the settlers. Only, I was the invader—and a thief at that—as I followed behind Jeph, unable to mimic his confidence and sense of belonging in a foreign world. I'd never felt self-conscious before, but wearing a strangers' clothing in a time period I didn't belong to while my enemy led me around a crowd of ancient strangers, made me feel extremely wary.

"Witches," a man said, spitting, his aura full of contempt.

"I's tellin' ya, they not real," his companion responded.

I slowed to listen.

"They is! And they's gon hex 'n curse us all. Vermin—erry last one o' them."

"You's been talkin' to Beardsley again, ain't ya?"

"He tell me there be a mad lord who—"

Before I could hear more of their conversation, Jeph turned and called my name. I'd fallen a little behind, too busy eavesdropping and gawking. He slowed, put a hand on my lower back, and nudged me in front of him. The brief touch made my heart lurch.

When we reached the center of the town, he led me over to a communal dining area. There were shabby, weather-worn tables lining a wide, open field, with rickety stools full of townspeople chatting and eating. Toward the center of the clearing, there were large fires and huge pots with food inside. Daring to hope and finding my wishes crushed, they were filled with oats. Gruel it was.

Acting like we totally belonged, Jeph grabbed two bowls out of his bag—when had he gotten those?—and handed one to me. I eyed it suspiciously, concerned for his streak as a kleptomaniac. My tummy gave a loud gurgle, and I took the stupid bowl from him. He smirked, and we got in line behind a few men scooping oatmeal from the pot.

"Ya hear 'bout the ruckus 'n *Wintan-Ceastre*?" one of the men asked, ladling oatmeal into his bowl.

"Yea, Beardsley. Heard there was a squabble," another man responded.

"Naht jus' a squabble, Carden—thems Hunters are lookin' fer some criminals," the third said.

"Ferget *Wintan-Ceastre*, Hagley!" Carden said. "Didja hear King's at it again?"

"Nah!" Beardsley protested while his friends dished up. "What that criminal do now?"

"I heard King lifted a mountain from da plains near da ocean," Carden said.

"That's naht what I heard!" Hagley said excitedly. "He *drown* the mountains with the ocean."

"Ya crazy! King *moved* the mountain *and* the oceans—with *magic*." Beardsley looked smug as if knowing this information made him special.

"You's the crazy one!" Cardan protested. "There ain't no such thing as magic."

"No! Really," Beardsley insisted, gesturing. "King kept the Jutes out of *Cantwareburh*! They'd'uh been overrun if he hadn't."

"You's still crazy."

"Excuse me," Jeph said, addressing the men. "Who's this 'King' you keep talking about?"

Beardsley's lip curled back. "What a Roman doin' here?"

Jeph's brow furrowed. "Pardon?"

"That skin. That accent. Roman."

"That ain't no Roman," Cardan said. "That one of them Italians."

"That no Italian accent—ain't it like, one of thems slave's... what's thems called again?" Hagley asked.

"Ya mean thems Greeks that says theys Roman?" Beardsley inclined his head. "Dunno. Ain't met one."

"Me either," Cardan mumbled. "Thought most'o'em died in the wars."

"Naw, naw," Hagley looked excited. "Some them flee."

"Ya met one?"

"Once—when I wus a boy in da Empire." Hagley squinted his eyes at Jeph.

"You recognize my accent?" Jeph asked, frowning. "You must be mistaken—"

"Hear dat? Greek thinks he better'n me."

"No—I just—" Jeph sputtered.

"I heard 'em," Beardsley said, spitting at Jeph's feet.

"What a Greek doin' this far north?" Cardan asked. "Didn't Romans snuff out yer kind?"

"Nah," Hagley retorted. "I thought da Romans were da ones that lost da war."

"Romans did." Beardsley smirked. "But theys ancestors en- slaved lotsa Greeks."

"You's a deserter, Greek?"

Jeph's jaw set, his magic flaring with his rage. I put my hand on his bicep and squeezed. He couldn't make a scene, even if *I* wanted to beat them all senseless. My Native ancestors had known centuries of slavery and oppression; even hearing some- one talk so lightly about a nation that had been conquered and enslaved pissed me off. It was the way of the world, but the world was wrong.

Jeph's muscles were coiled with anger, so I dug my fingers in, and little by little, he relaxed. His aura told me he was still contemplating their murders. Unfortunately, *something* they did was important to the timeline. Well, Beardsley wasn't, but the other two? Yes. My intuition flared with that truth—not that I would tell Jeph that. Killing Norms for the hell of it—even if they were out of line—was wrong.

"Excuse me," I tried the same kindness Jeph had started with. "Could you tell *me* about King?"

The three men stared at me for a long minute, apparently trying to categorize me. Unlike Jeph, I had an accent from growing up in Seattle. Not only would they not be able to place it, I also didn't fit a nice category. Between my Cherokee mother and my Caucasian father, I was a conundrum all unto myself.

"The wo'man is talkin'," Beardsley said, and I was rethinking my decision to deck him.

"Pretty lil' thing."

"But why she talkin'?" Cardan asked.

"Is this you's wo'man?" Beardsley asked Jeph.

He arched a brow.

"He's my brother," I lied. "About King—"

"Git you's sister outta men's talk!"

Before I could punch one of them in the face, Jeph guided me around the men to the pot of food. We both dished up, his jaw twitching with his anger.

"Apparently, women are to be seen and not heard," he whispered.

"I'll give them something to hear," I muttered, violently scooping the oats into my bowl.

"Just ignore it."

"Don't act like you aren't seething right now."

"Oh, I'd happily gut all three of them like fish. But you're going to harp on me if I do. *The timeline! The timeline!*" he mocked.

I scowled. "You're a dick—but yes."

The guys made some more rude comments when we brushed by them.

"Let's just eat and head for *Cantwareburh*," Jeph said.

"Why there?"

"You heard those assholes. If King can do even half of what they said he can, he might be able to help us."

"What, like you think he can do a ritual?"

"Something like that. If he doesn't know how to help, maybe he knows someone who can. Besides, we can't stick around here."

"Because we're wanted criminals," I muttered.

"That was a given. But now we know the Hunters are around."

Jeph led us to the tree line, and I sat on a large, relatively dry rock with my back against a tree. He sat to my left facing me, apparently unconcerned that the ground was wet.

"Wait. How are we supposed to go to *Cant-Cant*-wherever if we don't even know where it is?"

"It's east," he said, blowing on his oatmeal.

"How could you possibly know that? *I* don't even know where we are and I'm the one that brought us here."

"Because I can, and I do."

"Uh-huh. Cuz you just *magically* know where we are?"

"Weren't you listening to those men talking?" he asked.

"Yeah! They were insulting us both."

"You're not very detail oriented, are you, precious?"

"Oh, please, Mr. Wise Council Mage," I said mockingly, "what did I miss?"

"If we caused a ruckus in *Wintan-Ceastre* last night, then we're west of *Cantwareburh*."

"Oh, cuz you know where either of those are?"

"Yup." He took a sip of his oatmeal and cussed. "Hot."

"No shit, genius. It just came out of a piping hot cauldron hanging over a fire."

"Anyway," he said, ignoring me, "we're in Great Britain—England, to be precise."

"Now I *know* you're full of shit."

"If you would shut up and just listen to me for half a second, I could tell you how I know where we are."

I glared at him but stayed quiet.

"First of all, these people are a bunch of whities—"

"That's rude!"

"—second of all, they were talking about the fall of Rome like it *just* happened. The only people who would care about that would be the people it affected: Europe—Anglo-Saxons, Jutes, Franks. Third of all, *Wintan-Ceastre* is Old English for Winchester and *Cantwareburh* is Canterbury."

My mouth opened and closed as several questions raced through my mind. *He knows geography? He knows history—no! Ancient history! He knows Old English?*

What I settled on was, "How come the translation spell didn't work for the towns?"

"Because they're proper names. Your name is Samantha, not *listener*, which would be the meaning if literally translated."

My heart beat a little faster hearing him say my name. Not just Sam but *Samantha*. I stared into my oatmeal, trying to convince myself I didn't like the way my name sounded on his lips, the way his accent made it sound a little foreign and exotic.

We ate in silence, sipping our oatmeal.

"So," I drawled. "You seemed surprised about those guys bringing up your accent."

Jeph didn't comment.

"Are you? Greek, I mean."

He shrugged.

"Are you always this forthcoming?"

"Are *you* always this intrusive?" he snapped.

"Yes."

"New rule: no more talking."

"Say something in your native tongue." I leaned toward him, curious.

"I just said—"

"Say something," I pressed.

"I literally just did." He shook his head in exasperation. "Translation spell, remember?"

"Turn it off—just for a minute."

"No. That's a waste of magical energy—and it could lead the Hunters to us."

"Don't be dramatic," I said, waving away his concerns. "That's not enough energy to alert them and we both know it."

He sighed, muttering a counter-enchantment under his breath.

"Okay, now say something."

He did, and it was the absolute most archaic thing I'd heard in years.

"What was that?" I asked.

He repeated himself but said more this time. He spoke too fast for me to even try to catch any of what he said, but the lyrical cadence of the language was pretty. The way he said it, the tone he used, it gave me goosebumps, and I leaned even closer, enthralled.

"Satisfied?" Jeph asked in English, jolting me from the thrall of his words.

"Oh…Yeah." I blinked. "What did you say?"

He smirked. "That you're a pain in my ass, and I hope you get bitten by mosquitoes."

I swatted his arm. "You did not!"

"How do you know?"

His eyes twinkled with mischief, his grin lighting up his whole face. It stole my breath, and I realized I was still leaning toward him, realized that he'd leaned toward me, realized that this was a dangerous game. I sat back, staring into my oatmeal.

"Because…I just know." Besides his aura flashing with his lie, my intuition told me I was right.

"Your turn," he said, and my head whipped up in surprise.

"My turn?"

"Yeah. Say something in Cherokee."

"How did you know I…?"

His brow furrowed. "You told me."

"No, I didn't."

He frowned. "Right. Anyway, say something. Turnabout is fair play and all that."

"Okay…but I've got the grammar of a toddler. Mom was teaching me but…"

But she died before she could teach me much. Before I could fully understand the words or how to use them. Died, and I fell out of practice and forgot…

"It doesn't have to make sense," he said, tone uncharacteristically gentle. "It's not like I'll know what you're saying."

I chewed my lip, trying to think of something to say. Seeing his genuine curiosity, his open sincerity, stirred something in my chest. There was no scowl, no judgment, mischief, or annoyance in his eyes. He wasn't mocking me for once. It frightened me, and that gave me an idea.

In the most horrifyingly botched grammar I'd ever used in my life, I tried to tell him that he scared me. Scared me because he was fierce, because he was deadly, because he was my enemy. Because he was a living, human being, and there was more to him than met the eye.

Because in moments like these, when I forgot we were enemies, he made my heart race.

"What did you say?" he asked.

"That you're a jerk."

"You really enjoy insulting me, don't you?"

"You really enjoy being a jerk, don't you?" I mocked.

He shrugged. "What does *ni-hi* mean?"

"You."

"And *a-yv*?"

I blushed. "Me."

"I think you said something like...*a-s-ga-s-di*?"

"Something like that," I agreed.

"Well?"

"That was the insult. Called you an unfortunate waste of space," I lied.

He scowled, putting the translation spell back in place. While he did, I scarfed down my meager meal. Then, I watched him sip at his oatmeal, eyeing his bowl longingly.

"Here," he muttered, holding it out to me.

"But that's yours."

"I'm not the one who needs to rebuild magical energy."

"Yeah? Well, you probably burn *way* more calories than I do, so you need it."

"Just eat the damn gruel."

I grimaced. "Don't call it that. That's *so* not appealing."

"Says the chick that just scarfed down a whole bowl." He shoved the dish toward me again. "Eat it."

"I dunno..." My stomach rumbled.

He smirked. "Take it before I feed it to you."

I snatched the dish, throwing it back and downing it.

I was so intent on avoiding his gaze, and he so busy gloating, that neither of us saw it coming. Jeph grunted, falling forward across my legs, his weight trapping me in place. I looked up and regretted it. Something smacked me in the face hard enough to bruise, and the world went dark.

hen I came to, I was draped over Jeph in the back of a wagon. Not just any wagon—one with bars on all sides and overhead. *Ah. So, we've been captured.* But if that was the case, why didn't I sense any of the Hunter's magical energy? I knew I was depleted, but I wasn't *that* depleted. Walking for hours and missing meals wasn't helping anything. I'd slept enough to recuperate *some* energy, maybe even enough to get us on the other side of these bars, but definitely not enough to get us to safety. Trying would just drain what little energy I had regained. It was probably better to wait for Jeph to come to than to waste energy that was just going to knock me on my ass. Then we'd be right back in the cage— with some seriously freaked out Norms guarding us.

I sat up, holding my throbbing temple as I looked around. We weren't the only ones in here. There was a brunette girl who couldn't have been older than fourteen or fifteen. Dirt and tear tracks stained her face, and I couldn't tell if she shared my coloring, or if she was simply that dirty. Then again, I also needed a bath. She was quiet, probably resigned to whatever fate lay ahead.

Outside the wagon, a horse pulled the cart and a few Norms walked on either side of the cage. With some irritation, I noticed one of the Norms had my pilfered bow and quiver. Another had Jeph's short sword. We were weaponless and confined inside a cage, going goddess only knew where.

"Hey," I whispered, drawing the girl's attention. "You okay?"

She stared at me with glossy, brown eyes.

I scooted closer, and she shied away. "I'm not gonna hurt you," I said gently, holding up my palms.

She looked from my hands to my smile before her eyes darted to the Norms, giving her head a slight shake and trying to turn away from me.

"I'm not gonna—"

"Quiet!" one of the men yelled, snapping a whip at the cage. If it had been at a different angle, it might've hit me through the bars. Instead, it slapped across them, and I suddenly understood why the girl didn't want to talk to me.

I glared my defiance at him, his eyes meeting mine. If I had that bow, he'd regret his scare tactics. "Where are you taking us?" I asked.

"None of your concern," the other man spat.

"Dude, just answer the question."

The whip flew toward me, angling through the bars. It snapped with a *crack*, the sound branding itself into my memory as it tore through my forearm, splitting my flesh wide. I screamed from deep in my core, tears filling my eyes, white-hot agony searing along my throbbing skin, oozing blood.

As if roused from the dead, Jeph was up and snatching the end of the whip before Bow Guy could pull it back out. He wrapped the end of the whip around his wrist and yanked, Bow Guy coming forward and smacking face-first into the bars. Then, he hooked a hand around the back of the man's neck, holding him there as his feet began to drag with the wagon.

It suddenly lurched to a stop, throwing the girl and me forward. I put my arms out, catching myself—which really was stupid because *wounded, Sam, wounded!* I screamed, the girl curled into a ball on her side, and Jeph's attention shifted to me. The distraction cost him.

Sword Guy whipped Jeph across the back, and he roared, releasing Bow Guy as his spine arched from the pain. Teeth bared, he snarled and raised his hands to either side of him, something dark snaking from them to wrap around each man's throat. It wrenched them forward, knocking their heads against the cage with a loud *crack!*

The girl started screaming, and I grabbed her, pulling her to my chest and hiding her face against my neck. Jeph froze in place, his eyes wide and wild. His chest heaved, sweat trickling down his temples. He looked around frantically, his aura and magic raging with malice and contempt. Fear crawled up my spine, and I unconsciously held the whimpering girl tighter.

His eyes locked on mine, and the longer I held his gaze, the more his aura calmed. But then he looked at the blood trickling down my arm and his aura rippled with darkness so black, it almost seemed to suck in the light around it. I shuddered when he tightened the grip on his magic, trapping both men in his spell. He pulled one man so close, his face strained against the bars.

"Hurt her again and I'll kill you," Jeph growled, his face an inch away from the Norm's, and he whimpered. "Now, tell me where you're taking us."

"T-T-To the mad lord's estate…" Bow Guy answered.

"Mad?" I asked.

He looked at me, eyes wild, and Jeph shook him. "Lord Edward…isn't right in the head."

"And who's Lord Edward?" Jeph demanded, and I swore the Norm wet himself. "Why are you taking us to him?"

"A s-s-slaver!" he shouted, his aura nauseating colors of black horror and red terror. "He wants champions for his arena."

"And we're…"

"The slaves," I finished for Jeph. "Figures." Even after overhearing the Three Stooges talking flippantly about slavery, I had trouble wrapping my mind around our situation.

"Where are we now?" Jeph asked.

"*Anderitum.* Lord Edward's estate is just over that hill." The Norm pointed, his arm trembling.

Jeph looked up at the sky, his scowl deepening. "It's midday."

The sun was high on the horizon, which meant we'd been on the move for several hours. It had barely been daybreak when we'd started eating. Now the question was: Were we closer to Canterbury or farther away? Jeph must've been wondering the same thing because he released the Norms from his magic before looking back at the skyline, a small smile curving his lips. I took that to mean we were heading in the right direction.

Bow Guy scrambled away, watching Jeph with terror in his eyes. He gave the cart a wide berth as he rounded it. I grimaced, noticing he had, in fact, wet himself. I didn't even blame him; Jeph was made of darkness and the stuff of nightmares. All he needed was *The Shining's* theme song playing in the background and he'd be the ultimate horror movie.

Bow Guy and Sword Guy ran to the front of the wagon, hurriedly pulling the horse's reins, and it lurched forward again. I held onto one of the bars to keep my balance, not wanting a repeat of minutes ago. That the Norms weren't throwing us out on our asses amazed me. If I were them, I'd be ditching the cart entirely and cutting my losses. They were wise enough to be scared but stupid enough to keep heading toward the estate.

Psh! Stupid? More like greedy.

Then, Jeph surprised me by taking my injured arm in his hands. His touch sent a shockwave of pain up to my shoulder. I hissed, yanking my arm, but he held firm, not letting me tuck it against my side like I wanted to.

"Hold still," he ordered.

"That hurts!"

His aura flashed with anger. "It's going to hurt—they ripped your skin open."

"And your back?" I challenged.

"It's fine."

I glared. He was always saying he was "fine." He was full of it.

The girl cowered, whimpering and trembling. She squeezed the breath from my lungs, burying her face in my shoulder. I shushed her, gently rubbing my good arm up and down her back. Jeph looked from my cut to the girl, to my face, and back to my wound again. Something flitted across his expression. He seemed baffled by me, as if comforting someone else while blood flowed from my wound was unheard of.

"Shouldn't we be escaping?" I asked.

He shook his head and frowned as he wiped the blood, trying to get a better look at my wound. "They're wimps—easily overpowered."

Before I could comment, he lifted my arm to his mouth and…and started *sucking* and *licking* the blood. I wanted to be disgusted—should've been mortified—but the feel of his lips and tongue on my skin did something weird to my stomach. The blissful expression on his face, eyes closed, brow furrowed in pleasure-pain, captivated me, and I stared, transfixed as he bent over me.

He pulled away and licked his lips, swallowing before meeting my eyes. His almost had a tint to them now, the irises a coppery-red color, but when he blinked, they looked normal again. It must've been a trick of the light.

"Sorry," he murmured, his hands still holding my wrist and elbow. "Not like there's exactly anything to clean it with."

I nodded, not sure I could speak.

"Good news is," he continued, looking at my arm, "it's not too deep, and it's clotting now."

My heart was erratic in my chest. "O-Oh. Okay."

Jeph set my hand on his thigh before gripping the end of his tunic and tearing off a strip of it. I squeaked in protest, but it was too late. He gently wrapped my forearm, taking care not to put too much pressure on the cut. My hand flexed nervously on his thigh and he arched a brow at me.

"Stings," I whispered hoarsely.

It did, but that wasn't what had me fidgeting. It was the way his hands deftly moved as they wrapped my injury. The delicate way he was taking care of me. The heat of his leg under my hand. How close he was sitting to me as he leaned over my arm.

"Sorry," he murmured, cinching down the knot on the makeshift bandage. Once he was done, he took my chin in his thumb and forefinger, turning my head and tracing a finger down my temple.

I winced, sucking air between my teeth. "How bad is it?"

"Well, you're rockin' a black eye."

"Of course," I muttered bitterly. "Stupid Three Stooges."

"Stooges?"

"Tweedle-Dumb, Dumber, and Dumbest."

"Those assholes did this?"

"Yup. Last thing I saw before lights-out."

Jeph cussed under his breath. "I should've known better than to stick around bigoted assholes."

"You couldn't have known this would happen."

"No, but I should've heard them coming. I was distracted and even left my back wide open."

I ignored the butterflies partying in my chest. *I'd* distracted him.

"Well, not much we can do about it now."

"Like hell there isn't. We're leaving," he muttered, turning to the girl. "You okay?"

She squeezed me tighter.

"It's okay, sweetie," I told her. "We won't hurt you."

She shook her head, clinging to me.

"I'm Jeph," he said softly. "And this is my friend, Sam. What's your name?"

One heartbeat.

Two.

"Ara."

Jeph and I shared a victorious smile.

"Want to come with us, Ara?" he asked, and she nodded against my shoulder.

Just then, the wagon came to a halt and knightly-looking guards surrounded us, swords in hand or bows raised. Looking fidgety and sporting the start of a black eye, Bow Guy unlatched the cage of the wagon while Sword Guy accepted money from another armed man.

"Come out," one of the guards commanded.

Jeph put his back to Ara and me, facing the open door and asking, "Can I kill them?"

"No," I hissed.

Several of them were important to the timeline, and with so many, I wouldn't be able to tell him who he could and couldn't kill if a fight broke out.

"Besides, she's terrified." I pulled Ara closer. "Don't... don't make her see that."

His aura soured. "Got any ideas, then?"

"Uh. Sure…" I lied. "Follow my lead."

"I hope you know what you're doing, precious."

I hope so too, I didn't say out loud, stepping past Jeph and exiting first.

As soon as I was out, someone snatched Ara away from me. I shouted, but it quickly turned into a scream when I was grabbed next. Jeph snarled, reaching for me, but I shook my head and he stopped. Several guards converged on him, and I grimaced. I had no doubt he could take most of them down, but they greatly outnumbered us and their weapons weren't for show. They'd likely kill one or both of us if they felt threatened. Jeph followed my order, mutiny in his eyes as they roughly tied our hands behind our backs.

Ara shook like a leaf, tears streaking down her dirty face again. I tried to catch her attention, to give her reassurance, but her gaze darted all over the place. The man holding her grabbed her roughly by the arm, dragging her away.

"No!" I shouted, trying to follow them.

A guard caught my arm, wheeling me back around. I snarled and yanked out of his grasp, getting three steps before he tackled me to the ground. I turned my head at the last second, and my already-bruised temple crashed against the cobblestone pathway, dazing me. He then grabbed me by the hair, using it to help me to my feet.

Jeph strained against the men holding him, his eyes locked on mine. His shoulders knocked into guards, banging their protective helmets into their noses. Some fell on their asses; others struggled to hold him at bay. Someone hit him over the head, dazing him with the butt of their sword, and he fell to his knees. Then, the man put his boot overtop the bloody wound on Jeph's back, pushing his foot into it and making him scream. He slumped to the ground, and his attacker stood over him, spitting on him and making a comment that had the rest of the guards laughing. I didn't hear what he said, but his ugly aura told me it was something derogatory. The sight made my blood boil, and I desperately wanted to show the guard the sharp end of one of my arrows.

The hand holding my hair didn't loosen as I was led through a tall, stone and wood gate and into a cobblestone castle. I was taken around a corner and up a hallway, then through another and another until I was lost. We descended deeper and deeper down an incline, the walls turning from stone to muddy earth and wood. Candelabra lined the walls every few feet, lighting our path. The air was so dingy and musky I struggled to breathe. Then, we stopped in front of a tiny prison cell. The man still gripped my hair while he drew a key, unlocked the cell, and shoved me in.

I tripped over my feet, turning and falling on my shoulder to avoid smacking my temple again. Because I was a certified dumbass, I shrieked when I landed on my bandaged arm instead. My spine arched, and I gnashed my teeth as wave after wave of searing agony jolted through my arm and shoulder.

The door to the cell clattered shut, and I barely managed to force my clamped eyes open. I was alone and couldn't sense Jeph's energy anywhere nearby. Unable to stand the pain any longer, I flashed in and out of Chaos, sans the rope. A silent scream formed on my lips, the magic draining my already-battered and beaten body. I shouldn't have done it, but having my hands free was worth every agonizing breath.

I could only hope I was deep enough below ground that my magic wouldn't attract the Hunters to us. If not, then they would have a general idea of which direction to travel. That was supposing Jeph's freak-out session in the wagon hadn't already alerted them to our presence. Either way, we weren't safe.

When some of the dizziness faded, I finally dared to get to my feet. I wobbled, listing to the side. My balance was so far gone, I was forced to catch myself against the wall. My skin was clammy and pale, I was trembling, and my hair was plastered to my face and neck. I leaned there, seconds passing like hours as I tried to breathe again. I'd taken one too many hits to the head, one too many bumps and bruises to the body, and the magic really had been stupid.

As I tried to breathe through the pain, a single thought replayed over and over in my mind: *I should've let Jeph slaughter the guards.*

It felt like eons before someone came to collect me. In reality, it couldn't have been more than a few hours. Hours of staring into space. Hours of contemplating my life and my pending death. Some days, I was ready for all the bullshit to end. Others, I wanted to put the world in its place. Today was the latter.

The guard grabbed my arm, yanking me to my feet. I'd been laying on the nasty straw-heap in the corner, trying to get some rest. *Okay, okay, I kinda blacked out for a minute or two.* But I wasn't too keen on being manhandled.

"Watch it," I snapped, glaring.

He didn't respond, pulling me along by my bicep. I only behaved myself because I was hoping he'd lead me to wherever Jeph and Ara were. It was a series of twisting and turning corridors before we headed up toward fresh air. I was led to a door with a gate in front of it, and my brow furrowed as I stared at the large arch. Excited murmuring and chatter came from the other side. As we got closer, I finally realized what was going on.

I dug in my heels and tugged on his hold, wanting the hell out of there. The man jerked me forward, and I just about toppled into him. I was weak and dizzy, tired and injured, my eye swelling bad enough I was having trouble seeing out of it. But I didn't need both my eyes to know I sure as hell didn't want to greet all the excited auras on the other side of the gate.

"Don't put me in there," I pleaded.

He ignored me.

Then, there was a loud *thump, thump, thump*. I looked through the gap in the bars, my gaze following the source of the noise. A fat man in his thirties held a fancy staff, hitting it on the floor of the raised platform he was standing on. Beneath him, high walls formed an arena in the shape of a ring. Behind those walls, a crowd of people looked at him.

"Friends," the fat man's voice carried, silencing the crowd. "It is with great honor that I, your Lord Edward, gathered you here for another stupendous round of festivities." He paused for dramatic effect. "Today will be full of excitement. Why, just a little while ago, I was informed we got lively, fresh blood in to entertain you."

The crowd roared, hooting, stomping, clapping, and whistling in excitement.

My stomach dropped.

The lord held his arms wide. "Let's bring in our competitors and give you a chance to see who you're rooting for."

The gate opened, and the guard pulled me forward. When I attempted to run again, he pulled a knife from his belt, holding it to my side. I stopped struggling, and he led me into the arena, which was almost big enough to fit a football field. The walls were constructed of mortar and cobblestone, erected over fifteen feet into the air. Above the safety of those walls, row after row of seats were packed in tight with onlookers. Only Lord Edward's platform was relatively roomy, and he was surrounded by guards.

I met his gaze as I was forced toward the center of the arena.

"This is our first contestant," Lord Edward said, smirking and turning his attention back to the crowd. "I'm told she was found with bow and arrow—perhaps a hunter for her people?"

My people? I thought incredulously. That was, until I remembered I must've looked rather dark compared to their fair complexions. The asshole probably thought I was some kind of barbarian. *I wonder what he'll think of Jeph, then. That guy's insane.*

Several spectators leaned forward in their seats, trying to get a good look at me. All of five foot four with little muscle to speak of, I was a toothpick. I could pack a good punch but only because my arm was strong from pulling back my bowstring over the years. TV made it look so easy, but it really wasn't. Some onlookers were quick to dismiss me, but mostly, I received suggestive leers. Their auras were a distinct pinkish-red that spoke of lust, and I shivered, wanting to cover myself from their gaze. Instead, I stood tall and defiant, eyes trained on my true threat.

"As in every competition, each contestant will be given the opportunity to demonstrate his skills," the lord continued. "If he is successful, remaining the lone Champion, he will be given more opportunities to thrive. Your Lord is nothing if not generous." He paused, soaking in the adoration of the crowd; it made me want to gag as they hung on every bullshit word that came out of his mouth. "A Champion who proves himself ten times over will be given a place in my court and the spoils that position offers—not that any Champion has survived long enough to claim that role…" He grinned impishly, and the crowd chuckled.

Yeah. I bet no one has…

"I notice you said *'he!'*" I shouted, and he started, his smile fading.

"Yes, well. The weaker sex *has* been Champion before—ruthless, evil witches, usually." He turned to the crowd, grinning coolly. "But we know what to do with witches, don't we?"

"*Let them burn! Let them burn! Let them burn!*" they chanted.

My stomach churned. If I won, I'd be accused of being a witch—and I was. If I lost, well, I'd be dead anyway. I needed to find Jeph and Ara and get the hell out of here.

The guard pulled me away, Lord Edward already introducing the next contestant. We didn't go far before I was shoved into a little room, the wooden door slamming shut and locking behind me. I screamed, kicking it in frustration. Then, I paced to the left, to the right, and back again, getting progressively more irritated as the minutes ticked by. It was four steps from end to end, dingy, and lit with a single candle overhead.

The door suddenly burst open, nearly smacking me in the face. Jeph stood there, that wild look back in his eyes. I stared in confusion, jumping when he strode the short distance to me, the door slamming shut behind him. Surprised, I retreated, my back hitting the wall. He grabbed my shoulders, turning me this way and that. My heart lurched at his nearness, at his intense scrutiny. When he seemed satisfied, he released me and stepped away.

"We need to leave," he said without preamble.

"Agreed," I whispered, trying to keep from trembling. "Got a plan?"

"Working on one." He inclined his head. "Why are you shaking?"

"I…" I grappled for any excuse but the truth. "I used magic earlier."

"I know." He stared at me. "I thought they might've hurt you."

Was that why he inspected me?

"Not exactly, but that little bit of magic wiped me out…"

He frowned. "Then all the more reason to get out of here."

"There are easily a hundred guards out there. We can't take down an army!"

"It's them or the arena."

"*That's* your plan?" I demanded. "Face-down trained guards and *hope* we're successful?"

"Oh, there's no 'hope' involved, precious. Don't forget who you're talking to."

"Like your arrogant-ass ever lets me forget," I muttered. "And FYI, you can't kill anyone if *that* was your plan."

He glowered. "Like hell, I can't."

"Jeph," I sighed, rubbing a hand down my face. "Do you even understand the consequences? We're *sixteen hundred* years in the past. These people might have a bearing on the future. What if one of these people's descendants turns out to be George Washington or something—can you even imagine the future we'll go home to?"

His jaw set. "I liked the odds better when I could slaughter them all."

"You can't kill anyone," I said sternly, my gut churning at just how serious he'd been when flippantly referring to the annihilation of a hundred men.

"I'm liking you less and less with every word out of your mouth," he muttered.

"Look, pal. Not all of us are sociopaths."

"I'm not a sociopath. I just have one goal and one goal alone: keep you alive long enough to get home."

"Gee, you're a real keeper, y'know that?"

His eyes narrowed, but before he could argue, a guard came in. The man backpedaled, clearly not expecting to find Jeph in the room. The Norm pulled a sword from his scabbard, pointing it at him. Jeph smirked, not looking threatened in the least—until several more guards filled the corridor, one of them with an arrow trained on him and another on me. Powerful or not, I didn't think Jeph could stop an arrow mid-flight.

"We're coming," I said, stepping in front of him. "Just—don't hurt us."

His angry aura grated along my back, ramping up when a guard roughly grabbed my arm and yanked me into the hall. I looked over my shoulder, meeting his eyes and giving my head a slight shake. He gritted his teeth but reeled in the magic seeping from him, that sinister, black magic that made my hair stand on end. How could these men not feel their lives being threatened? The palpable bloodlust of a madman willing to slaughter many for the sake of one—himself.

Since I had an arm guiding me, and Jeph was already projecting our location loud and clear to any Hunters actively tracking us, I looked into the future, stumbling over my feet when my vision split between real time and the images I was conjuring. My goal had been to learn who the Champion was and protect them at all costs, but I knew now that that wouldn't be necessary. No one in tonight's arena was ever going to survive, and as I watched strangers slaughter each other in desperation, thinking of only surviving to see another day, I felt a piece of my heart die. Did these people really believe their lives mattered more than the ones they cut down?

Maybe I was the naive one for finding more value in the life of a stranger—in the life of an enemy—than in my own. I had to be; that thought process—that mercy—had been what had trapped me here. If I'd just killed Jeph when he'd goaded me to, I wouldn't be here, in this time period, about to witness the truest cruelty I'd ever experienced. But...if I had, Jeph would be dead, and that thought bothered me more than I cared to admit.

We were shoved through one of the arched doors, the metal bars clanging shut behind us. I stared at the two dozen other people in the arena, their auras chaotic with dread, excitement, or anticipation. They ranged in age and gender, each face matching up with one I'd seen in the vision. Worst of all, Ara was clear across the battlefield, trembling and shaking.

My heart screamed and my knees felt like rubber. *I can save one, right? Just one?* I already knew the answer to that question.

I backed toward the bars, my pulse roaring in my ears, my breath stuck in my throat. *I can't do this. I absolutely can't do this.*

"I don't suppose you want me to let these ones live too?" Jeph asked drolly.

"They all die," I whispered breathlessly. "All of them…"

"And the girl?"

Tears stung my eyes as I shook my head.

He stepped between me and our opponents, turning to face the arena. "Watch my back, don't kill anyone, and stay out of the way," he called over his shoulder.

Lord Edward struck his platform with his staff. "Begin!"

 eapons rained from the sky as guards threw swords, daggers, bows, and quivers of arrows into the arena. Before the first one could hit the ground, Jeph ran, catching a sword in his right hand and a bow in his left. I grabbed a quiver that had fallen nearby, racing to meet him as several other people reached for swords and daggers.

He turned again, putting his back to mine, and we looked around. While some of the others had collected weapons, no one had made a move yet. My eyes shifted from person to person, and they either met my gaze, or their eyes darted away in shame. No one wanted to be the first to strike, to be the first to take a life.

Then, a man screamed, falling to the ground, an arrow sticking out of his back, but no one in the arena had attacked.

"Plenty more arrows where that one came from," Lord Edward announced, and everyone's heads jerked upward to stare at him. Grinning, he lifted his hand, and the guard standing next to him nocked another arrow. "I did say *begin*, didn't I?"

We stared, stunned, as the next arrow went into the fallen man's heart, killing him.

Pandemonium broke out as people nearest each other lunged for one another. Cries of terror and shouts of rage echoed off the walls, and the crowd roared and cheered, the noise deafening after the near-silence from moments before. But the worst sounds were the shrill shrieks followed by the dull thud of lifeless bodies hitting the ground.

The pressure of Jeph's back let up at the same time I heard metal scraping violently against metal. I didn't have time to think about his battle; someone was running toward me. I raised my bow, heart pounding as I aimed for my assailant's thigh. My arrow flew true, and the man screamed as he hit the ground. But he was far from defeated, his arm rearing back, dagger coming for me as he scrambled to his feet. The mania in his eyes terrified me, too close now for my bow to be useful.

I backpedaled, bumping into something solid. Before I could scream, Jeph wrapped an arm around my waist and whirled me behind him. Then, I heard a squelching noise that was paired with the thrusting of Jeph's sword arm. The man's screams fell silent, and the sickly-sweet scent of copper filled the air. I tried not to vomit at the implications.

Shouting, I wriggled out of Jeph's grasp when I saw a man going for Ara. My arrow hit her opponent in his dominant shoulder before I could process my actions. He roared, sword dropping from his hand, and I ran toward Ara.

Screw the damn timeline!

Before I could reach her, the man I'd shot was armed again, blocking my path. It took a minute—really, it shouldn't have—but my eyes went wide as I recognized faint magical energy coming from him. He was a mage.

"*You,*" he hissed, finger leveled on me. "Sibyl trash."

Scratch that—he's a Hunter.

"Oh, please," I said, sneering. "*I'm* not the one trying to kill a little girl."

"My survival outweighs hers."

Heat filled my chest. "*You* don't get to decide that."

Looking from her to me, his aura glowed with disgust. "Your apprentice?"

"Are you a moron? We both know she's a Norm."

"Doesn't mean she's not your acolyte."

I blinked at him. "And *this* is why I'm being hunted. You guys are *idiots!*"

He snarled, sword rearing back as he ran at me.

Well, shit.

I hit the deck and rolled, not sure what the hell else to do. He was too close for my bow to do me any good. We passed each other, and I got to my feet. At least Ara was behind me now, but that wouldn't do much good if I couldn't get to her soon. There were plenty of adversaries looking to pick off the weak. The Hunter raised his hand. We were both beaten and drained of magical energy, but that didn't stop him from—

My heart lurched, and I turned, launching myself at Ara. I reached her just as the energy blast rocketed into my back. It seared through me like a blazing fire, and I screeched, putting my hands behind Ara's neck and skull as we went sailing. We crashed into the ground, my hands smacking hard enough to numb my fingers. It was just as well because I'd dropped my bow—not that I could use it anytime soon; I'd need feeling in my battered digits.

Sweat beaded on my brow, and I pulled my hands from behind the girl's head, pushing myself up onto shaky arms. "Are you...okay?" I panted.

She coughed and wheezed, her gaze dazed as she blinked lazily, her eyes sliding over my face. I lightly slapped her cheek, and she jolted, her eyes focusing.

And then I howled. I couldn't believe a guild mage—of all people—was using magic in front of a literal crowd of Norms, but then again, they wouldn't be able to see it. But the blast that sent me flying was *just* a tad difficult to explain away. My temple crashed into the wall, and I must've lost some time because the next thing I knew, I was hauled to my feet—by my throat. I couldn't help myself, I laughed. It was a shrill, pitchy noise borne of hysteria, but it gave him pause.

"You mock me in the face of your death?" he snarled.

I grinned at all three of him while my vision danced, warm liquid dripping down the side of my face. "Choking...me," I wheezed around his grip.

"What?"

I wrapped his forearm in my hand, leaning closer to him, grin never slipping from my face. I wasn't sure why I was so amused, but I was. It just didn't seem to matter when or where I was—Ancient Egypt, the Dark Ages, the eighteen hundreds, or the twenty-first century—Hunters just couldn't seem to help but grab me by the throat.

My expression clearly disturbed him because he leaned away from me. The souring of his aura also told me the same, but him moving was much more helpful. I braced a foot on the wall and shoved into him. It hurt like a mother, my trachea calling me every name in the book, but we sprawled to the ground, me on top of him. His sword went skittering away when his hand hit the packed soil.

And then the goddess blessed me for once because there was a nice, shiny dagger right there. I reached for it, but he saw it too. He grabbed me with one arm, holding me in place while his free hand grappled for the blade. I turned my head and took his bicep in my mouth, chomping down. Vicious satisfaction flitted through me when he howled. At least, until he began punching me in the head. That didn't feel too good, and poor angle or not, he was still getting my ear. It made pain flare through my skull, so I bit down harder. My stomach churned when my teeth crunched and sank into muscle.

That must've been the last straw for him because he flipped us toward the dagger. Now I was on my back, trying not to retch as his muscles contracted between my teeth and lips. I let go, bringing my knee up when he straddled me. His scream was shrill this time, and I flailed as I crawled out from underneath his collapsed weight. I must've hit him harder than I thought because he seemed incapable of anything but holding himself.

I stumbled to my feet, listless and swaying, my eye swelling shut from his beating. In all fairness, he had been hitting the same side that was already "rockin' a black eye" as Jeph had put it. My eardrum might even be ruptured because I couldn't seem to stop swaying. I almost fell over when I took the dagger into my hands.

But now that I had it, I didn't know what to do with it. I'd shot with arrows, bit and scratched, punched and kneed, but I'd never *stabbed* anyone. Something about using a knife—about using my own hands—to tear into someone's flesh seemed more culpable than simply shooting them. When an arrow tore into someone, it was the weapon doing the damage, but me driving this dagger into him would be done by my own agency.

His angry blue eyes met mine, and I knew he saw my inde-cision, my hesitation, and he lifted a hand, magic already gather-ing to blast me again. It would be weak now that he was on his last dregs of magical energy but would still hurt. It would hinder me and give him the advantage.

Just like that, my resolve settled into my bones. It was like facing down the mages in the Magical Community from the night before. I'd become callous—the true embodiment of the Sibyl these people feared. I became her now, wrapping both hands around the dagger's hilt before I brought it down. The length of the blade sliced into the back of his hand, skewering his flesh as I drove it into the dirt.

Blood gushed, and the noise that tore from his throat would haunt my dreams until I died. While he tried futilely to pull the weapon free, I backed up the few steps necessary to pick up the sword he'd lost. I stared him in the eyes, taking slow, deliberate steps toward him. Each one was measured, like the seconds tick-ing on a clock as the hands marched toward the inevitable pass-ing of time.

Tick.

Tick.

Tick.

His time was up.

I drove the sword into his back, purposefully missing his heart. It was harder than I thought it would be, the resistance of his flesh as the blade tore through muscle and grazed along bone. I might've even broken a rib if that was what made the awful cracking noise. And the rasping, gurgling sound coming from his mouth told me I'd punctured his lung.

I knelt down next to him, still staring into his eyes. "Drown," I hissed. "Because any man who would willingly kill a defenseless girl for his own gain, when he's sworn to protect the lives of those like her, is filth."

His mouth floundered, but all he could do was choke on blood. Then, I got to my feet, turning my back to him.

Time froze when my eyes met Jeph's from across the arena. He held my gaze, something feral and untamed raging in his eyes, matching the anger in my soul. His eyes were alive, but his stance was the same eerie calm that existed within me. The creature inside of me recognized the beast within him. He was the calm before the storm, a prelude to the horrors to come, and I was the howling wind, provoked by the crashing of fire and ice.

From one heartbeat to the next, time marched on, the spell broken when Jeph's sword slashed across his next challenger. I blinked, coming back to myself. In my absence, he had amassed a body count and was drenched in crimson, his tan clothing soiled with the truth of his kills.

I nearly jumped out of my skin when someone touched my arm. Ara stood next to me, holding a bow out in offering. I took it, grabbing her hand and pulling her away from the dying man at our feet. I brought us over by the wall, putting her at my back.

"Stay behind me," I said.

"Thank you," she whispered, and her words cracked open a fissure in my heart. This was far from over, and I'd already seen her death once. I refused to see it happen again.

I lifted the bow, that eerie calm numbing me once more. Callously, I started sending arrow after arrow into dead men walking. As I hit thigh after thigh, calf after calf, others came along to finish them off. I couldn't stop to consider my complicity in their deaths.

They would've died regardless, I reminded myself. *That doesn't make it okay...*

I was so focused on enemies across the arena, I didn't notice the woman until she tackled us to the ground. The wind knocked from my lungs, and I landed on Ara. She gasped, her agony searing along my aura, and I wrestled the woman away from her. The bitch dug her nails into my forearms, ripping my wound open. I howled and returned the favor to her biceps, coating my fingers in warm, sticky blood. Then, we rolled over and over each other until I pinned her.

My small victory only lasted for a moment.

Something sharp cut along my shoulder blades, and I screeched, slumping onto the woman. She shoved me off of her, and my vision went white behind my eyelids. I moaned, rolling onto my good arm and trying not to pass out. She frantically grappled in the dirt next to us, raising a dagger over her head.

Just as she brought it down, her head and hand went flying. Her body fell across my legs, blood gushing over me. I gagged, my scream lodging in my throat.

Jeph kicked the corpse off of me, leaning down and wrapping an arm around my waist. He hauled me to my feet, and the pressure on my gut was all the encouragement my stomach needed—I vomited. He held me against his left side as his sword flashed, jerking me around with each parry and every blow. Through the roaring in my ears, I heard the screams of the dying, the cheers of the crowd, and the clinging and scraping of metal. Between the noises overwhelming my senses, the searing pain in my shoulder blades, and the dizziness setting in, I wasn't sure I'd be conscious much longer.

But when my eyes landed on Ara's mutilated body across the arena, blood drenching her from head to toe, my screams joined the fray. I wriggled out of Jeph's grasp, bending down to pick up the bow at my feet. With little regard for the corpse next to me, I ripped the arrow from its body. Fury fueled me, dulling the pain and clearing everything from my mind. I shot the man leaning over Ara, his blade slick with her blood.

He slumped to the ground, and I wasn't sure if my arrow killed him or not. For a vicious moment, I wished it had—*hoped* and *prayed* it had. If that made me a killer—a murderer—then so be it. And when his ghost came out of his body, I had my answer. The sins of today would forever stain my soul the way the blood of my victims stained my hands.

Now that I was looking, several bodies lay without auras, some with flickering ones. They were dead or dying, their ghosts hovering just outside their corpses, looking broken and confused. Some lingered, some winked into the ether the way Phoenix did, and others...others I stopped sensing altogether. A particularly angry ghost dive-bombed Lord Edward. He jolted, and I shivered with sympathy pains, watching the ghost unravel and dissolve on impact. She wasn't powerful enough to hurt anyone, and whatever she'd done, it had annihilated her.

That could've been me, I thought, remembering Phoenix's concern from just the other day.

I was pulled from my thoughts when Jeph wrapped a hand around my arm, yanking me behind him. A sword grazed along his bicep, cutting him deep. If he hadn't moved me, that would've been my throat. How many times had he saved my life now? How many times had he been hurt on my behalf? He released me, howling as he drove his sword into the woman's heart. Her eyes widened before turning glossy and lifeless as she fell to the ground.

Jeph stood there, chest heaving, drenched in gore and crimson. Then, he looked around, taking in the sight of the mangled and broken bodies, most of them dead, some of them bleeding out. I followed his gaze, realizing we were the last two standing.

"Can you shoot?" he asked.

"Probably not," I admitted, speckles flecking the edges of my vision.

He held my gaze. "Then we'll have to play this by ear."

"Play what by ear?"

"They want *a* Champion," he muttered, lifting his sword and driving it into the ground. Then, he stood tall, staring into Lord Edward's eyes.

I turned to face him too, raising my chin despite the agony roaring through me.

The stout man got to his feet, walking to the edge of his platform. "Kill the girl and become Champion, young warrior."

Jeph snorted. "Champion? Warrior? Try pawn—*slave*."

"If you won't kill the girl, then perhaps she will kill you?"

"No," I shouted, sweating buckets and swaying on my feet.

Lord Edward sneered down at us. "Guards!" he shouted, snapping his fingers, and two bowmen flanking him raised their weapons. "Kill them both."

"Shit," Jeph hissed under his breath.

I lifted my bow, but with my injury, pulling the string taut was too painful. It didn't matter either way. I was seeing double, my depth perception shit, thanks to my swollen eye.

"I've got a horrible idea," Jeph whispered as the guards loaded their bows. "Roll with it."

"What?" I hissed, dread pooling in my stomach.

"Before you kill us," he shouted, and Lord Edward held up a hand, stopping the bowmen, "could you at least give me a moment to say goodbye to my wife?"

I stiffened. *Wife?*

The crowd gasped in excitement, murmurs filling the arena.

Lord Edward arched a brow. "Your...wife?"

"Yes," Jeph said desperately, his words a plea. "We're in love—haven't you seen how I've defended her?"

The crowd got louder, excitedly making comments about how romantic it was that we'd fought side by side, how noble it was that we were willing to die together. Jeph's story appealed to them and they wanted us to put on a tragic, romantic show. Lord Edward looked at them, seeing their eager faces. He wanted them to be pleased, wanted them to be entertained. He cared what they thought, and Jeph was using the sick bastard's own motives against him.

"Go on then," he said dismissively.

"Thank you, my liege," Jeph said with a deep bow, and Lord Edward's aura glowed with satisfaction.

"What are you doing?" I hissed, panic coloring my tone.

"Trying to save your life," he replied, taking a step toward me.

My heart skipped a beat. "My life?"

"Yes. Your *life*." He leaned closer, and my breath caught.

"But I'm the Sibyl. It's your job to kill me..."

"Won't be my problem if I'm dead, now will it?"

My brow furrowed in confusion. "What?"

"If you die, I'm stuck here, and I'd rather not deal with that. If I die, they're going to put you back in this arena tomorrow—by yourself—but with those injuries, you're as good as dead. The only way we both survive is if we *both* get out of here alive."

I swallowed. "But I'm not your..."

"Obviously." He rolled his eyes. "Look, I could probably kill everyone here, but that would screw up the timeline, correct?"

I nodded.

"And I don't have the energy for a prolonged battle. So, if I can't kill them—"

"Why is killing always the solution with you?" I demanded, disgusted.

"A dead man won't try to stab me in the back while it's turned."

"Oh."

"So, it's either we do this and hope Lord Edward is entertained enough to let us live, or...we die. Your choice."

"But I don't even like you!"

A tick worked in his jaw. "Then pretend I'm someone else," he snapped, taking my face in his hands.

Someone else. *Someone else? He's a moron!*

But he was right. Our options were to give this a try or die. I really, really didn't like those options.

"I...I threw up," I whispered, mortified.

The edge of his lips quirked up. "You worry about the strangest things, precious."

Then, Jeph lowered his head slowly toward mine, so slowly my heart pounded in my chest. My palms tingled and fizzled. My gut turned over. And when he was a breath away, I couldn't seem to breathe at all. As soon as his lips touched mine, my ears began to roar. My lips sealed against his, a fit so perfect, it was as if his lips were made for this—made for me. I hated it. I hated him. I didn't want him to stop.

Despite the acidic taste still coating my tongue, he kissed me like a man possessed. I could scarcely breathe for how deeply his tongue stroked along mine, the taste of copper and dirt transferring from his mouth. The remnants of battle flavored his lips the way the remnants of fear flavored mine. It should've disgusted me, should've disgusted him, but it didn't.

I wasn't aware of wrapping my arms around him, but there they were, forearms cradling his back, fingers splayed over his strong shoulder blades. And when had I stretched up on my tiptoes? I didn't remember, and I didn't care. I wanted him closer.

He clung to me, his hands dropping to my waist and pulling my pelvis against his. I gasped, white-hot heat raging through my body, a frenzy ignited by his nearness. One hand held me firmly against him, and the other trailed delicately along my back. His fingers traced slowly over my neck, raising gooseflesh in their wake. And when they slid into the hair at the nape of my neck, I couldn't stop the shiver that traveled the length of my spine.

My lips crashed against his, our teeth clicking in desperation. Our tongues twined and stroked along each other's. I couldn't stop the low moans in the back of my throat, and Jeph groaned in response, his fingers burrowing into me as if he was trying to get closer, closer still. He was starving, a man dying and begging me to bring him to life, and I was a madwoman, living for what felt like the first time.

He was like fire against my skin. Like lightning striking my nerves. Like a storm sweeping me away, and I was powerless to stop it. Everything screamed with the need to stay here—right here—and never let go.

I forgot who I was, who Jeph was, but I needed to remember. He was the Hunter, and I, his prey. I was a rabbit caught in his trap. A mouse ensnared by his prowess. A deer standing before the hunter's gun. I was the fox, dead at the wolf's feet.

"Let them live! Let them live! Let them live!" It was a chorus booming from the stands, and it startled me enough that I pulled away.

Jeph and I panted, staring at each other bewildered, his already full lips swollen from our desperate kisses. His cheeks were as flushed as mine, and the sight of it did something funny to my stomach. I had the intense urge to pull him back to me, and that desire terrified me more than the arena had.

Lord Edward banged his staff against the floor, silencing the cheers and jeers of the crowd. He raised the staff and his free hand as he declared, "My friends, I give you"—he paused for dramatic effect—"your Champions!"

The crowd erupted into applause.

I was suddenly dizzy, and the world spun. Relief made my knees buckle, my hands fisting into the back of Jeph's tunic to stay standing. He held me against him, his hand cradling my head against his chest.

"We might survive this after all," he whispered next to my ear, his drumming heart nearly drowning out the words. Its steady rhythm lulled me into a false sense of comfort, into a false sense of security, because I felt safe in his arms...and that was the stupidest thought I'd had in my life. Once this was over, once we were home, we would be enemies, and that thought made tears sting the back of my eyes.

I need to get far, far away from him, was the last thought I had before I blacked out.

Sixteen

hen I came to, it was to find Jeph hovering over me, looking extremely irritated. "Those are going to get infected!" he snapped at someone.

"Not my problem if a slave dies," a man retorted. "Be glad Lord Edward allowed this much."

"*This much?*" Jeph growled. "Those crude stitches aren't even holding the skin together. Give me a damn needle and thread—I can do better than that."

"Silence, slave. Or I'll appeal to Lord Edward to execute you. He doesn't need two Champions."

"I'll kill y—"

"Jeph," I wheezed, my throat hoarse and my lips cracking.

"I'm right here," he said, leaning over me and cupping my cheek in his palm. "How do you feel?"

"Horrible," I croaked. It felt like I'd dunked my shoulder in a vat of lava. But that wasn't my only complaint. "I'm thirsty."

"She's got a fever." Jeph looked up when the man didn't respond. "She needs water and something for the pain."

I tried to sit up, but the tearing feeling in my shoulder made me scream and collapse against the cot. My stomach churned, and I clenched my eyes shut and ground my teeth together, fighting the urge to vomit.

"Ale," the man sneered.

"Excuse me?" Jeph snarled.

"We have ale for pains and ailments—but it will be wasted on a slave."

"If she dies, may the gods have mercy on all of you. I will rip you apart. Limb. By. Limb. And I'm coming for *you* last."

The man must've believed him because there was the sound of a hasty retreat, followed by a door opening and closing. When he came back, he snapped, "Lord Edward has benevolently granted this reward for winning. He expects you to fully entertain him tonight at dinner and again in the arena tomorrow." With a huff, he turned on his heel and strode out of the room.

"Are we alone?" I rasped, not daring to open my eyes yet.

"For now," Jeph muttered, standing up. "But there're guards posted outside the door." He walked to a table on the far side of the room, his back to me. "There to keep us from escaping, no doubt." He snorted. "As if they could, but...you're in no shape to go anywhere."

My eyes flicked around the small room. It was just as dingy and poorly-lit as most of the estate, having only candles and a small, paneless window with light filtering in. I was on a small cot, real wood making up the railing, while straw stuffed the linen I lay on—linen that was stained red and brown with fresh and dried blood. I didn't even want to consider what the other stains were. Other than that, the room appeared to be empty of anything else—except for a bucket in the corner, reeking of what I suspected was human excrement. *Lovely.* A real chamber pot.

"Where are we?" I asked.

"Infirmary—or what passes as one," he replied, not bothering to turn around.

"What are you doing?"

"Making sure this isn't laced with poison."

My brow furrowed, watching his shoulders move as he did something with the cup. "Why stitch me up just to poison me?"

"That man's a bigot; he doesn't care if you live or die." He came over, one hand curled tightly in a fist, the other holding the cup out to me. "Drink this. It'll help with the pain."

"I...can you help me sit up?"

He handed me the cup, which took my full concentration to hold upright while laying down. Sitting next to my head he gently lifted my shoulders with his open right hand and closed left fist. Very carefully, he put his legs on either side of me, pulling me to rest, sitting up against his chest. It was such an intimate position, I shivered. With his right hand, he helped me hold the cup and the other rested uselessly on his leg.

"What's wrong with your fist?"

"Nothing."

Not realizing how close he was, I turned my head to glare at him. My heartbeat spiked in my chest, and I quickly looked away, lifting the cup to my mouth. I took a tentative sip and spit it back out.

"Nasty!" I shouted, wiping a hand across my lips.

"Drink it."

"It's disgusting."

"It'll help you feel better," he sing-songed.

"No, it really won't."

"Don't be such a wuss." He lifted the cup toward my face again. "Just drink it."

"I don't want to."

"Sam," he growled next to my ear, and my breath caught. "Drink. The. Damn. Ale."

I had half a mind to argue with him, but the forcefulness of his tone had me turning my head again. My eyes met his, a steady blaze in his irises. I gulped, feeling hot all over again.

"I'll drink it if you show me your hand," I said evenly despite how breathless I felt.

His eyes narrowed, but he lifted his fist, uncurling his fingers. Fresh blood and a clean, healing cut stared up at me from his palm. I traced a finger next to it, confused.

"When did that happen?" I asked. "It wasn't there a minute ago."

"Yes, it was," he said so defensively, I looked at him again. "I got it in battle—it and several other cuts."

"No, it wasn't."

"Whatever you say, precious. I showed you my hand, now drink."

Grimacing, I tipped the cup to my lips, bubbles washing over my tongue. I held it in my mouth, trying not to spit it out again. It really did taste like a hobgoblin's foot. After a moment of collecting my courage, I swallowed, shuddering in disgust and fighting a belch of bile.

"Is it really that bad?" he asked, sounding amused.

"You try it." I held the awful cup toward him.

Shrugging, he took a tentative sip. "I've tasted worse," he said gruffly, coughing and handing the cup back to me. "Bottom's up."

"I think I'd rather eat my left hand."

"I don't recommend it."

"I was exaggerating."

"You don't say."

Rolling my eyes, I took another sip. It was just as awful as the first two attempts, but I plugged my nose, tilted the cup end-up, and chugged until it was empty. At the bottom, there was a thick glob of *something*, and it was like finding a hunk of rich chocolate in a cup of cocoa. I closed my eyes on a moan. Then, not particularly caring, I tossed the cup when it was empty, listening to it clink onto the ground.

"You could've just handed it to me," Jeph muttered. "What if that's the only cup they give us?"

I shrugged, wincing with the motion.

"Can you *not* hurt yourself for two seconds?"

"Probably not."

He sighed, exasperated. "You know, looking after you is a full-time job. How have you managed to stay alive this long?"

"I ask myself that every day."

"Incredible," he muttered; it clearly wasn't a compliment.

The alcohol sloshed warmly in my empty stomach, reminding me how hungry I was. How long had it been since breakfast? Half a day? More? If I was starving, I could only imagine how Jeph felt. Guilt knifed through me. I hadn't stopped to consider his needs, his hunger, or his pain. He had to be dehydrated, famished, and in agony. He'd received so many wounds in the arena and yet, here he was, seeing to my selfish, pathetic ass.

"I should've saved some ale for you."

"I'm fine," he protested. "You're the one sweating bullets."

That's attractive, I thought bitterly.

Then, I giggled, the idea of sweat-bullets suddenly entertaining. Everything was entertaining as a tingling sensation prickled along the top of my head. My mind slowly drifted from my body, the pain a distant worry now. The tension in my muscles smoothed away, and I was a little sleepy. I snuggled against Jeph, reclining as far as I could against him and closing my eyes, a contented smile claiming my lips.

"Try not to fall asleep yet," he said, his chest rumbling under me. "You need dinner."

"Mmm," I murmured, nuzzling my face against his chest. He was so warm and comfortable, so gentle and safe.

Not gentle, not safe—Scary-Bad-Man...I frowned. *Sexy-Scary-Bad-Man.* I giggled again.

Jeph smoothed my hair away from my forehead, whispering, "You really should learn to listen when people tell you things."

I didn't respond, darkness pulling me under.

When I woke up again, it was to find I'd rolled over. My head was cradled between Jeph's throat and shoulder, his chin resting on the top of my head. My hands were squished underneath me, fingers splayed on his chest. His heart beat slowly and evenly under my palms and ear. I rose and fell with each breath he took, and he was lightly snoring, his hands resting on my back, one just a little too low for comfort. I reached behind me to move it, but the motion caused me to wince and hiss. His eyes flew open, and he blinked, brow furrowing.

"What happened?" he asked, stretching with a yawn, his muscles rippling underneath me, causing my heart to nearly explode in my chest.

Could he *not* do that? How casual was he with strangers that he could spoon them and stretch with them draped across him like it was no big deal? Was he just that *active* in his life that having a woman in his lap was like breathing air? The thought made something foul and bitter curdle in my stomach—or maybe that was the ale.

Definitely the ale and not *jealousy*, I decided when nausea crept in.

"Your back doing okay?" he asked. "You look pained."

I pressed my lips together, wanting to bash my head into the nearest wall. Or to throw up. Either was entirely possible.

"It's fine."

"You don't look 'fine.' Here," he said, putting his hands on my shoulders and helping me up. "Turn so I can get a better look at it."

I did, mostly because I needed something to do—needed something to focus on, other than the familiar way he spoke to me now. Other than the careful way he was taking care of me. It was only because I was his ticket out of here, nothing more than a ride home.

That knowledge didn't stop me from shivering when his hot fingers brushed over my bare back. Didn't stop the gooseflesh that rose, trailing sparks with the caress. My jaw clenched. I hated how magnetizing he was, how warm and tingly he made me feel—even from the first moment I met him. There was something about his touch that made my skin hum in a familiar way.

"This looks a lot better," he said. "And it'll be even better after a little more rest."

Then, I felt something tug my skin.

"What are you...?" I trailed off, gagging when I realized he was pulling out my stitches.

"Don't make that noise."

"Stop," I wheezed.

"No. These are too loose. They're going to snag on something and tear your skin."

I gagged again.

"Don't be a baby," he muttered, tugging the next one out.

"Distract me," I said breathlessly. "Or I'm gonna hurl—again."

"How do you feel?"

I laughed bitterly. "That's not gonna take my mind off what you're doing to my back."

"But it's a legitimate question."

"Never better."

He snorted.

I gritted my teeth, feeling my skin pull away from muscle with the next stitch he tugged out. "You're not distracting me."

"I'm not? I thought I was."

"You're making me mad."

"Isn't that distracting?"

"No," I growled.

"Well, I suck at small talk."

"Gee, you don't say."

"Did you sleep okay?" he asked.

"Yup."

A beat of silence.

"How about *you* pick something to keep you distracted."

"Me? I'm not the one ripping thread from my flesh!" My hand flew to my mouth, something between a gag and a belch invading my throat.

"Don't say it like that if it's going to make you make that noise," he muttered, exasperated.

I swallowed back bile, shuddering the whole time. It settled unhappily into my stomach acid. I needed something to eat or I was going to throw up, but if I ate, I wasn't entirely sure I wouldn't vomit anyway.

Desperate for a distraction, I asked the first question that came to my mind. "What's your favorite color?"

"Black."

"Never would've guessed," I deadpanned.

"What's that supposed to mean?"

"Nothing."

More silence.

"And what's yours?" he asked, tugging another stitch.

"Purple," I said through gritted teeth. "This isn't working."

"I'm halfway done."

I whimpered. "That's it?"

"That's it."

His hands stilled on my shoulders, and the hair on the back of my neck rose. I could almost sense his contemplation. Whatever it was, I knew I wasn't going to like it. Then, I gasped, my whole chest seizing when his lips trailed over my exposed shoulder. My heart pounded erratically, and my breath came in shallow pants.

"What...what are you doing?" I whispered.

"Distracting you," he murmured against my skin, making me shiver.

"That's not…that's not what I had in mind."

"Then what is?" He nipped my shoulder, and I yelped.

"Anything else."

"Anything?" There was a smile in his voice.

"I take it back."

He chuckled, nibbling my earlobe. "Such a tease, precious."

I swallowed, my eyes closing and my head lolling of its own volition. Stupid neck. Stupid Jeph. Stupid lips with their stupid stupidness as they trailed slowly and wetly along my jaw, his tongue and teeth teasing my skin as he got closer. Closer. Just one more second—one more move—one breath and…

"All done," he whispered when his lips were right next to mine.

"What?" I asked, breathless and dizzy.

"Your stitches." He pulled back, running a finger above my wound. "They're all out."

"Oh." I blinked, trying to pull my head out of my ass. I ground my teeth together in annoyance. "Stop doing that."

"Stop doing what?"

"Touching me so casually."

He was silent for a long moment. "You said to distract you, so I did. Worked, didn't it?"

My blood boiled. "I didn't tell you to sexually harass me!"

"You said to do anything."

"And I said I took it back!"

"Well, stitches are out," he said, shrugging. "You going to keep biting my head off for helping you?"

"Yes!"

"Hmm. Why not try, 'Thank you, oh amazing, incredible, sexy Jeph, for helping me'?"

"Rot in Hell."

He nodded. "Every day of my life."

"I'm gonna kill you."

"You and everyone else," he muttered.

"You're not funny!"

"And you're not nice, precious."

My chest heaved in anger. "You're annoying."

"Owchies. That hurts my non-existent feelings," he said in a pretend pout.

"Asshole."

"If you're going to insult me, the least you could do is make it worthwhile. Like, Supreme Asshole. Or—"

"Dickhead from Hell. Arch Enemy."

He was quiet for a moment before whispering, "You're my enemy."

"And you're mine."

He chuckled.

"What's so funny?" I snapped.

"First you tell me not to be so casual with you, then you turn around and stake a claim on me? Make up your mind. My poor, little, black heart might get whiplash."

"What are you even—?"

"I'm *yours?* Really, precious? Where do you get off making possessive claims on me?"

It was like whiplash with this guy. *One second, he's being kind and gentle, the next, he's being mocking and cruel.* It was confusing and I couldn't decide if he was actually a somewhat decent human being or if he was just an asshole.

The door on the far wall slammed open.

"Lord Edward requests you wash before dinner."

Seventeen

e were given a washbasin and clean clothing to wear. Apparently, just because Lord Edward was dining with "filth," didn't mean he wanted us filthy—and we were covered in blood, dirt, and goddess knew what else. He probably didn't want us to ruin his appetite. If it weren't for the fact that it was *blood*, I would've stayed dirty just to spite the man.

This was going to be another awkward adventure of turned backs while we each attempted to sponge bathe. More annoyingly, Jeph insisted I wash up first while the water was the cleanest. But with my injured shoulder, I had a limited range of motion.

"Here," he said, holding his hand out behind him for the sponge after the third time I'd hissed in pain.

I was seriously getting sick of hearing that word. "I can do it!"

"If you weren't cussing like a sailor, I might believe you." He kept his back to me. "Are you decent enough for me to turn around?"

I grumbled under my breath. Of course, I was. I couldn't even move far enough to reach my knees without hurting my shoulder. I couldn't very well take off my damn dress. I'd resigned myself to a very mild sponge bath.

"Yes," I mumbled in defeat.

Jeph turned around, arching a brow. I was fully dressed, feet in the bucket of lukewarm water, skirt hiked up to my knees. The back of the dress had since fallen into the water. He pressed his lips together, but I could tell he wanted to laugh at me. He refrained—barely. Shaking his head, he retrieved a shoddy stool and brought it over to me, putting it on the far side of the bucket before grabbing my hips, turning me, and making me sit.

"Hey! What—"

"Just figured you might want your back to the door in case the guards decide they want a peek."

I flushed. "That's awfully considerate of a heathen like you."

"I also don't like my back to doors."

So, that's what it is. I rolled my eyes.

"Now"—he snatched the sponge from my hand, squatted next to the bucket, and hiked my skirt up to my thighs, making me scream—"let's get you cleaned up."

"No!"

He ignored me, grabbing my ankle in one hand and dipping the sponge in the water with the other. I flushed a brilliant shade of red when he began washing my calf and ankle. This was just like the stupid stitches all over again but felt one thousand times more intimate.

He's literally bathing *me!*

I watched him, irritation pounding in my chest. Anger boiled in my veins while something else stirred low in my stomach. The concentration on his face as he began scrubbing my filthy toes was cute—*I mean concerning!* Then, I yelped, jumping in my seat. He grinned, rubbing the sponge back over the arch of my foot, making me yelp again.

"Ticklish?" he asked, his eyes glittering with mischief, enjoying his revenge.

"Nope."

He did it again and again, and I gritted my teeth against the need to laugh, clenched every muscle in that foot and leg to keep from—

I jumped, splashing him with mucky water, and he smiled smugly.

"You're such a jerk!"

"Takes one to know one," he said triumphantly, taking my other ankle into his hand.

I glared, watching him work again, the water already a murky red-brown—*blood.* The blood of people who had died…

while I'd been *allowed* to live. No, not allowed to; I'd shot people down and rendered others defenseless. And what about the Hunter and the Norm I'd killed?

"Try not to think about it," Jeph said, pulling me out of my thoughts.

"You don't know what I'm thinking about."

His half-smile was grim. "You've got that *look*."

"What look?"

"Guilt. I've seen it before…too many times."

I shifted uncomfortably on the stool. "I'm not…"

He stopped washing my calf, looking up to meet my eyes. "Sam, don't think I didn't see what you did to that man. Besides, I used to lead a squad of…" He trailed off, gaze going distant. "I've seen that guilt in the eyes of boys younger than you. Too young."

"Does it…does it ever fade? The guilt, I mean?"

Jeph held my eyes before going back to cleaning between my toes. "Guilt is an emotion. You do with it what you will. Some people get eaten alive by their sins. Some people couldn't feel guilt if it slapped them on the ass and called them 'daddy.'"

"Charming," I muttered.

"Your demons are with you for life, but don't let them eat away at your soul. Regardless of whether or not you failed in your goal, you killed to save someone else, to protect someone worth protecting. People kill for less."

"Are you one of those people?"

Jeph put my clean foot outside the bucket, dropping the sponge in the water. He grabbed the meager towel we were given, drying me from calf to toe, first one leg, then the other. I could scarcely breathe while he handled me so carefully, so tenderly, even after I'd asked an accusing question. Then, he slapped the towel over his shoulder, scooting closer to me and taking one of my wrists. He picked up the sponge and began wiping.

"I can wash…" I trailed off with a gulp when his hard, brown eyes met mine.

"Yes."

"Yes?"

"I've killed for less. Much less."

Breathing became difficult, but Jeph didn't wait for a response. He went back to wiping my arm, and I gasped when the sponge ran over damaged skin. Frowning, he looked closer at my arm, taking it in his hand and turning it from side-to-side. The whip wound was deep but luckily, not too long. It even looked rather clean, despite the battles I'd been in.

"Deeper than I thought," he muttered to himself, gently wiping around it before moving on.

When he got to my wrist, he put the palm of my hand in his own. It was like lightning and fireworks fizzled from him to me. And when he held my fingers cradled in his like a prince might delicately hold a princess', I snatched my hand away. I couldn't help it, couldn't stop the knee-jerk reaction. My heart pounded, breathing nearly impossible. No man, no matter how gorgeous or handsome, no matter how kind or sweet, had ever made me feel so fuzzy and dizzy from such a light touch. This man was a murderer, yet made it impossible for me to think clearly.

He looked up, hands still held out in front of him, ready to clean the blood and dirt from my fingers. We stared at each other for a long, stunned minute. He hadn't expected my reaction any more than I had. My cheeks were flushed, my heart pounding, the vein in my neck jumping.

"Tickled," I lied, very slowly putting my hand back toward his. It shook and tingled, which was only made worse when he took it in his palm. To distract myself, I asked, "Why do you kill people?"

He shrugged. "I was an Elite Hunter once—like all Councilmembers."

Of course, he'd been an assassin. Someone didn't become a Councilmember by doing nothing. I wasn't sure *what* someone had to do to become one, especially at the top guild to ever exist, but it had to be *something* impressive. With over a hundred mages to choose from, it said a lot about Jeph that he'd been promoted so young. From how confidently he wore the authority, he'd been on the Council for a while.

"How young?"

"Hmm?" he hummed, not looking up as he started cleaning my other hand.

"How young were you when you made the Council?"

"Eighteen."

My age—how many people had he killed before he was my age? "So, that means you've been on the Council for...two years?"

"It'll be four years in November."

I guffawed. "You're twenty-two?"

"I will be in August."

"So, you'd *barely* turned eighteen, and they made you a Councilmember over men who were surely older and more experienced than you? Why?"

He shrugged. "I wonder that myself sometimes. There were two Elite Hunters due to ascend before me, yet the Guildmaster picked me instead."

"He must like you."

This time, he snorted. "Likes my power, more like it," he muttered, dropping the sponge in the bucket and grabbing my waist.

"Hey! Wait—!"

He pulled me to a standing position and walked behind me, putting his back to the door and nudging the stool out of the way. "I'm assuming you're still wearing this because your shoulder limits your range of motion?" He tugged on the dress, and I nodded. "Are you going to yell at me if I try to help you change into something clean?"

I chewed my lip, debating. I couldn't take off the dress myself, but I didn't like the idea of him stripping me. I also didn't like the blood staining me, marking the truth of what I'd seen and done.

"I won't," I breathed, barely audible to my own ears.

Jeph set the clean dress on the stool next to us, and my heart raced in my chest as he lifted my dress. I felt something brush against my legs when the bottom of the skirt was past my thighs. Nervous and confused, I turned my head. His weird, dark magic was lifting the towel along with the rise of the dress, covering my skin even as he exposed it.

He really was trying to be as chivalrous as possible. For all his flirting, rudeness, and lack of boundaries, it shocked me. At the same time, it didn't, not after the way he'd just gently washed me when he didn't have to. He could've easily left me soiled in the gruesome aftermath of our battle; the new dress would've covered the blood and mud. Instead, he'd insisted I use the clean water first, had told me not to dwell on the guilt of the arena, and now was respecting my boundaries the best he could.

"Arms up," he whispered, his voice throaty and gruff.

I complied, shivering as goosebumps broke out all over my flesh. The filthy dress slid over my head, and my hair caught and fell, cascading down my back and tickling my bare skin. My bra and panties were now the only things clothing me from his sight. The discarded dress hit the floor in a heap somewhere behind me. Before I could contemplate why that made me feel much too hot, the fabric of the clean dress tickled over my raised arms. Jeph's palms guided the dress, trailing fire with his touch. He released the skirt, and it fanned out around my legs. I held the top against my chest as his hands reached around me to grab the straps and secure them in place. Then, he grabbed my hair, gently pulling it out of the dress, and I winced, feeling it rub against my shoulder wound.

"Did I hurt you?" he asked, voice husky.

"Not really," I said breathily, stomach doing backflips.

"Well, it's my turn, so…"

I nodded, keeping my back to him as I moved away, the room filling with the sound of rustling clothing. He was likely in nothing more than his boxers—or was he a tighty-whities boy? There was a part of me that wanted to turn around. Since that was absolutely the stupidest thought I'd ever had, I brought up our conversation from before, listening to him wring out the sponge.

"Did you ever *not* kill someone?"

Jeph went so quiet behind me, I almost turned around to see his expression. I barely caught myself halfway, turning forward to face the wall again.

"Why?" His tone was a cross between playful and suspicious. "Hoping you can talk me out of killing you?"

I tried to laugh it off, but I was still trying to calm my erratic heart rate from nearly turning around. "Well, I hadn't thought about it, but that's not a bad idea."

"Yes."

"Yes, what?"

"Yes, there was a time when I didn't kill someone I was supposed to."

This time, I didn't catch myself, turning to gape at him. He arched both brows, and my face burned crimson. I slapped my hands over my eyes, turning back to the wall. *Boxers it is*, my brain inappropriately supplied for me. And that wasn't an image that was going to fade any time soon...*Goddess, that guy's ripped.* I knew he was, but...*wow.*

"Why didn't you kill them?" I asked, voice strained.

He chuckled, which wasn't helping anything. "Didn't feel like it."

"*Pfft! You?* Didn't feel like *killing* someone? Now we both know you're lying."

"If I were anyone else, precious, I might be offended by that."

"But I'm right."

"You are," he said, amused.

"So?" I asked impatiently. "Why didn't you?"

"He was innocent."

I whipped back around, shocked. This time even my modesty didn't register. I stared at him, at his aura, trying to catch his lie, but he was telling the truth. He really spared that man because he was innocent.

"How did you know—no, wait. Why did you *care?*"

He shrugged, dropping the sponge in the bucket and toweling off. I chose to look over his head, high enough I couldn't see all those tantalizing muscles—the dark tattoo curling over his pecks, shoulders, and biceps—but low enough I could spot his aura.

"I found out by accident." Jeph tossed the towel aside, grabbing the tunic and pulling it over his head. "The man was a good fighter, but that wasn't what saved his life that night. He had a portable alert-ward—first of its kind at the time. Just as I was about to slit his throat, it flared and scared the piss out of us both." His aura dipped out of sight as he leaned down to put his trousers and leggings on. "Gave him just enough warning to keep his head. If he'd been a less skilled fighter, he would've died regardless of that ward. I was already a skilled assassin, even then."

"Even then?" I echoed.

"I was only a Hunter."

That wasn't reassuring.

"I thought only the Elites went on assassination missions."

"Normally, but I was a special case."

Now that he was dressed, I met his eyes. "So, what happened?"

"He wanted to live, so like any desperate man, he began rambling and begging for his life."

"And?"

"And the more he spoke, the less my mission made sense."

"So," I drawled, "you spared him?"

"So, I spared him."

Either Jeph was a damn good liar, or he was telling the truth. His aura didn't waver in the slightest. At least, not regarding whether or not he was lying, but it did flash with various things I couldn't quite catch.

"How did you get away with it?" I asked. "Wouldn't the guild consider you a rogue for disobeying an order?"

That set his aura flaring with mistrust and fear.

"Nothing special." *Lie.*

"Oh?"

"It would bore you." *Lie.*

"Uh-huh."

"It's not important." *Lie.*

So, even he has secrets he wants to keep...

"Sure, sure," I mumbled, walking closer to him. "You missed a spot."

He looked at his hands. "Where?"

"Right," I drawled, picking up the sponge and wringing it out before cupping his cheek and putting the sponge to his face, "here."

We both froze, staring at each other.

I took one breath, two, and then I centered myself, going back to the task. He'd gone to town on those poor people in the arena, and he'd gotten their blood all over his face. They hadn't deserved to die like that, but they would've died regardless of our interference. In a way, this had been better. Jeph had killed swiftly, making painless deaths out of what would've been violent suffering. It had been my arrows that had been cruel.

"Close your eyes," I whispered.

He did, without hesitation.

I wiped the sponge just under his eyes, trying to scrub the dirt away. It was proving stubborn, and I grumbled under my breath, moving my hand from his cheek to the back of his neck, holding him steady as I started scrubbing harder. His hair was softer than I'd imagined it would be. Silkier, the curls at the nape of his neck gliding between my fingers. As I scrubbed violently at his face, I absentmindedly played with the locks of his hair.

Jeph's eyes snapped open, one hand snaking around my waist and pulling me to him, the other winding into my hair. I yelped in shock, my breath catching when his mouth was just an inch away from mine. My heart pounded with anticipation, and I licked my lips. But he just held me there, our shallow breaths mingling, his fingers playing with my hair the way mine had with his.

I didn't dare speak or move.

As the seconds dragged by, I could only take short, shuddering breaths. My pulse roared in my ears, my limbs had long since lost circulation, but a fire existed everywhere his skin touched mine, everywhere his body pressed against mine. I couldn't stop myself from wavering, ever so slightly, toward him. Our noses brushed, and Jeph growled, releasing me so quickly I fell into a heap of skirts and limbs on the floor.

I looked up to find him on the far side of the room, staring at me with wild eyes. Fear lurked in his aura, fear and hope, regret and…desire. It sent warmth coursing through my veins. Jeph wanted me, and for some reason, that scared him.

e entered the dining room to find Lord Edward already seated at a long, rectangular table. Why he wanted to eat dinner with us was beyond me. That was, until I realized most of his court was there to greet us, all looking excited and expectant to see the "happy couple."

Lord Edward's eyes narrowed on us, and Jeph instantly took my hand in his, putting himself just in front of me. It was both possessive and protective. He was back in "husband" mode. If it was the story keeping us alive, then it was the appearance we were going to have to give. So long as they didn't ask us to start boinking in front of all of them, I was roughly seventy-three percent sure I could make it through whatever they threw at us. But the memory of Jeph's kisses—both in the arena and along my shoulder, and then that near-kiss just minutes ago—had my stomach doing weird things.

I wanted to hit myself.

"My friends, your Champions have arrived," Lord Edward said, standing and holding his arms wide. His posse clapped, eager grins on their faces.

Jeph's hand squeezed mine harder. "Can I kill them?" he asked so low, I almost couldn't hear him. "I'll even ask nicely. *Please?*"

I shook my head, rolling my eyes. "Most of these people have impacts on the timeline—whether directly or indirectly, I'm not sure. It could be them—it could be their descendants five hundred years from now."

"How do you know?"

"Intuition—it's a perk of these awful powers."

He arched a brow but continued forward, taking the empty seat set aside for us. There was only the one, which left Jeph pulling me onto his lap. I also noticed we only had one place setting in front of us. We were going to have to share our meal, which wasn't reassuring after how little we'd had to eat since we arrived in this goddess-forsaken time period.

I would have thought this was further hazing and cruelty on Lord Edward's part, but he had only wanted one Champion. We'd relegated ourselves to this position when we'd refused to follow the rules. Rather, we'd relegated ourselves to a lot of messed up shit just because I'd hesitated when Jeph had suggested leaving.

"Now that our honored guests have arrived, we can begin the meal," Lord Edward said.

He waved over a man standing against the wall, and the servant walked to us, presenting us with a long loaf of bread. Jeph took it, breaking a piece off before offering it back to the servant. He then moved to the other end of the table, offering it to Lord Edward. While he took his piece, the men at the table—because I was the only woman—chatted among themselves. Then, more food was brought out, and a hunk of ham and two chicken legs were put on a plate in front of us, along with cheese, cabbage, and beans. In our cup, of course, there was more ale.

How were we ever going to fight tomorrow if we weren't even sober?

"Eat," Jeph said against my ear, and I had to fight the urge to jump.

"You need to eat, too," I protested.

"I'll eat whatever you don't."

I glowered, picking up the chicken leg and holding it toward him, hoping he'd take it. Ever so slightly, he shook his head, his eyes boring into mine. Glaring, I took an angry bite. Triumph lit his eyes when I moaned softly. I was *famished*, and the meat was heaven on my starved tongue. Turning back to the plate, I practically inhaled the food. Between gulps of ale, I took bites of this and that, sampling the various flavors. I was a little over halfway through the plate when I remembered Jeph still hadn't eaten.

Very carefully, I set a bite of cheese back onto the plate. I doubted we'd be offered seconds, and Jeph needed his strength if we were going to escape. Magic would draw the guild mages to us, so that was out of the question. We had to rely on Norm tactics if we didn't want a battle once we fled the estate.

"I'm full," I whispered, daring a glance over my shoulder.

One dubious eyebrow arched at me, a hint of a smile on his lips. I got the distinct impression he was mocking me. He didn't say anything as he reached past me, grabbing the cheese I'd been about to eat. That eyebrow stayed high on his forehead as he popped it in his mouth, his smile turning into a smirk.

Annoyed, I turned back to the table, picking up the ale. I was pretty sure, now that I'd had—how much had I had? The cup, unlike my plate, kept seeming to magically refill itself. Anyway, I was sure I was nearing something like a buzz. I assumed this was part of Lord Edward's ploy to keep us docile and from trying to escape tonight. Or maybe it was just the culture here. The ale was quickly muddling my thoughts—at least it didn't taste bad. It was actually kind of sweet; probably the "good stuff," unlike the swill they'd given me in the infirmary.

Jeph snatched the cup from me, taking a long, deep drink, tilting the cup back, back, back as he chugged it down. I pouted, staring longingly at it. My back and arm weren't hurting per se, but the alcohol was definitely tuning out the dull throb. It was also starting to make things floaty enough that stuff was *just* a bit funny. I smiled, looking around the table at all the men. They were eating and talking, paying us no mind. One pudgy man had food all over his face, and it made me giggle. He looked like a fat little piggy.

"Oink, oink," I murmured, turning to look at the man seated next to Piggy.

He was thinner than Piggy but had a long, unruly beard. There was food in it. He had more hair on his chin than he had on top of his balding head, which shined and gleamed in the candlelight. I giggled again.

"Chrome Dome," I whispered to myself.

I tried to look at the other men, but it was getting difficult to see now that my vision was swimming. My head felt light and airy, but my body felt like a ton of bricks. I wobbled, and Jeph's hands caught my waist before I could dump myself onto the floor.

"Careful," he murmured against my ear, sending a shiver down my spine. His grip tightened on my waist. "With your luck, you'll fall off my lap and break your neck on the way down."

My head bob-lolled as I turned to glare at him. "You're nah nice," I slurred.

His eyes glittered with mischief. "So you've told me—at least a dozen times now."

"Good—cuz you're nah."

His slow smile drew my gaze. Licking my lips, I leaned ever so slightly toward him. I must've been drunk because I wanted to taste his lips, wanted him to kiss me the way he had in the arena. I wanted to turn around, crawl into his lap, press him against the chair, and—

"You doing okay, there, precious?" Jeph grinned. "You're looking a little cross-eyed."

I jolted, blinking and giving my head a slight shake. "I tol' yoo ta stahp callin' me thah," I complained, glaring at him again.

"And I decided to ignore you."

"You're—"

"Rude? Yes. You've said that. Now, sit still while I finish eating. And no more ale—you're cut off, Drunkie."

I insulted him under my breath.

"And how are our Champions enjoying their meal?" Lord Edward smirked at us, revealing the food stuck in his teeth.

My nose crinkled in disgust.

"Just fine," Jeph snipped, taking another bite of pork.

"And the lady?"

"Would be better if I had my own chair," I managed to say without slurring.

The men apparently found my forwardness entertaining be-cause they all chuckled.

"I would think you'd enjoy the nearness to your beloved," a man to my right—it was Piggy—said. "Especially after the enthusiasm you two showed us in the arena."

"Ah, yes. Young love is always so...*passionate*, is it not?" Chrome Dome asked suggestively. There was a sick gleam in his eyes as he raked his gaze over my body.

Jeph wrapped an arm around my waist, turning me toward him and nuzzling his face against my neck. It put most of my back to the man leering at me. If he hadn't turned me, I would've missed the disgust raging in his aura, the anger burning brighter than the sun. But to anyone who was looking at his calm expression, they would see a man affectionately embracing his woman.

"Yes," Jeph replied coolly, calm façade never leaving his face. His teeth gleamed threateningly. "My wife is extremely important to me. Which is why I'm hoping my kind and benevolent Lord"—he turned to Lord Edward, his sneer softening into a kind smile—"might grant us the privilege of sharing our lodging tonight?"

I tried to protest—*I'm so not sleeping next to him again!*—but something shadowy wrapped around my mouth, silencing me. Jeph's magic radiated from it, but his gaze never left Lord Edward, even as my fingernails dug angrily into his arm.

The men shared knowing smiles, lustful gleams in their eyes. They chuckled to themselves as if they were sharing some kind of secret. Even Jeph's expression matched theirs as if this was all just fun and games between equals. The only thing that told another story was the murderous threat in his aura.

"Who could blame you for wanting to take your wife to bed after that...*eager* display earlier?" Lord Edward asked with a leer. "Why, I think several would agree that you're quite the lucky man to have such a...*bewitching* little thing for a wife."

Heat seemed to flare from Jeph, and his fingers burrowed into my waist. "I'm a lucky man indeed," he gritted out.

"I do suppose I could grant this one thing to our Champions," Lord Edward murmured, an undertone to his words. "Wouldn't want to keep you from celebrating your victory, now would we?"

"We're grateful for your kindness," Jeph replied.

Like hell we are!

Dirty, dingy, or otherwise, I'd been looking forward to sleeping alone in my cell tonight. Specifically, *without* the man who'd been frisking me in some capacity for the last forty-eight hours, the man who was going to kill me if I didn't make it to the twenty-first century alone...*the man I can't leave here without because he's* just *enough of an asshole, he'd screw up the entire timeline just to spite me.*

Jeph's magic finally slithered away from my mouth, and irritated, I reached for the refilled cup of ale, throwing it back and chugging. If I had to sleep next to him again, this time I was doing it drunk. My nerves were on fire just being this close to him—or was that the buzz from the alcohol? He snatched the cup away from me, and I belched at him, not even caring how disgusting or unattractive it was.

"Now for the real fun," Lord Edward said, his words met with enthusiasm. He got to his feet, his stooges following suit. "Come. Let us rejoice further." He motioned for Jeph and me to do the same. He didn't wait for us long though, looking eager to get wherever he was going.

I got to my feet, stumbling and tripping against the table.

Jeph sighed. "Really, precious? Can't hold your liquor?"

"Mmm nah drunnnk," I slurred.

"I beg to differ," he muttered, wrapping an arm around my waist to keep me standing. "You can't even stand up without falling over."

"Can too," I sing-songed.

"And I'm Jesus."

"No, you're nah," I drawled. "You Satan."

He rolled his eyes at me. "Sure. I'm Satan. Whatever. Now can you at least *try* to stand upright?"

My brow furrowed, my head rolling in a wide arc as I tried to look at my feet. I had four of them. I blinked a few times and squinted, trying to figure out which of the four feet I should try to stand on. Two of them, right? But four would be more stable. *Totes more stable*, I mused to myself, giggling.

"Sam!"

I jumped. "Hmm?"

"You're wasted."

"Nuh-uh."

He scrubbed a hand down his face. "You just love making things difficult, don't you?"

"Nooo." My voice was high and long, reminding me of Dory making whale calls in *Finding Nemo*. I bit my lip, giggling again. "*You* make the difficult."

"What are—*Ugh*." He looked like he was ready to kill me. "Whatever. Just—stop talking. You sound like a dying cat."

"Rude!"

Ignoring me, Jeph held me in one arm while he held out the other hand. Food from the table flew toward his outstretched palm.

"Ack!" I shouted, burying my face against his shoulder, waiting for it to hit me. When it didn't, I dared to peek at the food. It was gone, all of it, except the piece of bread he was now munching on.

"Let's go before they notice we're missing," he said. "I'd hate to die after surviving this much bullshit."

I nodded, trying to take a step…and falling forward. His grip around my waist was the only thing that kept me on my feet. He grumbled under his breath, holding the hunk of bread between his teeth as he used his other hand to help right me. He held me there for a minute, waiting for me to stop swaying. When he realized it was an impossible task, he pulled me against his side and walked slowly. I stumbled over my feet and nearly face-planted.

"Eat some of this, it might help," he said, pulling the bread from his mouth and shoving it in mine.

It was super dry, and there was nothing to wash it down with, so I tried to spit it out, but Jeph just held it in my mouth. When the need for air prevailed, I took a bite, chewing and swallowing. Then, I opened my mouth to yell at him, but he just shoved more bread in. After the third failed attempt, I gave up, snatching the bread from him and angrily munching on it. When the last of the bread was down, I still felt kinda fuzzy-brained but better.

"Better?" he asked, eyes alight with mischief.

"You're a dick," I said perfectly.

"I'll take that as a yes."

He kept his grip on my waist as he led me in the direction the rest of the dinner party guests had gone. They weren't moving particularly fast, so it wasn't like it was difficult to find them. They hadn't seemed to even notice we were gone. Rather, they must've. A few of them grinned and leered at us over their shoulders when they heard us coming.

Ah. So, they thought they'd been giving us some "privacy." Not like it had been real privacy; there were guards posted at the end of every hall. No doubt they, or the dinner party guests themselves, would've come running if they'd heard particular *activities* playing out. *Cretins.*

But those thoughts were quickly wiped away when I realized where we were heading. We were going toward the arena. Jeph seemed to realize it too because his gait slowed. His face pinched in disgust long before we arrived. When we did, his jaw set in anger. It took me a minute to catch on in my drunken state, but when I did, I quickly sobered, not nearly enough, but I finally understood. I wasn't sure if I wanted to be further from my mind or closer.

The first thing my eyes landed on as we walked under the arch, the metal bars of the cage raised, was the large pile of small stones. It was so unassuming but completely out of place. The stack was deliberate, the size and shape of each stone similar. The rocks hadn't been in the arena before, so why place them there now?

I already knew.

If I didn't, the large, gleaming sword resting on the small table next to the pile told me more. It was much too wide to ever wield in battle, and the shape of it put too much emphasis on the weight of the blade itself, instead of balance. It wasn't for fighting. The implication of its presence was even more startling than the pile of small, smooth stones.

But that wasn't what had my knees trembling.

I'd thought Ara had been killed in the arena...I'd been wrong. She was still alive—barely. That she was even breathing at all was a miracle. She was naked, had deep cuts all over her body, and was trussed up, attached to a wooden pole staked to the ground in the middle of the arena. There was wood and a bale of hay dispersed around her feet.

"Now for a grand spectacle!" Lord Edward announced, arms wide and a lecherous grin spreading across his face.

"Disgusting piece of filth," Jeph muttered under his breath.

"This little *vixen* survived when she should not have," Lord Edward said, his eyes boring into mine.

I knew he was implying I should've died, knew he was implying he thought *I* should be the one tied to that pole, knew that he'd called her a vixen because he'd...he'd...I was going to be sick. Ara had survived, but she would've been better off dead. I never should've interfered, never should've killed that man, but he'd been trying to kill her. He'd reveled in the idea of her slow, painful death.

Not all of the people in the arena had been victims. Some of them had deserved worse than the clean kills they'd gotten. Some of them had been in there because they'd been criminals...but it was a little late for Chaos and my intuition to tell me that, too late to undo what Lord Edward had done to the girl, the humiliation she'd suffered—the pain—or the death she was about to endure.

Meddling always made it worse, always made everything so much worse.

"How...?" I whimpered. *How could I let this happen?*

"Her cuts were shallow," Jeph said quietly, misunderstanding my question. "She likely only passed out earlier, presumed dead."

"I saw her weave witchery during the battle—sending her attackers away so that she might survive!" one of Lord Edward's stooges proclaimed.

*The Hunter...*They'd seen the Hunter knock me off of her.

I couldn't breathe. Ara wasn't a witch; she was a Norm girl, but I couldn't say that without outing myself as one. From the tone the man just used, I really didn't think I wanted them to know. From his aura, I knew the truth wouldn't matter anyway.

"She's dangerous!" another man shouted.

"She'll hex us all!"

"She should've died in the arena! She uses her spells, even now, to keep breathing."

"No..." I whimpered, my knees giving out. "She's just a girl..."

Jeph caught me, keeping me standing.

"*Witch, witch, witch!*" the men chanted until Lord Edward held up a hand, silencing them.

"We know her crime, gentlemen, but what of her punishment?" he asked, gesturing with wide arms at the collection of death instruments.

"Behead her!" Piggy said, walking toward the sword.

My teeth ground together, tears springing to my eyes and rage filling me. Jeph's grip on my waist was a warning, his fingers digging painfully into my skin. *Be silent*, they urged. *Don't draw attention to us.* He was right; Lord Edward already wanted me dead.

"We did that last time," Chrome Dome complained, walking over to the stones and picking one up. He examined it in his palm, a small grin on his face. "We should stone this one to death." To make his point, he turned, hurling it at Ara.

Jeph's hand silenced my scream faster than it could tear from my throat. It didn't matter anyway; no one heard me. Ara's bloodcurdling wail echoed off the arena walls when the rock pelted her in the eye.

"Stonings are so slow and boring," one of the other men said.

"And annoying," another added, hands clamped over his ears.

"Well," Lord Edward hedged, a gleam in his eyes as he walked toward a torch in one of the candelabra on the wall. He pulled it from the iron, holding it in his hand as he slowly approached Ara. "There's always *my* personal favorite."

"Ah," Piggy sighed. "You do put on an excellent show, don't you, my lord?"

"I do love a good burning," he responded. "Something about watching a practitioner of evil burn before she meets the real Hell flames brings me a certain...*joy*." When he was mere paces away from Ara, he stopped and turned to me, a full grin on his face. "And now, we burn the witch!"

He threw the torch at her feet.

Nineteen

J stared at the flames, transfixed. They licked higher and higher, closer and closer to her feet.

"Don't look," Jeph said.

"I can save her," I breathed, reaching a hand toward Ara.

"You can"—his voice was careful—"but at risk to us both."

Lord Edward watched us—watched me. He wanted to burn me alive because he was frustrated Jeph had conned him, had used the crowd and court against him. He was mad I had survived—because what had he told me? *"The weaker sex has been Champion before—ruthless, evil witches, usually. But we know what to do with witches, don't we?"*

Let. Them. Burn.

Ara started pleading and begging, screaming and crying. She hurt herself, straining against her bindings. So much blood already covered her from the arena, from her cuts, from what Lord Edward did to her. I needed to help her, needed to save her. If I just tried to get her into Chaos…but I would have to go over there, would have to be touching her. I couldn't do that—not without revealing my power. Not without drawing the Hunters to Jeph and me. Not without draining what little magical energy I'd barely started to regain. Not unless I wanted to change the course of history forever. I'd already done that enough for too many lifetimes.

But those screams—Ara's *screams*—echoed in my ears and reverberated through my soul.

I took an unsteady step toward her, hand still outstretched, and Jeph pulled me to him, stopping me. I stared in horror, watching as the flames nearly touched her now. They were close enough to scorch her flesh, to bathe her naked skin in an eerie

red glow. Or was that the blood? *So much blood...* And her aura—a small cry escaped my lips, her aura searing agony and terror along my own.

"Sam," Jeph growled, grabbing my cheeks in his hands and
turning my face to his. "Don't. Watch."

My head turned, seeking Ara again, wanting to help her, to
soothe her, to suffer with her. Silent tears rolled down my
cheeks.

My fault. My fault. My fault!

"Look at me," Jeph demanded, shaking my face.

I did.

His eyes held mine captive, his angry, vengeful eyes. He
covered my ears, but I could still hear her screaming behind me.
Could hear the shouts and jeers of Lord Edward and his court,
"Witch, witch, burn the witch!" Could still feel the stark terror
in Ara's aura. Could still see it in my mind's eye—a color so
awful, I never dreamed I'd ever live to see it.

But what loomed before me held my gaze transfixed: Jeph.
Disgust shone in his aura, in his eyes, in the set of his jaw, and
in the pressure of his hands crushing against my skull. Not just
disgust, but anger, *real* anger. I thought I'd seen dangerous and
threatening before, but that had nothing on the fury burning in
his dark eyes now.

Then, the soft heat of the encroaching fire kicked up. I
thought I felt magic behind me, thought I felt Jeph's hands heat
against my ears, but I was too drunk to be sure, too mesmerized
by the flames reflected in his eyes. It was likely just the fire
catching on the timber, likely just the blistering heat of the
blaze, scorching Ara's body to ash, but the temperature didn't
dwindle or fade. The heat blazed much too hot, hotter than I
could stand, searing my flesh. It burned along my open wound,
even though the flames were nowhere near me.

At some point, all I could hear was the muffled sound of the
roaring fire. It had long since silenced Ara, swallowing up her
screams along with her life. This time, I knew she was dead.
She'd been dead for minutes now. If the raging inferno hadn't
killed her swiftly, then the smoke surely had.

Suddenly, the heat vanished. It was like a vacuum opened up and sucked it away. There were nothing but embers now. Embers, and the ash that had flaked onto my skin and hair, onto Jeph's skin and hair. We were bathed in more death. I would never be clean of the lives lost in this arena today.

The gore and carnage had already been awful. This was worse. It was cruel, *monstrous*. Lord Edward was a monster, and this was a power play. It was a warning and a threat. He didn't know who he was fucking with.

With the death of the flames, Jeph finally released my ears, his eyes still holding mine, angry flames dancing in the depths of them. "She didn't suffer," he whispered, gently pulling me to him.

I clung to him, trembling and sobbing, my tears mingling with Ara's ashes.

"She can't feel pain now."

I couldn't respond, my mouth too dry, my blood too toxic, my brain swimming with ale, dread, and hollowness. Then, there was Jeph, with his steady warmth and cold kindness. I leaned into his comforting embrace, and he smoothed down my hair while I clutched the back of his tunic.

"That was fun!" Lord Edward announced, and Jeph caught my head and held it firmly against his chest, preventing me from looking at the vile man. "But I think our Champions need their rest now. Wouldn't want you to be too tired for tomorrow's match, now would we?"

Jeph growled so low, I could only hear it because I was pressed up against him. I wanted to give the Lord a piece of my mind, but Jeph's chest was suffocating me.

"Guards," Lord Edward called, his tone smug. "If you would show our Champions to their cell? They've got a *lot* of goodbyes to say tonight. We'll only have *one* Champion tomorrow."

We were thrown into a cell with bars and a lock. Unlike the infirmary, this was an *actual* prison cell. It was maybe eight feet by six feet wide, the only light coming in from the candelabra lining the hall. There was a chamber pot—I would die before I ever used it—making the cell reek of rancid piss and shit. The straw mattress was filthy from repeated use and had likely never seen any sort of cleaning or replacing. Despite being thoroughly repulsed, I was too tired and numb not to sit on it.

I also had a pounding headache from the ale, and Jeph was only making it worse. He paced like a caged animal. Correction—he *was* a caged animal. It showed in each step, every stride as he glided back and forth, every muscle tense and coiled as if he could leap into a killing spree at the slightest disturbance. For all his cool, calm façade, *this* was a whole new side of him I hadn't seen before. *No*, that wasn't true. This was the Jeph who defended like an alpha wolf caring for his pack, spoke in low, gravelly tones, touched with fierce aggression, and kissed like a man possessed.

I shivered, my fingers going to my now-tingling lips.

He threw back his head and roared, the sound like a gunshot in the dead of night. I flinched, my palms covering my ears. His hands dug into his hair, pulling at it before he stopped in front of the wall. He stared at it as if he wasn't really seeing it, as if it wasn't really there. Then, he punched it—*hard*—his knuckles splitting open.

Pain flared through his aura before it was replaced with… with what? I couldn't get a read on his aura. It was so dark, so grim, so stained. I'd never seen anything that close to black in my life, but I couldn't figure out why it was like that. Some people had flecks of black in their auras, usually from trauma, deep sadness, or the taint of their "sins," but Jeph had a *black* aura with flecks of *color*. Flecks of red for rage, gray for pain, and orange that I associated with heat and fire, but everything else was difficult to discern against the darkness of it.

He became eerily still after he punched the wall, going from chaotic energy to just standing there, staring at his fist as blood oozed over his knuckles and standing so still I wasn't sure he was breathing. His aura had even stopped spiraling and raging. The sudden stillness, his sudden silence, made gooseflesh creep over my skin and the hair on the back of my neck rise.

The tiniest shift in his moods and aura affected me, unlike anyone I'd ever encountered before. Those shifts spoke louder than Hunters who'd attacked, yelled at, or hurt me. Even meeting him had terrified me. He hadn't threatened or attacked me, he'd just stood there, holding me upright while his overwhelming energy had nearly knocked me on my ass. Now that I understood him a bit better, I didn't think he'd done that intentionally.

I got to my feet, slowly walking the short distance across the cell to stand next to him. He didn't even seem to notice me as he stared, transfixed by his own blood. My heart raced, and my hand trembled as I reached for him, my palm coming up to rest on his bloody knuckles. Once I covered it, he blinked, his intense focus landing on me.

His gaze on me was matched by how determinedly he'd stared at his own fist. For a minute, I couldn't breathe, look away, or move. The world seemed to shrink around me, consumed by the gravity in his eyes. Then, he blinked, pulling his fist away...it was like that moment never existed at all.

Sitting on the mattress, he examined his split knuckles with mild disinterest. Then, totally grossing me out, he licked the blood from his wound. I knew we didn't have soap or water to clean it with, but that wasn't sanitary either. His brow furrowed, his whole face pinching in what looked like pain, which—*no duh!*

I walked up to him, heaving a sigh as I crouched down in front of him and grabbed his wrist. I pulled it away from him, inspecting the wound. To my surprise, it wasn't as bad as I'd thought it was. In fact, it was so shallow and small, I was shocked there'd been so much blood. Or, had I only thought there was more?

Jeph arched a brow, and I examined his knuckles further, turning his hand over to check the cut he'd had on his palm. It was gone. Like, not healing, not scarring, just *gone*. He snatched his hand away, and I stared up at him. He stared right back, and my eyes narrowed.

His knuckles *had* been split worse than that. There was too much blood on my palm and wall. And the gash on his palm? He'd only gotten it hours ago! I studied him, realizing I hadn't seen my teeth marks in his forearm. Those cuts he'd told me about getting in the arena? The one that should've been on his bicep—that I should've seen when he was bathing? Also gone. And if those were gone…

I reached for the hem of his shirt, lifting it as he gasped in shock. I didn't know what he thought I was doing, but he was apparently too stunned to protest when I ran my hand along the smooth, unbandaged skin of his waist. His waist, which should've had a deep gash in the side of it, a deep gash that I'd dressed just last night.

No wonder the creep keeps saying he'll be fine!

He must've finally realized what I was doing, because he snatched my wrist, pulling it away from his side. He held it firmly as he glared me down. Two could play at that game.

"Your wound is healed," I said, my tone daring him to lie.

He didn't respond.

I wished I could get a better read on his aura. It wouldn't tell me what he was thinking, but it would at least let me know what he was feeling. The two were strongly related. If he was happy, I could count on him having positive thoughts. If he was angry, then it would be the opposite. But Jeph wore a mask the way one might wear a poker face.

The problem was, I couldn't figure out which part of him was the mask and which part was the real him. Every time I thought I'd figured it out, he did something completely out of character—like force me to look away from an innocent girl's execution or punch a wall because he couldn't stop her murder. Yet he took pride in being a killer. He was such a mystery, between those cheeky smirks and those dirty comments, his no-nonsense attitude and his complete disregard for my personal space, his quick wit and his obnoxious cockiness, I didn't know *who* Jeph was. I didn't think I ever would.

Then, there were moments like this. If I stared into his eyes long enough, I could almost see through the carefully constructed walls guarding his true self—guarding his heart—protecting him from those he perceived as a threat. I was a threat.

"You should get some rest," he finally said. "We're breaking out of here at daybreak."

That was another thing. He was always looking ahead, always planning for what came next. He'd been smart enough to find us clothing, and now, he was already looking ahead to our escape. It was so unlike me; I usually flew by the seat of my pants.

"Right," I murmured, getting to my feet.

He stood, offering me the straw mattress.

"Aren't you gonna sleep?" I asked.

"One of us needs to be awake so we don't oversleep."

"That's ridiculous!" I protested. "How do you plan to function if you're not eating or sleeping?"

"I don't need to function. I'm not the one who's going to get us home."

"Yeah, but…you're no good to either of us if you drop dead from exhaustion."

"I'll be fine."

"No, Jeph. You really won't."

He cocked his head to the side. "Looking into my future?"

"No," I said, approaching him and looking up into his face. "I don't need magic to predict that your body is going to shut down after barely eating, battling for your life, bleeding and being injured—even if those wounds seem to *miraculously* be gone—and barely sleeping last night. And *don't* tell me you slept. You were gone and back with provisions by the time I woke up."

A tick worked in his jaw, and now that I was looking, I could see the faint shadows under his eyes. I reached up, tracing those circles with the tip of my finger. He watched me, those calculating eyes trying to read me.

"Get a few hours of sleep," I said gently. "If you're that worried about daybreak, I'll stay up."

"No."

"No?"

"You need to sleep more than me."

"And you need sleep period!"

He glared.

I glared back. "If you don't sleep, I'll leave your ass here when my magical energy comes back," I threatened.

Jeph scoffed. "Like you would—you're like, a goodie-goodie two-shoes."

I crossed my arms over my chest. "Try me."

"Why demand I rest if you're just going to leave me here to rot?"

I shrugged. "Opportunity to rid myself of an enemy."

That was the wrong thing to say.

His entire face closed off, expression becoming blank and gaze going distant. "Go to sleep," he said dismissively, turning his back on me and staring at the bars.

"No."

He whirled back around, a crazed look in his eyes. "No?"

"No." I arched a haughty brow. "If you're not sleeping, then I'm not sleeping either. We can just leave now."

"It's the middle of the night in a foreign world, Sam!" He threw his hands in the air. "We're safer in here until it's light out. At least there's shelter and relative protection here."

"If neither of us is sleeping, then what's the point of shelter?" I shrugged. "Let's just go."

He growled, getting right in my face. I didn't flinch, meeting him growl for growl.

"You. Are. *Infuriating!*" he ground out.

"Says the obnoxious asshole! Besides, why request we be tossed in here together if you wouldn't be able to sleep?"

"Are you dense?" Jeph demanded. "Did you see how those pigs were looking at you? Who knows what one of them would've tried if you were left in a cell on your own!"

My mouth was suddenly dry. "You...you did this for... *me?*"

"No, I did it because I clearly hate myself," he muttered sarcastically, but there was no lie in his aura. Before I could contemplate that, he barreled on. "I may be your enemy, but I'm not about to let some disgusting, ancient man violate you! And trust me, precious, at least one or two of them was thinking about it."

"I'm literally filthy and smell horrible; they wouldn't want—"

"Jesus! You've got to be the stupidest woman I've ever met!"

"Excuse me?" I hissed, two seconds from strangling him.

"You don't even know how goddamn beautiful you are, do you?" Jeph snapped, making my heart leap in my chest, but his next words had me shaking all over. "You think a little dirt is going to stop them from…from—" His lip curled back in disgust. "They're cruel, vicious men who don't care about anyone but themselves and their own pleasures. They force people to *kill* each other for entertainment, Sam. You really think any of them will care if you *smell?* If you're *dirty?* Did you see how disgusting their own hygiene is? They wouldn't even think twice about it."

My stomach curdled, fear churning and making me nauseous. Because he was right. Lord Edward had made it clear he wanted me dead. Had made it clear he expected either me, Jeph, or both of us to die in the arena tomorrow. What would he care if someone assaulted me? What if Lord Edward himself came to do to me what he'd done to Ara…

"I may be a monster, but even I have morals," Jeph whispered, his gaze far, far away.

Monster.

Was Jeph a monster? He was rude, controlling, and mischievous, but that wasn't enough to make him a monster on its own. It just meant he was obnoxious and an ass. He was also a liar, a thief, and a conman, but that still didn't make him a monster—immoral, but not a monster, per se. He *was* a murderer, though, but was that because he was a Hunter or because he truly enjoyed killing people? Did it matter either way?

A soldier killed men defending their country, or sometimes—most times—it was a battle over the stupidest, pettiest things. Oil. Land. Money. All resources the wealthier party didn't actually need, but things they simply wanted. Did that make the soldier a monster for going to war, or just someone caught in the web of patriotism? Did that make the commander the monster? The man at the very top? Or were none of them monsters at all?

A soldier might say he wasn't a monster, even if he was. Some might be, most wouldn't be, but morals and intentions factored into every individual interaction. Was it ever truly okay to take a life?

If Jeph was a soldier of his guild and he viewed himself as a monster, could he really be one? Only monsters thought themselves guilt-free. Only psychopaths thought themselves sane. Only murderers thought themselves justified. Jeph was holding himself accountable for his sins. And suddenly his aura made sense—so, so much sense. He harbored the weight of every kill because he felt it in his heart and soul.

But that brought the question full circle: Was Jeph a monster or not? He'd killed and felt guilt—but he'd done it anyway. *But what about the innocent man? The man he'd spared because that man hadn't deserved his sentence?* That didn't sound like a monster. Neither did someone who'd had the forethought to keep me from potential danger tonight. Someone who'd been grieving Ara's death right along with me—I just hadn't realized it until now.

And what about me? I'd killed someone. It hadn't been the first time, not by a long shot. But it was the first time I'd held the weapon—pulled the trigger, so to speak. It had been the first time I'd known what I was doing—the potential consequences of my actions. Did that make me a monster?

"Try not to think about it," Jeph had said. *"Don't let it eat away at your soul."*

Could a monster—a true monster in heart and soul—really say something so compassionate? He knew guilt, regret, pain, suffering, and sorrow. He was damn good at hiding it, damn good at putting on a show, but his aura told me everything he refused to say aloud. He wasn't a monster; he just thought he was.

I swallowed, hesitantly reaching a hand toward him, but he straightened up, stepped away, and stomped past me, slumping onto the bed in anger.

He laid down, glaring at me. "Either get over here and sleep, or I'm going to strangle you until you pass out—don't think I won't."

And he's back to being a dick.

"That's counter-productive!" I yelled.

"Try me," he mocked.

I stomped over to the bed, my huffing and puffing nowhere near as grand or dramatic as his had been. Once there, I briefly contemplated my life and how it had come to this—to sharing a small sleeping space with my enemy…with a man who would kill me…with a man who'd kissed me to save my life. I *so* wasn't going there right now.

I plopped down onto the straw bed, hissing when it pulled my shoulder wound.

"Could you be any more reckless?" he snapped.

"Yes!"

"*Don't.*"

"Is that a challenge?"

"No, precious, it's not. Now turn over."

"You turn over," I muttered. "I'll be big spoon this time."

His eyes narrowed. "Are you making a joke?"

"Are you laughing?"

"Nope."

"Didn't think so."

I turned over, and despite there being more than enough room for us both, Jeph pulled me flush against him, fitting our bodies together like a glove. I would've protested, but he was shaking. His fingers curled into the skirt of my dress so tightly, I had no doubt his knuckles were white. He was upset, and I didn't think it had anything to do with our yelling match. Biting my lip, I pressed against him, trying to provide him some comfort. His steady warmth enveloped me, and his grip loosened ever so slightly.

It didn't take long for exhaustion to pull me under, the screams of the dead following me into my dreams.

I woke up to a mild headache and the worst taste in my mouth. I wasn't sure if I just had ale-breath, or if I'd secretly eaten a village of trolls in my sleep. I *did* have a bit of a hangover, I realized, as the room seemed to spin around me.

Tackling one thing at a time, I tried to work up some saliva, licking something crusty and flaky from my lips. It tasted irony and mildly sweet, familiar, almost. But I couldn't place it. Next, I sat up and blinked myself awake, my eyes landing on Jeph's back. Then, I rubbed my eyes because I couldn't be seeing things right.

No, still there...

Somehow, he had materialized the food from last night. My brain was a little foggy on the details, but I did remember the food disappearing. Where had he even been keeping it? I vaguely remembered him gathering it with his magic, but there was no way he'd had that on him all this time...Had he?

"Come eat," he said, not looking up from the food he was laying out on a piece of cloth.

"How did you know I was awake?"

"You're the loudest mouth-breather I've ever met."

"I am *not!*" I screeched.

"And you snore."

"No, I don't!"

"They say denial's not just a river in Egypt."

I would've snapped back at him, but his words had my heart lurching in my chest. This situation was so similar to my adventures before, it was unreal. While Ancient Egypt might have started the legend of the Sibyl, that legacy carried on nearly one thousand years later into this era. But that wasn't what had me upset.

I missed Phoenix. I never thought I'd live to feel that way, considering nine days out of seven we were at each other's throats, but I did. I missed his simple presence when we were on good terms, how we could coexist in a space without needing to say a word, how he understood me, and how he was always there for me—even if he ripped me a new asshole later for being reckless or careless. I missed having someone to confide in, to talk to, who would hear me out, who would plan with me and scheme, keeping me ducking and dodging enemies.

He'd been in my life every day since I'd met him in Ancient Egypt. When I was thirteen, he'd been the kind young man who'd helped me recover from the desert. When I returned home, he'd been the very dead ghost who'd told me stories of what had happened after I left. After he'd died...

Died. That was such a mild term for what had happened. *Phoenix hadn't simply* died *at the age of twenty, he'd...*

My lips quivered, tears springing to my eyes. Jeph looked over his shoulder, and I had to look away. I didn't want him to see my guilt, my shame, my secret, my pain. I wished Phoenix would hate me.

Goddess, it would be so much easier to bear if he would just hate me.

"Are you going to eat or not?" Jeph asked, turning back to the food. "We need to get moving."

Squatting next to him, I grabbed a hunk of lukewarm chicken and grimaced. I was going to get food poisoning, but I couldn't exactly be picky or choosy. We ate in silence, finishing off most of what he had gathered. By the time we were done, there were only a few small pieces of cheese left. He scratched his cheek, contemplating what to do with it. I didn't think it would hold over much longer. It was bad enough we'd already eaten what was likely spoiling food, but tossing out any food at all would be a waste. He must've come to the same conclusion, because he wrapped it back up, putting it in his pack from the other day.

When had he gotten that back?

"Where did you get that?"

His brow arched. "Get what?"

"The pack. I thought the slavers took it."

"They did."

"When did you...?" I trailed off, overwhelmed—and mildly terrified—by all the new surprises Jeph presented me with.

First, he could spar like a ninja. Next, I learned he could dual-wield swords. Then, he had that creepy darkness that seemed sentient in the way Chaos was, and he could heal like nobody's business. In addition to being ruthless, a thief, and a conman, he was also apparently adept at sleight of hand. And he had magical energy for days or something because he was *powerful*.

"Took it when our whip-happy friend and I were having our nice little chat."

"Right," I drawled before changing the subject. "Did you sleep?"

"Yup."

Jeph shifted behind me, taking my shoulders in his hands. He traced a finger over my wound, sparks and gooseflesh following his touch. I shivered, unable to stop myself. It seemed like the tingles were getting worse with each passing day— stronger—as if something was growing between us. Which was stupid, because I definitely thought he was an asshole.

I don't have feelings for him or anything. Not even a little. Nope.

But only one other person had had that tingle to their touch. Just one. Yet I'd danced with many Norms over the years, had battled many Hunters, had crushed on boys in high school, and the kinds of butterflies those guys had given me were nowhere near what simply being in the same room with Jeph did to me.

And I don't even like him.

"So, what the hell is it?"

"What the hell is what?" Jeph asked.

My heart shriveled. *Did I say that out loud?*

I cleared my throat. "N-Nothing."

"Sounds like something."

"No," I drawled. "It's nothing."

"*It's* nothing? So, it's something," he said wryly, his thumbs rubbing over my shoulders. I wasn't sure if he was doing that on purpose or if he knew he was doing it at all, but it sent more sparks shooting along my skin.

"Stop that," I said breathily, hating myself for it.

"Stop what?"

"Whatever spell you're using."

"What spell? I'm not using a spell."

"Yes," I gritted out, "you are."

"Do you feel me using magical energy?"

"No."

"Then I'm not using a spell. That would be stupid. We're trying to avoid the Hunters, not attract them to us."

"Then why does it—" I cut off abruptly, realizing I'd just dug my own grave.

"Why does 'it' *what?*"

"Why does…Why does…" I was so, so screwed. "Why does it feel like that?"

"Why does what feel like what? You're not making any sense."

"Your touch," I whispered, hating how nervous the words made me feel.

"What about it?" There was something sly in his tone, cocky as if he was enjoying my squirming. "Are you saying you like my touch?" He traced a hand along my back again, fiery heat blazing over my skin, and I gasped, the feeling a hundred times worse than before. "I'll take that as a yes." He chuckled. "Naughty, naughty, precious."

"No!" I tried to sound less breathless than I felt. "Don't you feel that?"

"Feel what? The goosebumps on your skin?"

"No," I gritted out, irritated with how smug he sounded. "The"—I hated myself—"*tingles.*"

Jeph's hand stilled on my back. I didn't know whether to take that as "yes" or "no." He was probably laughing at me. Perhaps he was insulting me in his head. Or…or maybe he felt them too.

"So, I make you all tingly?" he asked, tone mocking. "*Precious, precious.* You do know this is all just an act, right? The false relationship, the protective act, the *kiss.*"

I'd finally had enough. Embarrassed or not, I'd asked an honest question, and he was being a dick. "Your bravado," I shouted, turning and glaring him down. "Your bullshit and lies!"

His eyes widened. "What?"

"You're so full of shit!"

"We all are—intestines and all that."

"You're not funny!"

"I'm hilarious," he said, grinning.

"You're an asshole."

"And *you*"—he poked the tip of my nose—"apparently like it."

"I hate you!"

Jeph's expression didn't change, but his aura flinched like I'd physically slapped him. "As you should."

"I do."

"Good," he said, almost sounding...*relieved?*

I opened my mouth to argue more, but stopped, brow furrowing when the motion of raising my arm, angry finger leveled at his nose, didn't hurt. I'd been so distracted by his touch, so distracted by him and his stupid nearness, it took me longer than it should've to notice what I *hadn't* felt when he'd touched my wound. There hadn't been pain. When I reached behind me to touch the puckered flesh, all I found was *smooth* skin.

"Can I ask you a question?" he asked, not meeting my gaze.

"You're going to anyways, so why not?"

"Did you ever," he paused, scratching the stubble on his cheek, "meet someone?"

"I've met lots of people," I muttered sarcastically.

"In the graveyard."

"How did you know I go to the graveyard?"

"Reports." *Lie.*

I glowered. "If you've read the reports, then you should know the answer to that question."

"Did you meet a boy?"

"A boy? That's not very specific..."

"Blonde, probably. With hazel eyes."

My brow furrowed. "That's...That's a really random question."

"Just"—his fists clenched and unclenched—"answer it."

I'd met a blonde earth elemental the same day I'd met Jeph, but since he'd been lying about the reports, there was no way he would know that I battled mages from another guild. Even if he did, I wasn't sure if Mr. Mother-Nature had hazel eyes or not. I hadn't gotten close enough to find out.

"Not that I recall," I said, hoping that would end his insistent line of questioning.

"Six years ago."

"What?"

"On Halloween. He would've been about thirteen."

Now, I was really confused. He was getting more and more specific with each thing said, more nervous, too. His aura swirled with fear and hope, dread and regret.

I'd first visited my mother's grave alone six years ago. I'd done it on Halloween, while my dad had been at work, after my aunt had dropped me off following a night of trick-or-treating with my cousin. They didn't know I'd snuck back out. Hecate was my favorite goddess, and I'd believed she would grant me the sight to see my mother's spirit, the ability to commune with the person I missed most in the world. I'd been twelve and naïve as to what I'd been hoping for. My mother's spirit had been long gone, but the spirits who remained were obnoxious.

But how could Jeph possibly know I'd been there that long ago?

"What does this have to do with anything?" I asked.

"It has everything to do with nothing."

He turned his head to meet my gaze, something sad, haunted, and lonely—something *vulnerable*—lurking in his eyes. My answer mattered to him, not that I had the slightest clue why. Did he think I'd met someone he'd known? He wasn't blonde or hazel-eyed. Not to mention, with the age difference between the boy and himself, it couldn't have been him.

"I never met a boy on Halloween," I finally said.

Jeph became eerily still. "You didn't?"

"Nope."

"You're sure?"

"Yup."

"You really did forget…" he whispered, staring at the wall.

"Forget what?"

"We need to get going," he said, getting up.

"Wait," I scrambled to my feet, standing in front of him. "What did I forget?"

"Nothing." *Lie.*

"Who did I meet?"

"No one important." *Lie.*

He tried to brush past me, but I grabbed his arm.

"It was you, wasn't it?" I didn't know why I asked. Nothing he'd said added up, but my gut screamed *jackpot!*

His eyes bore into mine. "Either you remember the boy or you don't. Make up your mind."

"I *don't* remember meeting anyone, Jeph. I went trick-or-treating with family, snuck out when no one was looking, danced for my mom, and went home."

"You didn't dance *for* your mom, you danced *on* her grave."

My eyes widened in shock. "How did you…?"

"Because I *saw* you."

"You…" My heart lurched. "The guilds…this whole time…they've…"

No, no, no, no, no! Not safe. Nothing and nowhere is safe.

"I didn't know who you were," he said. "I thought you were a Norm."

"A Norm? A *Norm!* Ha! Goddess, I *wish!*" Then, I dissolved into hysterical laughter, fingers skimming along my scalp as I grabbed fistfuls of my hair.

"Sam."

I kept laughing, mania setting in.

"*Sam!*" He grabbed my shoulders and shook me.

"You're going to take everything from me, aren't you?" A single tear escaped my watering eyes, rolling down my cheek. "My sanctuary. My sanity. My life. I wish you'd just kill me now and get it over with."

"I'm not going to kill you." *True.*

"Of course not! You need me—my *magic*. This stupid, *stupid* magic!"

"I do need you," he whispered. *True.*

"Just do me a favor and make it quick when you kill me. I don't want to suffer."

His jaw set. "Any other requests?"

"Tell me."

"Tell you what?"

"Tell me what I don't remember—*why* don't I remember?"

"I don't know why you don't! I just thought you didn't recognize me because of my costume."

"Then what don't I remember?"

"If you don't remember, then I'm not telling you."

I scoffed getting right in his face. "Then why bring it up at all?"

"Because!"

"Because why?"

"Because of your stupid question!"

"What question?"

"This!" Jeph shouted, running a hand along my cheek and down my neck. It sizzled with his touch, sparks and tingles trailing along my skin.

I gasped, eyes closing against the assault.

"*You* hexed *me*," he growled, his breath dancing over my face and lips. He was close, so close, but I couldn't bring myself to pull away.

I shivered, and his nails lightly dug into my shoulder as he continued to run his hand along my skin. "I didn't," I breathed. I'd been twelve and hadn't had magic, let alone the knowledge to perform spells.

"You branded me that night."

"How?"

"Like this," he whispered, his lips ghosting over mine.

Gasping, my hands fisted in his tunic, and I stretched up on my toes, pressing my lips more firmly against his. He growled, pulling me to him, his lips burning fire over mine. I moaned, trembling in his arms as he fit me closer and closer against him, so close I couldn't breathe—I didn't want to.

My fingers tangled into his hair, holding him to me as his lips slanted against mine, tongue stroked along mine. His taste was heady, and it set my body on fire. Everything tingled. Everything sizzled. There was a hunger in my soul, and it screamed for him. It cried, *mine, mine, this is mine!* But he wasn't; I wasn't his, either.

Terrified, I tore away and shoved him, making us stumble backward.

We panted, him looking as wild-eyed and bewildered as I felt. When I could breathe again, I ran the back of my hand over my mouth, trying—and failing—to rub away the feel of him, the taste of him, the irrational need to grab him and kiss him again.

"So, an accidental hex," I breathed. "Is that a thing?"

"Depends on the spell you used."

"But—!"

"You don't remember," he muttered bitterly. "There are only two ways to break a charm, curse, or hex—well, three, depending on how powerful the spell is."

"And those are?"

"The first is to break or disenchant any talisman holding the spell."

"I wouldn't have used a talisman." I didn't even know what I could use as one to begin with.

"The second is for the caster to undo the curse. Or, if the victim knows they are being spelled and knows the counter curse, they can reverse it."

"And the third option?" Since I didn't know any curses now, there was no way I knew curses six years ago.

"You deplete the magical energy fueling the hex."

"But that would…"

He stared into my eyes. "Kill the caster, yes."

"So…My death would…"

"Would free me from your spell? Yes, it would."

Twenty-One

"We've wasted enough time," Jeph said, turning his back on me and heading to the cell door.

He held a hand out, and it clicked open. That was it. Just a swipe of his hand and the damn thing swung open. I suddenly felt a hell of a lot less secure about my apartment. I knew the door wouldn't hold if Hunters came crashing through, but I'd at least thought the locks would slow them down.

No wonder Evander thought I was a moron. No wonder his compound was warded out the ears. If I survived long enough, I would seriously need to consider buying wards of my own—if I could even figure out *where* to buy them or *how* to use them. Maybe if I was sly enough, I could get Evander to answer those questions. Hell, considering his high and mighty superiority complex, he might grill me on the information like a drill sergeant.

I followed Jeph down the corridor, all but running to keep up with his clipped pace. I wasn't sure if he was just ready to be out of this infernal dungeon or if there was a need to be hasty. Or maybe he just wanted to get as far away from me as possible. We made several twists and turns, and I was just starting to question why we hadn't run into any guards…when we did.

Jeph turned a corner and collided into someone. The two bounced off each other, staggering backward. The good news was the guard was alone. The bad news was that he had a sword. We had nothing. Which, as it turned out, wasn't a problem at all. Jeph used magery to quicken his step, appearing behind the guard in a flash, a roundhouse kick sending him smashing into the far wall. His iron and chainmail armor clattered against the stone, and we both grimaced, the sound echoing down the corridor.

"Did you hear that?" a voice asked from not far behind us.

"Time to go," Jeph hissed, grabbing my hand and pulling me.

We ran, and I panted with the effort of trying to keep up. I kept stumbling and tripping over my feet and the uneven dirt ground. Jeph was fast—*really* fast—and I hated that I was slowing him down. If he didn't have to worry about me, he'd likely be out of the winding halls of the dungeon already.

Feet pounded the ground behind us, making my heart shrivel. Chainmail clinked angrily as the footfalls grew faster and shouts erupted in the corridor. Jeph threw a glance over his shoulder. His eyes went wide as he skidded to a stop, catching me against his chest. Then, he whirled us around, right as—

He growled, teeth bared, eyes clenched shut, his head bowing backward, an arrow sticking out of his back.

"Oh, goddess!" I breathed.

"After them!" a guard yelled.

"Sound the alarm!" another shouted, followed by a sharp, high-pitched noise, splitting the silence. A bell tolled, and my blood turned to ice.

"Run!" Jeph barked, shoving me in front of him.

I did, and we rounded another corridor, finding more guards. I skidded to a stop, and Jeph grabbed me around the waist, turning us and shoving me toward the other hallway. We sprinted, and I shrieked as arrows flew past us. They pinged off the walls and embedded into the dirt floor in front of us, the volley slowing me down. I kept throwing my hands up to protect my face from debris when dirt flew and arrows broke, ricocheting off the walls. One slashed me across the cheek, the metal tip whizzing past my head when I turned my face a moment too late.

Jeph grunted, and I looked over my shoulder. He'd been hit in the calf, but that wasn't all I saw. My gaze met the eyes of a guard as he pulled his arrow back, stopping and aiming for the center of Jeph's back. My gut twisted. He was close enough not to miss. Panicked, I rammed my shoulder into Jeph, sending us crashing into the wall.

The guard's arrow whizzed past us, and Jeph roared in pain. The one in his back had snapped on impact. Our forward momentum dragged us painfully along the jagged, stone wall, wrenching an agonized scream from my core. It was worse when we tripped over each other, rolling over the dirty ground. Arrows scraped and bruised my skin as we crushed them under our combined weight. We came to a stop, the guards getting closer. I sprawled across Jeph, body beaten and battered from our tumble. Groaning, I reached for my throbbing forehead. I didn't remember hitting it on anything, but the blood that came away on my hand told another story.

"Fuck!" Jeph shouted, lifting his hand and shooting a bolt of magical energy at the guards. They flew backward, crashing into each other and falling to the ground. It wouldn't be enough to keep them down, but it would buy us a few minutes.

"You can't use magic!" I hissed. "The Hunters!"

"I *am* a Hunter! We'll deal with them when they get here."

He wobbled to his feet, hand braced against the wall, dragging me up with him. I gasped in agony, every muscle feeling torn apart. I was too scared to look down. If I didn't remember hitting my head and *it* was bleeding, I was terrified to discover how many gashes I might find everywhere else.

"Keep going!" he yelled.

I didn't know where the willpower came from, but I kept going.

We emerged from the underground, finally hitting ground-level. Servants screamed as we passed, covered in blood, dirt, and goddess only knew what else. We must've looked terrifying because they jumped out of our way as we barreled up the hall toward the main entrance.

When we reached the end of the corridor, someone came around the corner, and I plowed right into them. We tumbled, rolling across the floor and smacking into the far wall. My head cracked against the cobblestone, dazing me and stealing the hearing in my right ear. It rang, and my vision danced like lightning bugs in the night sky. Blinking the darkness from my eyes, I pushed myself to a sitting position and found Lord Edward doing the same thing under me. I'd landed on him, I realized, at the same time he did. His expression ranged from pain to shock before settling on rage.

He reached for me, but I was quicker and angrier. My fingers curled around his neck, savagery I didn't know I possessed taking over. But I didn't just choke him—oh, no—I began bashing his head into the floor. His hands wrapped around my throat, him bucking and flailing wildly to get me off of him. But I wasn't going anywhere; he'd have to kill me. I didn't care if he did—so long as I killed him first.

Then, Jeph was there, wrapping strong arms around my waist and tugging at me. But I didn't let go. I held onto Lord Edward's throat, and my prey snarled, holding onto mine. I wasn't breathing, but I didn't care. If I couldn't breathe, then neither could he because I could see the welts my thumbs had left in his throat, could see his face purpling from lack of oxygen, could see his eyes bulging, and I'd reveled in the sound of his skull cracking against the floor. But I couldn't do that now, not with Jeph still trying to pull me away.

"We need to go," he hissed in my ear.

"Not 'til he's dead!" I tried to screech, but it came out garbled.

"He's not worth it."

"He killed her!"

"Sam, listen to me," Jeph said urgently, giving me a tug. "He's important to the timeline, right?"

I didn't respond, still pressing harder into the lord's throat, his chunky, thick throat.

"You're not a killer, Sam. And the consequences aren't worth this man's life."

I let out a keening laugh. "Says the murderer."

"Let go, Sam. The guards are almost here."

I gritted my teeth stubbornly, my eyes boring hatefully into Lord Edward's. Disgust filled his eyes—hatred, malice, and fear. Fear of *me*. In the darkness of his pupils, I could see my snarling face reflecting at me, and it was so startling I let go.

"That's it, precious," Jeph murmured against my ear, ripping Lord Edward's hands from my throat. "He's not worth sinning for."

Before he could get me far enough away, I pulled my fist back and clocked the vile piece of shit in the face, reveling in the sound of his nose crunching. It hurt my fist—hurt really bad—but the sight of Lord Edward's blood gushing down his face brought me inner peace.

"For Ara," I whispered to myself, and I swore, out of the corner of my eye, I saw her smiling face, grinning cheekily, right before her translucent form vibrated and vanished into the ether.

"I think she'll appreciate that," Jeph murmured, setting me on my feet.

I nodded once, and we turned back toward the front entrance, running out the door and across the courtyard. So close—we were so, so close! We made it to the closed gate, and I skidded to a stop. Jeph flung his hands wide, and it exploded under the force of his magic. Splinters of wood rained down, snagging in my hair and on my clothes, and we sprinted through the opening, into a field.

"Almost there!" he shouted, dragging me, my hand sweating in his. "Don't look back!"

An arrow whizzed by my head, so close it nearly grazed me. I screamed, and more arrows rained down from the sky, some way off course, others too close for comfort. I was just glad cannons hadn't been invented yet because even if they missed, I wasn't sure we'd survive the debris. Well, maybe; Jeph had scary-good timing and reflexes.

Every muscle screamed and protested as we ran through the field, dodging fire. Even worse, my already pained calves burned as we climbed the hill toward the forest. I slipped, my legs giving out, and Jeph caught me, carrying me the rest of the distance. Our enemies couldn't reach us with their arrows now, but if they gave chase, we'd be sitting ducks. Jeph stopped when we reached the tree line and set me down.

Then, he raised both arms, tendrils of black darkness snaking away from him and reaching for the guards chasing us. It slithered around them, trapping them in place. Sweat beaded on his brow, and magical energy rolled off him in waves. The darkness yanked their swords from their hands, and bile rose in my throat, watching the weapons turn on the guards, non-fatally wounding them all. The shouts and screams, the sound of flesh rendering open, the smell of blood on the air, would forever haunt me. Then, a sword, bow, and quiver came floating to us, and Jeph snatched them out of the air, looping the sword's sheath over his chest before handing the bow and quiver to me.

I gaped at him, terror clawing at my heart. *This* was the power of a Councilmember. *This* was Jeph's power, and I had no doubt that had been only a small demonstration of what he was truly capable of. I had never, and would never, stand a chance in a battle against him, but now wasn't the time to think of him as my enemy; now was the time to praise him as my ally.

Swallowing, I whispered, "If you could've done that…"

"I was trying *not* to draw the Hunters to us."

"But we nearly died!"

"Which is why we need to haul ass out of here."

"Yes, but—"

"Let's go."

He turned to walk away, but I grabbed a fist-full of his tunic, forcing him to stop. I reached up, grabbing the broken arrow shaft in his back, and he roared when I tore it out. Cursing under his breath, he mercilessly did the same with the one in his calf before throwing it to the ground.

"You just enjoy making me bleed, don't you?" he gritted out, limping as he walked away.

"It had to come out," I said. "It's probably gonna get infected."

"It'll be fine."

"You *always* say that," I muttered, following him.

His calf and back were bleeding, although not as much as I would've expected. Staring at his wounds reminded me how he'd nearly died, and the thought made my heart squeeze. I'd nearly died, too—but he'd saved me. That arrow had landed low on his back, but at my height, it would've hit my lungs.

I grabbed his shoulder, halting him again, and he whirled around to stare me down.

"What?" he snapped.

"Thank you," I murmured meekly.

He looked dumbfounded. "Huh?"

"The arrow. It would've hit me."

"Just trying to keep the Sibyl alive," he muttered, turning around and trudging on.

I stood there, chewing the inside of my cheek and staring after him. His words were true, but also a lie. Inclining my head, I tried to see other things in his aura, other truths that he wouldn't speak aloud, but his aura had quieted again, locking me out of his mind.

He glanced over his shoulder. "You coming?"

I nodded, walking carefully through the wild forest. He forged a path, pushing aside underbrush, vines, thorns, and other obstacles. When we came to fallen trees, he'd climb up first, turn to me, and offer me a hand. Then, he'd climb down, holding his hands out to help me down. Hours passed, and I became so exhausted, I tripped. Jeph caught me with that billowing darkness that always hovered around him. It was like a second skin, like it was a piece of him, and I wanted to ask what it was, but I didn't want to know.

"We should rest," he said.

I sank onto a patch of mossy ground. Feeling like a sack of leaden potatoes, I sprawled there, eyes fluttering shut. My sore muscles throbbed and pulsed hotly, and I drifted to a place between awake and asleep.

"Do you think we'll make it?" Jeph asked, jolting me from sleep.

"Hmm?"

"To the present. Do you think we'll make it back?"

"I always do," I murmured drowsily. "It's just a little farther away this time."

Well, it was a hell of a lot closer than Ancient Egypt had been. But that time, I'd only had myself to contend with—myself, more patience, and a smaller reputation with the guilds. Having an extra person would take more magical energy, and if we didn't find King, I wasn't entirely sure we *would* make it back. I still didn't know how we'd made it this far. Chaos had nearly exhausted all of my magical energy, but someone else must've shared the burden of that trip. It should've killed me. I hadn't even been *trying* to time travel. I'd only been trying to go from point A to point B. *Something* forced my time magic to flare, but it hadn't been me.

"You make it sound like you make a habit of this," Jeph said.

"My magic is kind of an ass."

"What else can your magic do?"

"What can *your* magic do?" I countered.

He didn't respond.

"That's what I thought," I muttered. "I can't give away all my secrets. It's bad enough you're going to take this much information with you when we…" I trailed off, realizing I'd be so vulnerable when we returned to Seattle, he'd be able to kill me then and there. "Are you going to kill me when we get back?"

He was silent for so long I didn't think he would answer. "I'm not sure."

I arched a brow, sitting up to look at him. He was seated across from me, his back propped against a tree. He'd been watching me, and that knowledge made me hot and cold all over.

"Why not?" I asked. "Don't you wanna break the hex?"

"There're counter curses. I don't *have* to kill you to break it."

"Okay, fine. It's like, your job then."

"You're technically not even my mark. That's Evander's job."

I frowned. "Is that why you came back?"

"Is what why I came back?"

"To check on Evander's progress?"

"What progress?" Jeph snorted. "He's keeping the Sibyl in his home. Those aren't his orders."

"Obviously." I tilted my head to the side. "If not that, why did you come back?"

He shrugged. "It pleases my dark, little heart to piss Evander off."

"That's rude."

"Like you've said, I'm a rude person."

There was so much more to him than he was letting on. He wore many masks, many faces, but none of them were *quite* right. Both his expressions and his aura were hard to read, but I was finally starting to figure him out.

I stared into those dark, dark eyes—eyes made of fire and steel, mischief and wonder, mystery and lies, gravity and stars. "You're not as bad as you pretend to be."

"Who said I'm pretending to be anything?"

"I do."

He was across the clearing and in my face faster than I could blink. I sucked air, my heart leaping into my throat. Something menacing, feral, and animalistic lurked in the depths of his eyes. It made me shiver with trepidation.

He put his lips right next to my ear, speaking low. "Don't presume to know me, precious. I'm more monster than human, and if I want you dead, then I'll kill you. For now, you're my ticket home. For now, you're my plaything—just another defenseless, wounded creature, caught in the hunt leading to your death."

I gulped as he slowly, purposefully pulled away, a cruel sneer covering his lips.

"Enough resting," he said. "Let's go find King."

Twenty-Two

e walked in silence after Jeph's threat, leaving me time to consider his words. The more I thought about them, the more they seemed like a defense mechanism. He *might* kill me as he said, but he might not. Between him constantly harassing me, threatening me, and silencing me, I was left to wonder what he was afraid of me uncovering.

What truth was he trying so desperately to hide?

Twilight was less than an hour away now, and the sky was rapidly darkening under the canopy of dense trees. Jeph stopped walking, turning to evaluate our surroundings. He didn't look at me as he cursed under his breath. Apparently, he didn't like the idea of camping in the woods. I didn't either.

"I should've taken more provisions," he muttered to himself, not looking at me.

"Not like we were in any position to *take* provisions."

He didn't respond, pursing his lips as he looked around.

I scowled. "Did you hear me?"

He still didn't answer.

"So now you're ignoring me?" I snapped, taking a step toward him.

He arched a brow.

I threw my hands in the air. "I didn't even do anything!"

The other brow rose.

I took another step toward him. "Wow. Real mature."

The edge of his lips quirked up.

"What's even your problem?" I demanded, advancing toward him. "I said one little thing and, now, you're throwing a temper tantrum? Grow up!"

He watched me, arms crossed over his chest.

"And y'know what? I've been pretty nice, considering—y'know? Like. You're the big bad Councilmember. Yet I've helped bandage your wounds and stuff! I even saved your ass back there!" I gestured behind me, although Lord Edward's estate was miles away now. "And I keep trying to tell you to take care of yourself—but you won't! It's so infuriating! Like, you need to eat and sleep, too. Maybe that's why you're so grumpy!"

If possible, that pesky eyebrow got even higher on his forehead.

"And it's not like I've pressed you for info or anything—like, you *obviously* have some sort of crazy magic healing power or something—but I'm minding my own business like a decent human being. Just trying to survive, y'know? Get back to my life—which, when we get back, you're gonna kill me while I'm floundering on the ground, trying not to die. Again."

I stood close enough to him that I had to tilt my head back to stare into his eyes. My blood boiled with frustration. There was an almost imperceptible gleam in his eyes, and he was smirking now.

The sick jerk's enjoying himself! Oh, I'll give him something to smirk about!

"And you know what else?" I demanded, chest heaving.

"Hmm, *precious?*" Fire danced in his eyes, challenge filling his tone. His hands fell away from his chest, a grin on his face, and—*damn.* "What else?" His voice was low and husky, his hand rising to tuck a stray piece of hair behind my ear. The brush of his fingertips sent heat and tingles coursing along the side of my face, and I swallowed, my lips parting and my breath catching.

And then my erratic emotions gave way to a vision I didn't want or need to see.

Jeph leans down, his lips capturing Samantha's, cradling her jaw in his hands. She gasps, hands raising, one wrapping around his neck while the other curls into his dark, unruly locks. He moans against her mouth, opening hers with his lips, his tongue stroking along hers. She groans, leaning into him, and he digs his fingers into her waist, walking her backward until her spine hits a tree.

Her hands explore his chest, palms trailing over bare skin as he trembles, gooseflesh following her touch. Her nails dig into his back, and he jerks away with a hiss, head tipping back, eyes clenching shut. Their chests heave, and his mouth covers hers again, his hands seeking and exploring her body. She writhes and moans while he trails kisses along her jaw and down her neck, stopping at her bare clavicle.

Her eyes fly open, a soft cry escaping her lips when he bites her. It's then that she sees the Hunter sneaking up on them. Before she can speak, the man drives his sword into Jeph's back. His dying gasp is raspy, and she screams.

I couldn't breathe, the vision leaving as quickly as it'd come, Jeph already leaning toward me.

"We need to run!" I shouted, grabbing his hand and pulling him.

He only hesitated for a second, my fear enough to convince him something was wrong. We ran deeper into the woods, my legs screaming in protest. It felt like I was running on quicksand, the damp ground sucking at my shoes with each pounding step. And then I tripped, nearly taking Jeph down with me. He tugged my hand, and I came flying back up, my front colliding against his chest. He held me there, both of us panting.

"What are we running from?" he whispered.

"Hunters—they found us."

"And you know that how?"

"I...I saw them. In a vision."

"How many of them?" he asked. "Where are they hiding?"

"I—I don't know."

"Then how do you know they're out there at all? I don't sense anyone."

"They..." I swallowed back bile. "One of them snuck up on us and stabbed you through the back."

He looked skeptical. "I would've sensed them."

"You weren't exactly paying attention to our surroundings…" I flushed, heart rate spiking at the memory of our almost-embrace.

He arched a brow. "Oh?"

"Just—trust me. We need to get moving before—"

An arrow sailed past us, and I screamed, clinging tighter to Jeph. When I looked around the clearing, I realized we were surrounded. Archers, swordsmen, mages—*Hunters*. We were so, so screwed.

"Ah," Jeph muttered. "That would explain it."

"What would explain what?" I hissed.

"Wards."

"Surrender now, Sibyl, and we shall spare you," a Hunter said.

Jeph snorted in disbelief, and for once, I agreed with him.

"I've got a better idea," he said, a haughty smirk on his face. "Wanted to keep this one to myself, but desperate times and all that."

He stretched out his hands and the world fell into darkness. It was reminiscent of going into Chaos, only I didn't *go* anywhere, and there were no twinkling rainbow lights. I blinked, realizing it hadn't gotten dark. Jeph's magic had engulfed us, and it was so dense I couldn't see anything but him. Even he was shades of gray.

He scooped me up in his arms, princess style, and ran.

"I can walk!" I shouted…and then promptly found myself gagged by magic.

"Quiet!" he hissed. "They'll hear you."

I'm gonna strangle him!

Everything was a dark blur as he ran so fast my hair painfully whipped my face. I'd known the guy could haul ass, but goddess in the sky above, this was *insane*.

Magic blasted around us, and I tried to scream while Jeph cursed up a storm. Dirt and chunks of earth spewed into the air, raining down on us. Trees exploded, splinters and hunks of wood flying everywhere. Large rocks and branches went airborne. I was dusted by debris while Jeph dodged and weaved attack after attack.

One nearly clipped us, and my fingers dug deep enough into Jeph's shoulders I was sure I'd drawn blood. He didn't seem to notice, too busy spouting a string of words, sending some of the debris shooting back at our pursuers. I watched over his shoulder as Hunters flew off their feet, some hitting the ground or smacking trees. But for every one that went down, another seemed to materialize out of nowhere, taking his ally's place.

We're going to die!

I almost preferred the arrows of the Norm guards from Lord Edward's estate. These Hunters weren't messing around. I'd had some close calls in my time, but this was nuts! They clearly had zero respect for the land, but I had to wonder if my encounters in Seattle had been milder because of the dense population and infrastructure.

I couldn't imagine present-day Hunters wreaking this kind of havoc just to kill me. The Norms would lose their shit. The damage to the city would be irrevocable. It would cause a war, considering *this* kind of display would scream: *Magic is real, and we're coming for you!* And while magic was real, it was the goal of the guilds to maintain peace and balance by keeping the Magical Community a secret. I was starting to think assholes like these morons were a part of that decree—as in, their stupidity made the need to hide magic a necessity. I would fear magic, too, if this was the demonstration I was given.

Oh. Wait.

Jeph sent the coiled whip of his power shooting behind us. It clotheslined the mages, who acted as if they couldn't see it. When they went down, Jeph put on a burst of speed before suddenly stopping, his chest heaving with his exhaustion. He set me down behind a tree with a firm, "Stay here!" and was gone. I was too dizzy from the sudden stop to protest.

Then, I heard screaming, and I was terrified to look. Grown men shouldn't make that noise, not when they were Hunters, and not when it was just Jeph fighting them—*right?* Gritting my teeth, I turned to look around the tree—and slapped a hand to my mouth, the contents of my breakfast trying to find its way back up. Blood bathed everything in a sea of red. With sickening realization, my brain processed that the lumps on the ground were the bodies of Hunters. They were just *slightly* mangled and *totally* bleeding. A strangled, hysterical laugh escaped my lips.

My knees went weak, and I had to catch myself against the tree. I pushed myself upright, taking leaden, wobbly steps toward the carnage. When I reached the first body, I squatted down, searching for a pulse, and breathed a sigh of relief. Jeph hadn't killed him, but he was gravely wounded.

I stood again, staring at the blood covering my fingers. The man's blood soaked the hem of my skirt. But in all fairness, my dress was already soiled with blood and dirt from escaping the guards earlier. What was a little more blood when I would never be free? Never be clean of sin?

I deserve this; it's only fair after what I did...

The air seized in my lungs as I walked around the fallen mage, heading deeper into the woods to look for Jeph. He'd told me to stay put, but I couldn't, not when he was capable of this— capable of so much more than I ever imagined. I followed the trail of bodies and carnage, winding around trees, debris, and the underbrush. When I got closer, I heard his voice. I couldn't tell what he was saying, but something about it made me stop walking. Malevolent magic brushed over my skin, making the hair on the back of my neck rise. I forced my feet forward, trying to locate which direction his voice was coming from.

"Take this...Give to...Forget..."

I could only make out every other word Jeph said because he was on the far side of the clearing, his back to me. He held a blood-soaked mage around the throat, pressing him against a tree. From this angle, it almost looked like Jeph was... whispering in his ear? That didn't make sense, he'd just been talking to him.

"Jeph..." I called softly, a tremble in my voice.

His back went rigid, his head raising slowly as he stood up straight, not turning around. After a long, silent moment, nothing but the sound of my heart drumming in my ears, Jeph released the Hunter.

"I thought I told you to stay put, precious." His voice was low, silky—*sinister*.

The mage's eyes were vacant as he walked toward me, something clutched in his hand. It was a tall vial of something— maybe a spell or potion. Whatever it was, it was the same color as the blood dripping down the man's chin and neck, which was smeared from Jeph's grip on his throat. One side was bloodless, a lightly puckered scar running the length of his artery.

Adrenaline and fear coursed through my veins as the mage came closer and closer, but Jeph made no move to stop him. Then, my stomach curdled. The Hunter's eyes were glazed, hooded, and *red*. The irises were as crimson as the blood running down his face. There were no wounds, yet he was drenched in gore. He walked past me, not even looking my way, and it unsettled me to my core.

My eyes fell on Jeph's back again. He was still standing there, unmoving. Every nerve ending in my body screamed for me to flee. Every ounce of my skin prickled with fear. Every hair on my arms and neck rose.

When he finally moved, it was to lift his hand to his face and run the back of his arm across his mouth. I waited, breath lodged in my throat, until he finally turned around. His eyes were closed, his entire front covered in gore. It was splashed across him in spurts and splotches, staining his tunic and trousers red. Blood was smeared across his lips and cheeks, splashed along his temples, nose, and forehead.

When he opened his eyes, a soft cry escaped my lips, and I stumbled backward, my foot finding an uneven root. I began to fall, but before I got far—before I could breathe, or blink, or scream—Jeph was there. He caught my waist with his blood-drenched hands, staining me. His fingers held me captive in a vice-like grip, and I stared into irises so red, they were like rubies.

"I said," he murmured in the inhumanly silky voice, making me tremble, "I thought I told you to *stay put*."

He traced a single finger along my jaw and down the vein in my neck, stopping at the base of my throat. My heart lurched, and I couldn't breathe. He leaned forward, and I clenched my eyes shut, turning my face away in fear. His breath ghosted over my ear, making gooseflesh travel down my skin.

"You're right to fear me, precious." It was a whisper—a threat and a promise. It was a death sentence.

A small whimper escaped me, my lips quivering. His teeth sank into the vein he'd just traced, and I cried out. It didn't break the skin, but it hurt. It hurt and…butterflies and anticipation hammered in my chest. I was disgusted with myself, morbid desire filling me. But he was a bloodthirsty creature intent on taking my life. He would kill me if I didn't stop him.

"Jeph…" I breathed, my pulse racing.

He growled against my throat, and I bit back a sob.

"We need…we need to find King," I whispered.

He didn't move, but the pressure of his bite let up.

"We're gonna have to walk in the dark." I laughed, high-pitched and strained. "Can't stay here with the Hunters."

His teeth left my skin, and I took a shallow breath, relief nearly knocking me to my knees. Turning my head, I opened my eyes and just about jumped out of my skin. I stared into brown eyes, not three inches away from my own.

"We can't walk through the night," he said, sounding like himself again. "You need rest."

A high-pitched keening noise escaped my throat. It was supposed to be a laugh but sounded more like a drowning kitten sobbing. Tears pricked the back of my eyes, my whole body starting to shake. First, the adrenaline from this morning had wiped me out, then we'd walked for hours. Now, there was this. Another harsh laugh escaped me. One, then another. Soon, tears leaked down my face as I half-sobbed, half-laughed. My lips trembled as much as my body, teeth chattering between the keening noises coming from deep, deep in the recesses of my fractured sanity.

Jeph watched me, his head cocked to the side. "And they say *I'm* insane," he muttered under his breath.

"You are!" I shouted, so far gone, I was basking in Bat-Shit Crazy Ville. "You, me, the mages! All of us!" I laughed, and this time it was throaty with my receding tears. "The whole damn Magical Community! A bunch of mother trucking *nutcases!*"

His lips twitched up before turning into a frown. "Now isn't the time to have a mental breakdown, precious."

"*Sam!*" I screamed in his face. "My. Name. Is. *Sam!*" I grabbed his cheeks, moving his jaw as I repeated my name. "Sam. *Sam!* That's my name, and if you don't start using it, I'm gonna strangle you! But you know what? You seem like the sick kinda fuck that might actually like that—so, better yet, if you don't, I'm just gonna leave you here to rot! See if I give a damn, you *bloodthirsty psychopath!*"

"*God*, I love it when you insult me."

It felt like I'd just smacked an invisible wall. "What?"

He grinned, running the backs of his fingers down my cheek. "I love your quick wit and your smart tongue." He chuckled. "You're such a hotheaded spitfire, precious. It's what made me like you from the first moment we met."

My mouth gaped like a goldfish.

Did he just say he likes *me?*

"That…you don't mean that," I whispered, but I'd seen the truth in his aura.

"There you go again, assuming you know me." His words were gentle, soft. "While you're wrong about *that*, you're one of the few people who seems to understand me. But…you understood me even then…" His eyes stared through me, face pinching in pain. "Why don't you remember me?"

I couldn't answer that question any more than he could, but that wasn't what had my head reeling and my heart lurching. It was the naked, raw truth in his expression—in his aura. *This* was Jeph. *This* was him, the real him, and he was sharing himself with me.

"Why?" My voice trembled, frustrated tears filling my eyes.

"Why what?"

"Why have you been so cruel?"

His eyes snapped to mine, sadness lurking in them. "Because I'm a monster, precious. Monsters are cruel."

"You're not—"

"Stop!" he roared at me. "You don't know the things I've done. The horrible things."

I ran my thumbs over his cheeks. "Jeph…"

"No." His expression closed off, and he pulled my hands from his face. "We're not doing this."

He was pushing me away…again. The only time he didn't was…

"There's no hex, is there?" I whispered, heart sinking.

"There's no hex."

"You lied to me!"

"Newsflash, precious! I lie to *everyone*."

If his aura hadn't been so bitterly pained, I would've been mad.

"Then what is this?" I asked.

"I don't know—and I don't care to find out."

I smirked, reading his aura. "Liar."

"Excuse me?"

"Oh, you heard me, *pal*. I called you a liar. Like you said, you lie to everyone. Even yourself."

"Stop doing that!"

"Stop doing what?" I got a thrill out of baiting him, out of being in control for once, and sick creature that I was, I *liked* arguing with him.

"Stop analyzing me."

"Can't."

"Oh, precious. You don't want to play games with me."

I arched a brow. "Oh, yeah?"

"Yeah," he breathed, eyes flicking to my lips. "You won't like what I do."

"Try me."

He chuckled low and sensual. "Hasn't anyone ever told you playing with fire will get you burned?"

"Burn me, then."

Jeph closed the distance between us, his lips devouring my own. They were hungry. Wild. *Mad.* Hot and insistent, sliding against mine. Over. And over. And over again.

I was frustrated with him. Angry. So, so *furious*. And I wanted him with insanity so profound, I should've been committed. I didn't even care that he was covered in blood—tasted like blood. Didn't care that he'd almost killed me—that he *would* kill me. I just wanted him—*needed* him—and I needed him now.

He kept pushing me away—kept lying—but I wasn't taking "no" for an answer anymore.

I wound my fingers into his hair, yanking it as I pulled him closer. He growled, low and feral. My heart raced, my chest exploding with butterflies and heat when he pressed against me. His tongue found mine, and I moaned, wrapping my arms around his neck. He grabbed my hips, lifting my weight against him, and I wrapped my legs around him, eliciting a groan from us both. Everything inside of me went supernova.

The forest suddenly erupted into flames around us. Terrified the Hunters had come for us, I pulled back, frantically searching the trees. When I didn't find any danger, I looked at Jeph, his eyes hooded with desire, and my heart exploded all over again.

"Fire…" I panted.

"Mmm. Yes. I'm afraid I might've lost control for a second."

My mouth dropped open. "*You* did that?"

His grin was the sexiest thing I'd ever seen. "I told you you were playing with fire."

"Literally…" And then my heart stopped. "Ara!"

"Painless—as quickly and as hotly as I could make the flames burn."

"Jeph…" My chest squeezed, realizing he felt the weight of her death more than I could've ever known.

"Shh," he cooed, brushing his lips over mine. "It's okay. She's—"

I stole his lips, my heart overwhelmed by his compassion and kindness; he really was just one big pretender.

The fire raged hotter around us, our kisses becoming sloppy and desperate, tongues twining, teeth nipping and biting, lips colliding. Nails scraped over flesh, and hair was tugged and pulled. We were nothing more than each new touch, nothing less than the craze overtaking us, and I couldn't think, couldn't breathe. I was pretty sure my heart had exploded minutes ago. I was certain my stomach flew away with butterflies. And my skin? It hummed like a hive of bees had swarmed it, burned like I was drowning in lava, screamed, because Jeph's hands weren't touching nearly enough of it.

He trailed kisses down my neck, moaning and reciting my name like a prayer. "*Sam*," he breathed. "*Sam. Sam. Sam.*"

I shivered, eyes lolling shut, head falling back.

"You're mine," he growled against my skin. "*Mine, mine, mine.*"

"Yes," I sighed. "Keep me, kill me—I don't care. Just don't stop kissing me."

"Oh, precious. I'm *going* to keep you." He kissed me long and deep. "But there's something I have to do first."

I couldn't think, drowning in the feel of him. "Hmm?"

"And you…you have to forget."

My eyes snapped open. "What—"

"I'm sorry," he whispered against my ear. "It's not safe yet."

"J—!"

Darkness blinded me, and something like iron and honey spilled into my mouth. I tried to fight, but Jeph's magic held me firm, held me still as something heady and toxic drained down my throat. I finally placed the taste, finally figured it out, but it was too little, too late. My vision swam, and my head went blurry, fuzzy, and light as a feather. I wasn't just drunk, I was high.

"Forget," he murmured. "Forget this night."

"But…"

"Shh," he whispered against my lips. "No one can know my secret—not even you."

"Jeph, please—"

"And you have to keep hating me. It's the only way to keep you safe."

"No," I whimpered.

"Go to sleep now, precious, perfect Sam." His words were soft, reverent, sad. "It was a fantasy anyway. Only ever a dream…"

Before I could protest again, I felt my thoughts slipping away, my memory stretching thinner and thinner. Where was I? What was I doing? What had happened? What was…? What…?

I slept, dreams of hungry kisses haunting me.

Kisses, and red, red eyes.

The taste of blood stained my lips.

Twenty-Three

J woke up groggy, my head pounding, my mouth dry as cotton, yet my body felt like a million bucks. I sat up, looking around in alarm. I was alone inside a room I didn't recognize, and I didn't remember how I got here. In fact, I couldn't remember...What couldn't I remember?

Jeph and I had woken up, eaten, ran from guards, escaped Lord Edward's estate, walked the forest for hours and hours, and...that was it. That was all I remembered. Everything afterward was a blank. There was nothing there, hours of my life, just—*gone*.

I looked down at myself, finding another new outfit. That set my heart pounding even worse than the gap in my memory. Someone had dressed me, which also meant someone had *undressed* me. And with no memory of it, I wasn't entirely sure that person had been me.

I got to my feet, sparks dancing behind my eyes, my body listing toward the ground. A few blinks later, accompanied by a lot of stumbling and flailing, I managed to stay standing. Turning—slowly this time—I looked around the tiny room. The good news was, it wasn't a prison cell. It was a little room made of wood and a thatched roof.

To my left, there was a small bench for sitting. To my right, some folded clothing and other household supplies sat in neat order. At my feet was a blanket and hay-stuffed mattress, looking cleaner than what I had seen in forever. In the middle of the room, a small fireplace set into the floor, coal lightly burning. A pot was nestled in the embers, an aroma tickling my nose and making me salivate. I stepped toward it, and the door across from me opened. I jumped back, looking for an exit or a place to hide but found nothing.

An old woman's voice came to me, jovial and kind. She was speaking to someone over her shoulder. My heart pounded, arms stretched out at my sides, seeking something—anything—I might be able to use as a weapon. I wasn't sure if the woman was a threat, but the unseen person she was talking to likely was.

Then, she saw me and our gazes met. "Ah, finally awake." A smile broke across her face. "Yous husband has been worried sick 'bout you—poor thing has been beside himself." She came in alone, closing the door behind her.

"My husband?" At first, my brow crinkled in confusion, then my cheeks modeled with embarrassment. Apparently, Jeph was still keeping up the ruse we were married.

The old woman chuckled, walking the three short steps necessary to reach the center of the room. She bent down, picking up a ladle and stirring the pot. "Gave the poor thing quite the scare, you know?" she mused, scooping soup into a dish. "Passin' out in the middle of yous long journey east—was terrified you wouldn't wake up."

"I…passed out?" I asked, my words slow as I tried to piece together the new information. I *had* been exhausted, and I'd definitely taken a blow to the head. I probably even had a concussion or something. I'd likely blacked out after the fourth or fifth hour of walking. It wasn't like I'd had much to eat the last few days, and I hadn't had much time to rest, either.

The woman smiled at me, clucking her tongue as she came around the hearth, holding the soup out to me. "Go on, chil'. You need to rebuild yous strength before you continue yous travels to Canterbury. It still a day's journey off by foot—maybe two."

I took the bowl, trying to understand this woman's kindness and the fact that she knew where we were heading. Jeph must've told her, but that didn't sound like the liar and thief I knew. "And my"—I faltered—"husband?"

"Ah." She smiled wryly. "I chase him outta here a while ago. Stuck to yous side, that one was."

My brow furrowed. "He was?"

She chuckled again. "Eat." She waited until I sipped at my soup—I moaned at the flavor—before she continued. "You poor thin'. Must've been terrified when you woke up in a strange place. I sorry, sweetums. I'd meant to be back before you woke."

I shrugged and kept slurping down the hot soup, not caring that it was scalding my mouth. I was *starving*.

"How's 'bout I start at the beginnin', hmm?" She walked over to the bench and sat down, patting the spot next to her, and I sat. "It was pitch dark by the time yous got to town, yous husband carryin' yous unconscious body. I'd happened to be up late, preparin' sup' for the morrow"—she gestured to the pot of food—"when he stumbled through town, lookin' haggard an' frantic. Yous was both covered in dirt an' mud, your clothin' tattered an' ripped from walkin' the forest. I ask' the poor darlin' why he hadn't come by way of the road, but he said yous was chased off it by thieves an' vagabonds. Scared out his mind, he was."

I had to hold my snort at the thieves and vagabonds comment, considering that described Jeph's behavior these last few days.

"So concerned for you he was, I offered the shelter of my home. Ain't never seen a more dutiful, concerned husband in my life. Fussed over you most the night. I finally tol' him to go get washed up an' changed while I clean you up."

Relief spread through me. This woman had been the one to dress me. Not wanting to worry her, I didn't tell her that the dirt and cuts were from escaping a dungeon.

I was also stuck on just how overstated her claims of Jeph's care were. But…they weren't overstated at all. Jeph had done nothing *but* fuss over my safety. He'd been rude about it, but he'd done everything he could to help me rebuild my strength. He'd fought the Hunters when we'd arrived in the fifth century, had kept me warm through the night, had fought to protect me in the arena, had lied to a Lord to keep me safe, had given up rations of his food and his sleep, and then he'd literally taken an arrow for me *and* had carried my heavy, unconscious ass through the woods when he'd been bleeding and wounded. Even after all that, he'd *still* fussed over me.

My heart pounded, and my palms did a funny tingly thing. That didn't sound like a man only concerned about getting home. That sounded like a man who genuinely...*cared*.

Oblivious to my internal babble, the woman went on. "Yous husband is helpin' the other menfolk right now. Puttin' him to work to keep him from hoverin' over you."

"I'm sorry we intruded on your home. And I'll be sure to return these clothes before we—"

"Nonsense!" She swatted her hand through the air. "I happy to help a charmin' young couple such as youselves. An' I don't need that dress back, chil'. It belong to my daughter before she passed..." Her gaze went distant, and my heart screamed for her pain. "I have no need of it, not when a sweet chil' like yous self does."

"I couldn't possibly—"

"It a gift, sweetums! Don't argue with Granny Edith!"

"Yes, ma'am."

She nodded, appeased. "Now, let's see if we can track down that husband of yous."

I followed Edith into the bustling town. It was awash with blue eyes, blonde hair, and pale skin, and every passerby stopped to greet Edith. Several asked her how she was doing after the loss of her daughter. Others asked where her husband had gotten off to. Children ran up to give her hugs, asking if they could come listen to her storytelling tonight.

My heart felt both light and heavy with each of these interactions. The auras of the Norms told me their inquiries were sincere. These people cared about Edith, and they were genuinely sad that her daughter and the baby had died in childbirth just a few months ago. I wanted to cry and demand Edith take back the clothes she'd gifted me.

I knew what it was like to lose a mother, and I couldn't imagine how it felt to lose not only her child but her grandchild as well. Her aura was still rife with her grief, but she smiled anyway. It was a real smile, too. She loved these people as much as they loved and cared for her. I admired her strength, knowing it had taken me time to recover from my own losses. Seeing ghosts helped me understand my mother's soul was in a better place, hopefully watching over me.

When we reached the edge of town, we finally found the menfolk who were hard at work replacing a fence for some of the town's cattle. From what Edith had told me on our way here, the town had chipped in to purchase a few dairy cows and sheep. It was a communal lifestyle, and they shared the milk and wool. There was no real money in this town, only hard work and pitching in.

As we drew closer, I felt Jeph, my magical energy sensing him as if he were standing right next to me, an insistent hum making my heart jump in my chest. I was hyper-aware of his presence, but I wasn't sure why. He'd been attached to my side for the last few days, however. Perhaps I'd gotten used to his constant companionship. Perhaps I was just codependent upon him the way I was upon Phoenix. My dreams probably hadn't helped anything either.

Then, I saw him, and my stomach tingled.

Stupid, stupid dreams!

His head suddenly jerked up, his eyes locking on mine, and I stopped breathing, watching a gentle smile spread over his lips. A real, genuine smile. My dumb ass shyly smiled back, waving a hand nervously. I wanted to kick myself.

"Ah, young love," Edith murmured, grinning.

"We're n—" I swallowed my protest, remembering the ruse.

Jeph was playing these people like the conman he was, putting on a show for their benefit. He'd needed shelter for us both, and he'd preyed on Edith's kindness. Nothing more. Nothing less.

Then why can't I look away?

He suddenly cursed, yanking his hand back and shoving his thumb in his mouth. I grimaced as the man working with Jeph apologized for smashing his finger with the hammer. He shook out his hand, repeatedly telling the man it was "okay." He meant it, too, which baffled me. Jeph even put his hand back in place, holding the nail again.

When they finished the last post, Jeph was thanked by several of the men—moshed, really—as the older men patted him on the back and shoulder or ruffled his hair. He smiled boyishly, trying to shrug off their gratitude, but they were having none of it. Hammer Man even wrapped an arm around Jeph's shoulders, giving him a little shake and following his gaze when he looked over at me again. Hammer Man said something in his ear, and Jeph nodded. Then, there was much whooping and more back-slapping and noogies, the townsmen moshing him again. Their behavior didn't tell me much more than their auras did; they were excited about something, but I didn't know what.

Jeph's aura was the closest to happiness I'd ever seen it, and that made my spirit feel light. His smile was doing strange things to the butterflies in my stomach, and the glances he kept throwing at me, while the men continued talking to him, had my heart doing pitter-pattery things in my chest. I felt hot and weak in the knees. I didn't think I was breathing, either.

The men finally stopped moshing him, Hammer Man slapping him on the back hard before shoving him in my direction. Jeph stumbled, but it was just an act. He was much too graceful and powerful to be put off his footing so easily, but the nerves in my gut when his gaze met mine weren't an act. He jogged over to Edith and me, scooping me up into his arms and twirling me around once before setting me on my feet and planting a wet one on me. The men behind him hooted and hollered, and their behavior finally made sense. They'd been teasing Jeph about his "wife."

Had they told him to do that? Or was this the act? What else had they said?

I couldn't handle this. My heart couldn't because it pounded in my chest from just a simple kiss. From just his hands holding my waist. From just being near him.

It's the hex, I reminded myself. *The hex is making you feel this way. And his behavior is just an act for the townsmen.*

Those thoughts hurt me in a way I didn't want to analyze.

When Jeph pulled away, his hands came up to cup my cheeks, his thumbs tracing over my face. He stared into my eyes, something so raw in his gaze, there wasn't enough air on the planet to keep me breathing. I didn't need to see his aura to see the truth of his gesture in his eyes. And then he completely closed off—his gaze, his aura, his smile—gone in the blink of an eye, leaving me reeling.

"I tol' you she be fine," Edith said, rather smugly.

Jeph stepped away from me, the distance like walking into the bitter cold of winter. "You did."

"I tol' you she jus' need rest."

"You did," he said again. "But she nearly slept for a whole day."

"A whole *day?*" I demanded, incredulous. "I slept an entire *day?*"

"You must've needed the sleep after…" He trailed off, eyes darting to Edith. "Visiting uncle Edward."

I shuddered, disgusted at the thought of that man as anyone's uncle.

"Yous had a long journey," Edith said, nodding. "Which is why yous can stay in my home tonight—an' this time"—she leveled her finger on Jeph—"you need to rest."

"You're *still* not sleeping?" I glared at him, folding my arms over my chest.

He lifted his hands, palms out. "I *did* sleep. Just not twenty-four hours like you, precious."

"Oh, don't give me none of that!" I wagged my finger in his face. "You barely slept at all—*again*—didn't you?"

"No! I really slept."

"Uh-huh, sure. And I bet you 'ate'"—I air quoted—"too, right?"

"I did eat!"

Edith snorted, laughing loud and sharp. "Such a sweet, young couple. My husband an' I bicker just like yous do."

Heat rose in my chest and neck, and I pointedly avoided Jeph's gaze. I'd never had a boyfriend before, so I wasn't sure what a relationship looked like. I'd seen people date in high school, of course, but being on the outside looking in wasn't the same thing. Was it normal to bicker? Or was that just proof that we could never work as a real couple?

Why am I even thinking about this?

"We'd be happy to stay with you and your family again," Jeph said, putting his hands on my shoulders. It made tingles race down my spine. "If we're not too much trouble?"

"Nonsense," Edith said emphatically. "Can't have yous traveling at night. Thems ruffians might come back around."

"Thank you, Granny Edith," Jeph said, his tone soft and sincere.

I wanted to turn around and look at him, at his aura, to see if that was genuine gratitude or just another manipulation tactic. With the strange way I'd been behaving today, I didn't dare.

"No trouble, sweetums! An' tonight, I be performing. Yous in for a treat!"

After dinner, everyone gathered around the bonfire, seated on logs, the grass, or simply standing as Granny Edith began to weave her story. It was a quaint little tale about a farm boy who wanted to become a knight.

"He try to appeal to the head knight, who laugh at him an' turn him away 'cause he was too scrawny. So the boy train his body. When he appeal to the head knight again, the man laugh, tellin' the boy he was too simple-minded.

"The boy went home, continuin' to work hard on the farm an' in his trainin', but now he had a tutor to teach him. When he learn to read an' write, an' learn about the histories, he went back to the head knight. The man laughed again, tellin' the boy he may be strong, an' he may be smart, but he too young to fight.

"Years went by where the boy work hard, learnin' an' studyin', an' when he turn sixteen, he finally went back to the head knight.

"The boy said, *'I'm smart an' strong, an' all grown up. I would like to be a knight.'*

"An' the head knight laugh again, saying, *'Come back when there's hair on your chest, young man!'*"

"What did the boy say?" a girl in the crowd asked.

Edith smiled cheekily, putting a finger to her nose before pointing to the girl. "Why, he become a rebel against the courts, of course."

"A rebel?" she whined in dismay.

The whole crowd leaned forward, wanting Edith's answer.

"Of course, sweetums." She chuckled wryly. "It be said the boy has since learn great sorcery—perhaps he knew it all along—but with it, he done many a great an' terrible things."

"Like what?" a little boy asked from Jeph's lap. Kipp had claimed that spot after his father, Hammer Man, came to apologize—again—for smashing Jeph's thumb.

Jeph ruffled Kipp's hair, and he scrunched up his face, scowling.

I bit my lip, seeing the playful gleam in Jeph's eyes.

Kipp liked Jeph's attention; his aura was glowing with admiration. I wondered if Jeph knew that the boy looked up to him. He'd been watching the men work during the day, helping bring nails and other small tools to them while they did the heavy lifting. Apparently, Jeph had taught Kipp how to use a hammer, showing him the proper way to hit the nail "just right" so that it went into the wood smoothly. Jeph would make a good father someday—if he stopped being a psychotic, murdering sadist from Hell.

"Some say he can shake mountains," Edith said, snapping me out of my musings. "Some say he can move the sky. Jus' the other day, he push and pull the ocean the way the moon kiss its surface, like a dance between lovers."

I leaned forward, my heart racing. *It couldn't be...*

"No way!" another child protested. "Yous lying, Granny!"

"It true! Or...so they say." Edith grinned.

"Next you gon' tell us he can dance with fire!" a man from the crowd said.

"He a sorcerer," Edith said, obviously relishing the effect she was having on the crowd. "He can do *anythin'*. Even rally rebel knights to follow him. That, my precious ones, why they call him King."

I couldn't breathe, and Jeph's hand encircled my wrist, squeezing hard enough it almost hurt. It wasn't perfect confirmation, but the fact that King had a reputation that spanned cities increased the odds of the tale being true.

The crowd erupted into shouts.

"You mean that no-good troublemaker from Canterbury?" one man demanded.

"He was a farm boy?" a woman asked.

"He a hero!"

"You mean, vagabond!"

"Disgrace!"

"He stop the Jutes!"

"You think he single?"

"When I get my hands on that punk—!"

On and on, the townsfolk ranted and raved, Edith grinning like a Cheshire cat. She was so small and unassuming with a heart so big, it was shocking to see her behave like a mischievous little girl. I liked her.

"Hush now, sweetums," Edith said, and, to my surprise, the crowd quieted. "It but a story—a legend. Perhaps, his tale. We may never know."

There was a long silence, and then slowly, the crowd began to clap. Their applause became thunderous when Edith performed a bow. Children ran up to hug her around the waist, and she patted them on their heads. There was a sliver of sadness in her aura; she was likely thinking of her own grandchild, whom she'd never get to tell stories to. I marveled again at her strong heart when she picked up one of the toddlers, settling him on her hip and tutting at the children's "ill manners."

Suddenly, a flute sounded a long, low whistle. I was confused for a moment, but then someone started strumming a lute, another person a lyre, and finally, drums began to beat. People clapped along to the tune, and my foot stomped with everyone else's. The music took over, and my need to dance flowed through me.

A grin spread across my face as I got to my feet, my hips rolling, my shoulders swaying, and my hands tracing patterns in the air. Men whistled, women gasped, and children laughed. My grin grew as the clapping got louder and the stomps harder. I closed my eyes, spinning and twirling, my hands clapping and my feet stomping, even as I moved and swayed to the rhythm of the beat. I couldn't stop moving, couldn't stop smiling, and when I felt Jeph's hands wrap around my waist, him moving in time to the music, I opened my eyes. There was a challenge in his, those brown orbs daring me to keep up. A question was in his smile, those full lips a smirk and something *more*.

I arched a brow: *I'm game.*

Jeph's hand pushed and pulled my waist, spinning me, twirling me. The other hand held mine as he led me in circles and twists. My head turned to face him, never losing sight of him, even as my body moved every which way. His gaze held mine. And as the song came to a close, Jeph pulled me to him, dipping me low.

I closed my eyes, feeling the searing heat of his palm against the small of my back, memorizing the feel of his fingers twined in mine as he held me balanced. I reveled in the sweat glistening over my body, the pounding of my heart so familiar I could almost pretend it was any other day at Terry's club. My breaths were shallow and quick, my lungs and throat searing with prolonged activity.

When Jeph pulled me back to standing, the last chord of the song struck, and I opened my eyes, staring into his—drowning in his—getting lost in the deep brown and the intense pull. Jeph was gravity, and I was the moon caught in his orbit. But he was also the waves of the ocean; he only seemed to push and pull when I was near. When we were this close. When...

We leaned toward each other, our eyes closing.

The townsfolk erupted into excited cheers, hoots, and hollers, and we sprang apart. Jeph's chest heaved like mine, and he quickly pulled his hands from me, reality setting in around us. We were in a crowd of people, in a town we didn't belong to, in a world that existed long, long ago. This wasn't real—not for us. And their thunderous applause and joyous laughter was like lightning striking my heart.

Trembling, smile stiff, I dared a curtsey. I didn't look at Jeph, but I felt his aura raging next to mine. He was shaken, and I didn't have the courage to look over at him. I was afraid of what I might see, was scared of what I might feel, was terrified of what I already felt.

Jeph walked away, and the townsmen crowded around me, each wanting a dance of their own. As the night went on, gentlemen young and gentlemen old stealing a dance, some handsy, some flirty, some plain adorable, I couldn't stop my gaze from searching the crowd. He was there, I knew he was, but I couldn't see him, couldn't find him...but I felt his gaze pulling me, his gravity always tugging me back to him.

When we retired for the night, I thought I might die. Jeph and I were given our "privacy" after the "rough evening" we'd had the night before. My heart pounded in my chest at the thought of being left alone with him in a small, little shack of a house, with the pretense of him being my husband, the whole town practically winking and nudging elbows at us. I couldn't seem to catch my breath.

My palms were a tingling mess, like when I got fits of anxiety. My body kept quaking with nervous energy, and I couldn't stop pacing. If I sat down, my legs would start to jump all over the place, *tap-tap-tapping* against the floor in a chaotic storm. I kept wringing my fingers and rubbing my palms, trying to get the pins and needles to stop. Even shaking them wasn't helping.

"You're going to wear a hole in the floor," Jeph said, his eyes trailing me as I walked back and forth, back and forth.

I didn't respond, my pacing matching my rapid pulse with the reminder he was sitting not three feet away. *Why* did I have to have those stupid dreams last night? *Why* did he have to smile at me—*look* at me—the way he had today? *Why* did he have to dance with me?

"Is this what you're like when you've had a good night's rest?" he asked.

I still didn't answer.

"Seriously, though. You're making me dizzy."

I stopped, turning to look at him. It was a horrible idea.

Jeph was lounging on the straw mattress, propped up on his elbow. He had one knee up, his free arm laying across his side. If that and the little bedding we'd been given to share wasn't enough to give me an ulcer, the damp lock of hair falling into his eyes as he looked up at me from under those long, long eyelashes was enough to give me a hernia.

Did I mention he isn't wearing a shirt? There wasn't enough spit in the world to stop my mouth from being this dry. *Could be worse...I could be drooling. That* so *isn't the mental encouragement I need right now.*

"Yeah?" I retorted, somewhat manically. "Sounds like a personal problem."

"Is it?"

"Why aren't you wearing a damn shirt?"

He arched a brow. "Because some of us did manual labor today and didn't want to smell like a pig's pen at bedtime."

"That doesn't explain where your shirt is!"

"Hanging up to dry." He smiled one of his cocky smiles. "Why? Does this bother you?"

"No. You're just horrifyingly disgusting to look at."

"Then stop looking, precious."

"I'm not!"

"Then I don't see what the problem is."

I stopped pacing again, not realizing I'd started back up. "I..." I stammered. "There isn't one."

"Okay," he drawled. "Then what's your problem? Hit your head too hard when you knocked yourself out last night?"

"I did *not* hit my head!"

"Oh, because you remember things that happened when you were blacked out?" His voice was laced with sarcasm.

"No!" I shouted, getting closer and closer to homicidal levels of anger.

"Don't tell me you *dreamed* about me, precious," he said suggestively. "I'm so flattered."

My cheeks flamed. "I wouldn't dream about your ugly mug if it was the last face I ever saw!"

He smirked, and it made me feel like he'd caught me lying. "Then what's your problem?"

"I'm just..." I grappled for an excuse. "I'm just..."

"Just...?"

"I'm ready for tomorrow. After what Edith said—I think King might actually be able to help us."

"That ready to get rid of me, are you?"

"I just wanna go home," I whined. "I miss my dad. I miss the indoors. I miss *toilets.*" If I had to squat in a bush one more time, I was going to scream. And I already knew I would have to in the morning.

Jeph blinked, then he threw his head back and laughed. And laughed. And kept right on laughing until his whole body was shaking, muscles rippling—not that I was looking—as he started coughing, he was so out of breath. I glowered at him, waiting for his little fit to end. He pressed his lips together, trying to stifle his laughs—failing miserably—tears glistening in his eyes.

"That's quite the list, precious."

"Would you stop that?" I asked, exasperated. "Just call me Sam."

"Call me Jeph."

"No thanks, pal."

"Okay, then, precious."

I growled, miming strangulation.

"Oh, make my day," he said, low and husky.

"You're a sick, sick puppy, y'know that?"

"I've been called worse."

I eyed him wearily, exhaustion creeping in. "I'm sure you have, *psychopath.*"

Something glittered in his eyes. "Not the worst, but still true."

I frowned. "Why do you do that?"

"Do what?"

"Put yourself down."

"And you aren't?"

"Well—I'm just being a dick. I kinda do that from time-to-time—especially when assholes like you are pissing me off."

"I piss you off?" He grinned. "I couldn't tell."

"Shut up! Just—why are *you* putting you down?"

He shrugged. "I've been put down my whole life."

"That's…" I frowned, pity filling me. "That's not okay."

"Says the woman putting me down."

"I—" I sighed. "I'm sorry."

"Apology *not* accepted, precious. You don't really mean it, so keep it to yourself."

"You're such a colossal *asshole!*"

"See?" He smirked. "You can't apologize and turn around and do the very thing you *just* apologized for. Naughty, naughty."

I was going to kill him, absolutely going to annihilate him.

"Whatever," I muttered. "I'm exhausted, so I'm going to bed."

I looked around me, frowning. The floor wasn't appealing, but Jeph was *too* appealing. Whether that was visibly appealing or *I'm actually going to strangle him* appealing, I wasn't sure. Muttering under my breath, I sat down, studiously avoiding the smirk on his face. He watched me, and I could practically feel his amusement from across the room. I probably did, considering he was near enough I could *just* touch the edge of his aura with my own.

I laid down, putting my back to him, and tucked my arm under my head, trying to pillow it against the floor. It was uncomfortable, and my arm was tingling in seconds, the blood flow stanched by my head. I heaved a sigh, curling into a ball, trying to stay warm. There were some embers lightly burning in the pit between us, but it wasn't doing much against the cool evening. I withheld my shivers, every muscle tense.

I closed my eyes and tried to sleep.

"Really?" Jeph finally asked, a smile in his voice.

"Really, what?"

"That can't be comfortable."

"It's not."

"I *do* have blankets and pillows over here—and what amounts to a mattress in this day and age."

"Cool for you."

"They were left for *us*."

"Neat."

"Would you like to sleep on the mattress?" he offered.

"Nope."

"I can trade you."

"I'm good."

"Why are you being difficult?"

"I'm trying to sleep, so keep it down, m'kay, pal?"

Jeph growled behind me, setting my hair on edge, but I didn't turn over.

"Don't make me come over there," he threatened.

"You stay on your side of the hut, and I'll stay on mine."

"Fine."

"Fine."

We were quiet, nothing but the sound of our ragged, angry breathing and the low sizzle of coals filling the room. There was rustling on his side—the sound of him settling under the blanket—and my muscles finally began to relax.

Then, something smacked me in the back of the head.

"Ow!"

I grabbed the offending article, rubbing my head. It was a pillow wrapped inside a blanket. When I turned over to glare at Jeph, his back was to me. He was under the blanket, off to the side of the mattress, leaving the decision to go over there up to me.

Even in the near-darkness, I realized I was seeing his tattoo for the first time. It was a stupid thing to notice, but something about it was just so…sinister it made me shiver. Not just sinister though, it drew my gaze like a magnet, like it had a power of its own.

It started at the base of his neck, a crimson skull staring me down. Black filigree snaked from it, curving up and under his ears. Tendrils of darkness laced over his shoulders, and I knew from seeing his front, they brushed the top of his pecs and wrapped around his biceps. It rippled over his shoulder blades, fanning out in a mockery of black, swirling and curling wings. The pattern raced down his spine, narrowing and thinning to a small line that ran the length of his back.

But even more frightening were the crimson droplets that intertwined with the black filigree. It made me think of blood—blood and death, like the skull laughing and winking at me in the flickering candlelight. I shuddered, feeling a premonition of my own death washing over me.

I so wasn't going over there.

Unwrapping the pillow, I put it under my head. Then, I unfurled the blanket, snapping it and letting it fall over my body. My back to Jeph again, I laid on my side and closed my eyes.

"You're not proving anything," he said. "You're just going to be in pain in the morning."

I didn't respond.

"Good night...Sam."

 slept fitfully, weird dreams coming and going too fast for me to catch.

Twelve-year-old Samantha dances atop her mother's grave in the moonlight.

Someone's approach stops her dance, and she turns to see the Grim Reaper walking toward her. She isn't scared, and she meets his gaze behind the plastic mask he wears. She looks at him with open curiosity, and he stares back.

"Why are you out here all alone?" he asks.

I tossed and turned, sweat beading on my body.

The Grim Reaper takes a startled step back when she grabs his mask, revealing the boy hiding underneath. He's young, around her age, with light blonde hair and hazel eyes.

She hands the mask to him, and they both jolt, looking at their hands when their fingers brush.

I gasped, cradling my tingling hand to my chest.

"You really shouldn't be out here by yourself," he warns. Like I said, it's dangerous."

She shrugs. "My goddess watches over me. She'd tell me if I was in danger."

"Your goddess?"

"Hecate." She nods. "She's why I feel safe here. This is her domain."

"Isn't Hecate a goddess of...of necromancy?"

"Yes," I mumbled in my sleep.

"You're strange," he says, smiling.

She grins. "I'd never want to be otherwise."

With admiration in his eyes, the boy leans down, pressing a kiss to her cheek. After a moment, he jerks away, stammering, "Oh. Uh. I...I didn't know I was going to do that."

"No takebacks," I murmured, turning over fitfully.

The boy watches Samantha warily as she takes a step toward him. Very slowly, she raises her hands, taking the boy's face in her palms. She stretches up on her tiptoes and gives him a chaste kiss on the lips.

My lips tingled, and I gasped.

"I have to go," he says, backing away.

"But you didn't tell me your name." She takes a step toward him.

"And I'm not going to," he snaps.

"Why not?" She crosses her arms over her chest, tapping her foot.

He pauses, watching her tapping before he continues his retreat. "Because I can't...It's dangerous."

"How is it dangerous?"

"It just is. Now, forget this ever happened."

"No." Samantha glares. "And my name's—"

"Shut up!" the boy hisses, moving inhumanly fast and slapping a hand over her mouth.

Her eyes widen in fear.

"Now do you understand?" He stares into her eyes beseechingly. "You're in danger—from me."

Tears fill her eyes, and his face contorts in pain.

"Leave. Go home and don't come back."

"But—"

"Now," he snarls, expression menacing.

Lips trembling, Samantha turns on her heel and runs out of the cemetery. The boy watches until she's out of sight. Then, he collapses to his knees, tears filling his eyes.

Tears spilled down my cheeks, and I sniffled.

She runs away from the graveyard, not paying attention to the city streets as she weaves further into the familiar maze.

"Are you lost?" a young woman asks.

"Oh, I'm—" Samantha stares at the woman. "My daddy told me not to talk to strangers."

"My name's Vi—Vivian Hart."

"That's cool and all, but I'm not telling you my name. My daddy didn't raise no fool."

"'My daddy didn't raise a fool,'" Vivian corrects.

"Yeah, whatever. I'm kinda in a hurry so..." Samantha shrugs.

"Are you always this rude?"

"Are you always so direct?"

"Kid, you need a serious spanking and a trip to your room."

"You're not the boss of me!"

"*You—*" Vivian grits her teeth. "*Fine. Whatever, kid. Do you live nearby? I can't, in my right mind, let a toddler walk home by herself. Do I need to call the non-emergency line and get a cop to take you?*"

"I'm not a toddler! And you're rude for a lady," I snapped, still asleep.

"*Look at that, Lady Clara,*" *a man's voice says.* "*I found you two perfect sacrifices.*"

"*Wonderful,*" *Lady Clara purrs.* "*Maiden blood is always so much more powerful, isn't it, Lord Hendrix?*"

"*Shit,*" *Vivian curses under her breath.*

Vivian puts herself between Samantha and the newcomers.

"*Who're you calling a maiden, meany-head?*" *Samantha demands.* "*I'll have you know, I'm a fairy princess.*"

"*Shut. Up,*" *Vivian hisses.*

"*A real princess?*" *Lady Clara drawls with curious menace.*

"*Make-believe!*" *Vivian snaps.* "*She's the biggest asshole this side of the planet, now if you'll excuse us, my sister is past due for her bedtime.*"

"Not…your sister," I murmured.

"*I think not,*" *Lord Hendrix says, standing on the other end of the street now.* "*We've got business with you both.*"

"*Don't worry,*" *Clara says, stalking toward them,* "*it won't hurt—much.*"

Hendrix smirks. "*Not after you're dead, that is.*"

"*Stars above,*" *Vivian curses.* "*Look, kid, I'm gonna distract them. As soon as they focus on me, you run. Got it?*"

"But—"

"No buts!" Vivian growls, reaching behind her back and drawing a sword out of thin air.

I writhed in my sleep, whimpering.

Vivian blocks Hendrix's strike, swords crossing. Pushing Hendrix back with the flat of her blade, she kicks Clara in the stomach, sending her flying. Hendrix snarls, launching himself back at Vivian, and Samantha screams.

"Go!" Vivian shouts. "Now!"

Clara is back on her feet, her daggers flashing, Vivian's sword grinding against Hendrix's. Clara's blades cut Vivian across the abdomen. She hisses in pain, jumping away from the pair and nearly tripping over Samantha. Vivian blasts the couple with magical energy, and they go sprawling.

"Goddess," I breathed, trembling.

"Get out of here, kid," Vivian pants.

"I'm scared," Samantha whispers.

"Back pocket—take my phone and call Orion. He'll get you to safety."

"But—"

"Enough buts! Take it and go hide!"

Samantha pulls Vivian's phone from her pocket and takes off for the alley.

"Pick up, pick up, pick up," I chanted, holding my fist against my ear.

"Do you know how late it is?" a man's deep voice booms from the other end of the phone.

"Are you Orion?" Samantha asks.

There's a long silence. "Who're you?"

"They're attacking her! Vivian said you could help. Please help her; they're hurting her—the crazy people with swords and stuff!"

"Vivian?" He sounds confused. "Ah. I see. Where are you?"

She tells him, and before she can finish speaking, a tall black man with dark, black-brown eyes stands before her, phone held to his ear.

He looks at her for a long moment, shock crossing his features. "Of all the people in the world he could run into... How do they always manage to make my life miserable?"

"Excuse me?" she demands.

He pats her on the head before taking her hand. "You'll learn soon enough, little one. I'll do what I can, but your existence puts both my life and my position in peril."

"I don't—"

"Tell me where Vivian is."

I tossed and turned, feeling like a huge pressure was weighing me down.

When Samantha and Orion come around the corner and back into the alley, Clara and Hendrix are dead, and Vivian is nowhere to be seen. Lying next to her sword is a beautiful blonde boy, covered in blood, with piercing blue eyes. He's older than the boy in the graveyard, and unlike him, this young man's eyes aren't haunted.

"Stars above, kid," Orion says. "You look like hell."

"Screw you, boss," he wheezes.

Orion snorts. "And here I thought you needed my help."

"Are you...are you Vivian?" Samantha asks.

Orion arches a brow at the young man. "Do you have any idea how confusing it was to get a call from a little girl claiming Vivian was being attacked by 'crazy people with swords and stuff'?"

"Can it," he pants.

"Here's your phone, Mr. Bloody-Dude," she says, holding it toward him.

Sweat drenched me.

"Well, are you feeling up to helping this girl with her... ah...impression of what happened here tonight, or will I be forced to assist her in other ways?" Orion asks.

"Give me a minute," he replies, slowly getting to his feet. "Kinda took a beating waiting for you."

"Sometimes, I think the Guildmaster put me in charge of you to torture me."

"Probably." The young man grins, although it's strained. "Could be worse—you could have to deal with Jeph, too."

"Even the Fates aren't that cruel. Now, hurry up so I can get back to bed."

"Dick," the young man mutters. "I'll get right on that."

He turns toward Samantha, and she takes a step back.

"I'm not gonna hurt you," he says. "Nothing personal, but some things are best forgotten."

"I...I don't wanna forget," she murmurs, taking another step back.

Orion and the young man share a look.

"It's better than the alternative," the older man says.

Samantha gulps.

"Mother of the stars, boss! Do you have to say it so ominously?"

"It's the truth." He shrugs. "And you know Norms aren't allowed to know—"

"Yeah, yeah. Order and peace. Blah, blah, bullshit."

Orion's eyes narrow. "Choose what you'll do. I don't have all night."

"Will it...will it hurt?" Samantha asks meekly.

The young man smiles at her. "It'll hurt me way more than it'll hurt you."

She nods. "Oh...okay."

The young man's hands tremble as he puts them on either side of Samantha's head, closing his eyes. Something tingly tears through her mind, and the boy's already-pale skin turns ashen, the expression on his face pinching.

Then, Samantha hears his voice inside her head.

"You went to the graveyard, danced upon your mother's grave, and found peace with her spirit and your goddess. You didn't meet anyone tonight, and you went straight to bed once you got home."

Then, with the suggestion to sleep, Samantha passes out in his arms.

"No!" I screamed, writhing in my sleep. "Don't take my—!"

"Sam," a voice said next to my ear. "Sam, wake up."

"You can't!" I said through soft sobs. "You can't take them!"

Heat stroked along my cheek.

"Wake up, Sam. You're having a bad dream."

"He's stealing my—"

"Shh."

My memories.

I finally opened my eyes, the insistent heat on my cheek pulling me from deep, gripping sleep.

"There you are, precious."

Jeph's hand caressed my cheek, his thumb running under my tear-soaked eyes, brow furrowing in concern, face hovering over mine. It was so dark I could barely make out his features. But that he was near me at all meant I was still sleeping, still dreaming. He would never look at me like that, never hold me so gently, not without an audience to fool.

Emboldened by the safety of my dream, my hand lifted to stroke his cheek, and he leaned into my touch. I traced my fingers along the stubble on his jaw, his eyebrows and cheekbones, his nose and lips. His soft, soft lips, ferocious and punishing, fierce and demanding.

He gasped, eyes lolling shut. "Sam…"

"Kiss me," I whispered. "Kiss me before I wake up."

"Wake up?" His face fell. "You think you're…"

"Please, Jeph."

"No, precious. I'm not going to."

"No?" I was incredulous. "It's my dream, damn it! How is that fair to me?"

"If you want to kiss me so badly, wake up and do it."

"Are you crazy? Real Jeph will kill me! Or…something. I dunno. He doesn't like me very much."

His lips quirked. "That guy *is* kind of a douche."

"Exactly!"

He grinned. "If you feel so strongly, why do you want to kiss me?"

Shrugging, I tangled my fingers in his silky, thick hair, playing with the curls while I tried to think of an answer to that question. "Well, I mean, you're hott."

He threw his head back and laughed, a twinkle in his eyes when he asked, "Is that all?"

"I dunno." I traced his smiling lips with the tip of my finger. "You're kinda nice in your own way."

"How so?" His tongue snaked out to taste my finger.

"You protect me," I rasped, breath caught in my throat.

"For my own gain."

"You take care of me, giving me food and stuff."

"Because I need you focused on healing."

"You think of everything I don't, like what needs to happen next."

"So we can get home faster."

"Your aura is so raw and full of pain I can't possibly believe you're as bad as you pretend to be."

"My…my *aura?*"

I traced it, noticing Dream Jeph had a lighter aura. It was still sad and dark, but it had a sort of happiness to it that Real Jeph didn't have. "What happened to you?" I whispered. "What broke your soul?"

When I met his eyes, they searched mine for a long, long time.

He grabbed my hand, turning his head to kiss my palm. "Maybe I'll tell you someday," he said against my skin. "Do you still want me to kiss you?"

The intensity in his eyes melted me, and I licked my lips and swallowed, nodding. Jeph pressed my wrist against the floor next to my head, and my breath caught in my throat when he hovered over me. My eyes closed, butterflies dancing in my stomach, and when I felt his breath on my lips, I shivered.

"Are you sure you want a monster to kiss you?" he whispered.

"There's no monster, only you."

"Oh, precious. You're so, so wrong."

Then, his lips brushed gently over mine. Just once, so softly, so tenderly, my heart pounded against my rib cage. Then, he kissed me again, and I gasped, the caress of his lips like the touch of a feather. This wasn't like my other dreams. Those had been hot, furious, and demanding. This was sweet, soft, and reverent, almost as if I was something delicate and fragile, as if he was afraid I would break.

"You're perfect," he whispered against my lips. "So perfect."

He kissed me again, sucking my bottom lip, his tongue flicking over it, tracing its curve. Sparks danced behind my eyelids, my heartbeat erratic in my chest. Then, he nibble-lick-nibbled my lip, the textures making it impossible to think, impossible to breathe. And when I thought I was going to die of need, his mouth covered mine.

He pressed against me, his body fitting to mine in all the right ways, and I twined my free hand into his hair, angling my head, parting his lips, and stroking his tongue with mine. He shuddered and groaned, and a surge of white-hot desire made my kisses feverish. He responded in kind, hungrily devouring me. I writhed underneath him, Jeph grinding against me in a way that made my heart stop, start, stop, start. Heat flooded me, fire racing through my veins. Everything tingled and ached with need, desire pooling low in my abdomen.

"Let me touch you," he rasped against my ear. "Please, Sam. Let me—"

"Yes," I hissed, my hands already greedily skimming over the bare skin of his back, nails digging in, clawing at him, trying to get closer, closer. I needed him closer.

His lips captured mine with renewed fervor, him pulling one lip, then the other, between his, slanting and angling his lips in new ways, discovering and exploring what felt best, what felt right. Every kiss pushed me closer to the brink, to the edge, driving me ever closer to insanity. Then, he slowly, painstakingly ran his tongue along mine, not ending the madness but drawing it out with each soft, tender stroke.

I couldn't breathe—couldn't think—couldn't stop my heart from racing. There was a pressure building in my chest, a scream ready to tear its way from my throat, an undeniable longing that needed, that demanded, that *wanted*. And when Jeph's hand trailed along my waist, stopping just under my breast, I trembled, arching into his touch. His thumb rubbed over its peak, and my mouth tore from his with a soft cry.

"So beautiful," he murmured against my throat, nipping my skin.

"Jeph," I sighed.

"Yes, precious?"

"Don't call me that."

"*Sam*," he murmured. "My Sam."

Yes, my soul screamed. *Mine, mine, mine.*

"*Yours*," I breathed.

"Awake or asleep."

"Hmm?"

"You're mine—awake or asleep."

"But…that doesn't make sense."

"Don't argue with me," he growled, his hand reversing course, trailing over my hip and down my thigh.

"Don't tell me what to do," I rasped.

He chuckled, tracing kisses along my jaw. "Wouldn't dream of it."

"Are…are we arguing? Or did you just concede?"

His thumb skimmed the inside of my thigh, my dress raising with his hand. "I'll do anything for you, precious."

For a moment, I couldn't think past the fire trailing with his touch, his agonizingly slow ascent up my thigh, making something clench low, low in my abdomen. His hand stopped, far enough away I had to stifle a whine but close enough I bit my lip hard, drawing blood.

"Anything?"

"Anything," he promised, rubbing his thumb over sensitive flesh.

I cried out, and he kissed me, pulling my bottom lip into his mouth. His entire body went rigid, his fingers digging into my leg, making me wince.

"You're bleeding…"

Before I could respond, he sucked my lip harder, moaning and groaning, tongue greedily running over my cut. Then, he drew my lip between his teeth and bit—*hard*. I screamed, and he pulled away, panting and wild-eyed.

"You bit me!"

"I didn't mean—I shouldn't—I'm so sorry, Sam."

"What's wrong with you?" I snapped.

"I told you, I'm a monster." His face contorted in pain, and my heart lurched at his misery, but I was still angry.

"Why did you do that?"

"You…you taste better than the sweetest ambrosia."

"What the hell does that mean?"

"I don't—I just meant—" He grabbed fistfuls of hair. "Fuck!"

I watched his aura rage and swirl: anger, frustration, self-loathing, desire, guilt.

Hunger, hunger, hunger.

"I can fix it," he said so quietly I had to strain to hear him. "I can make it better."

He looked at me, mania in his eyes. A shiver crawled up my spine, and I scooted away, but he was fast, so terrifyingly, frighteningly fast. I squeaked when he knelt between my legs, perched over me, one arm caging me in on one side, the wall blocking my retreat.

"Here," he said, holding out a dark liquid in his cupped palm.

My eyes darted to it, back to his face, then back to his palm. "What…what is that?"

"Something that'll make the pain stop."

"I don't think…"

"Drink it," he insisted, holding it closer to my face. "It'll make everything better."

Teeth chattering, I took his wrist and hand in mine, leaning forward and angling his palm toward my mouth. As soon as the liquid touched my tongue, I moaned, pulling his hand closer and drinking greedily. It was thick, sweet, and tasted of iron, salt, and copper. I licked his palm until it was clean of everything but my saliva, everything but the sweet tang coming from the gash in his palm. Moaning, I ran my tongue over it. It tasted like heaven, like magic, like *power*—so much power.

"Careful," Jeph whispered from behind me, his chest pressed against my back. I'd been so enthralled by the taste of perfection on my lips, I had no memory of getting there. "I don't know what too much will do."

He tried to pull his hand away, but I held firm, biting into his flesh. He hissed, but I didn't think it was in pain. I bit harder and he growled. A shiver of desire ran up my spine.

"If you don't stop that"—his voice was husky—"I'll do everything in my power to convince you to let me have my wicked way with you. I might even beg."

My stomach flipped, my breath caught, and my heart raced.

"No," I murmured, despite my body saying *yes*.

"Then stop that."

With great effort, I pulled his hand from my mouth, licking my lips—my *healed* lips. My head snapped around, and Jeph's red eyes met mine. I stared into them, the crimson color tickling a distant memory.

"Your irises…"

"I know."

"What is it?" I asked.

"Something that makes me extremely dangerous."

I studied his face, his eyes, his aura. "How dangerous?"

"Very."

"You are pretty scary."

He smiled, but it didn't reach his eyes. "That's an under-statement."

"Maybe if you were nicer…"

"Nice guys finish last, precious, and in the world I live in, it pays to be first." He cupped my cheek, pressing his lips against my forehead. He stayed there, his words tickling along my skin. "I spent six years hoping I'd see you again. Six years *fearing* I would. And when reports of the Sibyl cropped up, I think part of me knew she was you. And when Evander got your file, I'll admit, I was jealous." He chuckled, and it vibrated through me. "But then I got to see for myself. I was horrified to find you there—*terrified*—and so selfishly happy, I could scarcely control my own power."

I tried to pull away, but he held me firm.

"Why'd I go back?" I felt his smile as much as I felt his snort. "Because I'm clearly a masochist. I wanted to see you again. Didn't care if you hated me. I *needed* you to hate me—so I could walk away…So that I wouldn't put you at the mercy of my enemies. And then you were just so…*you*. The longer we sparred, the more I…" He blew out a breath. "Then we came here, and every second has been the bitterest torture and the sweetest hell. But you can't…*We* can't—I'll only get you killed."

"How?" I demanded, tilting my head back, his lips trailing over my nose. "I'm already being hunted."

"Right now, he simply wants the power of the Sibyl…If he knew what you are to me, he'd…he'd use you to break me. He'd torture you—keep you alive—just to…just to…You don't know what I would do for you, Sam." He pulled me into his lap, squeezing me painfully. "I'd be the monster he wants me to be."

"Who's 'he'?"

"My master," Jeph whispered.

My heart jolted, and my arms wrapped around him, holding him tight. He clung to me like a child, his fingers digging into my back. I found it difficult to believe that someone as strong as him could ever be owned by someone. Did that mean there was someone more powerful than him? Or did his master have something to hold over him? To keep him obedient, blackmailed, a *slave*. My breath caught, realizing how crazed Jeph had been when he'd woken up confined in the slaver's cart, how resigned he'd been when he'd learned we'd been sold to Lord Edward— his words to him in the arena: *"You mean pawns—slaves."*

I tilted my head further, my lips crashing against his. He responded immediately, pulling me closer, close enough I couldn't breathe. I didn't need air. How could I even ask for that when he'd been suffocating for so long?

"Tell me how to help you," I whispered.

"Leave Washington when we get back."

"I won't leave my family."

"Then stay far, far away from me."

His words stung like a slap, but I understood his fear. It wasn't *him* he wanted me to stay away from, it was the looming threat of those who opposed him, those who opposed me. I refused to accept those terms.

"I want to free you."

"You can't."

"Jeph, please."

"Do you really want to help me?"

"Yes."

"Then I want you to forget we ever had this conversation."

"What? No!"

"Sam, you asked me how you can help. Trust me."

I chewed my lip. "But then I'll think we're enemies again."

"We *are* enemies."

"I don't wanna be."

"Me either, precious. Me either."

Tears leaked down my cheeks, mourning the loss of *this* man, the one who was kind and passionate. The one who was self-sacrificing and noble. The one that had constructed a façade just to keep me at a distance…so that I wouldn't get attached to him—so that I wouldn't trust him, wouldn't like him, so that he didn't put me in danger.

I was already in danger, but that wasn't why I would do this. I would do this for him. I didn't care what happened to me. I probably would once I was captured, once the torture began, but I would survive that. I wouldn't be able to survive knowing that my feelings for him would lead to his suffering. He was a master of façades, his masks the perfect camouflage for whatever situation he had to endure, but my feelings would be written on my face.

My decisions had hurt so many people—too many people— I wouldn't hurt Jeph, too. If my hatred would spare him, then I would do this for him. He'd suffered enough; I wouldn't be selfish now. If this was what he needed from me, then I would do it for him.

"Promise me something," I whispered.

"Anything."

"Be a complete douchebag."

He sputtered. "What?"

"Your mask—it keeps slipping. I can't hate you if you keep making me like you."

"Say that again," he breathed, tone full of awe and wonder.

"I *like* you."

His forehead pressed painfully against mine. "I'll burn the world to the ground for you."

"Good." I smiled. "But start with the guilds."

"Precious, precious, precious," he breathed. "Just as soon as we get back...I'll make it safe for you. For *us*."

I shivered. "I like the sound of that."

"Just remember," Jeph whispered against my lips, "you're asleep." His power washed over my skin, humming in my veins and making my thoughts cloudy. "Dreaming pretty little dreams," he continued, stealing one last kiss. "But they aren't real."

My chest ached with longing, tears tracking down my cheeks.

"Don't cry," he murmured, wiping away the tears.

"Hold me?" I asked, sniffling.

He smiled gently and nodded. Then, we snuggled under my blanket, his strong arms holding me, one hand rubbing my scalp as he played with my hair. I listened to his heartbeat under my ear, rising and falling with each breath he took. His steady heat soothed me, and for the first time in years, I felt at peace.

I wish this was real, was my last thought before I fell deeper into sleep.

Twenty-Six

*E*verything hurt—my neck, my back, my arm—all of which I'd slept on wrong. I'd woken up feeling like I'd been run over by a freight train. I'd groaned as I rolled over, just to find Jeph staring at me, brow arched. He'd shaken his head, rolling his eyes as he got up and headed out of the house. When he'd come back, he had a pack full of supplies.

"Let's go," he'd muttered, not waiting for me to follow.

That was hours ago, and the long walk to reach Canterbury hadn't done my aching back any favors. Now my feet and legs screamed their dissent, and I kept trying to crack my neck, but I'd never learned that particular skill.

"We should make camp before nightfall."

"Uh-huh," I murmured, my head bouncing to the side as I tried—and failed—to crack it.

Jeph looked over at me. "What are you doing?"

"Trying to—y'know—crack my neck."

"Well, stop it. You look ridiculous."

"It hurts!"

"I told you not to sleep on the floor," he said calmly, despite the tick in his jaw.

"And I chose to."

"Then reap what you sow."

"If I could just get…" I tilted my head further, but I couldn't seem to push it far enough.

"Oh, for the love of the Northern Star," he muttered under his breath. "Come here."

"What?"

He held his hands out, fingers beckoning me. "Come. Here."

"Why?" I narrowed my eyes. "So you can break my neck?"

"Oh, for shit's sake." He reached out, grabbing my head, delicately cradling my jaw in his palms. "Relax."

All I could think was, *yeah frickin' right!* but I closed my eyes, willing my muscles to unclench. He turned my head back and forth, and…*Crack!* I yelped, snapping my eyes open. Then, I groaned, melting into his hands. *Crack!* Now, both sides felt like heaven, and the instant relief was almost enough to make me weep.

"Better?" he asked, his tone impatient, but he still held me, his thumbs lightly brushing over my cheeks.

"Yeah," I said breathlessly, stepping out of his hold. "Thanks."

He gave a curt nod and turned back to the forest. "It's not ideal, but we'll make camp here."

"What if Hunters find us?"

We'd had damn good luck evading them so far, but I doubted that luck would hold much longer.

"They won't." He paused. "Because we're not going to use any magic. Period."

"*Mi-mi-mi-mi-mi-mi-mi, we're not gonna use magic,*" I mocked. "That's kinda been the whole point of this awful journey, hasn't it?"

"Really? What are you, twelve?"

"Probably."

Jeph rolled his eyes, unstrapping his bag from his waist. He rummaged through it, pulling out a long, wide piece of linen.

"Please tell me you didn't steal that from those nice people."

He pressed his lips together, pulling more stuff from the pack.

"Jeph!"

"What?" he snapped, glaring up at me. "You told me not to tell you."

"That's not—! Ugh!" I threw my hands in the air. "Whatever. While you're doing that, I'm gonna go…"

"Take a leak? Have fun," he muttered, and my face flamed.

Stomping deeper into the forest, I looked for a place to squat. I really was getting sick and tired of peeing in the woods. It was mortifying, and I missed TP—*a lot*. After I finished my business, I started toward Jeph but halted in my tracks. The sound of running water had me turning around, heading deeper into the forest. I walked for several minutes before emerging into a clearing. In front of me was a wide river.

"Shit."

As awesome as Granny Edith had been, she'd forgotten to mention we'd need to cross a river. Daring to hope, I walked to the shore, looking up and downstream. There was no end in sight. We'd need to either cross tonight or tomorrow. It made more sense to do it now so we weren't walking in wet clothes all day.

But first...

I stripped my dress over my head, folding it and setting it on a dry rock. Next, I kicked off my socks and shoes, setting them aside as well. My fingers stilled on the hook of my bra. Deciding I wasn't *that* bold, I dropped my hands. I might want a bath, but I wasn't brave enough to go skinny-dipping.

I waded in, the cool water soothing my aching muscles, but I gritted my teeth when it reached my waist. Plugging my nose, I closed my eyes and dunked myself. I scrubbed my hands over my face, dirt and grime flaking away. When I felt satisfied, I began scratching and massaging my scalp. As I stayed submerged, the pressure in my chest threatened to suffocate me.

When I popped out of the water, panting and gulping for air, I screamed.

"*Ohmigoddess!*" I slapped my hands over my chest, resubmerging myself. "*Go away!*"

"I—uh—I couldn't find you..."

"*Go!*" I shrieked, picking up a rock and throwing it at Jeph.

He shielded his face, but it sailed past him, missing him by several feet. I lobbed rock after rock, and he retreated. Looking for more ammo, I reached farther and farther behind me. I finally clocked him in the forehead...at the same time I slipped, losing all footing on the bedrock.

The river swept me away, water surging and roaring in my ears. The current tossed me around, sucking me down. It was so dark I couldn't see, couldn't tell which way was up, and I flailed uselessly, trying to orient myself. My back ran along a sharp rock, and I screamed, inhaling water. Then, the back of my skull cracked against something, sparks dancing in my vision. I went over a small waterfall, crashing into the river, water pelting down on top of me.

Something hot encaged me, and I reached for it. I needed to get out, needed to grab...*Jeph?* He pulled us to the surface, and I coughed in his face, wheezing.

"Hold onto me!" he yelled, sputtering when the current sucked us under.

I clung to him, and his shoulders bounced as he desperately reached for something to hold onto. For the briefest moment, we stopped...then Jeph howled, and we spiraled downstream. My back collided with something, and his weight crashed against me, the last of my air gurgling from my lungs. Whatever we'd hit, he was able to grab ahold of it. Raging water beat against us when we surfaced, and I squeezed him so hard my muscles trembled with the effort.

His chest heaved against mine as we panted for air. My back throbbed, my lungs burned, and my head pounded. Sparkles wavered at the edge of my vision, darkness crowding in.

"Don't you dare pass out!" he barked. "Do you hear me, precious? Don't. Let. Go."

I nodded weakly, eyes rolling in their sockets. Every breath was like inhaling fire, and my skull pulsed hotly, probably oozing blood. My back ached and stung, and I felt heavy, so heavy. I closed my eyes.

"Sam!" he shouted, shaking me, and I jolted awake. "What did I just say?"

"Don' pass ou'," I slurred.

"That's right, precious."

We reached the shore, and he put a hand to my back, collapsing onto the bedrock, hovering over me and panting. His eyes were clenched shut, his head dipping lower and lower until his forehead pressed against mine.

"You really can't stay out of trouble, can you?" he asked, his breath dancing over my face.

I shook my head.

"You'll be the death of me," he muttered.

I was too exhausted to reply, too exhausted to move. He didn't move either, and we stayed there catching our breaths. My damp, exposed skin prickled in the breeze, and I shivered.

"Sam," he whispered, fingers flexing against my lower back.

I gasped, spine arching. "W-what?"

"I'm…I'm going to kiss you."

"You—what?" My heart raced at the prospect.

"Say yes," he rasped, his lips ghosting over mine.

My stomach flipped, heat flooding my veins. I knew it was the hex making me feel this way, the hex making him want to kiss me, but…I couldn't deny the part of *me* that wanted him, not any longer. Not after all the dreams I kept having, dreams where he kissed me like a man crazed, like a man cherishing something precious. Maybe that was the hex, too, but I wanted to experience it for real.

Besides…I was pretty sure he wanted me, too. No, I *knew* he did. I'd seen it in the way he looked at me, in the way he watched me, in the way he risked his life for mine, despite claiming he only protected me for his own gain. Why protect me if it resulted in his death…especially when his desire was to live—to make it home? He couldn't go anywhere if he was dead.

I took a chance and lifted my head, claiming his lips. His moved sweetly, tenderly, then hungrily as he parted my lips and stroked his tongue along mine. My hands ran over his back, gooseflesh breaking along his skin, and I dug my nails in. His mouth tore from mine with a gasp, and I trailed kisses along his jaw, stopping when I reached his earlobe. I bit it, and he shouted my name.

"Stop pretending," I whispered, unsure where the words came from.

"Pretending?"

"That you don't care."

His entire body tensed. "You can't know what you're talking about."

I pulled back, meeting his panicked eyes. "Stop lying to me."

"Lying? You think I'm lying?" He laughed mockingly. "Newsflash, precious, you're just—"

I kissed him, stopping his lies. He growled, pulling me against him as he sat up. He held me in his lap, trailing kisses along my jaw and down my neck, and my head fell back. He licked my collar bone, making my stomach flip and my palms tingle. And then, his lips kissed just below that...and just below that...and—

"Jeph!"

He chuckled wickedly, his chin grazing the top of my breast before he reversed course, nibbling my earlobe. My heart pounded, and part of me wished he hadn't stopped, that he'd gone lower and lower. That he explored me the way I wanted him to—*needed* him to—like he hadn't been able to in my dream last night.

"You want the truth, hmm, *precious?*" he asked sarcastically.

My lips trembled. "Don't..."

"I'm a hungry male holding a half-naked woman in his lap, and you don't seem opposed to whetting my appetite."

"Stop," I breathed, eyes stinging. "You don't mean that."

He laughed cruelly. "Don't I?"

"But..."

But what, Sam? How much of what I felt was real, and how much was the hex? Was all of it...magic? A curse? A spell? Nothing more, nothing less, and here I was, making a fool of myself? *I'm pathetic.*

"You'll take me home, then you're my prey," he continued. "I'll even let you live, precious, because it'll be more fun to draw out the chase."

"Stop..."

What are you clinging to, Sam? He doesn't care about you.

Hope.

I was clinging to hope.

"Why don't we have a little bit of fun first, hmm?" he hummed against my throat, teeth grazing my jugular, his hand dipping lower on my back. "Could be hot. Two enemies caving to their dirty fantasies and indulging in their lust."

He grabbed my ass, and I shoved away from him, slapping him across the face.

Tears filled my eyes, and I wanted to scream, wanted to hit him again when his head turned back to me, that stupid sneer on his face, wanted to strangle him and demand he stop lying. But that stupid leer stayed in place, that stupid, cocky smirk on his face, his eyes hard as steel. He wasn't idly taunting me...he *wanted* to hurt me.

I wasn't clinging to hope. I was clinging to a dream, a worthless, pathetic dream.

"I *hate* you," I sobbed, slapping his chest over and over. "*I-hate-you-I-hate-you-I-hate!*"

"I know, precious," he whispered, letting me hit him. "I know."

Twenty-Seven

My lips trembled when I got to my feet, stalking back upriver. I didn't even care that I was half-dressed, that he'd be getting an eyeful of my ass, didn't even care that his aura was raging behind me, screaming and howling in agony. My head throbbed, my back screeched in pain, and I kept stumbling. That was already a given, considering the ground was rocky, uneven, and I had all the grace of a rhino in a china shop. The exhaustion and having nearly drowned weren't helping anything either.

"Careful," Jeph said, grabbing my elbow to steady me when I almost face-planted onto a rock.

"Don't touch me!" I hissed, ripping my arm free of his grasp, which, of course, only served to make me wobble the other way. He had to catch me again. "What did I just say!"

He rolled his eyes, waiting until I stopped shaking before letting go. Well, until I mostly stopped shaking. My damn legs were seriously considering quitting on me, and at this point, I didn't blame them. I wanted to quit me, too. When I tripped not five seconds later, he heaved a sigh, wrapped an arm around my waist, pulled me to my feet, and picked me up. He cradled me against him, my skin sizzling everywhere it touched his.

"No! *No, no, no!*" I shouted, slapping his stupid chest. "Put me down! I'm not a princess to be carried!"

"Oh, don't worry. No one would ever mistake *you* for a princess."

Oh, I've had it up to here!

I wrapped my hands around his throat, squeezing and shaking him with all my might. He was so shocked, his step faltered, and with the uneven ground, we tumbled forward. I waited for my already-battered back to smack the ground. Instead, I landed on Jeph when he turned us, hitting his head on the way down.

I didn't even feel bad.

I kept strangling him, not really wanting to kill him but just so irritated with how big of an ass he'd been that I needed an outlet. Since he had a knack for recovering from physical wounds, this was the kindest solution to my problems. At least I didn't have something sharp; I wasn't entirely sure I wouldn't be stabbing him over, and over, and over again. I was ashamed to be assaulting him at all, but *c'est la* fucking *vie*, I thought viciously, digging my thumbs in.

Jeph just laid there, letting me strangle him, which wasn't what I wanted. I wanted him to put up a fight. I wanted him to battle me—to yell at me—*something*. But he didn't. He just stared me down, stupid brow arched on his stupid forehead as his stupid, full lips paled under the force of my hands.

Chill, Sam, I chided myself. *You're losing it. Actually, literally, losing it.*

Very slowly, I uncurled my fingers. This wasn't me, the anger and the violence. I'd never been this vindictive, this angry and volatile. But that wasn't true, was it? I'd tried to kill Lord Edward—over a girl I barely knew. And yet I'd never been so enraged on my own behalf.

What in the actual fuck is wrong with me?

I'd been somewhat cheerful and a little callous about shooting the Hunters who'd chased me over the years, but that was because it was do or die. I'd seen that up close—seen it when my friend Cole had been brutally murdered in front of me, simply because I was "the Sibyl." Because he was stupid enough to be near me—to try to help me—and it had cost him his life.

There were reasons I didn't have living friends, reasons I never would.

"At least you're a woman of your word," Jeph rasped after I stopped assaulting him. "Said you'd strangle me, and you finally did."

I didn't respond. I didn't *want* to respond. I was ashamed of my behavior, even if he deserved it, even if he was my enemy and I should kill him right now to save my own hide. But I couldn't, and I wouldn't, because he was human—he was *alive*. I wouldn't deny him that right the way his guild had denied it of my friend.

I closed my eyes, imagining Cole's face in my mind. His fluffy, dirty blonde hair with its wild waves and curls. His odd, hazel eyes, more blue than green. His thin lips, long nose, and his almond-shaped eyes with long, beautiful lashes. He'd been pretty for a boy—cute, even. He was one year my senior in high school, and he'd given up his status as the popular sports jock—and his gorgeous girlfriend—just to be *my* friend, just to defend me from *his* friends.

Then from my enemies.

And now he was dead.

He'd been dead for two years—two, long years that I felt every second of in my dark, dark soul. Cole wasn't the only person I'd gotten killed along the way, but I'd sworn to myself, he'd be the last. To honor his life, I'd sworn I would never take someone else's because losing someone was painful. I'd learned that when my mother had died, but I'd had some amount of time to prepare for her death. Cole had been there one minute and gone the next.

Now, I'd killed people and I felt it like a stain on my skin, heart, and soul. It didn't matter that those men were always meant to die. I'd been the one to kill them in the arena, the Hunter and the Norm.

I pushed myself off Jeph, staring blankly ahead as I walked along the rocky shore of the river. Its rapid currents filled my ears like white noise, the rushing, gurgling, and trickling of its shallows like a soundtrack to my misery—like a soundtrack for my life. The *crunch, crunch, crunch* of the rocks and sand under my feet only added to the music of my self-loathing. The chirps, crickets, and hoots of creatures-unseen were like the eerie undertone, setting the cadence of my guilt.

I followed the light of the moon back to camp, somehow managing to make it there without realizing time had passed. It was as if the moon had tranced me, as if the river had swept me along again, but this time, to my destination. It was as if the calls of the critters had lulled me into a walking sleep.

When we got back to where I'd fallen in, I grabbed my clothes, donning them as Jeph snatched up his own shirt, discarded haphazardly near the shore, and pulled it violently over his head. He pulled on his boots, too, before heading into the forest. Once I was dressed, I went to meet him at camp, but he'd already packed up and was back by the time I finished.

"Are you confident in your ability to swim across?" he asked.

I stared at him—really stared at him. He looked as exhausted and as drained as I felt. His aura was a swirling mess of blacks and grays, deep scarlets and violets. He was upset—extremely upset. But not a single crack in his façade shown on his face. His expression was neutral, his eyes focused, and he looked ready for anything. I, on the other hand, probably looked like a drowned rat about to keel over.

"No," I admitted. It was the first thing I'd said in a while, and it rasped from my water-abused throat.

He looked from the river to me and back again, scratching his cheek. "Well, we can do one of a few things."

"Here we go," I muttered.

He glared. "We can swim individually."

"Not gonna work."

"You can hold onto me while I swim us across."

"No thanks, pal."

"Or we can use magic and risk being slaughtered in our sleep."

"Fine," I muttered, walking over and standing in front of him, looking into his face. "But if you get handsy again, I'll skip the strangling and go right for the stabbing."

Both his eyebrows rose, a shocked "O" on his lips before it smoothed into a smile. "Talking dirty already, precious? At least wait until the honeymoon."

I punched him in the gut—hard.

He grinned, rubbing his abs. "That *almost* hurt."

"Keep it up and I'll aim below the belt."

"Again, with the honeymoon talk—"

I struck and he looked surprised, catching my wrist just short of my fist clocking him in the junk.

"Yeah. Let's get going then," he muttered, heading toward the river.

He waded in, stopping when he was waist-deep, turning to face me. He held out his arms, all business, and I grimaced first at him, then at the water. I could live my whole life with never looking at a body of water ever again—let alone *entering* one. I stepped in, a soft cry escaping my lips. The water was several degrees colder than it had been before. My teeth chattered, and I winced with each step.

When I reached Jeph, I stood there, shivering, my arms clenched against my chest for warmth, goosebumps covering my body from head to toe. He looked at me pityingly, and I was annoyed to see that he looked perfectly at ease. He didn't even look cold. Maybe he wasn't human after all because there was no way he wasn't freezing right now. Then again, his temperature always seemed to run hot.

"You're going to have to hold onto me," he said, arms still stretched wide.

"Give me a sec," I chattered. "I'm trying to adjust to the temperature."

"If you would just come over here, you'd be warm."

I narrowed my eyes, but I pulled my arms away from my chest before flinging myself at him, sobbing when his heat assaulted me. He was warm, and I was already so numb, I couldn't even be bothered to care that I was clinging to him like a monkey—a desperate monkey with no shame after having just yelled at him about touching me. I pressed my ear and cheek against his face, wrapped my arms and legs around his neck and waist, and squeezed him tightly as if that might help me assimilate his warmth faster. It didn't, but it helped cushion the shock of the river when he submerged us, fighting against the current as he swam across the half-mile long distance.

A few times, our heads went under, and I clenched my eyes and jaw, waiting for us to go spiraling downriver. We were being pushed along the current, but he managed to keep us moving across. By the time we made it to the opposite shore, we'd been carried a little way downstream, but not so much that we were too far off course.

I was so cold I refused to let go when we came out the other side. He either didn't care or my weight was no big deal to him because he kept walking until we were a safe distance up the bank, away from the rushing torrent of water behind us. When he finally stopped walking, he put both his hands on my waist, trying to pull me off of him.

"No!" I shouted. "It's cold!"

"If you let go, I can go find provisions for a fire."

"I'll freeze to death!"

"No, you really won't. It will only take me a minute to find something flammable. If you would just—"

"You're trying to kill me!"

"Why would I jump into a raging river—nearly getting myself killed in the process—just to let you die of hypothermia now, precious? Are you stupid?"

"Hey!" I snapped, pulling back to glare at him.

"What?" he demanded. "Just calling it like I see it."

"Whatever."

I grumbled under my breath, peeling myself away from him. My skin stuck to his, ripping away like the adhesive on a Band-Aid, leaving my skin pink and sore. Then, I sat on the bank while I waited for him to look for firewood. I really didn't have the energy or patience to help. If that made me a dick, then at least I was a very nice, big dick—and an asshole.

I must've fallen asleep because when I opened my eyes again, it was to find a large, roaring fire next to me. How long had I been asleep? It had to have been a while because my clothes were dry. I was also under a linen blanket. Where had that come from?

"If you're awake now," Jeph said, munching on something, "I found some nuts and berries."

I blinked sleepily. "Um, sure."

After I sat up, he put a handful of legumes and berries into my waiting palms. I tried to eat them slowly, but I was a little piggy and couldn't help but scarf them down. If Jeph, Hunters, or the wilderness didn't kill me, starvation would. With my luck, I'd accidentally walk off a cliff and kill myself.

"Slow down there, oinker," he said. "You're going to get a stomach ache."

I glowered. "You're such a dick."

"I know."

"And why is there a huge fire?" I demanded, gesturing at it. "The Hunters are going to find us!"

"They won't," he said coolly, staring into the flames. "But if they do, they won't be a problem."

A shiver ran down my spine, his words full of menace.

"Says you," I muttered. "I'll be dead in my sleep before I even realize anyone is here."

"Then it's a good thing *they* will be dead before they get anywhere near you."

"That's not funny!"

"It's not supposed to be."

"You can't kill them, Jeph. The—"

"Timeline, I know, I know." He crinkled his nose in disgust. "I'll be careful. Just don't worry about it. If anyone comes, I'll deal with it. Lord knows I've dealt with worse than a handful of Hunters."

My brow furrowed, and I studied him out of the corner of my eyes. He stared into the fire, his gaze distant. He was thinking about something—remembering something—because his aura kept shifting, but his eyes remained vacant. What had he dealt with that was worse than a squad of Hunters? I couldn't even begin to imagine and I really didn't want to know. Except...I kinda did.

"Jeph?"

"Hmm?" he hummed, still staring into the flames.

"What happened to you?"

A single brow arched, a small smile curving his lips, but his gaze stayed somewhere far in the past. "You're a consistent little creature, aren't you?"

"What?"

"Nothing."

"No," I said firmly, finally drawing his gaze. "What do you mean I'm consistent?"

"Your nagging questions, precious. Between presuming to know me and asking me stupid questions, you're just consistent is all."

I threw a small rock at him but he dodged it. "And you're an asshole. Nothing new there."

He shrugged, a bitter smile on his face. "I try."

Something about the way he said it had me pursing my lips. His aura read *true*, but I wasn't sure what that meant. Did he honestly *try* to be an asshole? Or was being an asshole true? Was it both? This was why reading auras was like trying to match two shades of the same color when shopping at different paint shops. They would never be exact, would never match up.

"Well?" I prompted. "What happened?"

"Nothing that concerns you...unless we're swapping bed-time stories and you're going to tell me all about the things that happened in your life that have shaped that aggression and reck-lessness—bordering on stupidity—that you wield like a shield, that is."

"Good night," I muttered, laying down on the rocky shore and turning my back to him.

Twenty-Eight

hen I woke up, there was a fire blazing and the smell of meat cooking.

"The mouth-breather awakens," Jeph said, which so wasn't what I wanted to wake up to today.

"Oh good, the douche lord still breathes," I returned, sitting up and shaking sand out of my hair.

I winced, my throbbing head screeching in protest. The cut along my back wasn't helping anything. My arms also had round, reddish indents from sleeping on rocks all night. I rubbed them, making them tingle painfully, then glared at Jeph.

"Barely," he muttered. "After your attempt to kill me yesterday."

"Keep being an ass this early in the morning, and I might try it again."

He grinned. "You know, I might like it if you do."

My face fell, and I stared at him like the idiot he was. Mischief danced in his eyes, and I hated how it made my heart flutter. I looked away, trying to remind myself he was public enemy number one. He was the man who would kill me.

My stomach gurgled pitifully, and he offered me a wooden spit with something hanging off the end of it—something warm, cooked, and smelling of heaven. It was juicy and cooked to perfection, the delicate meat gamey but reminiscent of chicken with a bitter undertone. I didn't care; it fell apart in my mouth. The greasy goodness of the meat dripped down my chin and fingers, the fat making my digits slick.

I scarfed it down before I thought to ask what it was.

"I'd say it was Bambi, but it was actually Thumper," Jeph said, shrugging.

I grimaced, regretting my decision to ask him anything.

"Here," he said, shoving a cup full of dark liquid at me. "I found some more berries and tried to make something decent to drink."

I eyed it warily, asking, "Is that why it looks like blood?"

He pursed his lips, shrugging. "Just trying to keep you hydrated."

"Pretty sure I drank a river yesterday. I'm good." I pushed the cup away from me. "And where did you get the damn cup?"

"Borrowed it from Granny." He shoved it back at me. "Now drink it. Poor joke aside, you really do need to stay hydrated."

"I don't want it."

This was quickly turning into a game of reverse tug-of-war.

"*Sam*," he growled.

"*Jeph*," I mocked.

"Don't make me mouth-feed it to you."

"You wouldn't—" I cut off watching him move the cup toward his lips. "No!"

I snatched it from him, glaring, but tried it—after a thorough sniffing to confirm it was, indeed, berries. Whatever type of berries they were, they tasted sweet and metallic, and I moaned into the cup, trying to lick it clean. When that failed, I stuck my fingers in, slurping the remnants from my digits. Then, I smacked my lips, feeling light and happy.

"See?" he asked, reaching for the cup. "Good."

I pulled it out of his reach, snarling at him. It was my cup, and there might be more deliciousness inside of it.

His brow pinched. "Sam?"

I growled when he reached for my cup again.

"Well *that* explains the aggression," he muttered to himself, pulling back his hand. "You can keep the cup—I won't take it."

My eyes narrowed, but he didn't try to take my cup again. He didn't do much of anything. He sat there, arms holding his knees as he stared into the fire, looking miserable. I felt oddly compelled to comfort him. It was a strong feeling as if something inside of me desired to see him happy, something that wasn't fundamentally me. It was almost like the strong urge I'd had to strangle Jeph last night—almost like the murderous rage I'd had to kill Lord Edward. I couldn't seem to control it.

Slowly, I reached a hand toward him. It trembled, two pieces of myself struggling against each other, the Not Me that wanted to comfort him and the Me that hated his guts for being a slimy asshole. I patted him on the head.

He glanced at me out of the corner of his eye. "Stop."

My hand stilled without me making the decision to do so, and Not Me eagerly awaited his next command. The thought made me scowl.

I don't want to take orders from him!

Not Me flipped me the bird.

"We should get on the road," he said, still side-eyeing me.

"Okay," I said, my hand resting on his head.

Not Me protested when I pulled it away.

Jeph got up, putting out the fire with a wave of his hand before grabbing the bag containing our meager supplies. I gaped at him, so many thoughts running through my head.

The fire.

"You didn't see me do that," he muttered, and Not Me tittered defiantly inside my head.

I blinked once and shook my head. "Didn't see you do what?"

"Exactly, precious."

"What are you talking about?"

"Nothing. Can't have you connecting the dots."

"What dots?"

He smirked at me, and my intuition told me he was about to lie. "Precious, precious, precious. You're rather dull today. Did you forget to sleep while you were tossing, turning, and screaming all night?"

"I—what?"

"Kept screaming my name. *'Jeph, Jeph,'*" he mocked. "*'Kiss me again, Jeph.'*"

I flushed. "I did *not!*"

He shrugged, slinging his sheath over his head and patting the sword to make sure it was in place. Then, he buckled the pack around his waist, turning to glare at me. "Any day now."

I scowled, ready to clobber him.

"Oh, precious. If you keep looking at me like that, we're never going to get anywhere."

"Like what?" I snarled.

"Like you're going to make all my dirty fantasies come true."

"Pretty sure I'm looking at you like that sword is about to go through your eye."

"As I said, dirty fantasies."

I didn't know whether he was joking or being serious. Either way, I was sick and tired of talking to him. Whatever had compelled me to kindness before was wearing off. I was left with a mild headache and a bad taste in my mouth. At the very least, the berries boosted my energy, and I hadn't noticed the throbbing at the base of my skull or the pain in my back.

Small miracles.

Shaking my head in disgust, I grabbed my quiver and bow, slinging them over my shoulder and around my waist. Then, I brushed past Jeph, heading east toward the rising sun. It was several hours before we made it to Canterbury.

Jeph stood at the edge of the town, glaring into the distance.

"There are mages and witches in there—but not enough to make up the population of a town that size," he said, inclining his head, eyes narrowed. "Which means there will be Norms."

"That's still a lot of magical people…"

"We'll need to be on our guard. There are going to be Hunters—especially if King's been causing as much trouble as the rumors say."

"They won't be happy that Norms are talking about him being a sorcerer."

"*Sorcerer*," he muttered. "What a sinister title."

"Like 'Sibyl?'"

He pressed his lips together, heading toward town.

I was shocked by the hustle and bustle. This place was already huge in comparison to the countryside houses we'd stayed in. Those had been little, one-bedroom homes. This town was bigger than that, with stone and wooden buildings lining dirt-compacted roads.

There were little shops everywhere, too. A baker's shop with a heavenly aroma coming from it. A blacksmith's forge made of brick and iron, heat wafting off of it. It was deafening, the roar of the fire and the clinking of metal pounding through the market. There was a butcher's shop where someone was leading a cow to be slaughtered. A weaver threaded fabric. A cobbler hammered nails into shoes. On and on the shops lined the streets, people in fancy clothing on par with Lord Edward's court milling up and down the street. People were talking, haggling, and bartering their own merchandise and coin.

This city was wealthy enough to function seamlessly, probably because of the gorgeous grazing fields full of cattle to the south and the harbor to the east. Wheat fields were to the north. And there were all sorts of herbs and plants growing, some of which I assumed were used for dye, considering how brightly colored some of the clothing was. I wondered how much of this city ran on trade—the farmer with his wheat given to the baker and farmers, who might trade leather and meat to the cobbler and butcher and vice versa—versus how much ran on coin.

Considering a blacksmith's work had to be more expensive, I assumed they would handle in coin and not trade. However, the Hunters and knights of this era wore chainmail and other armor and carried swords and shields. It was likely the blacksmiths were handsomely paid for their labor.

"Stay close," Jeph said, grabbing my elbow and pulling me near. "I don't want to get split up in this crowd. Not like in the arena."

"The difference is we're not under attack here."

"*Yet*," he muttered, dragging me along. "Not yet we aren't."

"Question."

"Answer."

"How are we supposed to know who we're looking for?"

"If he's anything like what they're saying, he'll have a tremendous magical presence."

"What if he doesn't?"

He stopped, turning to look at me. "What?"

"Well," I drawled, thinking through the gut feeling I was having. "We haven't sensed him yet, right?"

"Right."

"So, what if he doesn't have a noticeable energy?"

"Shit. He could have a ward—or just be containing it. I should've thought of that sooner. Especially because he'll have Hunters after him."

"What if he's not even here anymore?" I asked.

"Better start praying to your goddess he is."

"That doesn't make me feel very good."

"Chances are, he's here somewhere. This city is huge, and if he's as prone to exposing himself as he is, then where better to be than a large town?"

"So how do we find him supposing he *is* here? It's not like he's gonna have a neon light pointing at him."

His brow pinched, and he stared into the far distance. "I have a stupid idea."

"Don't."

"Don't what?"

"Last time you had a stupid idea, I was stuck playing the role of your wife."

"Like it was that bad? I bet you even liked it."

"Not in the least. You kiss like a slobbering dog."

"And you kiss like a virgin bride."

"Excuse you!"

He smirked. "Your anger means I'm right."

"It does *not!*"

"Prove it, then."

My mouth dropped open. "Absolutely not! I'm not subjecting myself to that torture again."

"Yeah? Then why did you kiss me last night, hmm, precious?"

"*You* kissed *me*, pal. And in my defense, I'd hit my head, so I was *clearly* delusional. Otherwise, I *never* would've let you anywhere near me."

"Sure, you wouldn't."

"Not even if pigs like you learned to fly," I muttered, crossing my arms over my chest.

Something glimmered in his eyes, and he glanced to my lips before meeting my eyes. My whole stomach turned to molten lava. He leaned toward me, and I gasped in shock, rooted in place. And when I felt his breath tickle over my lips, I shivered, waiting for his kiss.

His kiss…which never came.

He chuckled. "What were you saying?"

"Whatever," I muttered, flushing.

"Just admit it," he said, pulling away from me. "You kiss like a virgin bride."

I was going to strangle him.

"If you're done being an asshole, can we just go find King?"

He shrugged. "Do you want to hear my bad idea or not?"

"What is it?"

"Magical energy."

"What about it?"

"If King really is this wanna-be knight, he'll want to keep the people safe, right?"

"Right?" I drawled the word, confused.

"And if he felt someone was being threatened, he'd come running, right?"

"I don't get—" I cut off because I did. "Absolutely not!"

"Do you have a better idea?"

"If he doesn't come for us, the Hunters will!" I hissed under my breath. "Are you trying to get us killed?"

"That's not my primary goal, no."

"Jeph! That's got to be the stupidest plan I've ever heard."

"It's stupid, sure, but it's stupid enough that it just might work."

I glared. "Did you really just say that?"

"Yes or no? Because you get to play damsel—I'll play bait."

"What?"

"You'll get to be the innocent little witch being attacked by the Big Bad Mage."

"I already *am* the innocent witch being hunted by the bad mage!" I snapped at him, and he slapped a hand over my mouth, looking around frantically. No one seemed to be paying us any attention, but he led me into an alley anyway.

"Semantics. Best case scenario, we attract King."

"Worst case scenario, we bring the Hunters down on our heads!" I hissed.

"You'll be playing the victim—they'll come after *me*. I'll lead them away, and you can go barricade yourself in the tavern or something. Pretend to be a bar wench until I can come find you."

"That's the stupidest—"

"I'm trying to top myself today," he cut me off. "Yes. It's stupid, but it'll either work, or it won't. But we're not going to stumble across King by standing here, twiddling our thumbs."

"I don't...I don't like this."

"Trust me," he pleaded, looking into my eyes. "I won't let anything happen to you."

And wasn't that a loaded request?

"What do you need me to do?" I asked with a sigh. "But be forewarned—I *don't* trust you."

"Wise girl," he said seriously. "Just stand there and"—he grimaced—"look afraid."

"Why would I—" I yelped.

Jeph's magical energy assaulted me, screaming along my skin like fire and ice. It was hot—so hot it burned. But it was also cold and sinister—absolutely terrifying. I didn't need to pretend my fear; everything about his magical energy set my hair on end. It was absolutely heavy and dense with bloodlust and a desire to cause pain.

I stared into his eyes, watching as they shifted from Jeph to...*something*. As if his eyes were looking at me, but he wasn't the one looking out. It was like someone—*something*—else was sizing me up as if I was a treat at a dinner party. Very slowly, his hand came up and wrapped around my neck, holding me against the wall.

"Jeph..." I whispered, my voice trembling.

"Shh."

The pressure on my throat didn't increase, but he leaned closer, his face contorting into a snarl. My lips trembled, and I clenched my eyes shut, turning my head away. If this was him acting, I didn't want to see him serious. When he came for my head, I had no doubt he'd kill me before I could even touch the surface of Chaos.

"Someone's coming," he whispered against my ear.

And then, he went flying, a grunt escaping his lips. I screamed, and a cloaked figure put himself between Jeph and me, a dagger in his left hand and a short-sword in his right.

"Stay behind me!" the figure called over his shoulder, the hood obscuring his face.

Jeph sat up, holding his side. When he pulled his hand away, it was covered in blood. "Are you kidding me? I *just* got all the blood out!"

"This was *your* idea!" I snapped.

"I told you he'd come, though," he said smugly, getting to his feet. "Should've wagered a bet or something."

"Not into gambling my soul away, m'kay? Sorry-not-sorry," I said dryly.

"What's going on?" the cloaked figure asked, his defensive stance shifting. He held his dagger pointed at me and his sword toward Jeph, backing slowly toward the end of the alley.

"Are you King?" I asked. "Please tell me you're King."

"You...You did this on *purpose?*" he asked, which wasn't an answer. "Are you *insane?* The Hunters are gonna—"

"Stop right there!" a new man's deep, booming voice called from the end of the alley.

"Run!" Jeph reached for me, pulling me out of the way when the Hunter swung a sword. It crashed against the wall where I'd just been standing.

I guess these Hunters shoot first and ask questions later...

"Running!" I yelled, chasing the cloaked man. Until we confirmed whether or not he was King, we needed to keep him in our sights.

"Stop following me!" he called over his shoulder, swinging out with his sword, doing a neat turn as he pivoted back around to keep running.

"Not a chance!" Jeph snapped, catching a handful of his cloak.

"Less yelling, more running!" I shouted.

"Halt, Sibyl!" a Hunter yelled.

"Sibyl?" the cloaked mage demanded. "Oh, shit."

A hail of arrows came at us.

Jeph growled, releasing the cloak and lobbing energy blasts at the archers, knocking them off their feet. They returned fire, and I screamed, diving for the ground. I skidded to a stop, cursing and hissing in pain. Jeph stood over me, his dark magic lifting me to my feet while he sent more magic blasting at the Hunters. Even the mystery mage caught magic blasts and sent them back. His aura told me he was enjoying himself. At least, I assumed he was. I couldn't imagine anyone's aura looking that jovial if they thought their life was in real danger.

Jeph's magic gave me a nudge, and I ran deeper into the alley, him and the mystery mage backing up as they held off the Hunters still giving chase. We reached the end of the alley and looked around, assessing the walls surrounding us.

"Well, it's been fun," the mystery mage said. "Catch ya later!" Then, he ran and leapt at the wall, his hands and feet finding purchase as he scaled it.

"Oh no, you don't!" Jeph snapped, reaching for him.

The man kicked him in the face, causing him to rear back.

"Stop!" a Hunter yelled, dagger sailing for the retreating mage. It missed his hand by inches as it dug into the stone wall.

He yelped, losing his grip and plummeting toward the earth, but he turned, his magic pushing and pulling in green tendrils… and the earth rose to meet him, grabbing him and slowing his fall. He was an earth elemental, which was at least something. The stories about King *had* said he could move mountains.

"You any good with that sword?" Jeph asked the…*boy*, whose hood had just fallen back.

Now that it wasn't covering his head, I got a good look at a teenager that couldn't have been any older than seventeen or eighteen. His brunette hair was disheveled, his green eyes bright with adrenaline, and his bronze skin flushed with excitement.

"Got you with it, didn't I?" the boy snapped.

"That's because I *let* you get me. Now, give me that dagger and I'll show you how to *actually* use it."

I didn't understand why Jeph wanted a dagger when he had a sword, which reminded me…I pulled my bow from my back.

Hopefully, the Hunters wouldn't blast my arrows out of the air, but if I could help cause a distraction, then that would work, too.

"Whatever!" the boy shouted. "Like I'm gonna—"

We ducked a blast of water, hitting the deck. While it might have *seemed* harmless, it pounded the wall with a ferocity that told me I *so* didn't want to be anywhere near it. Not to mention, the water elemental could command that water to drown us. I'd had enough water to last me a lifetime.

"Give me the damn dagger!" Jeph barked.

"You've got your own blade!"

"Mines too long. Now, give!"

Now that he mentioned it, I realized the alley was pretty small. It would narrow the Hunters' range of motion as well, but they had numbers while we had…well, we had a psychopath, an unknown earth elemental, and me. We'd be surrounded before long if we didn't go on the offensive.

The boy handed over the dagger, muttering curses under his breath. Jeph sprinted at the Hunters, and the boy looked from him to me, to his sword, to the Hunters, and to the wall. Magic swirled around his fingertips, telling me he was about to take off.

"Don't. You. Dare," I growled, leveling my bow on him. I didn't particularly want to shoot him, but I would. If he was King, then we couldn't risk losing track of him. If he wasn't, then he deserved what he got for trying to leave us behind.

"You won't—"

I loosed my arrow, cutting his ear.

"Next one is your leg." I had another arrow loaded before his eyes could widen in shock. "Well?"

"I see the legends don't do you justice, lady." He grinned, winking at me before charging into the fray, sword clashing with a Hunter's.

Jeph had incapacitated several of them, his blows non-fatal. The boy was also careful with his attacks which was reassuring. I still didn't want anyone to die.

Then, it suddenly occurred to me that I had allies on my side—even if they were temporary. "Well, this is different," I muttered, sending an arrow sinking into the shoulder of a Hunter sneaking up on Jeph.

His eyes darted to mine, approval in them before he turned, slashing at another Hunter.

The battle drew on, and I injured those ganging up on my allies while they carefully wounded their assailants. It didn't take long for my quiver to empty out, and I frowned, feeling useless. Then, I felt even more useless when a Hunter snuck up on me, wrapping a beefy arm around my throat and cutting off my air supply.

"Surrender, and this will go better for you," he told me.

"Thanks, but no," I rasped, feeling Jeph's magic snaking toward us. It wrapped around the Hunter, yanking him away and smashing him into a wall. I wheezed, stepping away from his now-still body.

After a few more minutes, the Hunters were either unconscious or bleeding on the ground.

"They won't stay down for long!" the boy shouted, running through the fallen bodies with practiced grace.

Jeph grabbed my hand and we chased after him. My quick footsteps had me accidentally stepping on Hunter hands and limbs. It wasn't *my* fault they'd fallen in the alley, blocking the exit. They did make me trip and stumble, however.

Hunters make for a terrible floor, I mused, lips quirking.

We burst out of the alley and ran through the streets, dodging around Norms, mages, and witches. Some didn't move fast enough, and we ended up brushing their shoulders or shoving them out of the way. One man tripped into a stall, sending bread flying.

I grimaced, yelling, "Sorry!"

"In the name of the Hunters, clear the street!" a voice bellowed behind us.

Norms, mages, and witches scampered and tripped over each other, trying to obey.

"Shit!" the boy hissed, turning and raising his hands.

The ground rose high into the air, arrows sailing toward us. One broke through the wall where my face was because, of course, I was stupid enough to stop and gape. The tip was just shy of my nose.

"Why didn't you do that in the alley?" Jeph demanded.

"Ever have a building collapse on you?"

Jeph's eyes narrowed.

"Yeah, doesn't feel good," the boy muttered, turning to run again.

I followed, taking off at a sprint.

"Turn here!" the boy shouted over his shoulder.

We ducked into an alley. It snaked, twisting and turning, and we followed it to several forks, taking paths that felt like they were leading us in circles. We were all panting and breathless when we finally stopped. I leaned against the wall, chest heaving. The boy put his hands on his knees, trying to catch his breath. Jeph looked like he could keep running for hours.

"Who the hell are you guys?" the boy asked after he caught his breath. "Well, you." He pointed at Jeph. "She's the Sibyl."

"No," Jeph growled. "Who the hell are *you?*"

"Me?" His grin was cocky. "They call me King."

"Thank the goddess," I muttered.

"Hello, pretty lady." King turned his charm on me. "It's such an honor to be sought by the legendary Sibyl herself. I'm eternally at your service, my goddess." He bowed with a flourish, taking my hand and kissing it.

Jeph slapped King's hand away, stepping between us. "Look here, punk—"

"Puh—what?"

"—keep your grubby little mitts off her."

"My what?"

"Jeph," I said in warning, stepping around him. I smiled at the cheeky little brat in front of me. "Is it true that you're the most *incredible* mage around?" I was laying it on thick, but this ladies' man was much more likely to respond to honey than Jeph's...*jealousy?* "I would *love* to see one of your spells or tricks."

King wiggled his brows at Jeph, probably trying to assert his dominance in an imaginary contest neither of them was a part of. "If my lady would like"—he held his elbow out to me, and I linked my arm in his—"I would be *more* than willing to show you."

Then, my gut twisted when I felt a familiar pull.

"Oh, *goddess*—Jeph!" I screamed, reaching my hand toward him, but it was already too late.

King wasn't just a mage.

He could wield *Chaos*.

Twenty-Nine

"Here we are, m'lady," King said, cavalier. "But one trick for a beauty such as yourself."

"Take me back!" I snapped, not impressed with the inside of Chaos. Sure, it was beautiful with its glittering, rainbow lights shining in the black void around us, but this was a sight I was all too familiar with. And right now, I was more concerned with what sort of hell Jeph was raising without me there to keep him in line.

"The lady isn't impressed?"

"No, the lady is so far from impressed, you might as well have shown me a pile of horse dung."

His brow furrowed. "Do you not find the lights enchanting? The darkness…like mood lighting?" He grinned, brows wiggling.

"Gag me. Take me back to my friend or I'll show *you* a surprise next." I didn't want to use my own magic to exit Chaos if I didn't have to, but goddess above and below, I would. "And methinks you're not gonna like it."

"This always works," King muttered to himself. "Ladies are always impressed…"

"You *moron!*" I mimed strangulation. "Don't tell me you're actually showing off *Chaos!*"

His eyes went wide. "You know of this dimension? Did Guinevere tell you about it?"

"Guin—" Something in my stomach curdled, but I couldn't quite place why. "Just take me back to my friend. Right. Now."

That cocky smirk was on his face again, reminding me so much of Jeph's poor attitude, I wanted to smack him.

"As you wish." He flourished a bow. "But first, a little stop on the way."

"No—*wait!*"

King deposited us into a room. Several teens and young men looked up, brows arching. One of them put his cup of ale down, brows raising over familiar green eyes. But the eyes weren't the only familiar thing, his hair, skin, and face were familiar, too. The boy was a perfect duplicate for King.

"I dare say, Arthur, you do bring home the most interesting company."

"Did he just..." I couldn't breathe.

"Emrys, can you keep an eye on our guest? She's a lively one. I'll return shortly—with another *pleasant* guest."

I whirled, reaching for him. "King, wait!"

But I was too late. He was gone. I grimaced, knowing King was about to have a less than pleasant experience with Jeph. If there was one thing that set him off, it was my safety, and with us so close to making it home, he had to be livid.

Then, I cringed, feeling the weight of several gazes on me.

"Hello." I waved a hand.

Emrys—King's doppelgänger—sighed loudly. "Where did he pick you up from?"

"Excuse me?" I snapped, hands on hips. "You better watch that mouth of yours, young man. I'm in a seriously bad mood right now, and I've had it up to here with both of you!"

Emrys' eyes went wide.

The young blonde sitting next to him threw his head back and laughed, slapping Emrys on the shoulder. "You've done it now, Merlin. Offending every lass you come across."

My knees about gave out. "Mer...Merlin?"

"Nice going, Lancelot! You know you're not supposed to use my alias in front of strangers."

"I thought 'Emrys' was the alias?" a redhead man asked, and my mind reeled.

"No, Gawain, it's 'Merlin,'" Emrys said slowly.

"Gawain..." I breathed next, but they were all ignoring me.

"Whatever," the raven-haired boy muttered. "It's not like King didn't give you *both* those names."

"That's a secret, Percival!" Emrys snapped. "Would you all kindly shut your mouths and drink your ale!"

Percival. Gawain. Lancelot. Merlin. And mother trucking Arthur.

"Oh goddess," I breathed, grabbing my head.

I was standing in the middle of King Arthur's court. Only, Arthur wasn't a king at all—he was a miscreant, a hooligan, and a vigilante. And these men, ranging from age fifteen to twenty at the most, were his Knights of the Round Table. Was there even an Order for the knights yet? Or were the stories entirely glamorized and false? This was roughly seven hundred years prior to the creation of the Arthurian legends; I'd read that they'd been based on a war general and a madman—who knew those facts had been so, so wrong?

"Doing okay, there, lass?" Lancelot asked, looking genuinely concerned. "You look a little pale."

"Peachy," I wheezed, knees shaking. "Just need…just need a minute to process my life decisions."

This statement earned me several weird looks, followed by them looking at each other as if I might be insane. If we were making bets, I'd say I probably was.

"Get the girl some ale," Gawain said, shrugging.

That doesn't sound like a bad idea…

The ripple of Chaos tore through the room, and I barely managed to jump out of the way when a snarling Jeph and hollering King came crashing onto the floor, grappling and wrestling with each other. The knights were on their feet instantly, pulling swords from scabbards and pointing them toward the two men.

"Stop!" I shrieked, heart pounding in my chest. To my surprise, they did, more out of shock than obeying a command, but their hesitation was enough.

Jeph's head whipped up, his eyes locking on mine. Slowly, he released his hands from around King's throat, getting to his feet. My chest heaved from fear and adrenaline. I knew it was irrational, knew Jeph could take them all in a fight, but after learning who they were, I wasn't willing to take any risks.

"I'm fine, Jeph," I said, forcing a smile onto my face. I held my hands up for him to see. "Nothing happened."

Momentarily reassured, his focus shifted to the four knights, who were ready to hack and slash at him in a moment's notice. I knew he could have his sword drawn faster than I could blink, but a confrontation in this small room would be disastrous.

King hacked and coughed, sitting up and waving a hand at his friends. The other held his bruised throat. "I'm fine, I'm fine. Just a misunderstanding," he muttered, getting to his feet.

They hesitated a moment before putting their swords back in their scabbards.

Jeph was across the room in the blink of an eye, turning me left and right, tilting my chin side to side. When he seemed satisfied, he pulled me to his chest in a suffocating bear hug. He clung to me, fingers digging into my back and hair.

"I said I'm fine, pal," I said airily, trying to breathe.

"Don't take that tone with me," he said firmly. "One second you were standing in front of me, the next you scream and you're just *gone!*"

"It's not my fault Douche McGee can wield Chaos—I wasn't expecting that."

"Arthur!" Emrys snapped. "This girl knows about Chaos? You *fool!*" He swatted King upside the head.

"*Ow!*" King ducked his blows. "I didn't know she knew! I swear it!"

"They're at it again," Percival muttered.

"This could be a while," Gawain agreed.

"I think it's sweet," Lancelot said cheekily. "A lovers' quarrel."

Twin blasts of energy came from Emrys' and King's palms, sending Lancelot flying into the wall. I winced, watching his back and head crack against the stones, but the cheeky bastard kept grinning.

"What the hell is going on here?" Jeph demanded. "Why are there a bunch of children…" He trailed off, his finger pointing at Emrys, his eyes never leaving King. "Did he just say…*Arthur?*"

"Yes. That's Arthur, and his twin there is Emrys. Lancelot just hit the wall, the one drinking is Gawain, and that one's Percival." I pointed to them in turn.

The color drained from Jeph's face. "We can't stay here."

"Ya think?"

"What is this fixation on our names?" Emrys asked. "Do you know us?"

"N-N-No," I stuttered.

"She is lying," Gawain said. "Her aura is murky." He cocked his head to the side, looking at Jeph. "But yours is terrifying. How does one get an aura that bleak?"

"I can show you," he growled, taking a step toward Gawain.

I caught his arm, pulling him back as I stared at Gawain with wide eyes. "You can see auras?"

"A rare gift, I know. But a good one to have."

I'd never met anyone who'd had that ability before—no one besides me.

"What does mine look like?" I breathed, eager to know. "Please, *please* tell me." I couldn't see my own aura, and I'd always wondered what it looked like.

"Well, now it is absolutely blinding with your enthusiasm. Tone it down—you already shine rather brightly. Kinda like…" he trailed off, looking from me to King, to Emrys, and back again. "Oh, shit."

I scowled. "That doesn't tell me what it looks like!"

"What's wrong?" King asked, coming over to Gawain.

"Her aura…it is…"

"It matches ours, doesn't it?" Emrys asked, massaging his temples. "Arthur, what did you get us into now?"

It wasn't until he said that that I bothered to pay attention to their auras. They were unlike anything I'd ever seen before. And he was right, they were identical, but for twins, that was no surprise. Shining and translucent like all auras but like looking at a rainbow. Instead of each color representing a feeling or an emotion like in other people's auras—each person had a base color and patches of certain colors indicated their moods like a mood ring—their base color *was* the rainbow.

It was enthralling.

"Not exactly," Gawain muttered.

"Why would their auras match?" Percival asked, crowding in around us.

Lancelot came over, rubbing his head. "I sensed it too," he said. "To be honest, I just thought it was only yours and Emrys'—until you left and came back."

"Come on, guys. Stop leaving me out of the loop!" Percival shouted.

King stared me down, eyes narrowing. "I should've noticed her energy sooner. And her title...The *Sibyl* of Legend and Time." He cursed under his breath. "What era are you from?"

My eyes widened, but I supposed I shouldn't have been surprised. He could wield Chaos, after all. Not to mention, my reputation really did precede me. "The...the twenty-first century."

The room exploded into shouts and curses.

"How the blazes did you travel sixteen hundred years?" King demanded. "That should've killed you!"

"Well, it didn't—not that it didn't *feel* like it." I shrugged. "And you should ask me about Egypt."

"That has no meaning to me," King replied drolly.

"Never mind," I muttered.

"She can't stay here, Arthur," Emrys said, putting his hand on King's shoulder. "She'll damage the timeline."

"If she hasn't already," Lancelot said, inclining his head. "How long have you been here?"

"Long enough," Jeph muttered.

More shouts and curses filled the room.

"Please tell me you haven't spoken to anyone," Emrys demanded.

"Define 'spoken'..." I grimaced.

"Try hunted, chased all over England—do you guys even call it that yet?" Jeph asked. "Enslaved, put in an arena for a death match, chased off a Lord's estate, tracked by Hunters, and, well, there was that town of Norms several miles south of here. You don't know what miles are, do you?"

"Jeph!" I hissed, slapping him upside the head. "Wait... tracked?"

He glared, rubbing his head. "Don't worry about it."

Oh, I'm going to worry about it, all right. "Was that the night I blacked out?"

He shrugged.

"So, you really meant Hunters—and not ruffians—when you told Granny we'd been attacked?"

He shrugged again.

"How many of them did you kill?" I asked, exasperated.

"None." He pursed his lips, examining his nails. "Barely."

"Jeph!"

"She's *definitely* left an impact," Percival said, receiving glares from his friends.

"Look"—I turned to King—"I—*we*—just wanna go home. I don't know how we got here. I don't know *why* Chaos acted up—again—but here we are. I need your help."

"She's telling the truth," Gawain said, reading my aura. It was annoying, and I felt violated.

Way to be the pot calling the kettle black, I mused to myself. *And he still hasn't told me what mine looks like!*

"What do you mean by 'Chaos acted up?'" Emrys inclined his head. "You're a Kairos, are you not?"

"A what?" My brow furrowed.

"She can't be, Mer. She's a *girl*."

"Then explain how she's here!" Emrys snapped. "Do you not feel that magical energy? It's identical to—"

"I know it is!" King threw his hands in the air. "But she'd be *dead* if she were a Kairos. We *can't* do that, Mer. Especially not with the energy it would've taken her to carry this man along."

"Maybe she carries the amulet?" Emrys asked.

"We can sense her magic, she doesn't have the amulet, Mer." King pursed his lips. "Besides, that still wouldn't take her this far without killing her."

"Then I don't know, Arthur!" Emrys ran his hands down his face, and I had to admit, it was confusing watching them argue. With their identical looks, it was like watching someone have an argument with themselves. "How did she get here then?"

"The answer is simple," Percival said, drawing everyone's attention. I got the feeling he got the short end of the stick a lot, being the youngest in a room full of budding men. "Chaos did it."

I'd had the same thought myself, but it still didn't make sense. Even if Chaos kept me alive, it couldn't have helped me time travel. But...could Chaos fuel *my* magic and *force* me back through time? Was that how I'd gotten to Egypt, too?

"That's—" King held up a finger and just froze. Then, he turned to Emrys. "Do you think...?"

"It's possible. Gaia favored you, after all."

"But that's different."

"How so?"

"That was an exchange," King said. "What does Chaos get out of meddling in the timeline? Especially abandoning her where she can't get home on her own?"

Emrys shrugged. "Gods are fickle creatures."

Lancelot snorted. "You can say that again."

He went flying across the room, the twins blasting him.

"Wait. You're saying the gods..." I trailed off. Of course, the gods were real. I literally accessed Chaos—or at least touched the fringes of it—every day. "So, Chaos is a bully, big whoop. Can you help get us home or not?"

Emrys and King exchanged a look.

"We might be able to, but..." King started.

"It still might kill you," Emrys finished.

I didn't like the sound of that at all.

hat kind of ritual is going to bring the Hunters right to us, Arthur," Gawain said, several minutes later after Jeph and I had changed back into our sports clothes from the twenty-first century. There was no need to freak Evander out when we got back.

If we got back.

"We don't have a choice. She can't stay here."

"She's already influenced our perspectives of the future," Emrys complained.

"Not that that affects Arthur," Percival said.

"If it's the only way, then we should send them as soon as possible. What better time than when the guilds have already spotted you?" Lancelot gave King a pointed look.

"It wasn't my fault for once!"

Emrys snorted. "Sure, it wasn't."

"Says the jerk that moved the damn *mountain* and the *ocean* for fun!" King raged.

Emrys shrugged, a grin on his face.

"That was you?" I looked at him with awe.

"It was an accident, really. The elements got away from me…I was crafting with the goddess, and well, I lost focus for but a moment…" Emrys grimaced.

"Crafting? With the *goddess?*" My jaw dropped. If only I could get that kind of service from Hecate.

Emrys grinned, hand trailing lazily over the hilt of his sword. "It turned out okay in the end."

"He is just a show-off," Gawain whispered conspiratorially. "Likes to rub it in Arthur's face that he is *of* the elements."

"Yeah?" King asked haughtily. "Well I'm of time and space, so he can suck it!"

"Ah, young love," Lancelot murmured before he was blasted across the room again.

I winced, wondering why he continually made those comments if he knew they were going to attack him. And then, seeing Lancelot's gaze on King, I got it. *Ah.* Lancelot in the stories of Camelot cheated on his best friend by loving Guinevere. The truth was, if I was reading his aura right, the young man was in love with...

I bit my lip, fighting a smile. I wondered if King knew the depth of his friend's teasing and affection. Gawain caught my look, and his head inclined. A grin spread across his face in understanding, and he held his finger to his lips, winking. I grinned back at him, happy to see how supportive and considerate he was of his friends.

The longer I spent with the rowdy bunch, the more I liked them and the more I wanted to stay. And if it wasn't for the timeline, I think I would've liked to. I was hunted here, but so was King, and he'd managed to evade the guilds long enough to build his own legend in his own era. He'd even gained loyal friends and followers, as well as a *life.*

I briefly wondered if I could do the same in my own time. Could I find friends and happiness despite being hunted by the guilds? It was crazy to dream. I wouldn't dare to hope, not after what I did to my friends before. There was a reason my BFF was a dead man, a ghost, someone who couldn't be hurt, someone who couldn't die—again.

"If you're all done acting like a bunch of children, we'd really like to be on our way," Jeph said, glaring at them.

King looped an arm around my neck. "Where'd ya find this dolt? He's rather unpleasant. Is that what the ladies are into in the future?"

I pressed my lips together, both to keep from laughing and to keep from screaming. It was funny because *yes*, that kinda was the norm in the twenty-first century. It was annoying because Jeph and I weren't an item. I was getting really tired of everyone assuming that.

"We're not—whatever." I was done trying.

"We should get started, Arthur," Emrys said.

King clapped his hands together, rubbing his palms. "Circle up, boys."

"Which way's east?" Percival asked. "Wait. No. I sense it. Hold on." He walked toward the window on the far side of the room.

"If that is east," Gawain murmured, moving to Percival's left, "then this is south."

"West," Lancelot said, taking his place next.

"That makes me north," King said.

"And I'm the only spirit elemental of the lot of you," Emrys muttered, taking center. "You two, come stand next to me."

My eyes went wide when I realized what they were doing. They were going to cast a circle using the elements. I did this on a small scale in my own home, lighting colored pillar candles associated with each of the elements in cardinal order: air to the east, fire to the south, water to the west, earth to the north, and spirit in the middle. It was a way of praying to the gods or a way to enhance spells and ritual magic.

If I was understanding Emrys' words correctly, they were going to invoke the elements using their own magic. Not just their own magic, they were each an *elemental*. Percival controlled air, Gawain, fire, Lancelot, water, King, earth, and Emrys, spirit. I'd never met a full circle of elementals before. I'd had the occasional fireball thrown at me, but I'd never witnessed what they were about to do.

Jeph and I joined Emrys in the center of the circle.

"You'll love this," King said, grinning at me.

Emrys walked to Percival. "Air, I call on thee, come to this circle and strengthen me."

Air billowed around Percival and Emrys, and I watched in rapt fascination as Emrys cupped the air, holding it in his palm as he moved and controlled it. He wasn't just a spirit elemental—he was also *air*. The wind seemed to pick up, a torrent staying around Percival even after Emrys stopped touching the wisps of air.

Emrys moved clockwise to Gawain. "Fire, I call on thee, come to this circle and strengthen me."

Fire raged around Gawain, but he didn't look alarmed. Instead, he grinned, letting the flames dance around him. They didn't burn him, his clothing, or even the floor he was standing on. Emrys reached his hands into the flames, weaving them around himself before returning them to Gawain. A stray flame dashed toward Jeph, wrapping itself around him a few times before dashing back to Gawain.

Before I could ask what had just happened, Emrys moved on to Lancelot.

"Water, I call on thee, come to the circle and strengthen me."

Water matched air and fire, the clear liquid wrapping its way around the elemental, but not soaking his clothing. It clung to him, wisps dancing into Emrys' hands before he sent them back to Lancelot. I wasn't even shocked anymore; it was clear Emrys was something incredible. No mage could control more than one element, and yet…he was *Merlin*.

"Earth so strong and favorite of mine, I call on thee, come to the circle and strengthen me." Vines, lush with leaves and blooming flowers, climbed King's leg, the buds blooming under Emrys' touch.

When at last Emrys came back to the center, he grinned at me. I was too stunned to react.

"Spirit, I call on thee, come to the circle and strengthen me."

This time, there was nothing to *see*. I only knew air had been present because it had taken an off-white coloring, rustling Percival's and Emrys' hair. With spirit, it was like there was happiness expanding in my chest. I thought it was strange that I could feel it when the other elements hadn't affected me, but I also hadn't been standing directly next to the other knights like I was now.

Emrys closed his eyes, basking in the elements. I almost envied him, wondering what it would feel like to have all that elemental power flowing through me. It seemed like too much and too little all at once. As it was, I could barely control my own magical energy, so I couldn't imagine holding that much more power.

"Air, Fire, Water, Earth, Spirit, I call on thee," Emrys chanted, "open a path to Chaos, and help these travelers leave."

The space directly next to me ripped asunder, a path into Chaos manifesting right before my very eyes. It was like a gaping hole in this plane. Like a festering wound, erupting as the power of the void seeped into this dimension. It blew my hair from my face, the power acting like a torrent of air. I shielded my eyes with my hand, staring into the darkness, rainbow lights twinkling at me.

"I'll hold Chaos open," Emrys yelled to be heard over the roar of the void.

"And I'll push you as far as I can through time," King shouted next, drawing my gaze. "The elements will only give us so much extra strength. The rest is up to you."

I nodded. "Thank you."

"Safe travels, m'lady."

I grinned at King. "M'lord."

He winked, and I took Jeph's hand in mine. He looked from our clasped hands to me.

"Don't let go," I told him, and he nodded.

Together, we stepped into the storm.

Once we were inside Chaos, the noise stopped, all but a whistle of the primal power seeping into the mortal plane. I stopped just inside the void, turning to look out. It was strange being able to see out of Chaos the way one might look out of a window or through an open door. Normally, I pictured where I wanted to go and that would direct me through Chaos to the right "door" to open, even if it was seamless and literally doorless.

I met Emrys' eyes, and he turned his head, nodding to King. He lifted a hand, his magical energy reaching out, sending Jeph and me lurching through time, even if we appeared to physically go nowhere. With the rift, I could still see into the fifth century, still see the knights on the other side, but now I could feel the centuries passing me like water under a bridge.

It didn't take long for Emrys' face to contort first in pained-concentration, then in agony, holding primal magic open much longer than ever should've been possible. That he could touch Chaos at all still baffled me. That he could rip it open with the aid of the elements was terrifying.

King had to lift his other hand, the strain evident on his face as he pushed us further and further away. With each passing year, it was getting harder and harder for his magic to reach us, even if we were still physically standing right before them inside the void. But we weren't in front of them, not really. We were already eight centuries away. Sweat trickled down the side of his face, and he clenched his eyes shut, gritting his teeth.

I felt horrible for not helping, but I would need my strength to get us the rest of the way. Especially now that I could feel our progress slowing. It was trickling down to a handful of years as opposed to the centuries he'd been pushing us through before. Our movement was like traversing tar instead of swimming through water.

Emrys would lose hold of the rift in Chaos before long. It was already shrinking, already closing itself up as he held his hands in front of him, fingers hooked as if he might be able to pry the metaphysical wall open with his hands. And as it shrunk from the size of a double-door to the size of a large window, to the size of a small porthole, I felt the years we'd been being pushed forward turn to mere hours.

Emrys lost hold of Chaos, and King's magical energy vanished. The rift sealed itself, and Jeph and I were left alone, somewhere around the year 1600. I took a deep breath, clasping his other hand as I turned to face him.

"Sam—"

"Shh. I need to concentrate."

He stayed silent, and I tried not to think about how he'd used my name, about what he wanted to say, or why he'd spoken at all, his tone melancholy. I couldn't think about it; not if I was going to get us home safely, not if I was going to get us the remaining four hundred years.

I closed my eyes, calling on my magical energy and bringing it to the surface. It felt like fuzzy tingles in the tips of my fingers. It felt like the glow of embers just under the surface of my skin. It was like reaching for light and finding a sparkler instead. It was soft and warm, full and light, and it exploded within me like a car's engine backfiring and spitting smog.

I channeled it, guiding us forward in time. It was slow going and, unlike King doing the heavy work before, felt like I was slogging through molasses, moving decade by decade. His had been so powerfully seamless, it had been like breathing. Mine felt like I was running a marathon—and we were only halfway there.

My grip tightened on Jeph's hands, the magical output painful as it drained from me much too quickly. He squeezed my hands back, and I was glad he did. It grounded me inside the groundless void. I needed his stability, even if having him with me was causing me extra strain.

I pushed us into the twentieth century.

We were almost there, and I was sweating and panting with the effort. Hot liquid drained from my nose and over my lip, the last dregs of my magic leaving me. The edge of my vision sparkled, zooming in and out with the darkness. I was going to pass out...we weren't going to make it.

"Sam!" Jeph squeezed my hands hard. "Sam, stop."

There was no possible way he knew how close we were—how close, yet so far away. I could feel the time slapping against my skin like a belly flop, stinging me like a wasp, shredding me like a meat grinder. He wouldn't feel anything but me bleeding magical energy.

"You're using too much magic!" he yelled.

If I stopped now, we would never make it—*he* would never make it...because I already knew it was too late for me.

"Sam," he said urgently, right next to my ear. "You're not allowed to die."

It was a whisper, a command—a *plea*. And I knew, beyond a doubt, that he truly cared for me. It was a shame, really, to realize it after it was too late. All I could do now...was set him free.

I pushed my magic past the brink, a scream tearing from my lips, pain assaulting my every sense, and I knew I'd failed; if

Jeph was lucky, Chaos would release him, if not, he'd die here...like me. My knees buckled, and he caught me against him. I could scarcely breathe, and my vision swam. Numbness crept in, and I could feel myself fading, fading, fading. I was a light, and I was going to wink out...and then, everything went dark.

I couldn't feel anything—pain or cold, numbness or tingles. I couldn't feel my breath, my chest, my heart. Everything was silent—still—because I was dead. I was certain of that. My consciousness was slipping away, but before my soul could leave my body, before the ethereal world could take me in, something happened.

"Ah, Sammy Girl," a voice said. It sounded like my mother. It sounded like no one at all. It sounded like...*"You are my precious and favorite daughter."*

"Who...?" I couldn't speak the words; they wouldn't come, but she must've heard me because she spoke to me again.

"You have a choice to make, U-we-tsi-a-ge-yv. *You can come with me, and I'll take you to the Dead World, or..."*

"Or...?"

"Or you can accept a second life from this young man."

Jeph's tear-streaked face appeared in my mind's eye. The image did something horrible to me. I couldn't feel anything physically, but on a metaphysical level, it hurt everything—hurt *everywhere*. Was this true, unbridled pain? It was awful, like bathing in the aura of Depression and Anguish themselves.

"What do you mean, 'a second life?'"

"He's something special—something more. *If you come with me now, he can no longer reach you, and you will be free of the cruel fate this world has devised for you."*

"And if I stay?"

"Then his magic will raise you into a new life, a life full of grief and misery, happiness and friendship. You will have all, you will lose much, and you will suffer greatly. You will endure the most of all those you meet and inspire. You will share their burdens, feel their pain, and bring them sorrow, but without you, they will know no happiness to suffer at all."

"Gee, you're really selling yourself here." Apparently, even in death, I was still a sarcastic asshole.

The goddess chuckled, her laughter like tinkling bells. *"Ah, stubborn* U-we-tsi-a-ge-yv *of mine. How I forget your sharp wit and quick tongue."*

"Why do you keep calling me 'daughter'? And why in my mother's language?"

My essence felt something like a hand cupping my metaphysical cheek. I wished I could see her the way I could hear her so clearly. I knew her somehow, from somewhere…We'd met before. I was certain of it, but I couldn't remember. I'd worshipped her for so long, and yet praying to Hecate wasn't enough to overwhelm me with the feelings I had now. To overwhelm me with the urge I had to wrap her in a hug, feel her stroke a hand down my battle-braided hair, kiss both my cheeks, and say, "The strength of the heart is the strength of the warrior."

How did I know her?

"I call you daughter because you are mine. I use your familiar Cherokee because it's what your mother would do, is it not?"

"Well, yes…but…"

"Choose, U-we-tsi-a-ge-yv. *Time is running low."*

"But that's not—"

"Choose."

Life or death? That wasn't hard, was it? And yet…

"If I live, I'm going to be miserable and happy—I'm going to make other people miserable and happy…If I die?"

"A great deal will happen. A great deal will not. You already defy the Fates by existing. But I assure you, after what has transpired in your lifetime, your soul will not rest so easily. For every action, there are consequences."

"Great, so I'm screwed either way?"

Hecate didn't respond to my brattiness.

"If every action has consequences, then what are the consequences of letting my enemy save me?"

"A great many things, U-we-tsi-a-ge-yv.*"* There was a smile in her words. *"A great many things beautiful and cruel. I'll say no more. I have meddled enough...for now."*

Her cheeky smile radiated through whatever strange connection we had, and it was so impishly girlish, I was awestruck. For a moment, I could see her. If I'd still had working lungs, I didn't think I would've been able to breathe. She looked like...

"Mom...?"

"I'm afraid I'm not the mother you are seeking, although the description is still accurate in a way."

"What way?"

"You will learn soon enough, U-we-tsi-a-ge-yv. *Have you chosen?"*

"Will you...will you speak to me again?"

Her smile was sad this time. *"I'm afraid not. But from this boy's magic, I leave you another precious gift. You will need it if you are to defy destiny. Defy the Fates yet again and forge a new world for you and your friends, Sammy Girl."*

"I don't know what you mean!" I tried to shout at her, but she was already fading away from me. I couldn't sense her anymore, couldn't sense anything on the astral plane.

Everything suddenly felt *horrible*.

"Live."

I had no choice but to obey.

Epilogue

Jeph

"Don't you *dare* die!" The words tore from my throat. Sam was fading, and she was fading fast.

I compressed her chest again and again as I'd seen in the movies. I'd never learned CPR. I'd never had a reason to. I was a killer, a murderer, an executioner.

"You hear me, precious? You're not allowed to die!"

I leaned down, forcing air into her lungs. *God*, her still, unmoving lungs. I breathed for her again and again. Sam was alive. I could sense it—could *feel* it. She wasn't dead yet, but if I didn't do something, she was going to die. I wouldn't let that happen; I would never let it happen.

I began compressions again. She still wasn't breathing, her heart so faint against my palms, I wanted to scream. We'd survived the Dark Ages despite the odds—despite the complete and utter horse shit that had been thrown at us—I refused to see something as stupid as magical exhaustion take her life.

"You can't leave me! You don't get to leave me!"

This wasn't working.

Wasn't.

Working.

Desperate, I grabbed the dagger I'd snagged from King, ripping it across my wrist. The gash was short and deep, blood spilling over my arm. I ignored the delighted purr of the monster in the back of my mind. Pain. He loved all pain. Mine. Hers. It didn't matter. So long as there was blood. So long as there was something to revel in.

We wanted to drown in it.

I shook my head, refocusing on my purpose. *Sam, Sam, Sam.* She was my purpose, and my blood *had* to save her. There would be repercussions for this. There would be something... *something*, but I wasn't sure what. I'd never learned the consequences of my power because I feared it. Which meant I didn't know its limits. It could repair wounds, but could it stop death?

I was about to find out.

My blood was rife with my power, disgustingly riddled with it. It was a heady drug on the lips of others, addictive even, and it gave me temporary control over those who tasted it. I'd sworn to never use it again. I'd been successful...then I'd met Sam.

How many times had I poisoned her now? Three times? Four? It had to be more than that, but I couldn't remember. The rage was ever-present, and that had blotted out all else. The memory of how the slavers had whipped her. How the Norms in the arena had sliced into her. How the doctor hadn't actually treated her.

Then, she'd seen too much, and I'd taken those memories from her. I'd had to. The knowledge wasn't safe to me, to her, to anyone. And then, she'd wormed her way right back under my goddamned defenses, somehow getting me to spill more secrets she absolutely couldn't know.

So, I'd corrupted her.

I truly am a monster.

I put my wrist to my mouth, sucking the blood in. Sucking, sucking, sucking, trying not to think of the taste, trying not to moan at the power, trying not to swallow. *This isn't for me.* I didn't need it.

Sam did.

When my mouth was full, I leaned down, fitting my lips to hers. *Her lips.* Soft and precious, tender and sweet, fierce and demanding. *God*, when they'd been demanding. I could lose myself in the feel of her lips, in the taste of her tongue, in the sound of her voice.

I'd do anything if only she asked.

I cradled the back of her head in my palm, parting her lips and letting my blood trickle into her mouth. A small drop of it dribbled out of the corner, running down her cheek. I lifted her slightly off the ground, mouth still pressed against hers, tilting her head back. My blood slid down her throat, and I pulled away, licking my lips and using my finger to wipe the crimson rivulet from her face.

Then, I waited…

Sam's heart stopped.

"No," I whimpered, tears springing to my eyes as I felt for a pulse that I knew I wouldn't feel. I could sense her death, could scent it in the air like the sweetest perfume. "No, no, no, no, *no!*" I sobbed, my lungs seizing in my chest as my mind screamed and raged at me.

I killed her.

I killed her.

I killed her!

The monster echoed my thoughts, his grotesque pleasure slithering through my mind.

You killed her!

You killed her!

You killed her!

I couldn't breathe, trembling as I took her cheeks in my hands, my thumbs tracing over her skin. It was still warm. It was still flushed with color. It wouldn't be for long. I knew what a corpse looked like, felt like. Sam was…

"*No!*"

I threw my head back and roared from deep in my core, from the blackest recesses of my mind where the monster hid. That cruel beast who had plagued me my whole life. He was the only part of myself I truly knew, a part of myself no one else would understand. We were both killers, him and I, relishing the bloodshed and the pain of others. Delighting in darkness and death. Hiding within lies and shadows.

We were perfect for each other…yet I'd spent my entire life fighting him.

Now, it was time to embrace him. The monster had power I could use, and I had every intention of tapping into its source. I was a goddamn necromancer, but I was more than that, more than a dark mage. I was a fucking blood mage, and that was a sin all on its own—a sin and a curse—and fuck the gods, fuck the Fates, fuck death because I was *going* to call on that power now.

Closing my eyes, I looked within myself, searching for the darkest pit, the cruelest, muddiest, worst piece of me. He was there, those gleaming, red eyes leering at me out of the blackness. A feral, sharp-toothed grin greeted me, threatening to shred my sanity and devour my soul. He'd nearly succeeded once before.

As I stared him down, he entreated me to set him free, to let him wreak havoc; I'd kill us both before I ever let him try. But right now, I needed him. And sick, cruel bastards that we both were, he knew it. In my mind, he was bound, rows and rows of chains pinning him down, shackles around the indiscernible shape of him, steel bars holding him in, trapping him there. It never stopped his influence from reaching out to me. Never stopped his silky voice, his words like nails on a chalkboard, from calling to me.

Once, I had obeyed, had rampaged.

Then, I had locked him away.

Now, I was going to set him free.

Like the snapping of steel, clinking and shattering, I unleashed him, letting the monster guide the magic I knew so little about. My magical energy flared like a fire greedily drinking gasoline, surging white-hot through my veins and prickling like the spark along a fuse. If the spark reached my core, like a firework, I'd explode...and the monster would be in control.

I couldn't let him rule me.

Despite our differences in goals, he was eager to play.

I'll give you something to toy with.

Gritting my teeth, I pressed my forehead against Sam's, my forgotten tears dripping onto her face. With each second that passed, she would slip farther and farther from my reach. Her spirit hadn't left her yet, and I wasn't sure what would happen if it did. It wasn't like I made a habit of raising people from the dead. Hell, I never had. It was so much easier to put people in the ground than it was to try to bring rotting, soulless corpses back from the dead.

Ghosts were annoying but easily dealt with. Wraiths were tricky but could be subdued with some effort. Spirits fresh out of their still-warm corpses? I didn't know if I could command them back in. Even that had to be outside of my control. Some forces of nature wouldn't be denied.

But why hadn't Sam's spirit tried to leave her yet? It didn't matter; I wouldn't let her get far if she tried. As a precaution, I released my shadows from within me, wrapping them around us both.

"You can't escape me now, precious."

Then, I trailed my hand along her neck, feeling the blood in her body, every cell fizzling like static against my magic. I hadn't known I could sense it, hadn't known I could feel it—until now. I traced the artery to her heart, my hand resting over the unbeating muscle, and wrapped my magic around her blood, around her delicate tissue, around her heart.

Then, I pushed.

Buh-bump.

I pushed again.

Buh-bump.

Her blood spurted in her veins.

It wasn't enough.

I wrapped my magic around her major arteries, around her smallest veins, and pushed again.

Buh-bump. Buh-bump.

Still not enough.

The monster howled in my mind when he found the core of where her magic should've been stored, diving into it and dragging my power along. It was empty, completely void of the essence that should be there, but it wasn't any less heady or intoxicating to feel my magic pour into her, the monster trying to overtake her through our connection, the taint of our darkness stretching to fill her chakra channels. I gritted my teeth, trying to pull the magic back, but something inside her latched onto it with a vengeance, tearing my borrowed power from me in tendrils of magic so palpable, I could see it in the air between us, flecks of crimson, onyx, silver, and amber bleeding into her.

I roared in agony, the sizzling of the sparking fuse turning to a ticking bomb in my veins, shrapnel shredding me apart as I desperately fought Sam and the monster for control. Sweat beaded on my brow and dripped down my neck and spine, and my vision swam and danced, my breath becoming shallow and labored. The slow beat of my heart filled my ears; it, and a high-pitched ringing.

I was going to die.

No...

I am *dying*.

And then, I understood. Sam was draining my life force. The monster was giving it to her. The bastard was doing exactly what I asked, but he was trying to jump ship to a more vulnerable target...a more *powerful* target.

Over my dead body, you vindictive fuck.

With more effort than a half-dead man should've been capable of, I managed to get a leash around the monster, strangling him as I dragged him, inch by painstaking inch, back into myself. Black filled my vision and, for a moment, I thought that would be the end of me—the end of us. *No.* I refused to die here, refused to let Sam fade away because I wasn't powerful enough. Because I wasn't enough. I would never be enough, but this... this, I could manage. Trembling and shaking with fatigue, I took back only as much power as I needed to sustain myself, leaving the rest with Sam. She would need it more than I would.

With the monster safely secured back into the pits of my mind, I took a minute to breathe. It was then that I found it. *My blood.* Thanks to my magic pouring into her, it was finally there, finally finding its way to her bloodstream. I hadn't killed her; I simply hadn't been quick enough. But now, now it was within my grasp. I grinned, grabbing that blood and forcing it to absorb into her, to fill her, to fuel her. It would heal her.

Buh-bump.

Her chest lurched under the force of my power. I had to work fast. There was only a moment of time. Necromancy could only do so much, but my blood and magic could do so much more. All I needed was this one moment. All I needed was for her to hear me, and she would have no choice.

She would obey.

"*Live*," I commanded, the full force of my necromancy and blood magery twining together and filling the single word. Each alone wouldn't be enough, not for what I was trying to do. And gods above and demon spawn below, it *had* to work.

Buh-bump.

Buh-bump.

Buh-bump.

Buh-bump.

Her heart beat, again and again, already picking up pace.

My blood surged through her veins without my help now. It was taking over her blood, tainting it, contaminating it, making it *more*. I'd never realized what my blood felt like when it was separate from me. I'd known it was heady, delicious, and powerful; I hadn't realized it was raw, pure magic.

Sam gasped, her back arching when she took her first breath.

I pulled away, and her eyes snapped open—her *red* eyes, not a hint of green left to the irises. It was the most terrifying and beautiful thing I'd ever seen. My magic, her eyes, but she was alive. I'd raised her from the dead.

Her borrowed power flared around us, tearing us from the eerie void we'd been trapped within. We landed on the sparring mat in a mockery of the same position we'd been in when her magic had ripped us from this exact moment several days ago. Sam's eyes flickered between red and green as she burned through the remaining power my magic had lent her. When it was spent, she blacked out.

With a flick of my wrist, I expanded my shadows around us. We'd be invisible to Evander's prying eyes, but he was still trapped within the ward. He'd be powerless to do anything until I freed him. I would, but first, I needed a moment to collect myself—to breathe—because I'd almost lost her...*again*.

I wiped the blood from my face, licking my lips and wrist as I went. I told the blood to mend my wound so it wouldn't bleed. As exhausted as I was, all I could manage was to make the cut scab over, which was good enough for now. Then, I wiped my tears from Sam's cheeks, my hand lingering there as I stroked her soft skin.

I sat there, watching her parted lips as they moved with each breath. Her lashes fanned her cheeks, and her hair was a wild mess, haloing her head against the sparring mat. Last time we'd been here, I'd fought every urge begging me to kiss her. And when she'd thrashed underneath me...I'd thought I would go insane. Unable to resist now, I leaned forward, pressing my lips against hers. To my shock, her lips shaped against mine. I pulled away, but she was out cold.

I smiled, shaking my head. "You're perfect, precious," I whispered.

She was perfect, and I'd made her hate me—again. My heart seized in my chest. *She hates me.* She hated me, and she'd almost died not knowing what she meant to me, not knowing what she truly felt for me.

I had only ever loved two people in my life. One was my best friend. The other was a slave as much as I was. The first knew of my platonic affections, the latter didn't. Perhaps that was why we would never be friends—could never be friends—because I had made the boy hate me.

My affection was a death sentence. It painted a target on the backs of the people I cared for. It was why Vincent had to constantly look over his shoulder. It was why the boy didn't know. It was why I taunted and harassed the boy, even now. It was why Sam couldn't ever know how she'd haunted my thoughts and dreams for six years. She couldn't know how she'd filled my mind with hope—with "What if's" and "If only's." She would return my affection, and it would get her killed. To hope for anything at all would be suicide and murder. My master would learn of her and kill her. More than kill her, he'd destroy and break her. And if he let her live at all, it wouldn't be out of kindness, it would be to keep me on his leash—the leash I'd escaped just over three years ago.

I had thought I'd escaped my master when I'd made the Council. I thought I had finally escaped the man who'd tortured and harmed me, the man who'd threatened Vincent and the boy.

I'd been wrong. So, so wrong. In advancing to my so-called "freedom," I had damned the boy by leaving him to suffer alone with our master. I had been a buffer between them. As a Councilmember, I was no longer there to protect him.

I wonder if Evander will ever forgive me for that.

I knew I didn't deserve forgiveness.

And now, there was Sam.

If only I was that blonde-haired, hazel-eyed boy I'd appeared as on the day I'd met her six years ago. If only I hadn't been a slave then. If only I wasn't a cruel monster now. If only I'd never scared her away, but I had—because I'd been attached to her from the moment I laid eyes on her, dancing gracefully on top of her mother's grave. She was such a curious creature, such a beautiful temptation.

She's the purest light in a sea of darkness, a siren threatening to drag me under and cry while I drown.

It was far too late for that.

I was a goner long before now.

"You should hate me for what I've done," I murmured, stroking a hand down her cheek. "Should fear me for those I've mercilessly hunted and killed. I am everything bad in this world, and if I don't kill you, my master will."

I could never have her.

She was the legendary Sibyl.

My enemy.

My prey.

My heart.

She deserved better than a slave.

She deserved better than a monster.

"It was only a fantasy," I whispered. "Only ever a dream."

Then, I pulled away from her, from the dream, from what could've been and what couldn't be. Monsters didn't get to have beautiful dreams. Only nightmares. And I'd been asleep for so, so long.

"Wake up, precious."

She did.

Acknowledgments

To those who say writing happens in isolation, you sir, madam, dragon, unicorn, elf, orc—creature of any species—are a lunatic. It literally takes an army of brave warriors—of crazies dedicated to the fine craft of wordsmithing—to write a novel. I don't mean that they brandish pen or serve as a scribe while I word-vomit plot onto the page. No, no, no. After much editing, finagling, and other battering of said manuscript—my greatest adversary—there comes a time for the glorious Knights of Manuscript Editing to charge in and tear my writing to shreds.

And they do.

Without the overwhelming love and support of these faithful warriors, my first draft never would've seen the flames of the scorching forge where it underwent a metamorphosis, becoming the finely-crafted work it is now. A year and well over fifteen rewrites later, these are the fierce knights who gave me the strength to win my battles:

First, the biggest thanks to Gem, for whom, without her reading the shittiest first draft I ever could've written, I *never* would've taken the *Light of Chaos* series to where it is now. To you, I am entirely grateful. No, seriously. Your feedback allowed me to take garbage and turn it into rainbows and butterflies. You are a beautiful, majestic unicorn, my dear! All of the loves!

Nigel, Nigel, Nigel. You, too, helped me turn what was rainbows and butterflies into something magical and beyond. Thank you for having my back and not being afraid to call out my plot holes early on in the drafting stages. And yes, I knew the villains needed work. You forced me to face my demons—

quite literally. I hope they make your skin crawl now (they do mine).

Alice. Er. Mer. Gerd. I can't express how much your excited comments made a huge impact on the resulting scenes concerning Evander. You helped me not only identify places to improve his initial interactions with Sam, but your overall commentary helped me flesh out the world in ways I hadn't thought to do on my own. You were right, New Adult was DEF the way to go! ;D

Melinda, dear and crazy woman. Thank you for reading... and reading...and rereading *King's Chaos* and subsequent manuscripts as you've helped inform me, guide me, and mercilessly point out my weak spots, plot holes, and other hot garbage (my grammar). Thank you for being excited about not only my series but the blog that helped launch the first novel as well. You've read things as I've thrown them at you, helped me research, and helped me not go insane—you have been instrumental to this writing journey and I can't wait to keep blowing you away as the series progresses!

Selina my love, thank you for letting me talk your ear off about the lore and backstory of the Chaos Universe, as well as a dozen spoilers in ad nauseum. For falling in love with Sam and friends. For wanting to be a part of our journey. For being just as excited about the fate of my series as I am. For being a rock and a shoulder to cry on while I've gone through hell and back again these last several months. You are a saint, my love, and I couldn't have done this without you. P.S. I'm ready to drink more of your tears. *num-num-num-num-num*

Precious Hannah, thank you for being one of my biggest, most crazed fans, taking a risk on me and my characters...and falling in love with all of us. I can't thank you enough for how involved you've been in this grueling process—as I've nearly literally pulled my own hair out. Thank you for keeping me sane when I wanted to light my books on fire. *shifty eyes* You are my savior, love. Keep being perfection.

Paul, Mags, Amanda, Nefer, Kia—THANK YOU, THANK YOU, THANK YOU for being my willing victims in reading a universe that is much, much too large for any sane human to *want* to read. You each helped flesh out the finished draft of *King's Chaos* in ways that have only made it all the better. Seriously, though. You don't even know. I'm so grateful. Words cannot express—I cannot express...except to...*kidnaps you all and shoves you into my pockets* You're now stuck with me until the end of time.

Rachel, my wild and crazy friend, thank you for reading, copyediting, and loving my characters. Thank you for taking the time out of your day to be my third-fourth-fifth set of eyes on this bad boy. I look forward to further crushing your soul as the series progresses. >:}

To my writer's group, mi familia, my world, thank you times a million: Kayla, for letting me send all the Sam/Jeph tidbits as I wrote them. Akeel, for filling my head full of beautiful lies about my writing talent. Scarlett, for helping me with all the technical things that I never would've stopped to consider...or would've cried over while trying to figure them out. Trisha, for freaking out at me (in the best possible way) with your excitement as you read. Becka, for falling in love with Evander, sweetheart that he is. Caleb, for believing in me. Jessa, for every encouraging word and inspirational thought. Thank you all for your overwhelming love and support during this stressful process. I love you guys to the moon and back again. To the stars and back again. To infinity and... ;)

Gerardo, thank you for letting me literally send you novel-length messages about the series, drafting, and other such nonsense. Thank you for being one of my biggest fans, hardest shippers, and fiercest debaters. Thank you for listening to me ramble about this story for the last ten years—and *still* wanting to be my friend despite how truly obnoxious I really am. I love you, Gerry-poo-poo. ;P

Jimi, my Chaos-in-Arms friend. Thank you for squealing over my pending work and for answering the 9,001 questions I rapid-fired at you. I look forward to our universes sitting side-by-by side on our home bookshelves.

Tina and KayLee, you devilish creatures you! Thank you for your overwhelming love and support, your excitement when reading, and for nearly throwing my work across the room when you got to the ending. Nothing like your I-need-to-know-what-happens-next frustration to feed my inner ~~sadist~~ writer. I cherish you both. <3

Shellie and Kelly! Thank you for being excited about Sam and friends. I know you're eager for more. I'm sorry that I had a different version of my manuscript every time you asked about it...Every. Time. And *King's Chaos* is no different. Oops. (Have mercy on me!)

Tori, my lovely sweet, thank you for being here to support me along the way. You are magic in a world full of Norms. I love you to the edge of the edge of the world—the stars, the moon, the universe! I love you most-est-er! (Ha! It's in writing. Beat that, bish.)

Mom and Dad...I still don't know how *you* don't know how I can write an entire book...let alone the universe I've created. Thank you for listening to me ramble on, and on, and on, and on, and on...I love you, and I pray you never read my books. I never meant to write a romance novel...let alone an entire series of them. Please avert your eyes.

Reno...words cannot express the suffering you've endured while living with a writing-obsessed author. Just remember...this is all your fault. XOXO.

I love you, my knights in shining armor.
~Alex, your Queen of Chaos

About the Author

Alexandra Gardner, unofficial Queen of Chaos, writes action-adventure Dark Paranormal Romance. In her free time, she can be found sitting on the couch of doom with entirely too much coffee, her laptop (A.K.A. her other half), and two overly-affectionate cats laying across her wrists. She also enjoys roaming the Pacific Northwest, sleeping, and making up unrealistic, traumatizing scenarios for her characters. KING'S CHAOS is her debut novel.

Follow Alexandra

Website: www.agardnerbooks.com
Twitter: @agardner_author
Facebook: www.facebook.com/agardnerbooks
Instagram: @agardner_author

CPSIA information can be obtained
at www.ICGtesting.com
Printed in the USA
LVHW011826011219
639067LV00013B/576/P

9 781947 082717